By Suzanne Brockmann
Published by The Random House Publishing Group:

HEARTTHROB
BODYGUARD
THE UNSUNG HERO
THE DEFIANT HERO
OVER THE EDGE
OUT OF CONTROL
INTO THE NIGHT
GONE TOO FAR

OVER THE EDGE

Suzanne Brockmann

IVY BOOKS • NEW YORK

This book contains an excerpt from *Out of Control* by Suzanne Brockmann. This excerpt has been set for this edition only and may not reflect the content of the final edition.

An Ivy Book
Published by The Random House Publishing Group
Copyright © 2001 by Suzanne Brockmann
Excerpt from *Out of Control* by Suzanne Brockmann copyright © 2001 by Suzanne Brockmann

www.ballantinebooks.com

ISBN 0-8041-1970-8

Manufactured in the United States of America

First Edition: September 2001

OPM   20   19   18   17   16   15   14   13   12   11

For the brave men and women
who fought for freedom during the Second World War.
My most sincere and humble thanks.

ACKNOWLEDGMENTS

A million thanks from the bottom of my heart to Mike Freeman, for expert advice and countless hours spent reading notes and drafts. Thanks, also, to Frances Stepp for introducing me to Mike!

Thanks to my grandmother, Edna Schriever, whose ever-present smile, generous kindness, and sharp intellect were a vital part of my childhood. The warmth of her spirit is with me still.

Thanks to the men and women who took the time to record their accounts of the Holocaust in Denmark. That is a story we must never forget.

Thanks to all my readers, friends, and fans, who've shared with me the experiences of their mothers, fathers, and grandfathers during World War II. The matter-of-fact heroism and sacrifices continue to awe me.

Thanks as always to Deede Bergeron, Lee Brockmann, and Patricia McMahon—my personal support staff and early draft readers.

And thanks, of course, to Ed.

Any mistakes I've made or liberties I've taken are completely my own.

Prologue

THE MOON WAS hanging insolent and full in the sky just to the left of a billboard for a bankruptcy lawyer, and Stan knew.

It was the full moon's fault.

It *had* to be the goddamn full moon.

Senior Chief Petty Officer Stanley Wolchonok steadied himself, holding on to the side of a pickup truck in the parking lot of the Ladybug Lounge and praying to whatever god was listening that he wouldn't throw up.

His fever was spiking. He could feel his entire body break out in a sweat as a flash of intense heat gripped him. God *damn*, of all the times to get the flu . . . Of course, there was never a good time to get sick. This just happened to be a worse time than any other, coming back to the States after two relentless months away.

"Senior! Thank God you're here!"

Stan wasn't ready to thank anyone for anything—particularly not for his command performance tonight at this cheap-shit, lowlife bar where he hadn't come by choice in well over two years.

Which didn't mean he hadn't been here plenty of times in the past two years.

Cleaning up after whichever dumbass in the team had gone ballistic.

The average dumbass didn't get more than two strikes before he was out of the SEAL Teams—or at least out of the elite Team Sixteen Troubleshooters Squad.

Truth was, the average dumbass who was smart enough to become a SEAL learned rather quickly to be neither dumb nor an ass most of the time. But everyone had to blow off steam, particularly after two months away from loved ones, two months filled with high stress and not a hell of a lot of down time.

The married men—and the men whose relationships with their girlfriends had survived these past two very cold and lonely months of separation—were all home in their honeys' sweet arms tonight. The single guys were in bars like the Ladybug—an alcohol-doused location where it was extremely easy for the average dumbass to get into some serious trouble.

Tonight's dumbass was newly promoted Chief Petty Officer Ken Karmody, more affectionately known by his extremely accurate nickname WildCard. Unfortunately, there was nothing even remotely average about him.

This was, without a doubt, the seventeenth strike against him. Another man would've been out on his ear a long time ago. Problem was, another man couldn't do half the things to and with computers that WildCard Karmody could.

And Lieutenant Tom Paoletti, CO of SEAL Team Sixteen, honestly liked the little butthead. Truth was, Stan liked him, too.

But not tonight. He didn't like him at all right now.

And the million-dollar question was, what had WildCard done to live up to his nickname this time?

Chief Frank O'Leary had made the SOS call that had pulled Stan out of bed. A man of few words, O'Leary's usual lazy drawl was clipped and tight. He'd gotten right to the point. "Senior, WildCard's in deep shit. Sure could use you at the Bug, ASAP."

If it had been anyone else calling, Stan would have rolled over and moaned himself back to a feverish, near-sleep state. But O'Leary rarely asked for anything. So Stan had been up and dressed and in his truck inside three minutes.

He forced himself to straighten up now as Petty Officer Second Class Mark Jenkins scurried across the parking lot to him. "O'Leary and Lopez locked Karmody in the bathroom, and Starrett, Muldoon, Rick, Steve, and Junior are holding off about twenty jarheads who want to rip him to shreds."

Stan's head throbbed. "Sam Starrett and Mike Muldoon are here?" Fuck. They were officers. Despite the fact that

Sam was a mustang—an enlisted man who'd gone to OTS and made the leap to officer—and Muldoon damn near worshiped the ground Stan walked on, their presence here made cleaning this up more complicated.

And that wasn't even taking into consideration the twenty U.S. Marines who wanted—probably for some very good reason—to rip WildCard Karmody to shreds. *Twenty* Marines. Not two. Not three. *Twenty.* Beautiful. Just beautiful.

"Starrett swears he's blinded by the extremely generous, uh, charms of a young lady he met here tonight. He's seen nothing and will continue to see nothing. And Muldoon promised he'd be out the back door as soon as you arrived," Jenk reported in his schoolboy tenor. His cartoon-character voice matched the freckles on his deceptively honest face.

Stan managed to walk upright all the way to the Ladybug's door. Damn, he was dripping with sweat. The key to defusing a volatile situation like this was to come in looking completely calm and cool. He found his handkerchief, mopped his forehead, and prayed again that he wouldn't puke on the floor. "What happened?"

"I don't know exactly, Senior." Jenk, a veritable fountain of information and official team gossip, was coming up dry. When was the last time *that* had happened?

Stan cursed the full moon again. "Guess," he ordered the kid.

"I think WildCard went to see Adele again," Jenk told him. "And I think it probably didn't go too well. Again."

Adele Zakashansky. WildCard's high school sweetheart who had dumped him without ceremony after years of alleged devotion. At least that was WildCard's side of the story. The dumping had occurred a mayhem-filled six months ago. If Stan never heard her name again, it would be too soon.

"I was playing pool with Lopez and Rick," Jenk continued. "I didn't even see WildCard come in. Then there was this commotion, and I look up and he's going one on twenty with this bunch of Marines, like he's Jackie Chan or something. O'Leary was near the bar, and he grabbed WildCard and tossed him into the head. Muldoon got the Marines to agree to a temporary cease-fire. But it's only temporary."

God bless Chief Frank O'Leary and Ensign Mike Muldoon. "Anything broken?"

"A big mirror on the wall," Jenk said. "A coupla chairs." He laughed. "And a lot of Marine balls. The Card's a wild man."

The door opened and Mike Muldoon peeked out. "Senior! Thank God. You better get in here. The manager's about five seconds from calling the police, WildCard's shouting about getting out of the bathroom and finishing what he started, and the Marines are more than ready to rumble."

Stan mopped his face one more time and stepped inside. "I got it from here, Muldoon," he told the younger man.

"Oh, wow, Senior, you look really terrible. Man, you got the flu," Muldoon realized. He had one of those too-young, too-handsome faces with big expressive blue eyes that gave away everything he was feeling. And he wondered why he never won at poker. "You should be home, in bed—"

"And *you* need to get out of here," Stan said bluntly. "I can't fix this for Karmody with you here."

Muldoon looked as if he were about to cry. "But—"

"Get lost. *Sir.*"

Muldoon was no dummy, and with one more pained look on his pretty face, he vanished.

Stan glanced around the room. Marines, manager, man in the bathroom. The manager on duty tonight was Kevin Franklin—he knew the guy well. He was an asshole, but it was a devil-you-know situation—better than dealing with an unknown.

Yes, indeed, it was WildCard Karmody's lucky night— Stan could fix this. Provided he stayed on his feet and didn't barf on anyone.

Step one. Get the Marines out of here. With them gone, the manager would be less inclined to call in the local police. Stan aimed himself at the surly group.

The highest ranking Marine was only a corporal—Jesus, they were all children. That was either going to make it really easy or really hard.

"Tell Franklin to hold on," Stan murmured to Jenk. "Ask him—pretty please—to give me five minutes. Ten, tops. Tell him I'm going to clear the room, then see what I can do to make acceptable reparations for the damage that's been done."

Jenk slipped away.

"How about we all step outside, Corporal," Stan said to a big beefy kid who couldn't have been more than twenty-three tender years old. "I'm Senior Chief Stan Wolchonok, U.S. Navy, SEAL Team Sixteen. I'm not sure exactly what there is to say here, but a little fresh air can't hurt, huh?"

"Why should we be the ones to leave?" Another kid, even bigger and beefier—and more drunk than Corporal Biceps— stepped forward. "That stupid little shit started it."

Stan could hear WildCard—the stupid little shit in question—howling from the men's room, banging on the door and demanding to be let out.

"We'll go into the parking lot," another Marine suggested, "if you send *him* into the parking lot, too."

Stan sighed. "Can't do that, boys. If you want to fight him," he said, "and I really don't recommend it—he's small, but he's fast and he doesn't know the meaning of the word *quit*— what do you say I call your CO and we set up a time for your best guy to meet Chief Karmody in a boxing ring? Nice and clean, everyone sober, no one goes to jail afterward for drunk and disorderly."

Another of the Marines, a kid with recent Cro-Magnon ancestry, sidled forward, moving like a fighter. This was definitely their best guy, right here, in person. What'dya know?

Stan sized him up in one glance. Cocky and strong but inexperienced. Too inexperienced to know that inexperience could put you on the mat, facedown, lights out, faster than a ref could blink.

"I'd rather fight *you*, pops," the kid said, so full of himself, Stan could imagine his head exploding from an overinflated ego. Blam.

"You'd be more of a challenge," the kid continued. He grinned. "You look like you might even go a full two rounds before I knocked you out."

His dumbass friends laughed and nudged each other. They were on top of the world—but theirs was a very, very small planet. They were just too young and stupid to know it yet.

Kid Cro-Magnon edged closer, invading Stan's personal space. "And I say we do it right here. Right now."

Ah, crap. Stan didn't want to fight. Not four days from now in a ring, and especially not tonight. Tonight, all he wanted was to go home and go to bed.

He breathed on the kid, hoping he was contagious. Unfortunately this strain of the flu wasn't fast acting.

From all corners of the room, Stan could feel his men watching him. He could hear WildCard Karmody still shouting from the head. Christ, he still had to make things square with the asshole manager, and then talk Karmody down from whatever emotional ledge he was teetering on.

Cro-Magnon loomed over him, stinking of gin, and Stan knew in a flash that this was the perfect time to choose speed over finesse. Finesse required too much talking, and damn, his throat was sore.

"Fine. Let's do it. Someone say go," Stan said, his gaze never leaving Cro-Magnon.

"Go," Jenk shot back, good man.

A quick jab, a hard uppercut, and an elbow to the back of the head. Stan stepped back, and Cave Boy was down and not coming up any time soon.

It would've been even more effective if Stan hadn't been sweating as he stood there, light as a dancer on the balls of his feet. Light-headed from fever, too, but those fools didn't know that. He looked at the other jarheads, giving them his best dead eye gaze. Cold and emotionless. An absolute machine. "Who's next? Come on, line up, girls. I'll take you one at a time if that's what you want."

He definitely had their attention. He had his SEALs' attention, too.

"Stay back, Junior," he said evenly, without turning around to see who was shuffling his feet back behind him. He didn't have to turn. He knew his men.

And they knew him. But right now he'd surprised them because although he was a fighter by nature, in the past he'd usually preferred to talk things out.

The younger Marines were looking to the corporal for direction, and the Marine corporal, thank God, still had a few brain cells working. He stared down at his platoon's boxing champ, unconscious and drooling on the dirty barroom floor.

Stan watched while the corporal slowly did the math. If Stan could take their best man out in one point three seconds, then . . .

"What do you say I call your CO and we set up a time for your best guy to meet Karmody in a boxing ring?" Stan said again.

The corporal nodded jerkily, looking from Stan to the bathroom door, no doubt remembering Karmody with his mad scientist hair and his lean build, no doubt thinking that in the ring, their guy would be able to give him a thrashing.

If Stan didn't have the flu, he would've smiled. They were in for one big surprise. "What do you say you take Sleeping Beauty here and go on back to the base?" he suggested. Relentless repetition was usually needed when dealing with alcohol and idiots. "And tomorrow morning we'll set up that boxing match."

"Well . . ." the corporal finally said.

"Great," Stan bulldozed over him. "We've got a deal." He would've shaken the corporal's hand if his own hadn't been so damn sweaty. All he needed at this point was for the kid to think he was scared, so he tucked his hands behind his back in a modified parade rest. "Move it on out," he ordered.

Two of the Marines grabbed Cro-Magnon and they all shuffled away.

As the door closed behind them, the room seemed to take a collective sigh of relief. Not that there were a lot of people left. A few bikers who looked disappointed that there wasn't going to be a brawl. A pair of women eyeing Jay Lopez and Frank O'Leary as the SEALS stood holding the men's room door tightly closed. A few couples making out in the darkness of the corner booths, ignoring the rest of the world.

There was a time Stan had sat in one of those corner booths himself, getting very familiar with women who didn't care that he didn't look like Mel Gibson, who didn't care that he left town at the drop of a hat and sometimes didn't bother to come back. Candy, Julia, Molly, Val. Laura. Lisa. Linda. He'd met them all, if not here then in a dive very similar to this one. He should be feeling nostalgic, not nauseous.

But shit, all he wanted was to go home.

And he was only up to step two.

Lieutenant junior grade Sam Starrett intercepted him on his way to the bar and the waiting manager. Starrett had his arm around a woman who had, quite possibly, the biggest breasts in the world. He was grinning and a little tipsy—if that word could be used to describe a big, bad Navy SEAL.

The woman whispered something in his ear, brushing her enormous jugs against him, and Starrett laughed. Obviously he thought he'd found the right kind of solace for whatever had been eating him up these past few months.

"Senior Chief Stan Wolchonok," Starrett said, "meet the marvelous Miss Mary Lou Morrison."

Damn, did he look like he was here to attend a party? Starrett had had more to drink than Stan had thought if he couldn't see that Stan was dead on his feet. "Ma'am." He managed to nod politely. He had to work to look her in the eye instead of staring, hypnotized, down into that amazing Grand Canyon of cleavage.

Sweet lord.

He solved the problem by glaring at Starrett. "You shouldn't be here right now. Sir."

And the recently promoted lieutenant junior grade also shouldn't have been playing with fire by starting something with this Mary Lou Morrison. She was too young, too pretty, too desperately hopeful. While Starrett was looking only for a night in her bed, she was looking for a ring. Someone was going to end up disappointed.

"Yeah, I know, Senior," Starrett said in his cowboy twang, made thicker by all he'd had to drink, "but I do love to watch you work. And I'm not the only one impressed. Mary Lou's sister Janine over there was wondering what you're doing later."

Starrett gestured with his head toward the other side of the room, where a woman was standing. She gave Stan a little wave. Ah yes, she was definitely Mary Lou's sister.

A little bit older, not quite as pretty, but just as completely, amazingly stacked. She approached, but Stan escaped, nodding at the younger sister. "Excuse me. I need to speak to Kevin Franklin." He turned and ran.

But Janine was crafty. "Hi—Stan, isn't it?" She'd managed to circumnavigate her sister and Starrett and cut Stan off before he reached the bar, blocking his route. "I couldn't help noticing you."

She was sober. Amazing. Her eyes were blue and warm and she sipped what looked to be plain soda pop. And he'd been wrong. *She* was the prettier sister. Maybe not on the surface. But she was certainly the less desperate sister, and he'd always found lack of desperation to be particularly appealing.

"How's that for a come-on line?" she continued. Her gaze was frank and open and flat-out admiring, and her smile was friendly. He almost felt handsome. "You have any time later to pull up a chair and pretend to get to know me?"

Stan had to laugh at that. "Tempting, but believe me, ma'am, you don't want what I've got."

Her laughter was low, musical. "Want to bet?"

Oh, mama. "Seriously—Janine, right?" He dropped his voice. "Janine, I've got the flu and I've got about twenty more minutes, tops, before I'm going to fall over."

She lowered her voice, too, moved closer. "Oh, you poor thing. Then you need someone to take care of you, don't you? I make an awesome chicken soup, I'll have you know."

Someone to take care of him? "I don't think—"

"Well then, Stan, maybe you have a friend you could introduce me to. I'm not looking for long term, but this is a position I'd like to fill immediately. Forgive my bluntness, but we're both adults and we both know why people come to a place like this, don't we?"

Her honesty made him laugh again. "Truth is, I came here to talk to the manager and get my guy out of the men's room without him hurting anyone or himself. It wasn't by choice."

She bulldozed over him as completely as he'd run down the Marine corporal, reaching up to feel his forehead. Her hand was cool and soft against his too-hot skin. "God, you *are* burning up."

He stepped back, away from her. Guinness Book of World

Records breasts and pretty eyes be damned—he didn't want her touching him. Lately he didn't seem to want *any* woman touching him, except Teresa Howe.

Christ, where had *that* come from?

The fever. That was one goddamn feverish thought, no question. Because helo pilot and Naval Reservist Lieutenant junior grade Teri Howe was the last woman on earth who'd *want* to touch him. God, talk about beauty and the beast. Yeah, a woman like her hooked up with a guy like him only in a fairy tale.

And while his life was far from dull, it was no freaking fairy tale, that was for sure.

Meanwhile, he'd hurt Janine's feelings. "I'm sorry, but right now I really need to talk to—"

"It's all right," she said quietly. "You don't have to explain. It was nice meeting you."

Shit. Now she was walking away. What was he doing? She was pretty and funny and built like a Playboy Bunny and it had been months since he'd gotten laid. And yet he'd reacted to her touch as if she had the plague. What *was* he doing? Saving himself for Teri Howe? This fever was definitely addling his brain.

"Senior Chief." Kevin Franklin, the Bug's manager, called to him from behind the bar. "What are we going to do about that broken mirror?"

Ah, hell. Stan turned to him, forcing himself back to the business at hand, dismissing Janine as absolutely as he was usually able to dismiss all thoughts of ever being touched by Teri Howe.

Old Kev was more of an asshole than usual tonight. It was a pity Stan couldn't throw a few punches to shut him up, the way he'd done with that Marine. Instead he lived through an endless list of complaints and a whole lot of whining, entertaining himself by trying to guess exactly when his knees would finally give out, and what his men would do when that happened.

Stan tried his hardest not to listen, but there were a few things he couldn't help but hear. A, Franklin still wanted to call the police. And B, he was tired of bar fights on his watch, tired of WildCard Karmody in particular.

That made two of 'em.

"Here's the deal," Stan said flatly, when he finally got a chance to get a word in edgewise. "You don't press charges, and Karmody pays for the mirror and the chairs, *and* he never comes into the Bug again when you're working the night shift."

"He doesn't come in when I'm working *any* shift," Franklin countered, just as Stan had known he would. Good, let him feel as if he'd won a hard bargain.

"Well . . ." Stan pretended to think about it. "I guess so. I guess we got a deal." He held out his hand for the man to shake.

"Karmody's not going to go for this," Franklin warned.

"I'll handle Karmody."

Which was step three.

Christ, this was the part where Stan would go into the men's and sit down on the tile floor and talk to WildCard. "What happened this time, Karmody?" Through clenched teeth: "Nothing happened, Senior." A sigh from Stan. "Don't bullshit me, Kenny. I know you went to see Adele." "Fuck Adele!" Back and forth they'd go, with WildCard venting his anger, ranting and railing about whatever injustice Adele had done this time, until he was all ranted out and ready to go home and pass out.

Which was what Stan was ready to do right now.

Tomorrow WildCard would wake up all contrite and hungover. Stan would call him in to his office and do some ranting and railing of his own. WildCard was going to be feeling the repercussions of tonight's little hell party for a *long* time.

Stan made the trip from the bar to the men's room on legs that were leaden. Janine was still there, still watching him. He couldn't look at her, couldn't do more than put one foot in front of the other.

O'Leary was still guarding the door, but WildCard had stopped his pounding and shouting. It was quiet in there. Maybe the son of a bitch had knocked himself out from hitting his head on the tile walls.

No, that was too much to hope for, too much to ask.

O'Leary opened the door for him, and Stan went inside and . . . Oh, Christ.

"Shut the door and don't let anyone in here," Stan ordered O'Leary.

WildCard was crying.

He was sitting on the floor, arms around knees that were up close to his chest, head down, body shaking, sobbing as if his heart were breaking. Which it probably was, poor bastard.

Adele Zakashansky had no idea what she had lost by ditching him the way she had six months ago. Yes, WildCard could be completely obnoxious. Give him enough time, and he'd probably get on Mother Teresa's or Ghandi's nerves, but in all honesty, the man had a heart the size of California.

"Shit," Stan breathed, lowering himself gingerly down onto the floor next to him. He spoke gently. There'd be plenty of time tomorrow to yell at the man. "Why do you keep going to see her, Kenny? You know, you're doing this to yourself."

WildCard didn't answer. Stan hadn't really expected him to.

He put his hand on the kid's back, feeling completely inadequate here. Even when he wasn't fighting the flu, he wasn't the cry-on-my-shoulder type. He didn't do hugs, rarely touched the men in his team unless he had to—at least not much beyond the occasional high five or slap on the shoulder.

"She got a restraining order, Senior," WildCard lifted his tearstained face to tell him with the much too careful enunciation of the extremely drunk. He looked about five years old and completely bewildered. "How could she even *think* that I would hurt her? I *love* her."

Stan felt like weeping himself, his head throbbing in sympathy. God, being in love sucked.

"Yeah," he said. "*I* know that, Ken, and *you* know that, but maybe you haven't done such a great job over the past few months communicating that to Adele, you know? When you come at her all loud and angry, and completely shit-faced, too, well, that's got to be a little upsetting for her. I think you need to try to see it from her point of view, huh? She tells you it's over, and two weeks later, you've parked your Jeep in her flower garden at four in the morning, waking up the entire neighborhood by playing Michael Jackson at full volume on your car stereo."

"It was the Jackson 5," WildCard corrected him. " 'I Want You Back.' It seemed like a good idea at the time."

"And punching out her new boyfriend at the movie theater?"

"Yeah, that wasn't such a good idea."

"Calling her every fifteen minutes all night long? From Africa?"

"I just wanted to hear her voice."

Stan looked at him.

WildCard laughed. "Yeah, all right. I knew he was over there, with her. Goddamn Ronald from MIT. Getting it on for the first time. I wanted to make sure the evening was memorable for them." He wiped his eyes. "She's not going to take me back, is she?"

There was still hope in WildCard's heart. Hope that Stan crushed ruthlessly by flatly telling him, "No, she's not. Not tonight, not next week, not ever."

Hearing those words didn't make WildCard dissolve into more tears. Instead he wiped his nose on his sleeve. Sat up a little straighter. "I'm so damn tired of being alone, Senior Chief. I mean, when I was with Adele we weren't actually together that often, but she emailed me every day. I knew she was thinking about me." He looked at Stan with the pathetic earnestness of the truly drunk. "I just want to know someone's thinking about me. Is that really too much to ask?"

Stan looked at the kid. No, he wasn't a kid—he was well into his twenties, he was a full grown man. He just freaking *acted* like a kid most of the time. With his dark eyes and angular face, Ken Karmody wasn't a bad looking man. If you didn't pay too much attention to his Dr. Frankenstein haircut.

I'm not looking for long term. . . . Janine's pretty eyes and knockout body flashed to mind, and Stan knew what he had to do. He felt a brief flare of regret, but it passed quickly enough.

"You been with anyone else?" he asked WildCard. "You know, since Adele?"

WildCard looked away, looked embarrassed. Shook his head no, like that was something to be ashamed of.

"Maybe you need to," Stan said gently. "Maybe hooking up with someone for a while will put this thing with Adele into perspective. Yes, she was an important part of your life for a few years, but now that she's gone, your life's not over. There are plenty of women who would love to spend their time thinking about you." He pulled himself to his feet, amazed he could still stand. "Come on, let's get out of here, go rejoin the world."

WildCard pushed himself off the floor. "Senior Chief, I have to be straight with you. I was fighting before. I'm not sure exactly, but I think either the police or a whole bunch of jarheads might be waiting for me out in the bar."

"Franklin didn't call the police," Stan told him. "I took care of him—and the jarheads, too. Of course, you're going to have to pay for damages."

New hope lit his eyes. "You mean I'm not going to be arrested?"

"No. You're going to have to meet some seven-foot-tall Marine in a boxing ring in a few days. And you can't come back to the Bug if Kevin Franklin is on duty. Not ever again. We'll go over this, at length, tomorrow in my office."

Out of all the things Stan had said, it was only this last that gave WildCard pause. Tomorrow's little meeting wasn't going to be any fun for either of them. Stan was going to deliver an ultimatum. He gave him a small preview because although he was going to make sure WildCard was delivered safely home, there were still several hours before dawn, and the kid *was* a supreme dumbass.

"You need to know, Karmody, no shit, read my lips because this is serious: You break that restraining order, you're on your own. No senior chief to the rescue. It will be Lieutenant Paoletti who comes to see you in jail, and he will not be a happy man. And what he will tell you is good-bye and good luck. And good luck will be for surviving your eighteen months to three years in prison and then getting a job fixing computers in the back room of some CompUSA, provided you can find one with a manager who hires convicted felons. Do you understand what I am telling you?"

WildCard nodded, a dazed look in his eyes, and Stan knew he'd hit on the kid's worst nightmare. Good.

He pushed open the men's room door and WildCard followed him out into the bar. Home—and his bed—were so close, he could almost smell it. Only one more thing to do.

Sam Starrett had the younger sister out on the dance floor, taking advantage of a slow dance to get in a full body embrace. Janine stood by the jukebox, as if entranced by the list of songs, still sipping her soda.

Stan headed toward her. "Janine. That position still available?"

She looked up, looked from him to WildCard, noted the fact that the younger man's eyes were still red from crying. Her own gaze softened slightly before she glanced back at Stan, awareness and wisdom in her eyes, and he knew he was doing the right thing.

"Yes, it is."

WildCard didn't have a clue what was going on, still partially locked in the horror of that alternate reality Stan had described.

"I want you to meet Chief Ken Karmody of SEAL Team Sixteen," Stan said to Janine.

She looked at WildCard again. "I saw you earlier, with all those Marines. You didn't back down when they insulted you. You must be either really brave or really stupid, sailor."

"Really brave," Stan said at the exact same moment WildCard answered, "Really stupid," and she laughed.

She had a really nice, musical laugh, and WildCard woke up a little and actually looked at her. His eyes widened.

"You ever take a tour of the naval base?" Stan asked her.

She took a sip of her soda. "I don't believe that I have."

"Would you like to? Tomorrow?"

Janine looked at WildCard again, this time checking him out not quite as obviously as he was hypnotized by her breasts. She smiled. "Sure. Why not? How about right after church? Eleven-thirty?"

"Great," Stan said. "I'll have Chief Karmody here meet you at the gate."

"Me?" WildCard said in surprise.

Stan pushed him toward the door.

"I'll be there." Janine's eyes sent him a very definite message: *Your loss.*

It probably was. But right now he didn't want anything but his bed. And Teri Howe. He cursed this fever again. Stop thinking about her.

"Did you see the way she was looking at me?" WildCard asked as they stepped into the parking lot. The air wasn't any cooler, but it was less smoky. "Senior, if I go back in there maybe she'll—"

"Tomorrow at 1130 is early enough. That way you can impress her with your sparkling sobriety."

"Did you see her? She was *hot*, and I think she likes me! I *know* she likes me!" WildCard did a victory dance, punching the air. "Yeah! The hell with you, Adele! The hell with *you*!"

Mike Muldoon slipped down from where he'd been sitting on the hood of Stan's truck, staring at WildCard with amazement. He looked at Stan with something that normally would be uncomfortably similar to hero worship. But right now Stan appreciated the fact that Muldoon saw him through rose-colored superhero glasses—the kind that obscured the greenish tinge Stan knew was on his face.

"My God, Senior Chief," Muldoon said, "you really can fix anything, can't you?"

"Absolutely," Stan said, getting into his truck and starting the engine with a roar, praying that Muldoon wouldn't see the way his hands were shaking.

Christ, he was hurting. And he still had to call O'Leary when he got home, ask him to rouse WildCard in the morning, get him down to the front gate by 1130, order him to meet Stan in his office at 1300. Stan would ream him a new asshole then, using Janine Morrison to provide additional motivation to toe the line. He put down the window. "Do me a favor and get Karmody safely home."

"Of course, Senior Chief. But what about—"

"Thanks, Muldoon."

"—you?"

"I'm fine," Stan lied as he put the truck into gear and pulled out of the lot. No way was he letting Muldoon drive him home. His house was off-limits to the men in his team— even to Muldoon, who was the closest thing to a friend he'd ever had, despite their age difference, despite the fact that Muldoon was an officer and Stan was enlisted.

Stan made it all the way down the street and around the corner, holding tightly to the steering wheel, before he had to pull over.

And then he just sat there, shaking and sweating, sick as a dog and no longer needing to hide it.

God *damn*. That had been close. But it was okay. The illusion was intact. He'd gotten lucky again. Mighty Senior Chief Stan Wolchonok remained invincible, unstoppable, immortal. As Muldoon had said, he could fix any mistake, repair any screwup, find creative solutions to any problem, damn near walk on water if he had to.

Yeah, and if he didn't watch out, he was going to start believing his own hype.

Stan laughed at himself as he sat there, his teeth chattering from the sudden chill that gripped him. It took him, yes, him—the mighty senior chief—four tries to turn the heat up to high.

It was one thing to fool the men in his team. It was his job to do that. But there was no way he was going to fool himself into thinking he was some kind of god. No, he knew damn well what would happen if he truly tried to walk on water.

He'd sink like a stone.

It took him nearly an hour to make the five-minute trip home. But he made it. On his own.

One

LIEUTENANT COMMANDER JOEL Hogan grabbed her ass.

Right in the McDonald's on base. Right in front of . . .

A roomful of people who weren't paying either of them the slightest bit of attention.

Lt. (jg) Teri Howe didn't know whether to be bitterly disappointed or intensely relieved. She took her tray and moved away from Joel, purposefully ignoring him. She headed swiftly to the other side of the room. Evade and conceal. Run and hide. Do not engage the enemy at this time. Don't create a scene.

She sat at a small table already occupied by a female lieutenant who was deeply engrossed in a book. She glanced up quizzically at all of the other empty tables and then at Teri.

"Ass grabber on my six," Teri explained. "I'll be quiet, I promise. You don't have to stop reading."

The lieutenant smiled, sympathetic understanding in her eyes. "Some of these guys can be relentless in their pursuit. New here?"

"Reserves," Teri said. "I'm in between civilian jobs, so I took a short-term active duty assignment." A hundred and twenty days, with a hundred and fourteen to go, dodging Joel Hogan's wandering hands. God. It seemed like a long time, but at least there was an end in sight. It was pathetic, when all she wanted to do was fly. "I'm Teri Howe."

"Kate Takamoto." The lieutenant nodded, returning to her book, leaving Teri to her lunch.

Teri opened the wrapper of her sandwich, lifted the bun, and stared at the chicken, her appetite gone. No surprise there. She'd been on the Joel Hogan diet for a week now. It

18

was remarkably effective—the mere thought of the man turned the taste of food in her mouth into something unmentionable let alone unpalatable.

Teri glanced up, saw that Joel had been waylaid by several other officers. He smiled, laughed, his straight white teeth gleaming against the tan of his too-handsome face. His smarmy, smirking, God's-gift-to-all-women face.

There was a time when she'd actually found him attractive. It seemed impossible now, but it was true. There was a time she'd actually lusted after the King of Repugnancy. And her youth and stupidity were coming back now to bite her on the butt. Big time.

Don't touch me. She'd already said that to him too many times to count. *Don't talk to me, don't look at me, don't even think about me.* She hadn't said that. It was a far less reasonable request, considering they were going to work in the same area for the next 114 days.

God, it made her stomach hurt just to think about it.

She had to stay out of his way.

It was the smartest thing to do. She was going to have to stay on her toes, make sure there was always space between them.

From the corner of her eye, she saw Joel stand up, and she tensed. But he was only going to get milk for his coffee. She forced herself to take another bite of her sandwich and found herself looking straight into Senior Chief Stan Wolchonok's eyes.

He was sitting with Lieutenant Paoletti and a bunch of the other SEALs from Team Sixteen's Troubleshooter squad, both officers and enlisted. She'd worked with them before, and after ferrying them back and forth from a training op out in the desert this past week, she knew all of their nicknames.

Nilsson was Nils or Johnny. Starrett was called Sam. Jenkins was Jenk, Jacquette was Jazz, and Karmody was known as WildCard. Even the team's commanding officer, Lt. Paoletti, had his name shortened to L.T.

Everyone had a nickname but Stan Wolchonok, who was never called anything but "Senior Chief" or "Senior," and was always addressed in a most respectful and sometimes even reverent tone.

He was a scary looking man, not terribly tall but muscular—completely ripped, in fact—with a face that looked as if he'd spent a few years in a boxing ring. His broad cheekbones, big forehead, and heavy brow seemed made for the permanent glower he'd perfected. His jawline and chin were pugnacious and his nose listed very slightly to the left—broken one too many times, no doubt. His eyes were dark and capable of being cuttingly intense or soullessly flat and dead. His hair had lately outgrown his usual no frills crew cut and was thick and wavy and surprisingly blond. His skin was fair—too fair—and he was nearly always sun- or wind-burned, with ruddy cheeks and a peeling nose.

But the respect shown to him by his men and the officers in his SEAL team wasn't because he looked like someone you wouldn't necessarily want to meet in a dark alley. No, he was respected because his men knew that he would fight to the death for them, if it came down to that. No, he would even fight from *beyond* death for them, because not even death could stop mighty Senior Chief Wolchonok.

The man was a problem solver. A miracle worker, who expected as much—more—from himself than he did from his men.

And as she sat there, Teri found herself staring back at him. His scowling gaze flickered across the restaurant, landing briefly on Joel Hogan.

Oh, shoot, she'd been wrong. She forced herself to look down at her sandwich, feeling her cheeks heat. Someone *had* seen Joel cop a feel in the food line. Stan Wolchonok had seen.

God, how humiliating.

She choked down several more tasteless bites of her sandwich and finished her soda. Gathering up her trash, she said another quick thanks to Kate and headed outside, out of the building and toward the water, hoping that the fresh ocean air would help her regain her steadiness and calm.

But she heard the door open, as if someone were following her. Please don't let it be the senior chief. Please don't let it be—

"Hey, Teri, where you going in such a hurry?"

Well, that was a lesson in "be careful what you wish for." It wasn't Stan Wolchonok. It was Joel.

Evade and conceal.

Keep distance between them.

Run away.

Teri put her head down, pretending she hadn't heard him, and kept on walking.

The April morning should have been glorious. Crisp and clean with a bright blue sky and a breeze that proclaimed spring was finally here.

Helga Rosen awakened early with the strange sound of airplanes buzzing overhead. Lots and lots of airplanes.

She lingered in her room until eight, and then, like every other day, she went downstairs for a bowl of Fru Inger Gunvald's porridge, ready to curl up in a warm corner of the kitchen to enjoy her breakfast with a book. If she was lucky, she could get in at least an hour and a half of reading before she had to leave for school.

And if she was really lucky, Fru Gunvald would have brought her daughter Marte with her and they'd play one of Marte's marvelous make-believe games out in the yard.

Two years older, Marte was Helga's best friend in all the world.

But this morning Fru Gunvald was late. The kitchen hearth was cold, the room was empty.

Poppi was still home at this hour, arguing with Hershel.

Hershel! Helga ran to him. "What are you doing here?"

Her brother gave her a swift hug. "We've been invaded, mouse. The Germans are in Copenhagen. Classes are canceled."

"Invaded!" she gasped.

"Don't scare the child," her father scolded.

"*Some*one besides me ought to be frightened." Hershel turned back to her. "It happened in less than two hours, Helga. German soldiers came in on a coal ship before dawn. They're everywhere in the city now and the king surrendered with hardly a fight. It's bad news for all Danes." He grimly looked up at their father. "Worse for Danish Jews."

"Helga, go upstairs to your mother." Poppi's face was turning pink as he glared at Hershel. "Don't talk like that in front of her."

The sound of a wagon clattering out in the yard made them all jump. Helga's heart pounded. She'd read accounts of the roundups of Jews in Germany and Poland from underground newspapers Hershel had gotten at university and passed on to her, whispering to hide them from Poppi.

She ran to the window, but it wasn't Nazis in the yard. It was only Herr Gunvald. Marte's father.

He leapt down from his wagon, a big, broad-shouldered man, much taller than Dr. Rosen. He was a laborer, using his back to build houses—a profession that had always impressed Helga far more than her parents.

"Helga needs to know what's going on," Hershel said to their father, "what's happening in Germany—and all over Europe."

"That can't happen here," Poppi insisted. "This is Denmark. Rabbi Melchior says we must stay calm."

Herr Gunvald hammered on their door as if the hounds of hell were after him.

Helga opened it.

"Herr Rosen, have you heard?" he asked, talking to her father over her head. "We're part of Germany now."

"We've heard," Hershel said tightly.

"Where's Fru Gunvald?" Helga asked. There was no one else in the wagon.

"She's at home," Herr Gunvald told her. "Until we find out what's going on, I thought it best Inger and Marte stay there."

"Helga, go upstairs." Her father's pink face was turning red. Never a good sign.

Still, she didn't move.

"Helga, are you listening?"

"I'm going into Copenhagen to find Annebet—make sure she's all right," Herr Gunvald continued.

"Annebet!" Helga couldn't keep from exclaiming. Marte's

sister, Annebet, was in Copenhagen, still at university, with all those German soldiers. "Please bring her home!"

"I will. Inger asked me to stop here on my way into the city, let you know she wouldn't be in today." He bent down to speak directly to Helga. "Would you like to come to our house to play with Marte this morning?" He glanced up at her father. "You're all welcome to come if you're at all nervous about—"

"Helga?"

"My father says this is Denmark," Hershel said. "Despite the fact that German soldiers are in our streets, we must stay calm."

"Helga. Hello? Are you listening to me?"

"I'm trying to listen to Hershel, Poppi!"

"Okay, earth to Helga. Come back to me, woman. You've called me a lot of names through the years, some of them obscene, but Poppi?"

Helga blinked.

"Desmond Nyland." His familiar face was right in front of her, dark brown eyes studying her with concern. He looked as tired as she felt, lines of strain making him seem much older than she knew him to be.

"That's me, homegirl. You back with me?"

She nodded, shaken. Gone was Denmark. Gone were Poppi and Herr Gunvald. Gone was Hershel. Gone for so long, just yesterday she realized she could no longer recall his face. There were no photographs—not of him. Refugees usually didn't manage to have too many family photographs, and she had more than most.

"So where'd you go to?" Des sat down across from her desk, crossed his long legs. "Denmark?"

"Yeah," she admitted. She had been seven years old when the Germans invaded. "I must've fallen asleep."

"I don't think you were sleeping. Your eyes were open and you were talking to me."

She looked at her desk, her office. There were pictures on the desk of her husband, Avi, and her two tall sons. Her seven grandchildren. A picture of Desmond and his wife, Rachel, and their adopted daughter, Sara—black, white, and Asian.

They were quite the diverse family. Yes, Helga had plenty of photographs now, and a nice home—the same home for over forty years.

Not bad for a former refugee.

"Now, I know who Marte and Annebet Gunvald are," Des said. "Their family helped you hide from the Nazis. I've heard that story plenty of times. But who's Hershel? He's a new one to me."

Never forget. She'd lived her entire life making sure that the people she came into contact with knew that she was a Holocaust survivor. She'd told her story too many times to count. But Hershel she never spoke about. Nearly sixty years later, and it still hurt too much.

"You want to talk about this now or later?" Des asked, his voice gentle.

God, she was tired. Old and tired, with bones that hurt and a brain that had recently started time traveling. No, she didn't want to talk about this at all. "Later."

She frowned down at her desk, at her files there, at the page of notes she had written—in Danish. About . . . moving to Israel? Notes about safeguarding Mutti's furniture, some of which miraculously had been kept in perfect condition by neighbors while they'd been—

Oh, dear.

She pulled another file on top of it, and Des stood up. As her personal assistant for years, he knew enough not to press. "All right. Let me know if you need anything."

"I do need something. I need to find Marte Gunvald." Helga looked at him. "I've tried before, but now . . ." Maybe if she located Marte, found out about Annebet, made some kind of physical connection with the part of her past that she'd avoided for so long, she'd stop being haunted by these vivid memories that sucked her back in time and disoriented her so. "Can you help me find her? I know you still have some intelligence connections."

That was putting it mildly.

A former member of a U.S. Air Force elite rescue squad, Desmond had come to Israel in the early 1980s after marrying an Israeli woman and converting to Judaism. Those first few years, he'd worked with the unrivaled Israeli intelligence agency, Mossad. When he'd been appointed as her personal assistant several years later, Helga had suspected he'd been given the assignment because, with her, he could do things— go places and observe people—he otherwise wouldn't have been able to do, standing out rather visibly as a black man in a predominantly white world.

In all the years they'd been together, Helga had never asked Des a favor like this. She'd never played the intelligence card.

Until now.

It had never been this important.

He nodded. Got out the little leather-bound notepad he always carried in his inside jacket pocket. "Marte Gunvald," he said as he wrote. "I'll get right on it."

"Thank you," she said as he went out the door. "Give Rachel my love."

Des stopped. "Rachel's been dead for two years."

Merde. "I'm sorry. I'm—"

"Tired," he said. "Yeah, I know. I'm tired, too."

Stan watched Joel Hogan follow Teri Howe out of the fast food restaurant, swung his legs clear of the booth, and stood up.

"Excuse me, sir," he said, briefly meeting Tom Paoletti's eyes. Nodding to the other officers at the table, he headed for the same door through which both Howe and Hogan had exited.

Hogan was married, but men and women on the base sometimes had extramarital affairs, same as in the civilian world. And it was possible that what he'd just seen was some kind of kinky game Teri Howe was playing with the movie-star handsome lieutenant commander.

If that was the case, he'd find them in some closet, with Hogan's tongue in her mouth and his hand down her pants, breaking every rule in the book on appropriate behavior for an officer and a gentleman while on base.

That was if he found them at all.

But on the other hand, the tension he'd seen on Teri's face and in her shoulders and in the way she clutched her tray sure didn't look as if it came from playing some sex game. When she'd pulled away from Hogan back in the Mickey D's, every fiber of her being had been shouting for him to get his fucking hands offa her.

Of course, maybe that was just what Stan himself had felt like shouting.

God *damn*, the woman deserved a little respect. She was one of the best helo pilots he'd ever worked with, and he'd worked with plenty. But Howe was beyond solid. She was reliable. Efficient. Self-confident. Unshakable. Fearless in the air.

He'd seen her take her helo down and hover nearly motionless within yards of the radio tower on an oceanographic research vessel, a ship called the SS *Freedom*, out in the middle of the Pacific.

When the call from the *Freedom* had come in, she'd been transporting the Troubleshooter Squad home from a training op. They'd just spent three weeks aboard an aircraft carrier and were eager to get back to shore. Teri had been their taxi driver, so to speak.

But the distress call had come in, asking for any available assistance. Three teenaged students participating in some Jacques Cousteau–type onboard oceanography school had had a diving accident and were developing severe cases of the bends. The *Freedom* had a portable recompression chamber, but it had malfunctioned. The Coast Guard and even the Air Force pararescue jumpers were raring to come to their aid, but the ship was a good two-hour flight out—a four-hour round trip back to San Diego.

By sheer luck the SEALs were within minutes of the *Freedom*'s location. They could get the kids and bring them to the hospital in the shortest possible time.

The ship was too small for the helo to set down on the deck, but Teri Howe had brought them pretty damn close. They'd taken aboard the three students as if it were the easiest thing in the world to lift hospital baskets off a small ship being buffeted by healthy four-foot swells and gale force winds from a helo hovering overhead. Throughout, Teri's voice had come through Stan's headset, calm and composed and completely in control.

She'd gotten them all on board and flown them back to San Diego in record time, staying low to the water all the way in. It was a wild ride, and when they'd landed on the hospital grounds, as the medical team was unloading the kids, he'd gone forward in the helo to thank her face-to-face for a job well done. He'd been one of the men down on the deck of that ship, clipping the baskets to the line from the helo, and he knew firsthand that her skill as a pilot had helped save those kids' lives.

"Good job, ma'am." It was a simple compliment, yet she'd looked at him as if he'd given her a million dollars. With her cheeks flushed and her brown eyes sparkling, she'd looked so heart-stoppingly pretty, he'd quickly backed away.

"That's the way I like to fly," he'd heard her say. Fast as hell, apparently, and with lives at stake. She was tough, she was strong, she was capable.

So why the hell hadn't she broken Hogan's kneecap back there in the McDonald's when he'd grabbed her ass?

The air outside was cool and wet and smelled like the ocean—like salt and fish and great expectations.

Stan moved quietly around the corner of the building and toward the far parking lot, guessing by process of elimination that they'd headed that way. It was a pretty public location for a lovers' tryst, but if he did come upon them in a compromising position, he'd simply back quietly away.

He'd be disappointed, sure, but he wouldn't let it affect his opinion of Howe's skills as a pilot and as part of his team's support staff. He knew plenty of men who had excellent judgment when it came to their professions, but who were complete boneheads when dealing with their personal lives.

He could maybe even count himself among their number.

And then there they were. Teri Howe and Lieutenant Commander Hogan. In the parking lot. Standing much too close.

Except Teri was turned away from Hogan, as if she were trying to unlock the door of her truck.

Trying to get away.

Hogan leaned closer, his voice too low for Stan to make out the words.

Teri's answer was easier to hear. "I said, back off."

Stan moved toward them, picking up his pace. He wasn't sure if he was rushing to her rescue or merely moving closer to get a better view for when she kneed the asshole in the balls.

She'd managed to get the door unlocked, but she couldn't open it. Not without pressing up against Hogan. He was pinning her in place, one hand on either side of her, against the roof of the car.

"I told you before I'm not interested," Stan heard her say. "What part of that don't you understand?"

Hogan laughed, as if she'd made some kind of joke.

"The ice princess thing is a nice touch as far as your career goes, but come on, Teri. This is me you're talking to. We both know the real truth. How about I come over to your place tonight?" Hogan asked. "How about we—"

"Please."

Hogan was laughing, the asshole, like this was some kind of game. "You know you want me."

Her voice shook with anger. "What I want is for you to take your little pencil of a penis and keep it *far* away from me."

Stan wanted to laugh out loud, but the truth was, Teri Howe had made a serious mistake. When it came to assholes like Joel Hogan, you didn't insult their manhood, and you certainly didn't use the word *little* when talking about their personal package. She'd given him a direct invitation to prove her wrong.

And the bastard did. Or at least he tried to.

"You must be confusing me with someone else." From his angle Stan couldn't quite see everything, but he knew from the look on Teri's face that Hogan was touching her. Not with his hands—they were still on the car. But the son of a bitch had leaned even closer and was rubbing himself up against her.

And now he was going to die. She was going to elbow him in the ribs, maybe scrape the heel of her boot down his shin. Either way, it was going to hurt. Stan crossed his arms, settling in to watch.

But Teri didn't move, and Stan realized with a jolt of shock that she was frozen. That hadn't been anger making her voice shake. That had been fear. Damn, for some reason—and he didn't want to think why, the possibilities were too unpleasant—she was unable to move away or defend herself from this asshole.

Stan didn't hear what Hogan said to her, didn't hear what she said in reply, because he'd gone back around the corner, completely out of their sight.

"Excuse me, Lieutenant Howe," he called out, even before they could see him, pretending he'd just arrived.

And Hogan instantly backed off.

The look on Teri's face was one Stan would remember for the rest of his life. For the briefest instant, she looked at him as if he'd saved her, her eyes filled with relief, with echoes of fear and pure dread. But then she hid it all behind an almost expressionless perfunctory smile.

Hogan wasn't so smooth. Anger glittered in his eyes. He was pissed at Teri, and pissed at Stan, too, for interrupting them.

Although really, what was there left to say to a woman after she used those particular words to describe you?

Stan would've simply walked away, secure in his knowledge that she was misinformed. But maybe Hogan wasn't quite as emotionally well-endowed.

Stan kept his face as expressionless as Teri's, his own eyes devoid of emotion. He was just the enlisted messenger. The officers' servant. He knew that in Hogan's eyes, as a senior chief he was one step up from the butler. "Lieutenant Paoletti wanted me to go over a few points with you before this afternoon's training exercise," he said to Teri.

"We'll finish this conversation later," Hogan said.

Oh, yeah? How would he bring it up? *Say, Teri, about that pencil of a penis thing . . .*

"No need to bother," she told Hogan politely, in a voice that still wobbled a little. "I think we've covered all the ground necessary, sir."

"No," Hogan said. "I'll call you. At home." He turned his back on her protests and walked swiftly toward the administration building, nodding curtly to Stan as he passed.

"I know this is supposed to be your lunch break, ma'am,"

Stan told Teri, "so if you have some errands to run downtown, we could meet in my office at 1300."

"Oh," she said. "Yeah. That . . . That's a good idea." He knew she was far more shaken up than she was willing to let on. She was wearing a jacket, but she held her arms as if she were cold. Or as if her hands were shaking and she didn't want him to see. "Thank you, Senior Chief."

Enough already.

"Teri, I lied," Stan told her bluntly. "L.T. didn't ask me to talk to you. I saw you and Hogan. I *heard* you and Hogan."

She lifted her chin, finally met his gaze dead on. "I know." Her voice shook slightly. "Thank you, Senior Chief."

Ah, crap. Now she was forcing a smile, but with her eyes so huge in her thin face, she looked about twelve years old, and about as defenseless. Stan wanted to go find Hogan and beat him senseless.

He wanted to pull her into his arms and give her a reassuring embrace. But, Christ! *That* was the last thing she needed from him right now. Another man who wanted to touch her. No, she needed him to be cool and distant and professional.

She needed him to nod and walk away. To give her space to regain her equilibrium.

He couldn't do it.

"I couldn't help but notice that you seem to be having a problem, Lieutenant." He called her by her rank to cancel out the fact that he'd slipped and called her Teri a few moments earlier.

She didn't say anything, but she didn't run away either, so he kept going, choosing his words carefully.

"I'm not sure what's going on here." Much better, certainly more polite than flatly asking what the fuck was happening. "And I know that under normal circumstances, I'm probably—technically—the dead last person you should go to with a problem, but . . . I get the feeling that these are not normal circumstances."

She had been staring down at the ground, but now her gaze flicked up to his face, to his eyes, and then away.

"Look, I don't mean to embarrass you," Stan told her as gently as he could. The men he'd yelled at for being lazy sons of bitches during this morning's run would've been amazed. "I just want you to know that a problem that might seem insurmountable to you might not seem that way to someone like me."

He twisted his mouth up into what he hoped was a reassuring smile as she glanced up at him again.

"I'm here," he said as honestly as he possibly could, holding her gaze, hoping she understood that he meant what he said. It was probably wrong, he could probably get hammered even just for offering, but . . . "If you decide you want some help, Teri, I'm here. Okay?"

Oh, damn, her eyes filled with a sudden rush of tears.

And that wasn't even the biggest surprise. The biggest surprise was when she threw herself forward, into his arms.

Yes, the biggest surprise of the day, week, month, and possibly even the year was that he was standing in the parking lot, getting hugged by Teri Howe.

Stan's body reacted more quickly than his brain, and he was hugging her back before he had time to consider what exactly he should do in this particular circumstance.

But holy shit, she was an armful. Both soft and strong, she was warm and female—all soft breasts against his chest, and god *damn*, her hair smelled great. He buried his nose in it before he realized that probably wasn't such a good idea.

And then, almost before he registered the fact that, Christ, she was trembling, it was over. She pulled back, away from him, looking as surprised at herself as he was.

"I'm sorry," she said, hanging on to herself again as if she might explode into a thousand pieces. "God, I'm—"

Stan adjusted his face, wiping away the incredulous expression he knew he must've been wearing. "Did he hurt you?" he couldn't keep himself from asking. "Hogan," he added. "If he did, I'll—" *Fucking kill him.* He stopped himself from saying that in the nick of time.

"No," she said, glancing around, no doubt checking to see who'd witnessed her hugging SEAL Team Sixteen's senior chief. The parking lot was still empty, she was safe. She backed away. "No, it's not . . . I'm sorry." She turned and practically ran away. "Thank you, Senior Chief," she called back to him.

"No problem," he said, though she couldn't possibly hear him. "Teri."

Teri. Yeah, right. One weird hug, and she's permanently Teri in his head.

Okay, Mr. Fix Everything. Now what?

Teri—who would henceforth be thought of only as *Lieutenant Howe*—clearly was having some kind of problem—probably one of a sexual harassment nature—with Lieutenant Commander Hogan, who would henceforth be thought of as *that asshole*.

Stan had made it clear to Lieutenant Howe that if she wanted help, he was available. But he couldn't force her to tell him what the problem was. Confronting that asshole—as much as he was itching to do so—was not one of Stan's options right now.

Teri Howe was a big girl. If she wanted Stan's help, she would ask. Until then, the best he could do was sit tight. And keep an eye on her.

If Hogan was going to mess with Teri Howe again, well, damn, it wasn't going to happen on *Stan's* watch.

And that was for fucking sure.

Two

TERI HESITATED OUTSIDE the door, double-checking the address.

No, this was definitely it, 23 Hillside. Who would've guessed? Senior Chief Stan Wolchonok lived in a 1920s-era bungalow.

It was cute, it was small, and it was pristine, with what had to be the original leaded glass windows, a neatly kept yard, and one heck of an ocean view.

Living there would be kind of like having a portal to a different time. You could come home from work, close the door—and shut out most of the twentieth and twenty-first centuries.

Provided no one dropped by unannounced.

She should have called before coming over. What was she thinking, to drop in on the senior chief when he was off duty and relaxing, as if they were friends or something?

Truth was, she didn't want to go home. If Joel was waiting for her there, like yesterday . . .

Teri squared her shoulders and rang the bell.

Nothing.

A truck that looked like something the senior chief might own was parked in the driveway. He was home. He *had* to be home. She didn't think she would ever find the nerve to come back at another time if he wasn't home now.

She rang the bell again—just as the door swung open.

"Sorry," she said. Oh, that was a brilliant start. She tried to smile. "Hi." Even better.

Complete surprise crossed Senior Chief Wolchonok's face

as he looked at her. It didn't last long. It was just an almost imperceptible flash before he assumed the neutral expression she recognized as his parade rest face. It made him look completely inscrutable.

"I'm sorry," she said again. "This is probably a bad time."

She'd woken him up. That much was obvious. He wore a pair of shorts and a T-shirt, but his hair was a mess. It stuck straight up in places, and his feet were bare.

She turned to run away, but he stopped her. "No. I was— Are you all right?"

"Yeah, I'm . . ." Honest. She had to be completely honest with this man. It was the only way she could do this. She forced herself to look right into his eyes. They were blue—a fact she'd discovered to her surprise two days ago, when he'd followed her and Joel into the parking lot, when he was so impossibly kind to her.

She'd never dared to get close enough to the senior chief to really look into his eyes before.

"No, I'm not all right—I mean physically, I'm all right. Really," she quickly added as he started to react, "but . . ." She took a deep breath. "I'm taking you up on your offer of help, Senior Chief. That is, if it still stands."

"Of course." He didn't hesitate. "I just didn't expect . . . Um . . ."

She knew it. She shouldn't have come here, to his home. This was a mistake.

"I'm sorry. I wasn't comfortable with the idea of going to your office," she admitted, "and I wasn't even sure I was really going to come here at all until I came here and . . ." Her voice shook, dammit, but he saved her dignity by pretending he didn't notice.

"It's not a problem." He opened the door wider, stepping back. "Come in. Please. I'm not exactly dressed for visitors, and the house isn't really . . ." He tried to smile at her. "But now's a fine time. I *am* glad you came, Lieutenant. And it's absolutely fine for us to talk here. It is."

If he said *fine* one more time, she was going to turn and run.

But his entryway smelled like freshly brewed coffee, and she went inside instead. Teri had expected more of a men's locker room ambiance from the senior's house—old socks and dirty laundry—but not only was that coffee she smelled, it was *good* coffee.

And the interior of the bungalow was as perfect as the outside. The woodwork gleamed. The entryway wasn't an entryway, she realized, but rather a cozy living room. It had a fireplace made with huge smooth stones like giant, rounded beach pebbles. It was beautiful. The entire place was remarkable.

"Come on into the kitchen," he said. "Are you hungry?"

There was, however, no furniture in the room.

Only a mirror on the wall, and as the senior chief passed it, he caught sight of himself and quickly tried to fix his hair.

"God *damn*," she heard him mutter.

"You'll have to excuse me," he said more loudly. "I was up early this morning—I went out for a run. I have to go over to the base, but not for another few hours, so I was just kind of vegging out on the porch when you buzzed. Dreaming about breakfast. You caught me in scumball mode—I haven't even showered—so make sure you don't stand downwind. Coffee?"

"Thanks." The kitchen was right out of an old black-and-white movie starring Katharine Hepburn and Cary Grant. Big gas stove with a griddle. Rounded refrigerator. Separate pantry. There was a table in here, but it had only one chair.

As Teri watched, Stan took a pair of mugs from the pantry shelf and poured two steaming cups of coffee.

"I hope you like it black," he said. "I ran out of sugar and milk about two years ago." He set one of the mugs on the table beside her. "That's why I usually have to settle for dreams of breakfast—I'm too lazy to shop for anything but coffee. And I only buy that because I'm addicted." He toasted her with his mug and a smile.

He had a lovely smile. It completely transformed his face, and Teri found herself smiling tentatively back at him.

She knew what he was doing. He was talking to fill the potentially uncomfortable silence. He was trying to soothe her with his easygoing, quietly matter-of-fact, one-sided conversation, to make her feel less on edge. He was being impossibly nice—again—especially considering the way she'd barged in on his Sunday morning.

"Hmmm." He was looking at the single chair now, frowning at it as if it were at fault for not being two chairs. "Maybe we should go out onto the porch. Go ahead, Lieutenant, right through the back door there."

Holding her coffee, she obediently stepped outside onto a concrete terrace. It was surrounded by a low, rimmed concrete wall, with an overhang providing shade from the second floor of the house and two sturdy pillars in each corner.

There was only one chair out here, too, a beach style lounge chair. But Stan brought the kitchen chair with him in one hand, mug of coffee in the other.

He seemed to know that she'd prefer sitting in the kitchen chair. And instead of lying back in the recliner, he sat on the wall, facing her.

"So." He got down to business. "You want to tell me what's going on with you and Joel Hogan?"

Teri carefully set her mug down on the terrace, relieved he'd opened up the topic for her. "I'm not sure exactly where to begin."

"Why don't we start by agreeing that whatever you say here today doesn't leave this room." He looked around at the lack of walls and made a face. "You know what I mean."

She nodded. She did know. And she trusted him. She wouldn't have been here if she didn't. "Thank you."

"Why don't you get me up to speed on the ways Hogan's been harassing you. I know he's been touching you and making inappropriate comments. I witnessed that myself last week." His eyes were so kind and warm, it seemed crazy that she'd ever thought he was scary looking. "Anything else you think I need to know?"

God, there was a lot he needed to know, most of it embarrassing things she didn't want to remember, let alone share with anyone. And there were things he couldn't know, things she'd never told a soul. Things he'd probably wonder about, anyway.

If he asked her, point-blank, would she tell him the truth? She honestly didn't know.

She started with the easy stuff. "Last night Joel was waiting for me, on the porch of my apartment, when I got home."

"God *damn* it. What the f—" Stan took a deep breath. "Excuse me, please. I hear that, and I just don't know what this . . . guy is thinking."

Teri knew that there would never be a better time to say it. "He's probably thinking, 'Gee, I don't know what the problem is. She seemed to like having sex with me nine years ago.' "

She closed her eyes so she wouldn't have to see his reaction. But she heard him sigh heavily as she rubbed her forehead, her elbow on the arm of the chair.

"Okay," he said. "Yeah, I can see how a past relationship would complicate things."

She opened her eyes and looked out at him from between her fingers. "No, Senior Chief, it's worse than you think. There was no relationship."

He took a sip of his coffee, his eyes narrowing slightly as he gazed at her from behind the steam. He waited for her to continue.

She forced herself to put her hand down and look at him squarely. "Whatever you're thinking, it's ten times worse." Her stomach churned but she made herself continue. "In fact, it's about as bad as it can get. I picked him up in a bar. We had sex in the backseat of his car, in the bar parking lot. And no, I'd never done anything that stupid before, and I haven't done it since. But I did it. Once. With Joel Hogan."

There was no way the senior chief could know how much it cost her to tell him that. Her voice didn't shake. She refused to let her eyes fill with tears. But inside she was dying.

But his expression didn't change either. He'd blinked when she'd said the bit about the sex in the parking lot, but that was it.

Finally he smiled, then laughed very softly. Took a sip of coffee. Scratched his nose. Sighed.

And all the while his expression honestly didn't change. He just kept on looking at her with kindness in his eyes.

"Nine years ago, you were ... what?" he finally said. "Going to flight school? Just out of college?"

She nodded. "That's no excuse."

Neither was the fact that she'd stupidly assumed that having sex in the back of someone's car would be a major building block for a future relationship. But there was no way she was going to start yammering about all the little painful details of that night—such as the way she'd cleaned herself up after and went back into the bar, only to find out from a friend that Joel Hogan was engaged to be married in two weeks' time. God, she'd gone from being on top of the world to wanting to die. Right then and there.

"Maybe not," the senior chief said evenly, "but it's a rational explanation for stupidity. What, were you twenty-two years old? Twenty-three?"

"Nineteen."

He lifted an eyebrow.

"I graduated high school early," she explained.

"When you were *fifteen*?"

"Sixteen. I got my college degree in three years—in an accelerated program at MIT."

"Whoa." He was impressed. "A genius, huh?"

Teri snorted. "Obviously not."

He laughed softly at that. "Come on, you were young. He was probably just as flashy and good-looking then as he is now. And, oh, let me guess. You'd been drinking, right?"

She nodded and he laughed again.

"Alcohol is the one guaranteed ingredient in ninety-nine percent of the tales of woe and stupidity that I've heard down through the years," he told her. "And I've heard a lot of them, Teri. You're not the only one who did something really stupid nearly a decade ago. I made some pretty lousy choices myself, ten, twenty years ago. Do what I do, and give yourself a break."

"Easy for you to say," she said. "You didn't have sex with Joel Hogan."

He laughed loudly, and God, maybe he *was* a miracle

worker like everyone said, because for the first time ever, she could laugh about it, too.

She looked at him sitting there, with the deep blue late morning sky spreading out behind him, a gorgeous backdrop stretching all the way to the horizon where it met the sea.

Maybe this was what going to confession felt like. This sense of being absolved, of being forgiven. Of finally being safe because this awful secret had been shared. It wasn't really a secret anymore because someone else knew.

Maybe she should tell him everything. . . .

"So what are we going to do about this?" the senior chief asked. "I take it that the reason you haven't brought Hogan up on sexual harassment charges is because the details surrounding your previous relationship—and it was a relationship, it was just a really brief one—will become public. To your career and personal detriment."

She nodded.

He went on. "Teri, I've got to be honest with you. The best way to handle this might be to come clean with your boyfriend. And then have him show up at the base. Have him pick you up, give you a ride home, meet you for lunch, I don't know. Let Hogan see you with him. Maybe then he'll back down and . . . No?"

She was shaking her head.

"You don't want to tell him?" he asked.

"I don't have a boyfriend."

"Ah." She'd surprised him again. She suspected it wasn't easy to surprise the senior chief.

"I'm not very good at relationships," Teri admitted. "Men tend to avoid me." Ice princess, Joel had called her, just a few days ago. It was true. She came off as cool and aloof. It was better than scared to death, but only marginally. "I mean, they'll talk to me and flirt if they're in a group, but . . ." She smiled wanly. "Maybe I should look on the bright side. If the news about the sex in the parking lot gets out, maybe I'll finally get asked out on a date."

She liked making him laugh. She'd always thought of her sense of humor as being too dark, so she usually kept her mouth shut and her thoughts to herself. But Stan Wolchonok seemed to find her genuinely funny. And now that she no longer felt so dreadfully alone in this situation, she could see that there was an awful lot about it that was pretty hideously humorous.

However, there was still a great deal of it that was not funny at all.

"My concerns have to do with my career," she told Stan. "I'm between civilian jobs right now, and I'm considering taking a longer term OUTCONUS assignment after this one's up."

"OUTCONUS, huh?" he said. The acronym stood for outside the continental U.S. "You interested in traveling? In leaving California?"

She nodded. "Absolutely. I don't have any real ties to this area—my mother's back east. What I really want, Senior Chief, is to *fly*. No BS, no hassle, but . . ." She took another deep breath. "There's more you need to know. About one of my last civilian jobs . . . ?"

He smiled. "Don't look so worried. As long as you're not going to tell me that you had sex with the company president in the parking lot of the corporate headquarters, I'm not going to yell at you."

She laughed shakily, still amazed that she could laugh at all. "No, I did that only once."

"Yeah, I noted that you mentioned that. And I'm sorry, Lieutenant, I really shouldn't tease you about any of this."

"No," she said. "I like that you did. I like . . ." *You*. Oh, God, if she said that, he might think she'd come here for more than his help. "I don't know how to thank you. You've been so . . . sweet."

"Sweet?" That got laughter with a snort. "You can thank me by not repeating that in public. Please. My reputation will be shot to hell."

He was blushing. She'd embarrassed him, and he was trying to cover it up with a joke. As she watched, he gave up pretending and looked her in the eye.

"I like you, too," he said bluntly. "I like you as a pilot, I like you as a human being. I'm happy to be able to help you."

"Thank you," she said. She was happy, too. She was having

an almost ridiculously severe case of the warm fuzzies. He *liked* her! She hadn't felt this affected by those words since middle school.

"So let's get all the facts out on the table here," Stan continued. "There's something you think I need to know about this civilian job . . . ?"

She took a deep breath and told him. "I left Harmony Airlines because it was an unpleasant place for a woman to work." Understatement of the century. "The female employees were treated with disrespect. There was lots of sex talk and innuendo and just general ugliness. And I'm not talking about a bunch of guys sitting around occasionally joking about the size of their . . . of their—"

"Yeah," he said. "I get it."

"It was continuous, and it was meant to intimidate. It was mostly two individuals, and during my three years with the company, I did everything I could to make sure I wasn't scheduled with them. But it was a small airline and . . ."

It had been easier to leave, so she'd left.

"A few months after I handed in my resignation, I was approached by the lawyer of one of the other female pilots. She was suing them. For sexual harassment. I appeared as a witness. I testified in her behalf, she won, and the company offered me a settlement, too. I think they were afraid if they didn't, I'd turn around and sue as well." She took a deep breath. "If I make harassment charges against Joel Hogan, he'll get a lawyer. And if that lawyer digs, he'll find out about the settlement with Harmony. It was a completely different situation, but if it becomes public . . . Senior, I don't want to be known as the woman who cries harassment every six months."

He sat there nodding, his mouth slightly scrunched up in thought.

"But at the same time," she added, "I cannot handle Joel Hogan touching me." She needed Stan to understand how important it was to her that Joel be stopped. Somehow. "I don't want his hands on me, I don't want him . . ." Her voice shook.

Damn it, she'd been doing so well up to now.

"I'm scared I'm going to go home and he's going to be in-side my house, inside my bedroom," she admitted, needing to say it but unable to speak louder than a whisper. "That bastard has made me scared to go home, scared to *be* home, and that's going too damn far."

The senior chief set his coffee mug down.

"Okay," he said. Leaned forward slightly and looked her straight in the eye. "Here's what we're going to do."

"Don't even think about it."

The waiflike American girl in line at the World Airlines check-in counter was starting to cry, and Gina Vitagliano could feel Trent behind her, pushing her toward the gate.

"Come on, Gina, I'm serious," he continued, looking at her over the tops of his sunglasses, his blue eyes bored.

How could *Athens* be boring? She wondered for the twentieth time that afternoon what she'd ever seen in him.

Yes, okay, all right. So he was gorgeous with blond curls that rivaled Ryan Phillippe's. But it was only three days into this trip, and already, if she never saw him again—ever—it would be a hundred years too soon.

She'd tried to break up with him at lunch, but apparently he hadn't realized she was dead serious.

Her fault—she was always joking and teasing. Why should anyone ever take her seriously?

"It's just a con," he said, Mr. Blasé Know-It-All. "She comes to the counter just as the flight starts to board and bursts into tears. Some American sucker—" He paused, and although he didn't say *like you*, it was heavily implied. "—goes to help, and she tells them her credit card was stolen just this morn-ing on the way to the airport. They buy her a ticket and she promises that her rich daddy will send them a check, paying them back, and of course he never does because he doesn't exist. She's probably flown all over Europe this way."

"God, you are so jaded." Gina looked back at the girl, who was still pleading with the World Airlines attendants, her mascara starting to run. "I bet you don't believe in Santa Claus either, huh?"

But Casey was tugging on her sleeve now, too. With her

face pinched and worried, she looked about twelve. "Please, Gina," she said. "Let's just get on the plane. I can't wait to get *out* of here."

Gina had to admit that this airport, with its history of violence and terrorist threats, wasn't on her top ten list of favorite places to hang out.

Her father had been absolutely grim when she'd told him she was going to Europe with the university jazz band and that one of the tour cities was Athens. But she was twenty-one years old, and she'd earned the money for this trip herself. She'd weighed the potential risks in with the other pros and cons, and decided the opportunity was too good to pass up. There'd been no stopping her.

Ironically, one of the pros had been the chance of spending three weeks with dreamy Trent Engelman. Hah. Mr. Athens-is-so-dull, wake-me-when-the-bus-gets-to-the-airport Engelman.

What was *wrong* with him?

He was holding on to her by the waistband of her shorts, as if she were a dog on a leash, needing a firm hand to stay heeled. Maybe if he hadn't held her like that she would have just gotten onto the plane.

Instead she pulled away from him and out of the line. "I'll catch up." She said it to Casey, not Trent.

Poor Casey looked as if she were going to have a stroke, and Gina gave her a reassuring smile, waving her boarding pass. "It's not like I don't have a seat."

"There she goes again," Trent said with a long-suffering sigh. "Off to save the world, one pathetic loser at a time. You know, Gina, I'm not waiting for you."

He wasn't waiting for her. Okay. And she, well, *she* was never having sex with him again.

Between the two of them—and as long as the topic of *losers* had come up—she suspected *he* was the one who was going to be the most disappointed.

She smiled at him, too, then. As sweetly as possible. Looked pointedly at the long line behind them. "It's not like the plane's going to leave before everyone gets on."

Gina moved quickly away from them, before Casey could gulp at her again, before Trent could be any stupider.

Before she called him an asshole to his face.

Asshole.

"But my passport was stolen along with my boarding pass," the girl at the counter was saying. She had a remarkably perfect nose. "If I don't get on this plane—"

"I'm sorry, miss," the woman behind the counter replied in her British-tinged English-as-a-second-language accent. "I'm not sure how you got to this gate without a boarding pass, but I can't help. You have to go back to the ticket desk—"

"But I'll miss this flight!" The girl started to tear up again.

Except she wasn't a girl. Up close, Gina saw that she had to be a few years out of college. Older than Gina by at least two years. She merely *looked* seventeen, with long brown hair and delicate features that made her seem as if she came with a FRAGILE—HANDLE WITH CARE label sewn behind one of her perfect ears.

She looked a little bit like an anemic, thoroughbred version of Gina, with the same dark brown eyes and a faintly similar heart-shaped face.

They could've maybe been cousins.

It was possible this girl was what Gina would've looked like if she hadn't been born in East Meadow, Long Island, with three older brothers who continuously pounded on her until she learned to pound back, a mother who force-fed five-course Italian meals to anyone within shouting distance, a father who was a die-hard Mets fan and permanently depressed because of it, and about forty-seven aunts, uncles, and close family friends who spent their free time mucking up the lives of those unlucky enough to have been born in Gina's generation.

"I have no money at all," the girl continued. "What am I going to do?"

The World Airlines clerk had already turned away.

Yeah, this girl really had an amazing nose. It was a living tribute to some high priced plastic surgeon. Man-oh-man.

"Hi," Gina said. "I couldn't help but overhear. . . . Got your purse snatched, huh?"

The girl wiped that perfect nose on her sleeve. "My pocket was picked," she said tightly. "I wasn't even carrying a purse because I'd heard . . ." She shook her head, miserable. "This sucks. My father is going to kill me. If I'm not on that plane . . ." Her voice wobbled even harder—very Mary Tyler Moore at her most stressed. "I'm supposed to meet my sister at some hotel in Vienna and I have no way of getting in touch with her. I can't call the hotel collect and I'm *not* going to call my father!"

Gina could relate. Absolutely. "Write down your sister's name and the hotel, too," she suggested. "I'll call and leave a message for her as soon as the plane gets in."

Her long-lost half cousin's eyes widened. "You'd do that?"

"Sure. We Americans have to stick together. Got a pen?" There was one on the counter. Gina reached over and took it, handing it to the girl, along with the paper that had her luggage tags attached. "Write it on this. Do me a favor and try not to get any snot on it, okay?"

"Oh, God, I'm sorry!"

"That was a joke. I was kidding."

"It's the Hotel Rathauspark—I have the phone number for her room," the girl said. "If you could do this for me—"

"Consider it done," Gina said, glancing at the paper. The sister's name was Emily something and the hotel Ratsomething else but the number and extension were clear. "New York, right?"

The girl nodded.

"Me, too. I can always tell a fellow New Yorker. I'm Gina, by the way."

"Karen."

The line for boarding the plane was down to a businessman and a tired looking woman with a sleeping baby in a front-pack who'd come late to the gate.

Gina dug into her pocket. She had a single Greek bill there—10,000 drachmas. It was the equivalent of about twenty dollars, give or take a few.

She held it out to Karen. "Lookit, I'm not going to need this anymore. You might as well have it—buy yourself a hunk of whatever that crap is they try to pass off as hamburger. Save me the trouble of exchanging it."

The girl started to cry again. "Oh, my God, thank you so much."

"No problem. By the way, nice nose," Gina said, and got onto the plane.

Three

SAM STARRETT WAS fast asleep and dreaming that he was lying on the deck of John Nilsson's boat. It was vivid, and for a moment he was uncertain. Was he awake or was he asleep?

It was afternoon, and Nils had cut the engine. The boat was drifting while he and WildCard Karmody fished and Sam lazed in the sun—a pleasant sensation.

But Sam knew he had to be dreaming when Alyssa Locke came out onto the deck carrying two piña coladas and wearing a smile.

And absolutely nothing else.

Jesus, she was beautiful. Part black, part white, part Hispanic, part God knows what, Alyssa had a face that combined the very best features from every single race of humans around the world. Her ocean green eyes had a slightly exotic slant, and her nose was exactly the right size and shape to complement those eyes. Her smile was wide, her lips lush and full, and she had the most gorgeous, smooth as silk, mocha-colored skin. Her hair was wavy, with reddish tints. Her arms and legs were long and gracefully shaped, her body slender and athletic, yet soft in all the right places. Her breasts weren't large, but they were perfection. *She* was perfection.

He should know. He'd made love to her, thanks to the fact that she'd gotten completely shit-faced drunk and spent a night in his hotel room. One incredible, amazing night.

Of course the morning after hadn't been very much fun.

Because Alyssa Locke hated him. She'd always hated him. It had been hate at first sight and apparently a night filled

47

with the best sex of either of their lives wasn't enough to
change that.

A former U.S. Navy officer herself, Locke had resigned
her commission when she was tapped to join the FBI's
most elite counterterrorist team. A team that, at times—
unfortunately—worked closely with SEAL Team Sixteen's
Troubleshooters Squad.

Sam's team.

That night of heaven and morning of hellfire had happened
nearly six months ago. Six *long* months.

During which time Sam had dreamed about her constantly.
Hardly a night went by without Alyssa Locke showing up
in his dreams, usually naked, and so stupendously perfect
it hurt.

She smiled at him now, sitting down on top of him, straddling him right there on the lounge chair. And God, then he
was touching her again, running his hands across all that
smooth, beautiful skin.

"I missed you," she whispered, leaning down to kiss him,
her eyes filled with warmth and sparkling with amusement
and desire.

Why don't you leave me alone?

When Sam was awake, he always vowed to ask her that, the
next time he dreamed her into his life. But when he was
asleep and dreaming about her, he didn't want to say or do
anything that might make her vanish.

"I missed you, too," he whispered, heart in his throat. He
missed seeing her, missed talking to her, missed making her
laugh.

"Mmmm," she said, as she settled herself more completely
on top of him, pressing herself against the full length of his
erection. She kissed him again and then smiled. "Is that
for me?"

Stay asleep, he ordered himself. Whatever you do, *stay
asleep*.

In a heartbeat, both the drinks she was holding and his
bathing suit were gone. In a shift of the dream universe, he
was inside of her, and they were making love, moving together in perfect unison, skin slick with sweat. He was

laughing aloud, it was so damn good. She was laughing, too, her eyes alight with the same pure joy he was feeling.

"Lys," he said. He needed to tell her . . . It was important that she know . . .

Another shift, and he could hear her ragged breathing, feel each exhale against his skin, and he knew she was close, so close.

Stay asleep! Stay asleep, god damn it!

"Lys," he begged her. "Lys, please—"

"Who's Liss?" WildCard's voice cut through, and just like that, Alyssa Locke was gone and Sam was awake.

Shit.

Heart still pounding, drenched with sweat, Sam opened his eyes and stared up at the relentless blue of the sky.

WildCard handed him a bottle of beer, sat down on one of the built-in cushioned seats beside him.

Sam sat up, adjusting his shorts as he took a long, cooling slug of beer. It was probably a good thing WildCard had woken him up when he did. Another few minutes, and he would've had his first wet dream in years.

In public.

Jesus.

Johnny Nilsson sat down on the other side of him, sighing with contentment as he nursed his own beer.

"New girlfriend?" WildCard asked. "What, is Liss short for Alice or something? Do we know this girl?"

"No." Sam answered his first two questions, hoping he would apply it to the third as well, even though it wasn't true.

Yes, WildCard and Nils both knew Alyssa Locke. Sam hated the idea of lying to his friends, but he'd given Alyssa his word that he'd never tell a soul about the night they spent together.

He probably could've gotten away with confessing that he'd been dreaming about a woman he'd had a one nighter with and—didn't it always work that way?—he'd wanted more but she hadn't. But WildCard was one superintelligent son of a bitch, and it would be just Sam's luck if he put zero and zero together and came up with Alyssa Locke.

Besides, talking about it made him feel pathetic. So he drank his beer and gazed out at the horizon.

"So you're not seeing anyone these days?" WildCard persisted. "Because Janine gave me a call—I'm not with her anymore, but we're still friends—and she wanted me to ask you how come you won't return Mary Lou's phone calls?"

Ah, shit.

Sam gave him the same answer he'd told Mary Lou months ago. "It wasn't working out."

Nils opened his eyes. "I thought you said you really liked this woman."

"I did, but . . ."

"Man, you can't just not call her back," WildCard said. "I've been there, on the unanswered end of the telephone line, and it sucks."

"She was fun at first, but then it got un-fun," Sam admitted.

If he was going to withhold the truth about Alyssa from his best friends, he might as well come clean about Mary Lou. Well, as clean as he could without talking about the way he really felt.

"She's a party girl, you know?" he told them. "Every night was a Saturday night. And that body—Jesus! It was like going home with the winner of the wet T-shirt contest all the time."

Which was fun for about a week and a half.

Then reality cut through. He would lie in Mary Lou's bed, mere seconds after strenuous, gymnastic, heart-pounding, gut-wrenching sex, and instead of settling into the relaxing calm of orgasm-induced peace, his entire body would hum with dissatisfaction.

This wasn't enough.

He wanted—

No. There was no way he was going to let one night with Alyssa Locke ruin sex for him forever.

Maybe Mary Lou Morrison just wasn't the right woman. Maybe his dissatisfaction was because he was getting older, growing up, and he just didn't want every night to be a party anymore.

He didn't want empty sex with some stranger with big tits

who drank too much and had no real ambition besides hooking herself a SEAL for a husband.

"I thought she was into me for the fun," Sam admitted now to Nils and WildCard. "But she wants to join the Wives of Navy SEALs Club, and soon as she started talking about moving in, I cut her loose."

He'd actually started extracting himself from the relationship before that, pulling back instead of matching her beer for beer every night. Going home after she fell asleep.

He'd told himself it was because he couldn't stop dreaming about Alyssa Locke. She came to him relentlessly—even the nights he spent in Mary Lou's bed. He'd told himself that that wasn't fair to Mary Lou.

Truth was, Mary Lou in the morning was not a pretty sight.

"She wasn't in love with me," Sam said. "And I sure as hell am not in love with her." He looked at Nils sitting there, basking in the sunshine, all but dripping with contentment. "What we had going on was nothing like what you've got with Meg."

Newly married, with an instant family that included a ten-year-old stepdaughter and a gorgeous wife who was already pregnant with his child, John Nilsson was the poster model for true love. He walked around with a spring in his step, smiling for no apparent reason, as if he and the sun and the moon shared a private joke. Running home to Meg as soon as the day was done. Calling her if he had a few minutes free. Happier than he'd ever been before.

It would've been annoying if Sam and Nils weren't so tight. But since Sam couldn't have loved Nils more if the man were his own blood brother, he focused on being glad for him instead of envious.

And maybe that, too, was what made him decide to break it off with Mary Lou before she even started talking about the future.

Seeing Nils and Meg together.

Wanting what they'd found.

It was stupid. Sam was stupid. He didn't want what they'd found.

Couldn't you just see him with a baby on the way? He

wouldn't be calmly sitting around like Nils. He'd be in a dead panic.

What the hell did you do with a *baby*?

"Still," WildCard persisted. "You gotta call her back, man. Don't ignore her—you don't want to pull an Adele Zakashansky on her."

"The bitch," both Nils and Sam said in unison, and they all cracked up.

Except WildCard wasn't really laughing. He was just pretending to laugh. Ten whole months after he split with Adele, and he was still hurt.

Jesus, love was a crapshoot. Nils had won himself a happy-ever-after. But WildCard had lost his shirt.

And here Sam sat, between the two of them, safely single again and determined to stay that way. Unless, of course, Alyssa Locke came walking up from below, naked.

And that wasn't going to happen in this lifetime.

Sam closed his eyes and let himself drift as Nils started talking about the tracking system that WildCard, the boy genius, had developed, about patents and interest in the project from the FBI.

FBI. The name cut through his drowse.

His eyes still closed, Sam started paying attention, listening to see if, in their discussion of the FBI, either of them mentioned Alyssa Locke.

God, he was pathetic.

But he was saved from being too pathetic by the shrill sound of his cell phone.

WildCard's started shrieking a half second later.

They both grabbed for them.

Sam pulled up the antennae. "Starrett."

It was Jazz. "Get in. ASAP."

"What's up?" Sam asked, but the connection was already cut.

Sam looked at Nils, whose phone was silent. Nils shrugged as he stood up, moving back to get the motor going and head in to shore. "Nothing for me."

"Lieutenant Paoletti always did love you best," Sam told him. "You're going to be home in your own bed, with Meg in your arms tonight—while me and Karmody are getting eaten alive by mosquitos, crawling through some swamp, pretending to be terrorists while a platoon of Marines try to learn to tell their asses from their elbows."

WildCard snapped his own phone shut, "Alli, Alli, Ox in tree."

"It's a training op," Sam guessed.

"Gotta be, if Johnny didn't get called," WildCard agreed.

"Son of a bitch," Sam said. "On a *Sun*day." He complained, but the truth was, he loved getting called. Even when it wasn't real.

Sure, they were probably going to end up in some stinking, bug-infested swamp playing make-believe games with inexperienced troops, but maybe they'd get to do a HALO jump in. They'd exit the plane at a dangerously high altitude and would sky dive down, not opening their chutes until they'd almost reached the ground. That was a rush and a half—and worth all the aggravation that would come before and after.

On second thought, maybe Lieutenant Paoletti loved *Sam* best.

But then Nils's cell phone shrilled, too.

"They want us in fast," he reported. "Maybe this *is* real."

"Hang on!" WildCard gave that boat all it had, and like a rocket, they hurtled back to shore.

The adrenaline surge made Sam laugh out loud.

He didn't need Alyssa Locke, because times like this were better than sex.

Well . . . almost.

As Stan went into the hallway that led to Lt. Tom Paoletti's office, Kelly, Tom's fiancée, was coming out. Her face was pale, and her movements clipped.

"Hi, Stan." She smiled at him, but it was forced.

Great. He was here to ask his CO for a major favor, and his warm-up act had been a lovers' quarrel. Yeah, he was going to go through that door to find Tom in one hell of a bad mood.

Perfect.

"Everything okay?" he asked.

"Fine," she said shortly as she kept walking. But then she

stopped and turned back. "How can you stand working with him? He's so stubborn!"

He nodded. "Yes, ma'am, that's usually a good quality for a commanding officer."

"He won't let me pay for anything," she fumed. "Clothes. I can buy my own clothes. And I can buy him presents, but I can't buy him anything too expensive. Do you know how much money I inherited when my father died?"

Stan cleared his throat. "No, ma'am."

"Lots," she told him. "Piles. Mountains. Tom and I are set. We could both retire tomorrow and never have to work another day in our lives. Except he won't let me add his name to my bank accounts until after we're officially married. And you know what? I bet he's not even going to let me do it then."

It was really pretty amazing. Stan knew, not through his own experience but through watching his men, that the biggest source of conflict for a couple was money. But they usually fought because they didn't have enough of it.

Kelly and Tom, however, were arguing because they had too much.

"Do me a favor and just ignore me," Kelly said, and this time when she smiled it was much more natural. She was one of those sweet-looking little blondes. A real Gidget, girl-next-door type—at least on the surface.

But appearances often deceived. And Stan had once seen Kelly pull Tom with her into the ladies' room of a posh Washington, DC, restaurant while a very formal party was in full swing.

And it had been a full twenty minutes before they'd reemerged.

"I didn't mean to rant at you," she told him now. "Or to hold you up."

"Yeah," he said with a smile. "As if I'm in any kind of hurry to see him now."

She laughed as she walked away. "Just don't talk about money, and he'll be fine."

But Stan knew his CO and Kelly weren't really fighting about money. They were fighting because Tom wanted to get married and Kelly kept finding excuses not to set a wedding date.

A woman who didn't want to get married—it was one of the biggest mysteries Stan had ever encountered.

Or it had been up to about ten seconds ago. Ten seconds ago, Kelly had given Stan a big hint as to what her heel-dragging was about.

"She wants you to quit the Teams," Stan said as he went into Tom's office.

"What?" Tom Paoletti stared up at him from his desk. He was a big man with a ruggedly handsome face and warm hazel eyes that canceled out his rapidly retreating hairline. Retreating? Hell, his hair had damn near surrendered.

"Yeah," Stan said. "Kelly as much as said it, right there, out in the hall. She said she inherited enough money from her father so that you could both retire tomorrow. That's what this is all about, L.T. She doesn't want to marry some guy who's going to be gone for months at a time. Or die."

Tom shook his head. "No. Stan, I know you're usually right about these things, but this time . . . no. If there's one thing I'm certain of, it's that she's okay with me being CO of this team."

"Are you sure?"

"Yes," he said. "No. *Shit,* I don't know anything anymore, except . . . can we please not talk about this right now?"

"I'm sorry, sir," Stan said. "I thought I was helping."

"You were," Tom told him, sorting through the piles of paperwork on his desk. "You are. I just need to file it away and think about it later, when the squad's not hours from going wheels up."

"Sir, I know we discussed my not participating in this particular training op," Stan said. "But I'd like to go along."

This op was mostly a test to see how quickly Team Sixteen's Troubleshooters Squad could get in the air, across both the country and the Atlantic to the Azores.

Usually if something was up in that part of the world, a SEAL team based on the East Coast would be called in. But that didn't stop the powers-that-be from testing readiness and the ability to move quickly and efficiently from one distant spot on the globe to another.

And while they were there, the squad would be participating in a training op with an SAS team from England.

It was a silver bullet assignment—a reward for the hard-working men in Team Sixteen. The SAS were always a kick to work with, full of new tricks, potent dark English stout, and their twisted Monty Python senses of humor. And—bonus—at this time of year there were few nicer places on earth than the Azores islands.

Still, Stan had originally opted to stay behind, in garrison along with Paoletti, in an attempt to get caught up with the paperwork that threatened to overflow his desk. The team's XO, Lt. Jazz Jacquette, was in command of the training op, so his men were in good hands.

"I'd also like to call in a favor, sir. It has to do with Lt. Teri Howe," Stan continued. "I'd like you to request to bring her along to work with the team, as support for this operation."

Stan had the CO's full attention now. "She's Reserve," Tom pointed out. "This operation is OUTCONUS."

"She wants to do it, sir. I'll take care of whatever paperwork is necessary to transfer her wherever she needs to go to make this possible."

Lieutenant Paoletti was looking at him with that X-ray gaze that seemed able to penetrate a man's skull and see his very thoughts.

"What's going on, Senior Chief?" he asked. "Are you and Howe—"

"Whoa," Stan said. "L.T. Reality check. Have you seen this girl? And my use of the improper *girl* instead of the more feminist and PC *woman* is intentional, sir. She's very young."

"And very beautiful. Yes, I've certainly seen her. She's hard to miss. Nice as hell, too."

"And to be honest, I'm not unaffected by any of that," Stan admitted.

It was true. If it had been anyone besides Teri Howe ringing his doorbell, he wouldn't have let them inside of his house.

He had a rule that he never broke. His house was off-limits to everyone he worked with. It was his sanctuary. But along came Teri Howe with her amazing brown eyes, and he broke his unbreakable rule without hesitating.

"She came to me for help with a serious problem," he told the lieutenant. "I'm not going to go into details—it's something you definitely don't want to know about. But it would do her good to get out of Dodge for a few weeks."

"She came to you?" Tom asked. "Why would she do that?"

"Let's talk figuratively," Stan said. "Say one of the female officers was being sexually harassed by, oh, say, a lieutenant commander. And say I saw this asshole grabbing this female officer's ass—and say she knew I saw. And say I followed her out to where he'd cornered her in the parking lot and—"

"Damn." Tom sighed and rubbed his forehead. "There are proper channels for this kind of thing."

"Yes, sir, there are. But that doesn't apply in this particular unique situation."

Tom applied pressure to his eyes. Stan was definitely giving the man a headache.

Another sigh and Tom looked up at him. "You know, I could order you to tell me who this lieutenant commander is."

"Aye, sir," Stan agreed. "You could. But I know you'll trust that I have my good reasons when I ask you not to do that. Besides, we were talking figuratively, remember?"

Tom gazed at him for many long seconds. But then he laughed. "You know what's going to happen, don't you? You're going to marry Teri Howe before Kelly marries me."

Stan laughed, too. That was just plain silly. "Right."

"Yeah," Tom said. "It's going to be just like it was with Johnny Nilsson. I turn around, and wham, the kid's married. How did that happen? I've been engaged for forever, I'm dying to marry this fabulous woman I absolutely adore, only I can't seem to get it done. I swear to God, if you come back from the Azores and tell me you want to get married, I'll—"

"That's not going to happen," Stan insisted.

"Throw you a party," Tom finished with a tired smile.

"Muldoon," Stan said. "I'm going to set her up with Mike Muldoon. Not that you heard that from me."

He'd thought of it right away, when Teri Howe was lamenting the fact that she couldn't get a date. Who would be more perfect for her than Muldoon—the Troubleshooters' own personal version of Dudley Do-Right? Honest, sincere, squeaky clean, and disgustingly handsome. Stan had no trouble imagining the two of them together.

Tom looked at him. More X-ray vision. "Okay. You better get moving if you're going to do that paperwork. And somebody better tell Howe to get her gear together."

"Thank you, sir." Stan put the papers on the CO's desk. "She's all ready to go, and I have the paperwork right here."

"Of course you do." Tom smiled and signed.

Four

THEY WERE BEING hijacked.

The news came from the white-faced stewardesses who moved through the cabin, telling people in a variety of languages to remain seated and to please stay quiet and calm. There was a gunman in with the pilot, demanding they land the plane in Kazbekistan.

Gina held Casey's hand, glad to have something to do, someone to talk to, to soothe, to keep from going ballistic. It was keeping her from going ballistic herself.

"Stay calm," Dick McGann, the university band director, told the American students, although he looked as if his head were going to explode. "Stay quiet, stay in your seats."

Gee, thanks for the news flash, Dick. As if they hadn't heard the stewardess.

Casey was crying, but at least she was doing it silently now as the plane began its descent.

"We'll land in Kazabek," Gina told her friend, "and that'll be that. This guy probably just wants a ride home. He'll get off the plane and—"

"You really think so?" Casey's eyes were hopeful.

Gina was praying it was so. She didn't want to think about what might really be happening here. She'd taken a world cultures course last semester that had dealt primarily with the concept of terrorism.

She'd done a term paper on the psychological makeup of people who would willingly pick up a gun and take a roomful—or a planeful—of people hostage.

In order to do that, you had to be ready to be a martyr for your cause. To die.

59

And to kill.

Please, God, don't let the gunman start shooting and make the plane go down and . . .

They landed. The wheels touched down with a lurch and a jerk, and thank God at least falling out of the sky was no longer an option.

Somehow she managed to smile at Casey. "Yeah," she said. "Any minute now, he's going to get off the plane. I'm almost sure of it."

One of the big ironies of this situation was that Gina had used Kazbekistan when arguing the merits of this trip with her father. "It's not like we're going to Kazbekistan," she'd said.

Um, Dad? Change of plans . . .

And, crap, if they were delayed too long here in Kazabek, she wouldn't be able to call the Perfect Nose's sister at the Hotel Ratskywatsky or whatever was written on that piece of paper in her pocket.

"Think positively," she told Casey, told herself. "This is going to be over really soon."

The plane stopped rolling right there, on the middle of the runway, some distance from the terminal—if you could call the rundown Quonset hut and two-story concrete block structure a terminal. Come to think of it, this entire airport was barely an airport. It was a concrete strip in the middle of a field on the edge of marshlands, near the sea.

Two of the stewardesses moved purposefully at the front of the plane, the third moving back through the aisle to speak to the passengers.

"Please stay in your seats," she informed them. "The gunman has ordered us to open the door."

"See? So he can get off the plane," Gina whispered to Casey.

She could see out the window, see an awkward-looking cart with a disembarking ladder attached zooming across the concrete toward them. She could see it lurch to a stop. She could see . . .

Oh, God. Oh, tremendously powerful God . . .

"Don't do it!" Gina shouted over the hush. "Don't open the—"

The door opened.

And four camouflage-clad men carrying machine guns boarded.

Oh, *God*!

The chaos and noise was immediate, although most of it came from the intruders. They spoke loudly, in a language Gina didn't understand, but their meaning was clear. Close the doors.

The stewardesses didn't move quickly enough, and one of the men hit one of them—hard—in the back with the butt of his weapon.

A man in first class stood up as if to stop them and got savagely smashed in the head for his trouble. He went down, bleeding, and around Gina, everyone burst into tears.

She held on to Casey, who was sobbing uncontrollably. Dear God. Dear *God* . . .

Two rows up, she could see Trent, where he was sitting with Jack Lewis and Miles Foley.

He wasn't bored anymore.

Helga Shuler was losing it.

It. Her marbles. Her mind.

It was probably early stages Alzheimer's and it had caught Des completely by surprise. The worst of it was, he had no idea how long it had been going on.

The woman was a list maker. As long as he'd known her, she'd worked off of an entire legal pad of lists. Things that had to get done immediately. Things to do later. Things to start thinking about doing.

She made lists reminding her of the names of the people she was working with on various projects, lists of their spouses and children and birthdays. Lists of facts, lists of dates, lists of important information.

He simply hadn't known that that important information had probably included what year it was and what city she was working and living in and the fact that her husband, Avi, had died ten years ago.

He wondered if his name was on her current list. "Desmond

Nyland, personal assistant since 1986. His wife, Rachel—my former close friend—deceased two years. Adopted daughter, Sara, in first year at Harvard."

For years Helga Rosen Shuler had traveled all over the world as an envoy—a representative of Israel. She was sharply intelligent, marvelously eloquent, elegantly dignified, and warmly caring—one class act all the way. She was also a Holocaust survivor, a Danish Jew who never let an opportunity slide to remind the world of that fact.

She'd just turned sixty-eight. That was hardly old at all. She was still energetic, vibrant.

Maybe it wasn't Alzheimer's—her forgetting Rachel had been gone these past two years, her talking aloud to her Poppi and Marte and whatnot. Maybe she *was* simply overtired, overworked.

And maybe the man in the moon was coming over for dinner tonight.

So okay. He'd keep an eye on her for a while.

But if it happened again, Des was going to have to tell her that if she didn't resign voluntarily, he would need to inform both her bosses and his that she was no longer fit to do her job.

And wouldn't that be fun?

He knocked on the door to her office.

"Come in."

Helga was sitting behind her desk, looking up at him expectantly, with her usual friendly smile lighting her still pretty face as he came inside.

Des looked into her eyes. Did she even know who he was? He closed the door behind him, hating the fact that he would wonder that now, every time he saw her. "I found Marte Gunvald."

"Oh, my God, Des, you *did*? That quickly?"

Thank God. She knew who he was. "Luck played into it. And the news isn't all that good."

She was ready for it, already at peace with the idea. "She's dead."

He nodded. "Since 1980. Cancer." He handed her the file and sat down across from her desk, watching as she scanned it.

"So young," she murmured. "Her son was only what . . . ? Eighteen, poor thing, at the time. Stanley. Marte had a son named *Stanley*. It says he's from Chicago. Did she live in Chicago, too? Were there any other children?"

"I'll have more info for you in a few hours," Des told her. "Like I said, it was luck the information in this file was available. And I'm afraid your good luck is very bad luck for one hundred and twenty people on World Airlines flight 232 out of Athens. The reason this info came up so quickly is that two hours ago, terrorists hijacked that flight, forcing it to land in Kazbekistan. They're demanding the freedom of two prisoners—one in an American jail, and one in an Israeli jail—both charged with terrorism."

Des leaned forward to tap the file. "Marte's son—Senior Chief Stanley Wolchonok—is one of a team of U.S. Navy SEALs being called in to deal with the terrorist situation. He doesn't even know it yet. His CO probably just got the order himself."

And yet she and Des knew. There were questions in Helga's eyes, questions she knew better than to put into words. Questions he couldn't answer about his connection to Mossad, Israel's intelligence organization, questions about Mossad itself.

Instead she asked, "Who's going?"

Israel didn't negotiate. The terrorists could kill all of the people on that plane, one by one, and Israel still wouldn't let that prisoner go free.

But they would play the game. They'd send a representative to Kazbekistan to help buy the Americans the time they needed to get their team of SEALs in place and take down the plane.

Des shook his head. "Helga, believe me, you don't want to go to Kazbekistan." The godforsaken country was nicknamed the Pit. It was listed as the number-one nastiest place on the planet in the newly revised edition of *The World's Most Dangerous Places*.

"Yes, I do. Someone has to go, and I want it to be me." She had on her envoy face, used her envoy voice. "Do whatever you have to do to get me there."

* * *

Something big was up.

First Jazz Jacquette got a phone call.

Big and black, SEAL Team Sixteen's executive officer's default expression wasn't quite as dark a glower as Senior Chief Wolchonok's. His was more an expression of intensity, of ultimate concentration.

A taciturn, somewhat aloof man, Jazz seemed as if he were always on the verge of figuring out the cure for cancer or developing a theory that would enable him to defy gravity.

Teri had been a little nervous as she boarded the transport plane, when she'd found out that Jazz, not Tom Paoletti, was in command of this training op that she'd been sent along to participate in. But then she'd seen the senior chief. He'd met her gaze, sent her both a smile and a nod, and she'd relaxed.

Stan was here. She was safe.

It was a strange feeling—this sense of safety—and she refused to overanalyze it, to accidentally exorcise it by giving it too much thought.

As she watched, Jazz, still on the phone, called Stan over. He said something to Stan, and whatever he said, it made Stan instantly more alert.

Which was saying something. Stan Wolchonok usually stood like a fighter—on the balls of his feet and ready for anything. But as Teri watched, he went to DEFCON 1, to launch mode. There was really no other way to describe it.

He and Jazz had a conversation, with Jazz still holding the phone to his ear. And then, when Jazz gave his full attention back to the phone, Stan turned.

And looked at her. It was a little shocking, all that energy aimed directly at her.

Oh, fuck.

She usually wasn't very good at reading lips, but Stan's exclamation was impossible to miss.

But then he turned away and began talking to Sam Starrett, who had joined him and Jazz. Starrett, normally the king of laid-back cool, was all sharp movements and terse business, too.

"What's going on?"

Teri wasn't the only one who'd noticed something big was afoot. Ensign Mike Muldoon was sitting behind her and he leaned forward, concern in his eyes.

"I don't know," she said.

PO2 Mark Jenkins came down the aisle toward them. "A plane with Americans on board's been hijacked," he told them. "We're being rerouted to Kazbekistan."

Teri looked back at Stan, who was deep in conversation with both Starrett and Jazz. This mission had gone from make-believe to real life in the blink of an eye.

They were going to Kazbekistan—where U.S. Navy helo pilots were ordered to wear their flack jackets if they so much as set one foot outside of their garrison hotel.

Oh, fuck was putting it mildly.

FBI counterterrorist team agent Alyssa Locke came out of the elevator and into the lobby of her apartment building as Jules's car pulled up out front.

She ran out to meet him, opening the door to put her carry-on luggage into the backseat.

"Go," she said as she climbed into the front, and he pulled away from the curb before she even shut the door.

The flight to Kazbekistan was leaving in forty-five minutes. No way was it going to be delayed because of them.

Despite the fact that the call had come in less than an hour ago, despite the fact that Jules had been out of the office at the time, and despite the fact that they'd both been running nonstop ever since, they were not going to be late.

"I can't believe this," Jules said, driving fast, with both hands on the wheel. "Can you believe this?"

"No," Alyssa said.

FBI negotiator Max Bhagat had asked for both of them by name, requesting that they join a small group of FBI agents accompanying him to Kazbekistan to observe the negotiation and the actual takedown of the hijacked World Airlines flight.

Requesting. Sure. Bhagat's *requests* packed more power than a four-star's orders.

"Do you think he asked for us because he wants to sleep with you? And if so, are you going to do him?" Jules glanced at her, mischief lighting his eyes and too-pretty face, laughing at the dark look she shot him. "Aw, come on, I'd do him to boost *your* career. Of course, he is extremely hot."

"Please don't tell him that when we see him." Alyssa laughed at the thought of Jules Cassidy going up to the extremely straight Max Bhagat and ... "He's so obviously not—" She stopped herself. Because not all gay men were as blatantly out as her partner. And there *was* a certain tidiness to Bhagat. A well-manicured polish to his dark good looks. She looked at Jules. "I know it's none of my business, but ... *is* he?"

"A member of the Barbra Streisand Fan Club?" Jules asked. "Definitely not. Limited eye contact last time we met. But a boy can dream, can't he?" He fluttered his eyelashes at her.

"Dream away," Alyssa told him. "*After* we get on the plane, okay?"

"ETA—airport—thirteen minutes," Jules told her.

"Good."

His voice turned serious. "Why *do* you think we've been asked to observe?"

Alyssa shook her head. She didn't know. "I hope it's because Bhagat's recognized that we're good at what we do."

Jules nodded. "That would be nice. But ... what do you know about this situation?"

"Just what I told you on the phone."

World Airlines Flight 232 had taken off from Athens shortly before 8:00 A.M., local time. An hour into the trip an unidentified gunman had entered the cockpit, ordered the pilot to take him to Kazbekistan, ordered him to land at the airport in Kazabek, where four additional unidentified gunmen had entered the plane. At which time they'd sealed the plane, started making demands, and identified themselves.

"Five terrorists, claiming to be from a K-stani group called something that translates roughly to the People's Party, are aboard a 747 with one hundred twenty passengers," Alyssa summed it up, "an as yet unknown percentage of which are American citizens. They're demanding the release of two prisoners who are awaiting trial, charged with terrorism—

one being held in a U.S. federal prison, the other in a prison in Israel."

"Osman Razeen," Jules said.

She looked at him. "What?"

"The terrorist being held in the U.S. is Osman Razeen," Jules said.

Razeen was a GIK terrorist leader that Jules and Alyssa had helped apprehend less than six months ago.

"How do you know that?" Alyssa asked.

"The boss called on my cell phone a few minutes before I got to your place. He also said . . ." He glanced at her.

Uh-oh. "What?"

"Two things. Senator Andrew Crawford's daughter is on that flight."

Oh, God. "Do the terrorists know it?"

"Don't know."

"What else?" she asked him.

He hesitated again. "You're not going to like this."

"I didn't like the news about Crawford's daughter."

"This you're *really* not going to like."

"Just tell me."

"Okay." Jules glanced warily at her again.

How could a trained FBI agent who went up against crazed terrorists regularly in the line of duty be so afraid of her? What awful bomb was he going to drop?

He took a deep breath. "The K-stani government asked the U.S. for assistance in handling this crisis, and a team of Navy SEALS are already on their way to Kazabek."

Navy SEALS.

"Team Sixteen," Alyssa said with dread. It had to be. Just her luck.

"There's more. Lt. Sam Starrett's in charge of the actual takedown of the plane. He and his squad are who we're going to be observing."

"Shit!" Roger Starrett—nicknamed Sam for reasons that were too complicated to remember—was the last man on earth she ever wanted to see again.

Jules glanced at her. "Is there a chance that's why we're

along for this ride? Because Starrett asked for you to be there?"

Oh, dear *God*. "No! He's got no authority over Max Bhagat. I mean, he can't . . . he couldn't . . . Besides, he *wouldn't*."

She and Starrett had made a deal. They'd work together when they absolutely had to, but nothing else. The night they'd spent together nearly six months ago was forgotten. Erased. Deleted from their memories.

Except it wasn't. Not really.

In fact, it tended to pop into the forefront of Alyssa's mind at the most inopportune moments.

But that was to be expected, she'd told herself. After all, she was a red-blooded woman, and face it, the sex had been off the scale.

It was the man she'd had the sex with that she couldn't stand.

"You know, I know you slept with him," Jules said.

She turned to look at him, covered her shock with a laugh. "Get real."

"It was the night I went down to North Carolina," he said. "Or was it Virginia? I forget. But it was the night I was out of town and your sister Tyra had her baby."

She laughed again. "Jules. You don't *really* think—"

"It's okay, sweetie." His voice was gentle. "You don't have to say anything. That way you can pretend that you're still denying it without really lying to me. I just wanted you to know that, well . . . I know. I figured it out. Didn't even need my FBI decoder ring to do it."

Jules glanced at her again as he took the exit for the airport. But it wasn't because he expected her to say anything. On the contrary. "So if you ever want to talk about it . . ."

She was holding her breath, she realized, and she let it out in a rush.

"I got drunk," she confessed. "It was the stupidest thing I've ever done in my life. I mean, God help me—Roger *Starrett*."

Jules shrugged. "He's pretty cute. That cowboy attitude and the western drawl . . . Hard to resist."

"I would love to watch him hear you say that."

"Yeah, his homophobic tendencies are slightly less cute," Jules agreed with a smile.

"I don't want to see him again," Alyssa admitted. "Ever."

"It shouldn't be too bad if we keep our distance," Jules told her. "He's going to be pretty busy getting his team ready to go into the plane. Just keep it cool. Don't let him get to you."

Alyssa nodded. "Yeah." Cool. She was good at cool.

She'd be fine. As long as Starrett didn't touch her. Or talk to her. Or look at her.

If he came too close, she just might go up in flames.

Five

"SO." STAN SAT down next to Teri, fitting himself carefully into the less than spacious airline seat. "Two more hours, and we'll be in Kazbekistan. Did you know that it's called the Pit?"

She'd put down the novel she'd been reading and turned slightly in her seat to face him, all big brown eyes framed by short dark hair, small nose, delicately shaped lips, slightly pointed chin.

"Yeah," she said. "Are you all right?"

The question caught him by surprise. Of course he was—he was always all right. But on the other hand . . .

"I know how *I* get when my expectations aren't met," she told him. "I mean, you deal with it, sure, but . . . You were expecting something easy. The Azores. And you got K-stan. And a lot more work and worry. Something tells me this is the last time you're going to be sitting down all week."

He smiled at that. "I think you're probably right."

She smiled back at him. Christ, she was pretty. She twisted in her seat, trying to get more comfortable, and Stan looked down at his boots rather than at the way her body filled her shirt.

"I'm sorry this had to happen," she said.

"Me, too. But not because I mind the hard work." It was the fact that they were going to the Pit that pissed him off—no, it was the fact that he'd unwittingly dragged Teri Howe along with them that really rankled. "Kazbekistan's a dangerous place."

She nodded, her eyes serious now. "I know. Under normal

circumstances, I doubt I'd get an opportunity like this. To be part of something where I could really make a difference . . ."

Damn. She wanted to make a difference, and Stan didn't want her to get off the plane. If something happened to her while she was in K-stan, he'd never forgive himself.

But he wasn't going to attempt to do what he thought was best for her simply because *he* was scared. He respected her far too much to do that.

"Yeah," he said. "Okay. Because that's what I wanted to ask you—what you want to do about this mess."

"Really? *Ask?*" Her eyes lit up. "I thought you were here to break the news that I would only be in K-stan for all of two minutes—while I switched to a flight that would take me back to London."

"In all honesty, that's what I'd like you to do," he admitted. "And if I made enough noise about you being only Reserve . . . But you really want to stay, huh?"

"I really do, Senior Chief."

She was looking at him now as if he held her life in his hands, and he shook his head.

"Teri, the choice here is yours, okay? You want to stay, I won't be the one who makes you leave. But if you want to go back to the States, I'll make damn sure you go. Just do me a favor and really think it through."

"I have," she said.

"Think harder."

"I will."

"Good. See me before you get off the plane. I've got an extra flack jacket that I want you to wear. You leave your room, you put it on. Is that clear?"

Teri nodded. "Absolutely."

"Okay." He started to stand up, but she put her hand on his arm.

She took it away really fast as if she'd surprised herself by touching him. Or as if she'd been startled by how hot his skin felt compared to the coolness of her fingers.

He'd sure as hell been startled by her touch.

"Can't you sit for a minute or two?" she asked, startling him even more.

Holy God, was she hitting on him?

But then sanity returned and Stan had to laugh at himself for even daring to think the thought. Teri Howe. Hitting on *him*.

Right.

It was a typical male response. She was just being friendly, and he'd instantly jumped to the conclusion that sex was involved.

He'd thought he was better than that. But apparently not.

"You look a little tired," she said. And no, there was no promise of hot sex in her eyes, only warmth of a completely different kind.

She was being nice, and he . . . Damn, he must look worse than he usually did. But how did one politely mention that? *No thanks, Lieutenant, I'm not tired, just butt ugly.*

Except he *was* tired, and once this transport touched ground, he was going to be running nonstop. Lieutenant Paoletti and the team's language specialist, Johnny Nilsson, were a few hours behind them—not that they'd wait for L.T. and Nils to get started. In a situation like this, you just never knew when getting a few hours ahead of the game could save lives.

"Maybe you should try to catch a nap," Teri suggested. "I had a . . . good friend who was a SEAL. He served in Vietnam, and he used to talk about how part of the training included learning to take something he called combat naps. He told me if he could shut his eyes, even for ten minutes, it could make a big difference."

A good friend, huh?

The way she'd said it implied that whoever this guy was, he'd been far more than just a friend. But someone who did time in 'Nam had to be in their fifties. Or older.

" 'Nam, huh?" Stan said, wanting to know more, hating the idea of her hooked up with someone that old, someone who wasn't her equal in every way. "My father served three tours over there. Regular Navy."

"Career?" she asked.

He nodded. "Yeah. Master Chief Stanley Wolchonok Senior. He retired just a few years ago."

"He must be proud of you." She said it so wistfully.

"He is. We're not, you know, particularly close, but he was the one who urged me to join the SEAL Teams." His father had told him how hard it would be to get in—and oh, by the way, he was convinced Stan Junior had what it took to make it. Coming from the old bastard, that had meant a hell of a lot, particularly in those dark years right after his mother had died.

"How about you? Your father still alive?" he asked Teri, watching her eyes, wanting to know about her father, dreading to hear what she might tell him.

Maybe he was wrong, but he'd gotten the sense that somewhere, sometime, *some*one had really damaged her. He'd learned through his experiences as a senior chief, dealing in particular with the younger enlisted men, that more often than not if there was emotional damage, there was a father or mother lurking in the past who'd failed the first commandment of parenting—thou shalt not take thine own bad shit out on thy defenseless and trusting child.

"You mentioned your mother was living back east," he continued.

"Yeah, she's in Massachusetts—Cambridge. A literature professor at Harvard. As far as my dad . . ." The plane lurched and she looked away from him, out the window, assessing the cloud coverage below and the potential for turbulence with the calmly practiced glance of an experienced pilot.

She turned back to him and forced a smile. "This sounds awful, but I don't know if George Howe's still alive. He left before I turned two, and the few times I tried to get in touch with him starting when I was in middle school, he was so uninterested, I . . ." She laughed, embarrassed. "I kind of came to the conclusion that he was merely the guy my mother was married to when I was born. A handy name to put on the birth certificate. She was . . . adventurous, and it was the early '70s, and . . ." She shrugged. "I've asked her, and she insisted George was my father, but still . . . I don't believe her."

She was trying so hard to sound as if it didn't really matter to her, one way or another.

Stan wanted to hold her hand. Just like this morning, when she'd confessed her transgressions on his back porch, he wanted to pull her into his arms and hold her. He wanted to comfort her, to tell her that from now on he'd make everything all right.

But was that comfort really just an excuse to touch her, to get her into his arms again?

Probably.

He remembered how soft she'd felt when she'd hugged him last week—how good her hair had smelled. He sat back slightly, instead of leaning forward to see if her hair still smelled that delicious.

"Let me guess—when you joined the Navy, your mother wasn't exactly thrilled," he said.

That got him a real smile, although it was a wan one. "Good guess. Although *horrified* is the more appropriate word."

"Any brothers or sisters?" he asked. Surely there was *some*body in Teri's life who was proud of all she'd accomplished.

"None. You?"

Damn. "I have a sister," he told her, "who joined the Navy through marriage. She and Bob—my brother-in-law—are about to have their fifth kid, if you can believe that."

"Oh, my God, Uncle Stan! You and the other kids must be so excited," she said with another flash of her perfect teeth.

He laughed at that, gesturing for her to keep it down. "Shhh. Yes, I've got four nieces who can wrap me around their little fingers, but don't spread it around—my reputation as a tough assed senior chief will be completely shot."

"So did you always want to be a tough assed senior chief?" she asked, her smile still lighting her eyes.

If he were thinking with his dick, he might think she liked making him laugh—that she was actually flirting with him.

"Did you always want to be the best helo pilot in the Navy?" he countered, because what did it hurt to pretend that she was flirting, to flirt back a little bit, too, *and* let her know he thought she was first-rate, all at the same time.

"Yes." She blushed then, and he wasn't sure if it was the compliment in his question or her too-hasty response that implied that she was, indeed, the best, that made her cheeks turn pink. "Well, I mean, I've always wanted to be a pilot, you know, to fly. . . ."

"It's okay to be the best," he told her, suddenly wishing desperately that he looked like Mel Gibson.

And as long as he was wishing for things that he couldn't have, he wished that they weren't going to K-stan but instead were still headed to the Azores islands, where there would be enough down time to take Teri Howe away from the air base, away from anyone who knew them both, to spread a picnic blanket out on the sand of some deserted beach and *really* make her blush by taking off her clothes and . . .

Easy there, Mr. Wonderful. Thinking about fucking this girl blind while he sat here trying to be her friend was pretty goddamn rude. And where did he get off thinking she'd be even remotely interested in recreational sex, even if he *did* look like Mel Gibson?

She'd had sex with a good-looking stranger in the backseat of a car in a bar parking lot.

Once. Only once.

In her entire life.

And it *still* made her feel like crap, still cut a giant hole into her self-esteem.

Dear sweet Jesus, he'd sat there this morning, listening to her tell him about it, forcing himself not to react in any visible way at all. He hadn't burst out laughing, or burst into tears, or just plain burst from wishing it had been him with her in that car.

God *damn*, she'd been so embarrassed about it, all he could think about were the dozens upon dozens of far more stupid mistakes he'd made when *he* was nineteen.

She was so sweetly young and freshly untarnished despite her confession, he wanted to protect her from the world.

And he'd wanted to kill Joel Hogan, that was damn sure. He wanted to rip out his heart for using Teri that way all those years ago. He wanted to rip out the asshole's lungs for daring to take advantage of her one mistake all these years later. And he wanted to rip off his head for showing up at her house last night, for making her afraid to go home.

He was determined to protect her from Hogan.

And he knew that he would protect her from himself as well.

Stan knew how to deal with inappropriate feelings of lust. He knew what was and wasn't right between a man and a woman, between officer and enlisted, between himself and sweet Teri Howe.

Teri was a fantasy. Plain and simple. He could be honest and mature enough with himself to admit that. He was a big enough boy to know the difference between fantasy and reality.

And he *could* sit here with her, absolutely and truly being her friend, and still have moments of intense lust. He was human, he was male, she was amazing in every possible way.

She was smart, funny, and impossibly soft beneath that tough, efficient exterior. She had a face like an angel, a body to die for.

And yes, it was okay that he wanted her. But it wouldn't be okay to let her know it. And it sure as hell wouldn't be okay to act on it. So he wouldn't. Period. The end.

"I've wanted to fly since before I can even remember," she was telling him. "And then Lenny moved in and—"

"Lenny?" Stan asked, instantly jealous, then instantly incredulous and amused at himself. God, get a grip, Wolchonok.

"The former SEAL I was telling you about? Except he never told my mother that he was a veteran. It was bad enough she was living with a *Lenny*. I don't think she could have handled knowing he'd fought in Vietnam, too."

Lenny, the SEAL from 'Nam, was her *mother's* lover. Okay. *That* made sense. And it erased the troublesome and lingering pictures he'd had of Teri hooked up with a sixty-year-old man.

"He told me all about it, though," she told him. "As much as he hated 'Nam, he loved being a SEAL. It was the best thing that ever happened to him. And when he found out I wanted to fly, he . . ." She laughed, shook her head. "Do you really want to hear all this?"

"What, do I look like I'm falling asleep?"

"No. But I know your darkest secret, so . . ."

He scowled at her, but she was still laughing. Either she

knew he was hot for her and honestly didn't mind, or she didn't *really* know his darkest secret.

She leaned closer, and he got a whiff of her hair and an eyeful of her breasts, tight against the cotton of her shirt, nipples clearly outlined.

Oh, *shit.* Don't get a hard-on. Don't get a hard-on. As soon as he did, guaranteed, Jazz would need him and he'd have to stand up and . . .

"It's that despite the hard-ass reputation, you're really just a softy," Teri told him, her voice low so no one else could hear.

There was a delightful teasing light in her eyes, but Stan found himself hypnotized by her mouth, by the perfect, graceful shape of her lips, by the thought of those lips . . .

Oh, freaking perfect. He yanked his gaze away and waited for Jazz's inevitable summons. But it didn't come.

She'd just called him a *softy.*

The irony was unbelievably intense, and Stan couldn't keep himself from laughing. He heard himself make a sound that was remarkably close to a giggle, and that just pushed him even further over the edge.

Ah, dignity. It was overrated anyway.

Teri was laughing, too, clearly pleased with herself for making him crack up so completely, even though she didn't really understand what was making him laugh.

"I want to sit with you guys and have some of whatever it is you're drinking," WildCard said as he passed by on his way to the head at the back of the plane.

Stan finally caught his breath. "Lieutenant, believe me, I enjoy your company very much. I'm glad we're friends."

"Me, too, Senior Chief." She looked out the window again, as if she suddenly didn't want to meet his gaze.

Shit. What had he just said that had embarrassed her?

"So what did Lenny do when he found out you wanted to fly?" Stan asked, hoping he was misreading her body language. He hated the distance she'd put between them with the set of her shoulders. "How old were you, anyway?"

"I was eight when he moved in," she told him. "Twelve when he left."

Ouch. "That must've sucked," Stan said. She was looking at him again, thank God.

"He had his reasons," Teri said. "Of course, I didn't know them at the time. Still, without a doubt, he was the most important person in my life. Ever."

And she'd had him for only four years. Stan had thought losing his mother at eighteen was bad. Damn.

"I'm sorry he left," he said quietly.

"When he found out that I wanted to fly more than just about anything," she continued, "he hooked me up with the local CAP—you know, Civil Air Patrol. A friend of his was a member—Archie. He used to take us up in this little Cessna." She smiled, lost in the past, her eyes distant. "He used to let me take the controls. On my twelfth birthday, Lenny talked him into letting me make the landing, probably breaking every rule in the book."

"So where's Lenny now?" Stan asked.

"He died," she told him. "When I was fifteen, I got this letter from a lawyer's office, telling me that I'd inherited a quarter of a million dollars from someone named Leonard Jackson."

"Holy shit—pardon my French, but did you say . . . ?"

"A quarter," she said again. "Of a million. Yes. That was my reaction, too. He'd put it into a trust for me, so Audrey—my mother—couldn't touch it. You know, I never even knew Lenny's last name—I didn't realize at first that this Leonard Jackson was *my* Lenny. And when I did . . . I didn't want the money, Senior Chief. I wanted *him*. I'd always planned to go find him someday, because *he* was my real dad. He loved me even when I didn't get an A plus in school, you know?"

Stan nodded. He knew.

"Then to make things even worse," she continued, "I found out that he'd left back when I was twelve because he was diagnosed with cancer. My mother couldn't handle the fact that he was dying, so he just . . . left. He didn't tell me why he was going because he didn't want to make her look bad. So he died in a hospice, all alone." She looked bleak, as if she were reliving her loss all over again. "And I could have had his love for another three years."

Touching her was a stupid idea. Touching her in public was even stupider. But Stan did it anyway. He touched the softness of her hair, touched her cheek before sanity intervened and he pulled his hand away.

"You did have it," he told her gently. "You just didn't know it until later."

She gazed at him. "I never thought of it that way before."

"Well, there you go," he said, wishing . . . No, he wasn't going there. Not right now. Not ever. He had to look away.

"He wrote me a note," Teri told him. "He said, 'College first. Then, be all that you can be.' " She smiled. "He included the name and phone number of a friend who was a Navy recruiter."

Stan laughed at that. "So it's Lenny we have to thank, huh? Without him, we might've lost you to the Air Force."

"Without him, I wouldn't have made it into the sky at all," she confessed. "As soon as I was old enough, I used my inheritance to learn to fly—everything from Cessnas to small jets. I didn't tell my mother. She would've had a cow."

Wait a minute. "So you came into Navy flight school already knowing how to fly a *jet*?"

She nodded.

"And yet you chose to become a helo pilot?" Stan didn't quite get it.

"I wanted to work with the SEALs."

"Ah." God bless Lenny and the stories he'd told her.

"Excuse me, Senior Chief." Sam Starrett was in the aisle, looking curiously from Stan to Teri. "XO could use you in a minute or two. He asked me to wake you, but apparently you don't need waking." He smiled at Teri. "Hey, Lieutenant."

Instant tension. It was amazing the way Teri just tightened up. She nodded at Starrett, but her shoulders were practically up around her ears.

What was that about?

"How're you doing?" Starrett asked her.

"Fine, thanks." She met his eyes only briefly, looking away as if she were embarrassed.

It was a weird dynamic. If they'd been lovers and Starrett had ditched her, ending their relationship with his usual lack of grace and finesse, *he* would've been the one who was uncomfortable around her.

Unless *she'd* ditched Starrett . . . ? No, that didn't sit right, either.

Stan excused himself and stood up, grateful that enough time had passed so that he could do it without embarrassing himself.

Teri picked up her book, holding it like a shield against Sam Starrett. It was almost as if . . .

"Starrett, you got a sec?" Stan asked.

"Sure, Senior." The lanky lieutenant followed him toward the front of the plane.

And sure enough, Teri visibly relaxed.

"What's up?" Starrett drawled.

Stan didn't mince words. "Keep your fucking hands off Teri Howe."

"*My* hands? Whoa, wait a second, it was Admiral Tucker who was—" Starrett broke off at the look Stan knew must've been on his face. "I just told you something you didn't know, didn't I, Senior? *Shit.*"

"When was this?" Stan kept his voice quietly calm. Deadly calm. Starrett wasn't fooled.

"Hell, I don't know." He scratched his head. "A year ago maybe? Maybe more? Teri was doing two weeks of Reserve training, and three of the regular helo pilots got food poisoning and— I shouldn't be telling you this."

"Oh, yes, you should," Stan said.

Starrett cast an uneasy glance back toward Teri. Lowered his voice. "She was filling in, chauffeuring top brass in one of the puddle jumpers. She took Tucker back to the base after some dinner thing, but he'd had a few drinks too many, and she was intending to drive him home, too. She was helping him to her car in the parking lot—you know, seriously helping the man walk? Arm around him? He was pretty severely alcohol challenged and I guess he got the wrong idea."

"Christ," Stan said. Was this kind of thing so commonplace in Teri Howe's life that she simply hadn't bothered to tell Stan about an *admiral's* inappropriate behavior?

"That's when I made the scene," Starrett continued, his

voice still low. "Tucker had his hands all over her, and—it was the funniest thing, Senior—I was sure he was going to have a permanent handprint of her palm on his face, but she froze. I had to pull him off her, and as soon as I did, she ran.

"I loaded Tucker into my truck, drove him home, and then went over to Teri's house. I got her address from the phone book—I knew she lived in San Diego and I had to make sure she was okay. I couldn't get her face out of my head, you know? That look in her eyes—like the world was coming to an end. The weirdest part of it was that while she was upset, she wasn't half as upset as I would've expected," Starrett told Stan. "I mean, she was *way* more resigned about it than I would've been. She didn't want to tell anyone, didn't want to do anything—she just wanted to forget about it. She seemed convinced Tucker wouldn't remember any of it in the morning anyway, so . . ."

Stan was mad as hell at Admiral Tucker, at Teri, at Starrett, too. "And it didn't occur to you to come to me, Lieutenant?"

"No shit, Senior, I swear to God, I wanted to, but she asked me not to report the incident."

Stan looked back across the plane, at Teri. Who wasn't reading. She was watching him. She quickly looked down at her book as if he'd caught her being bad.

What the hell had made her freeze that way? Both with Hogan and with Tucker. She should have kicked both of them in the balls so hard their eyes would've been permanently crossed.

How had she made it so far in a world where women had to be twice as strong as their male counterparts to succeed?

Except she hadn't made it that far, had she? She was only a lieutenant junior grade after joining the Navy at age nineteen. And she'd gotten out of the regular Navy and into the Reserves. Running from something he didn't yet know about, perhaps? *Christ.*

And yet Teri Howe, the pilot, didn't run from anything when she was in her helo. She flew without hesitation. She was decisive, courageous, and a consistently excellent junior officer. She gave her opinion when asked and followed orders without question when she wasn't.

Stan turned back to Starrett. "I apologize for jumping to conclusions, sir."

"Don't sweat it, Stan. If I were hanging out with her, I'd be pretty possessive, too."

"No, we're just friends."

Starrett didn't wink, but it was there in his voice. "Sure thing, Senior."

Christ, what was wrong with everyone? Both Tom and Starrett thought he had something going on with Teri Howe. They must think he really was some kind of miracle worker.

He made a mental note to himself not to sit with her again. Not without Muldoon or one of the other guys, anyway. She didn't need rumors about her and him being spread around.

He headed toward Jacquette, psyching himself up so that he'd be prepared for anything thrown at him, and when he glanced back at Teri, he caught her watching him again.

She smiled, and he was instantly there.

Ready for anything.

King of the world.

Six

THE CHARTERED FLIGHT to Kazbekistan wouldn't land for several hours.

Helga Rosen Shuler sat, wondering what he looked like.

Stanley Wolchonok. Marte's son.

In all likelihood, she wouldn't be able to meet him right away. He was going to be in K-stan as part of the team of men who would launch an assault on the hijacked plane, gain entry, and kill the terrorists before they had time to kill any of the innocents on board.

Yes, he was going to be very busy. But after it was over, she would request some time with him.

Did he look like Marte, with light brown hair and blue-green eyes? Or did he take after the elder Gunvald sister, Annebet?

Annebet had been a goddess. Tall and blond and voluptuous, she took after her Viking ancestors, with flashing blue eyes and a strong hatred of the occupying Germans.

Like Helga's brother, Hershel, she had been studying to become a doctor before the Nazis came to Denmark.

She'd still kept studying, like Hershel, but it was harder to do with her frequent trips home to check on her family. Hershel was home more often, too.

Helga often went with Marte after school. Although the Gunvalds' house was much smaller, it was a far happier place, particularly after three years of Nazi occupation.

Marte's mother, Inger, would give them bread and butter as a snack, and they'd take it into the yard to eat.

And sooner or later Wilhelm Gruber, in his German army uniform, would show up as they played there. Mooning over

Annebet, waiting for her to come home, hoping for a glimpse of her.

Helga closed her eyes, remembering the day he'd brought them Swiss chocolate. It was late in the spring of 1943, she had just turned ten, and Marte was twelve. Tensions were rising, food was scarce, and Annebet had moved back home from Copenhagen for good.

"How do we know it's not poisoned?" Marte had asked suspiciously, giving the German soldier on the other side of the fence her darkest scowl and most deadly evil eye.

"I'm in love with your sister," Gruber proclaimed. "What good would it do me to upset her by poisoning you?"

He really wasn't that bad looking a fellow, Helga had to admit. A little stout from too much of that chocolate he always had in such quantities, he had a broad, friendly face, with blue eyes that were made larger by his wire-rimmed glasses.

From the terrible stories she'd heard of Nazis tearing Jewish babies in two, she'd expected him to have horns and a tail.

"Come on," Gruber encouraged with a smile, holding out the chocolate to the two girls. "What harm can it do to take it?"

Helga never would have considered taking anything from a German. She always ran to the other side of her own yard when German troops marched past. But Marte was Marte, afraid of no one and nothing. And her poppi didn't have extra money to buy things like sweets. For her, Gruber's chocolate was tempting.

Marte looked at Helga. And reached for it.

"What are you doing?" Annebet descended upon them from inside the house like an avenging angel. But it was Gruber she was angry at, not Marte and Helga. "Stay away from my sister, Nazi! Stay away from my house! I will *never* go out with you. I'm not a collaborator—I'd never fraternize with the *enemy*!"

She grabbed Marte with one hand and Helga with the other, and dragged them with her toward the barn.

"I'm *not* the enemy," Gruber protested, following them

along the outside of the fence. "This occupation is a friendly one. Your king Christian still sits on his throne. The Danish government still meets. There was no fighting when we arrived."

"There was, too," Annebet spun back to fire at him. "Lars Johansen was killed defending the king's palace!"

Marte looked at Helga and rolled her eyes. This was an argument Annebet and Gruber had had many times before. Now he would make a crack about Lars having been killed by the faulty backfire of his own inferior Danish gun.

But he didn't this time. He just sighed. "Sooner or later, Annebet, you will understand that the Germans and the Danes are friends. You are one of us—you have many freedoms here that you take for granted, that you would not have if you were our enemy. Even your Jews are not required to wear the yellow star—"

"Oh, yes, Herr Gruber," Annebet interrupted. "Let's discuss what you Germans—*you Germans,* not we Danes, and no, we are *not* one of *you*—" She said the word as if she were saying *pig shit.* "Let's talk about what *you* are doing to your citizens who happen to be Jewish. Have you heard of the death camps your Herr Himmler has built? I have. I've heard stories from people who were there, who saw it with their own eyes. Railroad cars of people—women and children— being gassed, simply because they are not *Aryan.*"

Gruber tried to smile. "But you *are.* You Danes don't have to worry about—"

Annebet thrust both Marte and Helga in front of her. "One of these two little *Danish* girls is Jewish. Which one?"

Helga stared up at Gruber, up at the complete surprise on his face, and tried not to be terrified. She was too big to tear in two. Wasn't she? Marte reached for her hand.

"You can't tell from looking, can you? So what will you do, try to take them both?" Annebet pushed the two girls behind her. "I would *die* before I let you take either of these two children. You would have to shoot me right there, right in the street, like a dog."

Gruber was shaking his head. "Look, I don't know, I'm not

a Nazi. I'm simply a good German. And lucky to be serving my country here instead of Russia."

"Your *good German* leaders are murderers and thieves."

Helga tugged on Annebet's arm, trying to pull her the rest of the way to the barn. This conversation was getting much too dangerous, and Gruber was starting to get angry.

"It's treasonous words like that that will force us to take away some of the freedoms you Danes enjoy. If you don't watch out . . ."

"What will you do?" Annebet's voice was suddenly very soft. But it was filled with an intensity that made Helga want to cry. "Will you round up all our Jews? Will you take away the rest of our communists? I know—maybe this time you'll arrest all of us who've ever had a single communistic thought. You'd have to take me, Herr Gruber. I still work one day a week at the free medical clinic in Copenhagen for no pay. Quick, call the Gestapo."

A vein stood out on his forehead. "Don't make jokes about that!"

"I'm not joking, Nazi. I don't joke about a Reich that wants to rule the world by oppression."

She was magnificent, standing there like that, all but shaking her fist at Gruber, but Helga was terrified that he would take his gun and shoot her. Shoot them all.

"Too bad, because it's *our* world now," he taunted.

"Yes," she said. "That *is* too bad."

With a regal sweep of her skirt, she turned and followed Helga and Marte into the relative safety of the barn.

She closed the door behind them and instantly turned to Marte. "If I *ever* catch you talking to him again . . . !"

"He comes to the gate and calls to me," Marte defended herself. "Am I supposed to ignore him?"

"Yes."

"No." They all looked up in surprise. Helga's brother stood just inside the door. "There's no point in making him angry."

Annebet straightened up, her eyes flashing. "I suppose you'll next recommend I have dinner with him."

It was funny. Helga had never seen Hershel like this, so

stern, so . . . strange. Something about him was different. And he was looking at Annebet as if Helga and Marte had ceased to exist.

"I would never recommend that," he countered softly.

Annebet had a flush of pink on her cheeks now, as if . . .

Helga looked at her brother. *Really* looked.

He wasn't handsome. Not like Jorgen Lund who sometimes came by the Gunvalds' to take Annebet to a concert or for a walk in the park. Hershel's hair was a plain shade of brown and his nose was big and his face was just a face. Not ugly, but nothing special either.

He was tall and skinny. Except as Helga looked at him, she realized he wasn't so skinny anymore. His shoulders were broad, and with his shirtsleeves rolled up, she could see that his arms were strong—muscular, even.

But that wasn't the thing that was so different about him today. No, the difference was in his eyes.

Helga had always thought that her brother had pretty eyes behind his wire-rimmed glasses. A rich shade of hazel and usually warm and brimming with good humor, they truly seemed to be the window to his good-natured soul.

But as he looked at Annebet, his eyes were intense, as if his soul had suddenly become heated to an extreme temperature and was about to explode.

"It's good to be friendly, even just polite," Hershel said to Annebet. "The Germans will relax and never suspect . . . anything. I'm Hershel Rosen, by the way. I'm here to fetch Helga home."

How did he even know she was here? He hadn't looked away from Annebet, not even once, since he'd entered the barn.

"I know who you are," Annebet told him. She was looking at Hershel in the same way. As if Helga and Marte had vanished off the face of the earth. "I've seen you at university."

"Really? I mean, well, I've seen you, of course, but I didn't realize you were Inger Gunvald's daughter."

Marte leaned close, cupping her hands around Helga's ear. "Look at them. They want to kiss."

Hershel and Annebet? Helga looked at her brother. At Marte's sister.

She tried to imagine them kissing. Not the way her mother and poppi kissed—as if they didn't want any part of them but the very tips of their lips to touch—but instead the way people kissed in the movies. As if they wanted to swallow each other whole and wrap themselves around each other until they turned inside out.

She wasn't sure Hershel would know how to kiss like that. He had always been so polite.

Annebet smiled at him. "I'm hard to miss, huh? Always ranting about the Germans."

"You should be more careful," Hershel warned her.

"Helga and I are going out to play," Marte announced, dragging Helga with her to the back door, behind the horse stall, past where Frita had just had her litter of puppies.

She banged the door, but didn't go outside. Instead she held her finger to her lips and led the way up the stairs to the loft.

Marte loved playing spy, and Helga, too, had learned how to move soundlessly out of necessity, to keep up with her friend. But it didn't seem right to spy on Hershel and Annebet.

"It seems funny that *you* should warn me to be careful," Helga heard Annebet say to her brother.

She tugged on Marte's shirt, shaking her head no when Marte turned to look at her.

Yes. Marte shook her head the other way.

"No," Helga whispered fiercely.

"I'm not sure why your family hasn't gone to Sweden," Annebet continued. "I worry about Helga. Sometimes I just want to get on a boat and take her there myself."

Marte pulled her close, cupped her hands around her ear, and breathed, "If they get married, you and I really *will* be sisters. *Forever.*"

Marte as a sister. Annebet as a sister-in-law. It was a wonderful dream.

Marte continued almost silently into her ear, "But how will we know if they're going to get married unless we watch to see if they're going to kiss, huh?"

It made sense in a Marte kind of way, and despite her misgivings, Helga found herself following her friend silently up the stairs.

"My father won't leave his house, his shop," Hershel was saying. "He says what's happened in the rest of Europe won't happen here—not in Denmark. He doesn't let himself truly believe the news we hear of the ghettos and camps."

"I've seen postcards," Annebet said. "With messages written in invisible ink. No one could make up those stories. The camps are real."

From their perch in the loft, Helga saw that Annebet had sat down on the edge of the Gunwalds' wooden wagon. Hershel had come farther into the room, but he still stood with his hat in his hands.

"I don't know how to make my father believe that."

"If there's any way I could help . . ." Annebet slipped down off the wagon and moved toward Hershel.

"Here it comes," Marte breathed.

But Annebet stopped an arm's length from Hershel.

"Thank you," he said. "But . . ." He shook his head. Looked away from her, looked at her again with a laugh. "You know, our sisters are such friends, I can't believe we haven't met before this."

"But we have," Annebet said. "I've been to your house many times."

He shook his head again, incredulous. "I can't believe that—"

"I've helped my mother serve food at your parents' parties," Annebet explained. "At least twice while you were home for the New Year. As a servant, I made sure I was properly invisible." She smiled at him. "No diatribes against the Germans with the creamed herring. No impassioned pleas for my Jewish friends to get themselves to safety as soon as possible with the dessert course."

Hershel laughed. "You could never be invisible."

"Yes, I could. In fact, your parents are having a party for your mother's birthday next week. I'll be there, but you won't even see me."

"Except now I'll be looking for you," Hershel countered.

Annebet smiled up at him, almost shyly.

Somehow they'd moved so that they stood closer together. Close enough now to kiss.

"Come on, Hershel," Marte whispered almost silently from their perch in the loft. "She wants you to, so kiss her. . . ."

But Hershel *was* too polite.

"I have to go," he told Annebet. "It was a pleasure meeting you."

And so it started.

It wasn't more than a few days later that Annebet and Marte came by Poppi's store on the pretense of looking for Helga, but really so that Annebet could see Hershel again.

Helga's parents had seen the way Hershel looked at her, the way she smiled at him, and that night at home, all hell had broken loose.

Helga had sat on the stairs and listened.

"She's after your money!"

"How could you say that?" Hershel's voice was thick with disbelief, with indignation. Hershel, who never raised his voice to anyone, was as close to getting loud as Helga had ever heard him. "Money is the *last* thing she cares about. If anything, she's a communist, all right? She's becoming a doctor so she can set up a free children's clinic. She's as beautiful inside as she is out!"

"Don't fight," Helga whispered, closing her eyes, wishing Marte were there beside her. "Please don't fight."

"Who's fighting?"

"Poppi and Hershel," she said. "Make them stop."

"Okay, how's this—it's 2001. Their fight's been over for years. Come on, Helga. Look at where you are, who you're with."

An airplane. She was on an airplane and Des was sitting beside her. Her heart pounded and her mouth was dry. She had no clue why she was here or where she was going. She wouldn't let herself panic. Instead she reached for her purse.

"We're getting ready to land," Des told her. "I should fill you in on some additional details that came in while you were resting."

Details. *Merde,* she needed far more than *details.*

"Can you get me something to drink?" she asked. "Please? Some tea?"

He looked at her. Then pulled himself to his feet. "With lemon?"

"Perfect." She smiled, and then, finally, thank God, he was gone.

Helga dug into her purse and found her memo pad. She flipped it open.

"Hijacked plane in Kazabek, Kazbekistani terrorists, Americans on board," she read, "including Senator Crawford's daughter Karen, age twenty-four. Demanding release of two prisoners, one in Israel, one in America. U.S. Navy SEAL Team Sixteen, Senior Chief Stanley Wolchonok is Marte Gunvald's son!"

Okay. Okay. Breathe.

She remembered. It made sense again, and she could even recall getting onto the plane. But, dear God, what was going to happen when she *couldn't* remember? When she looked at her list and read her own handwriting, yet couldn't recall putting her pen to the page?

Desmond came back down the aisle, carrying a hot cup with a cover. She flipped her memo pad closed and forced a smile as he handed the cup to her.

"Thank you—aren't you nice." She took a sip as he sat down and laughed. "Oh, that's odd. I was expecting coffee and it's tea. You know how strange that can be. . . ."

Des looked at her. "You asked for tea."

She had? "Sorry, I was . . . groggy." And focusing so much on trying to remember what she was here for, on getting a look at her memo pad . . .

He cleared his throat. "Okay. You ready for details?"

"I am."

"The SEALs landed in Kazbekistan about five hours ago. They've already constructed a wooden mock-up of a 747 at a former military airfield just south of Kazabek, and they've begun using it to practice boarding the hijacked aircraft.

"The man in charge of the takedown is Lieutenant junior grade Roger Starrett. Your guy, Senior Chief Stan Wolchonok, will be working closely with him. One Lieutenant junior grade Casper Jacquette, the executive officer—XO—of the SEAL team, is in charge of surveillance, and he's already got a rotation of men surrounding the hijacked plane, looking in the windows, trying to get a sense of the situation inside.

"Lieutenant Tom Paoletti is the team's CO, and he's the man in charge of the entire operation. He's the one who'll say go when it's time to kick down the doors.

"FBI negotiator Max Bhagat will handle all communications with the terrorists—he's in place, but they've been silent aside from their initial demands. We've both worked with Bhagat before. Many times."

"Yes, of course," Helga told Des. "I know Max quite well."

He looked at her, but she couldn't read the expression in his eyes. "Last but not least, there are believed to be only five terrorists on board, all heavily armed."

Helga nodded.

"Starrett, Jacquette, Paoletti, and Bhagat," Des repeated. He lowered his voice, leaned closer. "You might want to write those names down in your little pad so you'll know who they are the next time you come up blank."

Helga didn't know what to say.

Des reached over and took her memo pad. He opened it to a blank page, looking at her the whole time.

He took a pen from his inside jacket pocket and, finally looking away from her, started to write.

When he was done, he recapped his pen, put it back into his pocket. He stood up, handed her the memo pad, and walked to another seat at the front of the plane.

Still shocked, Helga looked at her pad. He'd listed the names, titles, and positions of the men about whom he'd just briefed her. And underneath he'd written in his clear block printing, "I know your secret."

"Who is Karen Crawford?"

Gina held tightly to Casey as two of the gunmen moved to the back of the plane, both shouting in heavily accented English, "Who is Karen Crawford?"

It was terrifyingly bizarre, like the answer to some twisted round of *Jeopardy!* with machine-gun toting contestants.

The blond stewardess dared to intercede. "Americans," she called out. "They are looking for an American woman named Karen Crawford."

Not too surprisingly, no one stood up.

"Please," the stewardess said. "Miss Karen Crawford!"

Oh, yeah, like if *she* were Karen Crawford, *she'd* step forward right about now. No, thank you very much.

One of the gunmen waited. He was about Gina's age, with long, dark hair pulled back into a tight ponytail and a face that could have made him a fortune had he joined a boy band instead of choosing a career in international terrorism. He looked at them—in particular at the obviously American group of students sitting around her.

The sound of crying played like an annoying soundtrack to the fear. There were babies on the plane. They'd no doubt picked up on the tension and were inconsolable.

As was Casey.

Gina's own eyes were dry, but inside she was quaking and ready to be sick. She couldn't remember ever being this frightened of anything. *Silence of the Lambs* had scared the crap out of her, but it wasn't *any*thing like this.

This was real.

Those guns held real bullets. This wasn't some make-believe game, some movie where the director could call out "cut" and they'd all go home after the day was done.

Slight pressure from one finger and a sweep of one arm, and they would all be dead or dying.

Gina had never given it much thought before, but right now she knew. She didn't want to die.

And for the first time since she was eleven, she wanted her mother.

The other terrorist on the Find Karen Crawford Team paced, a dangerous panther of a man. Smaller than the Backstreet Boy, the expression on his face was even more frightening than those enormous guns.

He was angry and getting angrier by the minute. He spoke in a language that wasn't English, and Backstreet translated.

"We know United States Senator Crawford's daughter Karen is on this plane." Backstreet's English was very good, his smooth voice a gentle, soothing baritone, as pretty as his face. "We realize she most likely travels under a different name, so checking passports is a waste of our time. We can do this nicely. Or not."

Nicely. This was *nicely*? With guns and threats and fear souring all of their mouths?

Why couldn't the university jazz band have decided to tour Ohio?

Backstreet waited, watching them, but still no one moved.

Except for the snarly pantherman, who turned and brought the butt of his gun smashing down on trombonist Ray Hernandez's head.

Oh, God!

Ray slumped in his seat as Casey cried even harder.

"Oh, my God," she sobbed. "Is he dead?"

"I don't know." Gina's voice shook. Okay, now it was time to step forward. Other people were getting hurt. Come on, Karen—

Gina's world tilted.

Karen.

Was it possible . . . ? Could it be . . . ?

Gina reached for the piece of paper with her luggage tags, the one upon which the perfect-nosed girl in the airport had scribbled her sister's name and phone number in Vienna. Karen. That girl's name was Karen and her sister was Emily Something. . . .

Gina unfolded the paper.

Emily Crawford.

Dear, sweet baby Jesus. Karen Crawford couldn't step forward. Her boarding pass had been stolen and she wasn't on this flight.

Alyssa Locke was in Kazbekistan.

She was here—right here—at this run-down military airstrip south of Kazabek, where they'd just spent the past few hours constructing a wooden mock-up of the hijacked plane.

Sam Starrett concentrated on breathing, on keeping the air going into and out of his lungs, on keeping his heart pumping blood through his body.

Having the SEAL lieutenant in charge of the planned take-down of the hijacked plane faint would not be cool. Especially not in front of the parade of dignitaries who'd come to check them out.

And especially not in front of Alyssa Locke.

She was actually here. This wasn't a dream.

She had all her clothes on. A dark pantsuit with a blouse that buttoned right up to her chin. Dark sunglasses that covered her eyes.

God, he wanted to see her eyes.

He could hear Lieutenant Paoletti making introductions, Nils beside him—called in because of his ability to speak the language—repeating the lieutenant's words in the local dialect for a swarm of K-stani officials.

As Sam shook hands, he tried to bring himself back, to pay attention. All the major players had gathered, and it would be useful to remember their names.

He met Israeli envoy Helga Shuler and her assistant, Desmond Nyland, an older black man who was a former operator. Had to be. He was probably in his fifties, but he still moved as if he'd spent years in Special Forces.

Senator Andrew Crawford, whose daughter was on that flight, was also there, his million dollar campaign smile nowhere in sight, poor bastard.

FBI negotiator Max Bhagat had his usual cool on, but Sam knew Bhagat was as impatient as he was to get these introductions over with and get back to work. Alyssa and what's his name—her funky little fruitcake of a partner—were with Bhagat, no doubt to sit on the sidelines and watch the man work.

Good. Lock Alyssa in the negotiators' room that was being set up twenty miles away, over at the Kazabek airport, within visual range of the hijacked 747. If Sam was lucky, he wouldn't have to see her again for the rest of this op.

But then it was Alyssa's turn to be introduced. She took off her sunglasses as she shook hands with Mrs. Shuler, with Lieutenant Paoletti, and . . .

Sam took her hand. He had to. There was no way he could avoid it.

"Ma'am," he said, looking into her eyes for the first time in five months, three weeks and three very long days.

Her fingers were cool, fingers she'd once wrapped around his—

She jerked her hand free, as if she could read his mind.

". . . from the FBI. They'll be observing Lieutenant Starrett's preparations for the takedown of the hijacked plane," Tom Paoletti was saying as Sam briefly shook her partner's hand. Jules Cassidy. That was the little fruit's name.

And then Paoletti's words sunk in. Observing. Takedown. No. *No.*

But yes. Shit, yes. Alyssa Locke was here to watch *him.*

She wouldn't look at him. She was purposely looking over at the mock-up of the plane, out to where the senior chief and the other men assigned to his squad for this op were walking through their relatively simple insertion plan.

She was going to be watching as his team popped the doors as quietly as possible. They would enter with a bang and a flash of light, with detailed information from the surveillance team as to the five tangos' exact locations inside the plane. Once inside, they'd make head shots and take out the terrorists. Swift and deadly.

After they got the doors open, the entire operation would take a matter of seconds and run like a well-oiled clock.

But the reason it would run so smoothly was because Starrett and his men would practice. They would run the drill over and over and *over*, for as many days as the negotiators could give them, until they could do it in their sleep.

That kind of practice required complete concentration. And Sam was going to have to run the whole show here in Distraction City, with Alyssa Locke watching him.

He wanted her to look at him now, god damn it. Come on, *look* at him.

She finally glanced over.

He made a motion with his head and, what do you know?

she actually followed as he stepped slightly back, away from the rest of the group.

"How are you, Lieutenant?" she asked coolly, not even trying to pretend that she really wanted him to answer that, not trying to pretend she actually gave a flying fuck.

He tried to ungrit his teeth. "As fine as I can be knowing that the lives of one hundred twenty people on board that World Airlines 747 depend on what my team and I do over the next few days or even hours."

She gazed at him, so pristine and well put together in her neat little suit, hair pulled back, makeup perfect.

Hours ago, Sam had stripped down to a pair of shorts and a T-shirt he'd since caught on a nail and torn. He was sweaty and dusty and he needed a shave.

"This is going to be hard enough," Sam continued, his voice lowered, "without the added stress of—"

She lifted an eyebrow. "Does Lieutenant Paoletti know that you have doubts about your ability to—"

Fuck *that*! "Excuse me, I don't have *doubts*." Jesus.

There was nothing in her eyes, not even the slightest flash of memories from that night. Not the least little sliver of shared intimacies. "Then there should be no problem."

They'd have to forget about it, to pretend it just never happened, she'd said—the fact that she'd come to his hotel room and they'd made love not once but four times. Four. All night long, and then once in the morning, even. In the shower.

She'd been furious with him at the time, until her anger had shifted to passion. But now . . . Now she obviously felt nothing at all.

Sam turned away, unwilling to let her see the anger he couldn't hide in his face, his eyes. But then—screw *that*—he looked at her. Right into her eyes.

And he let himself remember.

The expression on her perfect face as he'd made her come. The way she'd smiled as she'd touched him, first with the tip of her tongue and then with her lips and then . . .

He smiled at her, remembering it all and letting her see it in his face, but she didn't blink, didn't flinch, didn't blush. She just put her sunglasses on, gazed back at him coolly through the slightly purple-tinted lenses, and then turned away.

Well, shit.

Apparently *she* wasn't haunted by dreams of *him* at night.

Apparently she'd successfully exorcised him. Of course that was assuming he'd ever possessed her in the first place.

Sam managed to catch Paoletti's eye and got a nod of dismissal. Striding back to the wooden mock-up, he tried to focus his anger at her—and at himself for caring so goddamn much—into a more helpful form of energy.

Determination.

"Okay," he said grimly to his squad. "Let's do this right."

Seven

"IS YOUR ROOM okay?" the senior chief asked as Teri came out of the elevator and met him in the hotel lobby. "You're facing the inside courtyard, right?"

"Oh," she said, trying to remember which side of the hall her room had been on. "I didn't have time to do more than throw my bag inside and wash my face, but yeah, I'm over-looking the swimming pool."

She smiled at him, happy to see him, glad she had a full ten hours before she had another shift. She suspected Stan didn't have that much down time and still couldn't quite believe he'd chosen to spend some of his spare free moments with her. "The room has running water, so how can I complain?"

The Kazabek Grande was a hotel that had clearly seen better days.

Of course, all of Kazabek had seen better days.

"Don't drink it. Bottled water only. And put that flack jacket *on*. What, do you think carrying it's going to do you any good?"

"It's so heavy. And hot."

"Put it on anyway. And don't take the elevator again," Stan instructed as they crossed the lobby. "Electricity here comes and goes—there's not enough to power the whole city at once. I was told the Grande goes black for at least four hours a day, usually starting just after sunset, but it can happen any time, and if you're on the elevator . . ."

Her room was on the seventh floor, the restaurant near the lobby, and the heliport was on the roof. If she was going to have to trudge up and down the stairs wearing that heavy jacket ... "This assignment is going to be great for my thighs. What a perk."

Stan looked at her in obvious disbelief. "Yeah, like you really need to lose any weight. What is it with women these days? I was thinking earlier that I was going to make sure you had dessert tonight—even if I had to force-feed you."

"Gee, that sounds like fun."

He looked at her sharply, and she realized she'd said the words not quite aloud but pretty darn close. Had he heard? She didn't know for sure, but she suspected he had.

She should hold his gaze. She should smile, maybe wiggle her eyebrows at him. Make it clear that she was flirting—or at least she would be flirting if she weren't such a social reject.

She held his gaze and even somehow managed to smile, but Stan looked away. He'd definitely flirted with her on the plane. What had happened between then and now?

He cleared his throat. "We've, uh, taken over half of the restaurant as our mess area. You can go down there any time you're off duty to get something to eat. If the kitchen's closed, there'll be wrapped sandwiches—not the greatest setup, but it's the best we can do for now."

He held open the door to a stairwell and stepped back for her to go first.

Down? "But . . ." Teri pointed across the lobby, completely confused. "The sign says . . ." That the restaurant, which boasted nightly karaoke, was up on the mezzanine level.

"They moved it," Stan told her.

She went in, waiting for him to lead the way.

"This is the east tower," he told her as he headed down the stairs. "The Grande has four connected towers arranged in a square around the lobby and the courtyard with the pool. We're garrisoned in the west and south towers—you're in the west, right?"

Teri nodded.

"Me, too. Just make sure you find the west stairwell when you want to go back up to your room. The floors to the different towers don't all connect. The restaurant's down here, in a ballroom in the basement beneath the east tower." His voice echoed. "It's in a room that doesn't have windows. In Kaz-abek, hotels tend to lose business when their customers are killed by flying glass. And glass tends to fly when a car bomb goes off out in the street. Which it does here with an annoying frequency."

"God."

He stopped, hand on the knob to the door leading out to the basement level. "Teri, you're not supposed to be here. You can decide you've had enough at any time, and no one will think any less of you for leaving."

She loved it when he looked at her like that, direct and to the point, right into her eyes. She also liked the way he'd looked at her on the plane—as if he'd wanted to kiss her.

But then he'd called her Lieutenant, clearly pulling back from any kind of intimacy. Yet now she was Teri again.

Which was it, Stan?

She didn't dare ask. Didn't dare call him by *his* first name, either. He was Senior Chief or Senior and calling him any-thing else seemed much too disrespectful. Besides, maybe he was as confused by this energy that seemed to buzz between them as she was.

"I'm not leaving. I just had one of the best days of my life," she admitted.

It had started this morning—God, had it really only been this morning?—when she'd found the nerve to ring his door-bell and ask him for help.

No, that had been yesterday morning. Traveling all the way around the world had compressed the end of Sunday, and they'd arrived in K-stan late Sunday night California time, but Monday afternoon, K-stani time. It was nearly 1800 now and it had been way more than twenty-four hours since she'd slept. No wonder everything seemed a little blurry around the edges.

He nodded. "Well . . . I'm glad."

And still he stood there. Just looking at her. In the privacy of the stairwell. Where no one could see him if he gently touched her hair the way he'd done in the transport plane. Where no one would know if he kissed her.

Teri's heart pounded nearly as much as it had when he'd casually asked her to meet him in the lobby before dinner.

She wanted him to kiss her, to touch her again.

Please, Senior Chief, force-feed me dessert.

Yeah, *that* would really work. She was going to have to do it. She was going to have to call the man *Stan*.

After all, he *had* asked her to dinner. And she knew he liked her. He'd told her as much himself.

But he turned away before she got up the nerve to say or do anything at all. He opened the door. Held it for her.

"Let's get something hot to eat before the power goes out and the kitchen closes. If I have to have another sandwich, I'm going to cry." He smiled at her, if not with his mouth then certainly with his eyes. "And if you tell any of the squad that I was whining, I'll deny it."

Teri laughed, walking beside him into what, even in its heyday, must have been a cheap imitation of opulence. Shabby now, the hotel ballroom was musty and dark, with candles on every table, presumably in place for when the power went out.

The tables were covered with cheap plastic cloths, the chairs didn't match. The acoustic tile in the ceiling was missing in places, with pipes and wires showing through.

Buckets were scattered around, catching drips from the leaky plumbing.

And yet it was exotic.

Or maybe the fact that she was walking into it at the senior chief's side was what made it seem so alluringly foreign and filled with romantic potential.

He held out a chair for her at a table and she slid into it, looking up to smile her thanks. Her mother would have purposely sat in another seat and scowled.

She slipped off her flack jacket. Surely she was safe in here.

Stan sat down across from her instead of next to her. "Good, Muldoon's right on time."

Teri turned, and sure enough, Ens. Mike Muldoon was crossing the worn carpeting, looking around the room.

The senior chief stood up.

Muldoon smiled, but then hesitated midstep as he saw Teri

sitting at the table. Still, he kept coming, but his smile now was a little forced and nervous.

"Hey," Stan greeted the younger man. "Have you officially met Teri Howe?"

"Uh, no, Senior, not officially."

"Ens. Michael Muldoon," Stan said. "Lt. (jg) Teresa Howe. You guys both went to MIT."

And with that, Teri knew.

Stan had asked her to dinner in order to set her up with Muldoon.

This dinner invitation wasn't really a dinner invitation.

And the way he'd touched her on the plane, God, now that she stopped to think about it, that had really been nothing more than a comforting pat on the head, hadn't it?

Oh, Lord. She was such a fool.

Teri supposed she was lucky he'd overheard her inappropriate comment, "That sounds like fun," when Stan—completely innocently, no doubt—had teased her about force-feeding her dessert. Lucky because the sheer humiliation and embarrassment distracted her from the disappointment.

She got to her feet as Muldoon shook her hand, glad to have something to do besides shrinking back in her chair and wishing she were trapped all alone on the elevator.

"To be honest," Muldoon told her, with an apologetic smile that made his handsome face even more handsome, "I went to MIT for only one semester."

"That's more than I ever did," Stan said. "Come on, sit down."

He sat first, opened his menu.

And as much as Teri wanted to make her excuses and run, she couldn't do it. If Stan didn't already know that she'd been hoping for more from him than friendship and an intro to his cute friend, her leaving would give her away.

Besides, friendship with Stan Wolchonok was better than nothing.

Wasn't it?

"So," she said to Muldoon, mostly because Stan glanced at her, because he expected her to say *some*thing. "When were you at MIT?"

"About seven years ago," the ensign told her. "First semester of my freshman year. But then my father got sick, so I transferred to a school closer to home."

Mike Muldoon was three years younger than she was. He was also almost impossibly handsome. Big eyes that were an even deeper shade of blue than Stan's. Golden brown hair that was thick and wavy, with a lock that fell attractively over his forehead—perhaps a touch of the rebel despite the squeaky-clean length in the back. His jaw was square, he had cheekbones to die for, and a nose that could have come directly from a Greek statue.

"Where's home?" she asked because Stan obviously wanted her to ask.

"At that time it was Florida," Muldoon said. "Before that, Maine. Kinda one extreme to another, you know? How about you?"

"Cambridge, Massachusetts," she told him. "From birth till college graduation."

He gave her another of those beautiful smiles, this one a little shy. Was this guy for real? "That must've been nice," he said.

Nice. Teri glanced at Stan, who was watching her. She didn't want to tell Mike Muldoon that it *hadn't* been nice, that she'd lived those last few years counting the days until she could leave home for good.

She forced a vague smile, then looked down at her menu, tired of small talk, tired of disappointments, tired.

"Go vegetarian tonight," Stan recommended, taking over the conversational ball. "Remember that the refrigeration cuts out for four hours every day. We'll be having our own food brought in. Starting tomorrow, hopefully."

A waiter came, clearly overworked, bringing bottles of water and breadsticks, and they ordered. Teri asked for exactly what Stan was having and he smiled at her. God, the way her heart raced when he did that was pathetic.

"Is there a reason we're not being billeted over at the airfield, Senior?" Muldoon asked. "I had a chance to look around out there, and there are two separate buildings that aren't being used. It wouldn't take much to clean them up and—"

"There's a very big reason," Stan said. "A GIK terrorist splinter group stole missile launchers from the K-stani army."

"Whoa." Teri sat back in her chair. "How do you steal a missile launcher?"

"From the K-stani army? Apparently pretty easily. They got two of 'em."

"Wait a minute." She tried to make sense of it. "Are you saying that if we set up living quarters in one of the buildings at the military airfield where the team built that mock-up of the 747—"

"We'd be an obvious and easy target," Stan finished for her. "Yes."

She looked from Stan to Muldoon and back. "And we're not a target *here*?"

"Think of it this way—a missile launched at an isolated building on a remote airfield versus a missile launched into the heart of Kazabek, where the civilian casualty rate would be outrageously high . . ." Stan shook his head. "Even factoring in the dangers of being in the city, we determined we'd be safer at this hotel."

"Okay," Muldoon said. "*I'm* going to sleep really well tonight."

From across the ballroom came a sudden blast of music and they all jumped. The volume was quickly adjusted, but it had caught the attention of everyone in the room.

As Teri watched, a skinny man climbed onto a wobbly makeshift stage. He started to sing "New York, New York" in a voice that shouldn't have been allowed within fifty feet of a microphone.

"Oh, Christ," Stan said, with complete and utter despair.

The man was singing in the local dialect, which had too many syllables to fit the notes.

It was beyond absurd and she met Stan's eyes. Disbelief, horror, and amusement were combined with the warmth of his somehow knowing that she, too, was dangerously close to losing it.

"Welcome to hell," he told her.

She had to clench her teeth to keep from laughing. Or crying.

"He's not *that* bad," Muldoon protested. "It takes a lot of nerve to get up in front of a crowd of strangers like this."

"Excuse me, Senior Chief."

It was Chief Wayne Jefferson—small, black, energetic, and well-known for his skills as an expert sharpshooter. He and Chief Frank O'Leary—tall, skinny, and laconic to the point of near-coma—were the team's snipers. The two men couldn't have been less alike.

"We've got a snafu with some of the rooms. Silverman, Jenk, Scooter," Jefferson listed on his fingers, "Cosmo, Horse, and Izzy all got rooms facing the street. I just spent an hour using sign language and baby talk with the hotel manager, getting them reassigned—and their *new* rooms all face the street. Normally I wouldn't bother you with this, Senior, but these men are tired as hell. I need to get them into their rooms *now*, and I recognized that my urge to grab this bastard and rip his smug racist smirk off his motherfucking face wouldn't speed up the process." He glanced at Teri. "I beg your pardon, ma'am."

"Good call, Chief." Stan stood up, looked from Muldoon to Teri. "You'll have to excuse me. This could take a while. If the food comes—eat. Don't wait for me." He turned to Jefferson. "Find me Lt. Johnny Nilsson. And then come back here and get yourself fed."

Jefferson was staring at the karaoke man in disbelief. "I don't think so, Senior. I'll be getting mine to go."

"Nilsson speaks the local language," Muldoon told her as Stan and Jefferson headed toward the door. "He flew out yesterday with L.T.—Lieutenant Paoletti."

"Yeah," Teri said. "I've met him. Nilsson, I mean."

The awkward silence that fell was daunting. Silence, that is, except for the sound created by the Karaoke Man, who hit an impossibly flat note and held it out impossibly long. Ouch.

Muldoon fidgeted in his seat. He was even more uncomfortable now that they were alone.

She prayed for Stan's swift return. How long could it take to get rooms reassigned in a hotel that was only filled to one-quarter capacity?

"So what's the deal with the rooms? Inside facing instead

of outside . . . ?" Teri asked, searching for something, *any*-thing to say. Stan had asked her about her room, too. *You're facing the inside courtyard, right?*

"Outside rooms—" Muldoon leapt upon the topic, ob-viously desperately glad to have something to talk about. "—rooms that have windows looking onto the street—are dangerous. This is a city where drive-by shootings and sniper attacks happen regularly. In a room facing the street, you need to put your mattress up in front of the window to protect against stray bullets, maybe even sleep in the bathtub. Which is about as comfortable as it sounds."

God, there were people in this city trying to raise children. How on earth did they ever let their kids go outside to play amid the continuous threat of death and destruction?

"Those inner rooms—the ones that face onto that courtyard—are significantly safer than the others," Muldoon continued. "It's one of the two main reasons Uncle Sam uses this hotel for billeting troops."

Teri nodded. "And the other reason—let me guess—is not just the heliport on the roof, but the fact that it's one of the tallest buildings in this part of the city. When we're on the roof, only a few people are going to be shooting down at us." As opposed to some of the other hotels, where they'd be sur-rounded by taller buildings on all sides.

"You got it." He relaxed enough to reach for a breadstick, snap it in two. "There's only one other building that's taller in this part of the city—and we've got Marines posted on that rooftop. The only real potential threat comes from the east-facing windows of the top two floors of that building—and we're working on getting men stationed in those areas as well. Until then—well, you got the instructions about swift landings and immediate takeoffs, right?"

Teri nodded as she took a sip of the bottled water the waiter had brought. Whenever approaching the hotel, she was to set the helo down fast. Like her passengers, she was to disem-bark as quickly as possible, running in a zigzag pattern across the roof to the stairwell. Boarding and takeoffs were similarly done. And once in the air, she was to fly like a bat out of hell, as swiftly away from the taller building as possible.

She'd done it three times today already.

Teri put down her glass to find that they'd slipped, once again, into a tense silence.

"I'm not good at this," Muldoon blurted. "I apologize."

"No," Teri said, "don't. It's not—"

"Women look at me and they expect—"

"—what you think," Teri talked over him, but he wasn't listening.

"—me to be someone else, someone cool and, I don't know, charismatic, and I'm not, I'm just an engineering nerd and I *suck* at this and, God, I end up disappointing all but the ones who just want sex, and *they* end up disappointing *me*."

Whoa. Teri could tell from the look on his face that he'd surprised himself with that outburst as much as he'd surprised her.

"Excuse me," he said, his face starting to turn red. "You probably didn't want to know that."

"I didn't ask Stan to set us up," Teri told him. *Stan*. She could do it, she could use his given name—just not to his face. "He did that completely on his own."

Muldoon cringed. "Oh, God, now I'm *really* embarrassed."

"Don't be—I thought maybe *you'd* asked Stan to introduce us, so . . ."

"No," he said. "I didn't."

"Obviously." She couldn't keep a giggle from slipping out.

He pushed his chair back from the table. "Excuse me. I have to go die now."

She grabbed for his hand. "Please don't leave. You can't imagine how glad I am that you said that. No one's ever honest, and I'm always second-guessing them, and God, I hate it. I mean, just a few minutes ago, I was thinking one thing and you were thinking another, but we were both wrong. And now we know—and we don't have to be nervous anymore."

Mike Muldoon was holding Teri Howe's hand.

Christ, that was fast.

Stan stood in the doorway of the restaurant, back in the shadows, watching them. He'd been waylaid in the hall by

Lieutenant Paoletti, and he hadn't been able to resist walking back with the CO toward the restaurant and looking in to see how things were going.

Apparently things were going pretty damn well.

Teri leaned closer to Muldoon and said something, and they both laughed.

She pulled her hand free, but the touch was perpetuated by the way they smiled into each other's eyes.

Fuck.

Hey, Yente. This was what you wanted, wasn't it?

No.

Yes. Look at them. They were so freaking cute together.

And Teri wasn't afraid of Muldoon. Her shoulders were relaxed—it was obvious she liked him. Which made sense. Muldoon was a great guy.

Stan had to back off on the envy overdose.

Which was easier said than done—but he'd done plenty of difficult things before. As hard as it was going to be, he could do this, too.

Stan had watched Teri all day today, and he'd made note of the way she'd practically flinched when some of the more, shall we say, *exuberant* men said hello to her. She'd tensed up, as if she were preparing for battle. Bracing herself for attack.

She needed someone steady, like Muldoon, in her life.

She'd needed more from Stan than a quick fix—he could certainly see that now. By taking her away from San Diego, he'd provided nothing more than a geographic cure.

Teri Howe's problem wasn't Lt. Comdr. Joel Hogan.

Teri Howe's problem was Teri Howe.

How in the hell was he going to fix *that*?

His cell phone rang.

"Sorry to bother you, Senior Chief, but there's a problem." Jenk delivered the news with his usual good cheer. "Gilligan's stuck in the elevator, and the hotel maintenance crew won't let us get him out ourselves."

Amazing. And the power hadn't even gone out yet.

"He's going to have to wait in line," Stan told the kid. "I have to wrangle some asshole at the front desk first. Find Sam

Starrett and WildCard Karmody," he ordered, thinking aloud as he walked swiftly to the stairs. "Tell them to bulldoze over the maintenance crew—to just keep agreeing with them—and get Gilligan the hell out of there anyway. And if I'm not there by the time he gets free, tell Karmody to do his best imitation of me and slice Gilligan into little quivering pieces. What the fuck is he doing getting into an elevator, goddamn knucklehead? Go."

"Aye aye, Senior Chief." Jenk signed off.

Fucking Gilligan. Christ. Tonight was off to a roaring start.

Ray Hernandez was going to die.

Gina's mother was a trauma nurse, and she'd taught all of her children enough first aid for Gina to be certain that unless Ray got to a hospital soon, that blow to the head he'd received from the butt of the hijacker's gun could very well prove fatal.

That is, if he wasn't dead already.

A blow like that had probably broken his skull.

Yeah, Ray was going to die. But maybe he was one of the lucky ones—because the way it was looking, they were all going down. At least by being unconscious, he wasn't scared anymore.

And it *was* inevitable, really. One by one the hijackers would go through them, smashing their skulls. Starting first with the boys, demanding Karen Crawford step forward.

But Karen couldn't step forward. She was still back in Athens.

"Karen Crawford," the too-handsome hijacker—the Backstreet Boy with the pleasant voice and pretty face—said again.

"She's not in *our* group." Dick McGann wept. "I *assure* you, if she were . . ."

He'd throw her to the wolves. No doubt about it.

"I will count to three," Backstreet said. "One."

They probably all would. Gina couldn't even say that—if Karen Crawford *were* here—she herself wouldn't be pointing her out to the gunmen right this very moment.

"Two."

Gina had always thought of herself as strong and principled, but it was easy to be strong and principled without guns held to your head.

The presence of those guns changed things a whole lot.

"Three."

No one moved.

Backstreet sighed wearily.

Gina had thought the shorter, more ferocious, snarly pantherman was the leader, but now she saw Backstreet give him a signal. Go ahead.

Pantherman pulled back the butt of his gun, ready to pulverize Trent Engelman's pretty head.

And Gina yanked herself free from Casey and stood up, stooping to keep from hitting her own head on the overhead luggage compartment. "Don't!" The word was out of her mouth almost before she realized what she was doing. What the hell *was* she doing?

She was looking at Backstreet, but she could see Trent from the corner of her eye, his face incredulous. She could also see Mr. McGann gaping at her, too.

"I'm Karen," she said. Her voice shook, so she said it again. Louder. "I'm Karen Crawford. Please don't hurt anyone else."

Eight

STANLEY WOLCHONOK HAD Marte's smile.

As far as Helga could tell, SEAL Team Sixteen's senior chief hadn't stopped moving since his plane had set down in Kazabek, but she'd caught enough of a glimpse of him to see that he had his mother's smile. And the glint of sharp intelligence in his eyes—that was pure Marte as well.

Out of all her regrets in her life, not searching more strenuously for Marte back in the 1960s, when they both would have been about the age Stanley was now, was exceedingly high on the list.

But Helga had been afraid it would hurt too much.

And here she was now, an old woman, forced to find Marte in her grown son's smile.

She was going to come face-to-face with Stanley later. At a meeting with FBI negotiator Max Bhagat and the SEAL commanders, whose names she had to consult her memo pad to keep straight.

I know your secret.

Every time she opened her pad, the words Des had written there seemed to jump out at her.

Her secret. That she was losing her mind—her brilliant, wonderful, God's gift of a mind.

Helga didn't want to think about it, didn't want to acknowledge it, hoping that if she didn't call it by name, it would disappear.

Knowing that *that* wasn't going to happen.

Des had said nothing more to her. But then again, he hadn't had time to. He'd vanished upon arrival in K-stan, and she could only guess where he'd gone, whom he might be contacting, what he might be doing.

Because she knew his secret, too. He wasn't *formerly* with Mossad. He was *still* with Mossad.

She tried to imagine him slinking around in the shadows like James Bond. Like the games Marte used to play—always moving silently and eavesdropping on everyone from the butcher to her sister, Annebet. She'd forced Helga to learn to climb out of her window and creep around without being heard.

"You never know when this will come in handy," Marte had told her, in complete seriousness.

And it had. Her ability to move soundlessly had come in very handy on that night when her parents and Hershel had fought.

At first it had been all loud voices. Poppi shouting about gold diggers after the family money. Her mother outraged that Hershel would even consider *any* kind of liaison with a girl like Annebet Gunvald. She wasn't even Jewish.

But then her mother stormed upstairs, leaving Hershel and their father. Their voices calmed and Helga had silently crept closer—close to the door of her father's study.

"She's a beautiful girl," she heard Poppi say through the door. "Very tempting. Particularly if she offers—"

"She hasn't offered anything," Hershel cut him off, his voice tight.

"These girls at university," Poppi continued, "freethinking young women who believe, what? That they're actually going to be *doctors* . . . ?"

"Yes," Hershel said. "Annebet believes that, and I believe it, too. She's wonderful, Father—"

"If it's marriage you want—"

"Marriage? I just met her."

"A man in your position must wait until marriage to . . ." Poppi cleared his throat. "Still, you've become a man and a man has needs. . . ."

Hershel was silent.

"As you get older, you'll learn to see beneath the obvious outward trappings of a girl like this. With age, you'll see her coarseness, her . . . lack of the more lasting virtues. Taking a girl like this as your mistress might seem like a good idea now—"

"Her name is Annebet, and I have no intention of insulting her by making her my mistress." Hershel was angry. He usually didn't get loud when he was very angry. He got quiet. Poppi didn't realize that, but Helga did.

"Good. That's . . . good." Poppi cleared his throat again. "Your mother and I weren't intending to arrange a marriage for you, like our parents did for us. We hoped you would pick your own wife. But if you're . . . hesitant to approach a certain girl, a Jewish girl from another well-to-do family, we could speak to her parents and—"

"Well, *that's* a hell of a reason to get married, isn't it?" Hershel sounded strangled. "Simply to get laid?"

"*Don't* use that language in my house!" Poppi exploded, and Helga shrank back from the door. "How *dare* you?"

"How dare *you*?" Hershel shot back quietly, intensely. "You don't even know Annebet, and you assume because she's not Jewish and because her family has to labor for a living that she's less than we are. Well, she's not. She's *more*. She's so much more. And I pity you for not being able to see that."

"I forbid you to see her again!"

"Or you'll do what?" Hershel asked. "Write me out of your will? Fair enough. Consider it done. I don't want your money. I have better things to do than sit around counting something that doesn't really exist."

Hershel pulled open the door. He didn't slam it behind him. He shut it instead with a much more final-sounding click. He took the stairs up to his bedroom calmly. If Helga didn't know him as well as she did, she wouldn't have guessed that he was furious.

She followed him up and into his room, watching as he started to pack, throwing his leather bag onto his bed and taking all of his undergarments from his drawer, putting them inside.

"I can't believe he still thinks I'm—" Hershel cut himself off.

"What?" she asked.

He shook his head. "Never mind."

"Are you really leaving?" Her heart was in her throat. "If you go back to Copenhagen, how will I know you're safe?"

Hershel sat down on his bed, took off his glasses, and rubbed his eyes. He sighed, looking at his suitcase. "Annebet told me she's not going back to university this term—I think the Gunvalds' are struggling more than ever to make ends meet. If I leave, I won't be able to see her again." He looked at Helga. "I'm *dying* to see her again."

"What does it mean—*get laid*?"

"You heard that, huh, mouse? Terrific." He stood up, dumped the contents of his bag back into his drawer.

"You're not going to tell me?" she asked, relief clogging her throat. He wasn't leaving.

"No."

"Are you sure? I suppose I could always ask Poppi . . ."

He laughed at that—as she'd hoped he would—some of the tension leaving his face. But he didn't tell her.

It didn't matter. She'd ask Marte. Marte knew everything.

Helga turned to leave, but Hershel stopped her.

"Does Annebet . . . Has she ever . . . mentioned me?"

Helga shook her head. "I haven't seen her since the day in the barn, and today in the store."

He looked so disappointed. "But Marte says Annebet looks at you like she wants to kiss you," she continued.

Her brother's face lit up. "Yeah?"

"Mrs. Shuler? Mr. Bhagat is ready to see you, ma'am."

Helga blinked.

An earnest young man stood in front of her. He couldn't have been more than twelve. Okay. Twenty-five. He just *looked* twelve.

Helga flipped through her notepad, skimming the words written there in her own familiar handwriting.

Hijacked plane. One hundred twenty passengers. Terrorists from the People's Party. Demanding release of prisoners, one in Israel. Max Bhagat—FBI negotiator.

I know your secret, in Desmond's bold hand.

Merde. When had he written that?

She rose to her feet and followed the young man into the other room.

"They haven't contacted us again," Max Bhagat was saying. "Not since they spoke to the tower in Kazabek before they landed. We've tried to raise them a number of times, but they're not talking."

Stan stood near the door to this room in the airport terminal that had been set up as the negotiators' headquarters. The building overlooked runway two, where the hijacked plane was parked.

This room had no windows, but just down the hallway was a waiting area with a floor-to-ceiling view of the 747. And, of course, the negotiators' room had banks of video screens, upon which were broadcast images of the plane from every imaginable angle, courtesy of the cameras put into place by the SEALs in Jazz Jacquette's surveillance squad.

They were out there right now, four men hidden on their bellies in the swampy grass surrounding runway two. Two teams of two on two-hour shifts, rotating out every hour.

"They haven't pulled the window shades," Bhagat continued, "so we've got a pretty clear look into the cabin. There appears to be only five terrorists—"

"I wouldn't set that into stone just yet," Lieutenant Jacquette interrupted. "Wait until we get the minicams and mikes into place in the body of the plane. I have a three-man team all set to move in after 0200."

The SEALs in Jazz's squad would approach the aircraft from its blind side—the rear—and work their way forward, staying beneath it. It would take time, moving slowly so as to make no noise, but they'd gain access to the luggage compartment and thread miniaturized cameras and microphones up into the passenger compartment and the cockpit of the plane.

Stan tried to stay focused, tried not to let his thoughts slip to Teri and Muldoon, who had surely finished dinner, even if they'd lingered over coffee. They were probably both in bed by now.

Maybe even together.

God *damn* it.

He was tired and cranky.

So what if Teri had hit it off so well with Muldoon that she had invited him back to her room? So what if he were there right now, skimming his hands and mouth across her naked body? So what if he were pushing himself inside of her as she clung to him, eyes closed and head thrown back, sweat glistening on her perfect breasts?

Ah, Christ. Stan wanted to double over from the longing and envy that gripped him. Instead he pushed it away, forcing himself to stand tall, to stand strong.

It would be great if Muldoon and Teri hooked up. He knew that was true. Because then Teri would be Muldoon's problem. Stan could stop thinking about her once and for all. He could stop trying to figure out how the hell to help her deal with not just the big threats in her life, but the day-to-day ones as well.

Stan could be her friend, period, the end. No obligations, no responsibilities, no temptation. Yeah, all temptation would be gone. Because no way in hell would he mess around with Mike Muldoon's girlfriend. No way. He could want her so badly he was bleeding from the ears, but he wouldn't touch her if she were involved with Mike.

Lieutenant Paoletti and Max Bhagat were deep in a conversation about timing and best and worst case scenarios—nothing Stan didn't already know. Still, he needed to pay attention, so he tried to wake himself up by standing a little straighter and resolutely pushing the last of the images of Teri Howe getting it on with Mike Muldoon out of his head.

Mrs. Shuler, the envoy from Israel, was watching him—apparently he wasn't the only one whose attention had wandered. She gave him a smile and a nod before they both focused on Max Bhagat.

But then the conversation and the meeting was over. And Stan followed Paoletti to the door. If he were lucky, he'd encounter no more emergencies between this building and his hotel room pillow.

Please, God, let him get just an hour of sleep tonight. . . .

But Mrs. Shuler intercepted him, turning to greet him with a handshake in the hallway.

The Israeli envoy was a small, pleasantly round woman in her midsixties with soft gray hair that curled around a still-youthful face.

"I don't want to take up too much of your time, Senior Chief," she told him in an accent that reminded him sharply, sweetly of his mother's laughter-filled voice. "I know you must be even more tired than I am. But I did want to meet you and introduce myself. When I was a little girl, back in Denmark, I was friends with your mother."

Stan had to laugh. "No kidding?"

Mrs. Shuler nodded, warmth in her eyes. "Marte and her family—the Gunvalds—helped save my life when the Germans rounded up the Danish Jews in 1943."

No shit? "She never talked about Denmark," Stan admitted. "At least not to me, not in any depth. I mean, I knew her parents died there when she was pretty young, right after the war. And family legend has it that her older sister, Annebet, hocked an important piece of jewelry, some kind of heirloom, I think it was, to buy them passage on a ship to New York, but other than that . . ."

"My brother's ring." Mrs. Shuler suddenly had to reach for the wall to hold herself up.

Stan took her elbow, afraid she was going to do a half gainer right on her face, this woman who had known his mother, who had known the grandparents he himself had never met. "Are you all right, ma'am?"

She looked at him with eyes that were no longer filled with energy and light, but instead were confused and frightened.

"Ah, Helga, there you are." Her assistant, the tall black former operator, breezed down the hall toward them. "I see you've met Senior Chief Wolchonok—Marte Gunvald's son. I'm sure there'll be a more opportune time to talk after this situation has been properly dealt with."

"Marte's son," Mrs. Shuler repeated, looking at Stan, her face now showing every single day of her sixty-something years of life.

"Is that okay with you, Senior Chief?" the assistant said. "Maybe you can share a flight back to London with Mrs. Shuler."

"I'd like that," Stan said. "You know, my sister's name is Helga."

Mrs. Shuler's eyes filled with tears. "I didn't know," she said.

And then she was gone. Whisked back into the negotiators' room.

Stan opened the door to his hotel room, peeling off his shirt and T-shirt and unfastening his pants as he went inside.

It was as freaking hot in there as it was out in the hallway. Hot and close. His vivid imagination conjured up the fragrant scent of the curried noodles and vegetables he'd ordered for dinner, back about a million years ago.

His stomach rumbled.

It was some realistic hallucination, because it overpowered the stench of his own clothes. He smelled like fatigue and nonstop stress, armpits and old feet. Tired, aching, stinky old feet.

He slapped on the light and sat down in one of the room's tattered easy chairs to take his boots off. His left boot was off and in his hands before he saw it.

Dinner—main course covered with a metal plate warmer— had been laid out on the small table in the corner of the room.

And—holy shit!—Teri Howe was curled up in the middle of his bed, fast asleep.

He was wearing only his briefs. His pants were down around his knees, his T-shirt and shirt back by the door where he'd dropped them.

His fingers fumbled, and his boot hit the floor with a thump, and Teri sprang awake. It was remarkable to watch, at least for the part of him that wasn't completely horrified by coming face-to-face with her in his current state of undress.

One instant she was sound asleep, and the next she was on her feet, back against the wall, staring at him, eyes wide, as if he were some flasher who'd dropped his pants in the park.

"Excuse me," he said. "I didn't realize I wasn't alone."

He stood to pull up and zip his pants—his turn to move fast. But then he was standing there, without a shirt on, his belt undone. As she edged even farther away from him, he quickly sat back down. Getting his shirt was a priority, but he'd have to walk past her to do it, and the last thing he wanted to appear was threatening to her in any way, especially when she was still off balance from sleep and on the verge of being extremely spooked.

As he watched, she looked around the room and got her bearings.

"Oh, my God," she said as breathlessly as if she'd just run five miles. "I must've fallen asleep. I'm sorry, I didn't mean to invade your privacy. I just . . . I heard that you had to go to a meeting, that you didn't get any dinner, so I ordered room service, only they wouldn't bring it here if someone wasn't in the room, so I found Duke—Chief Jefferson—who has a master key, and he let me in so I could wait for it, only after the food arrived I couldn't leave because I couldn't get the door to lock behind me and I didn't want to leave the room unlocked with your seabag in here."

She finally inhaled as she pointed to his duffel bag lying on the floor by the door, where he'd left it when he'd first been as-signed this room.

"I'm so sorry, Senior Chief," she said again, as if she'd committed some cardinal sin.

She'd ordered him dinner. Stan didn't know what to say. He couldn't remember the last time someone had ordered him dinner. He was always the man in charge of making sure everyone else had everything they needed, and his own needs often went ignored. He cleared his throat. "I'm, um, going to put my shirt back on, okay?"

"You don't have to. It's hot in here and you don't . . . have to . . ." Teri watched as he crossed the room and picked up his T-shirt, as he turned it right-side out and pulled it over his head.

"Did I say thank you yet?" Stan asked.

She shook her head.

"Thank you."

"I probably broke all kinds of rules, being in here like this." She was embarrassed as hell and looked as if she were ready to bolt from the room. "It really wasn't my intention to be in your room when you got back, like some kind of . . . of . . . weird stalker or something."

"Actually, the situation *did* have a Goldilocks and the three bears feel to it." He tried to make his voice light as he jammed his foot back into his boot. "Only you brought the porridge with you and your hair is dark brown. By the way, to get the door to lock, you need to pull up on the knob, let the latch click into place. So how was the karaoke? Did you get up and sing?"

She laughed—a short burst of surprised air. "Me?"

Stan felt far more in control with most of his clothes back on. "Not your style, huh?"

He crossed to the table and lifted the metal lid to find a fragrant mountain of vegetables, noodles, and chunks of tofu. Thank you, Jesus and Teri. He touched it with his finger and found that it was still faintly warm. Life was good.

"To get up in front of a bunch of people I work with and make a total fool of myself?" She laughed again. "No, thanks."

Stan glanced up at her. "Want some?"

She shook her head, her shoulders more relaxed now. "I had dinner."

With Mike Muldoon. Yeah, he knew. And yet she was here in Stan's room now.

If he hadn't seen her holding Muldoon's hand in the restaurant, he'd be wildly imagining a night filled with more than a good meal, a shower, and a few hours of deep, dreamless sleep. And okay, he had a very vivid imagination and it *was* going wild. But because he'd seen her with Muldoon, he knew reality was going to be very different from all he was imagining.

Still, he let himself enjoy the thought of Teri, stretched out naked on his bed, all long legs and full breasts and soft skin.

Oh, yeah.

As far as fantasies went, it was a good one.

She glanced toward the door. "I should go."

Stan put the lid back on both his libido and his dinner. "I'll walk you to your room."

She laughed. "Don't be ridiculous. You don't need to *walk* me—"

"There," he interrupted her. "That's the attitude you need.

Instead of shrinking when someone bigger than you so much as looks at you—"

"I don't *shrink*."

She was only pretending to stand her ground. Stan gave her two seconds to fold. "You wanna bet?"

"I *don't*." Her gaze shifted and she was done. "I mean, I *try* not to—"

"I've been watching you for a while, Teri." He moved so that she had to look at him. "Your body language is all about retreating when you should be holding your ground."

She looked down at the floor. He would've had to lie down to put himself into her line of sight. Or touch her, tugging her chin up so that she was forced to look into his eyes.

He did neither.

"Out in the parking lot," he said as gently as he could, "with Joel Hogan . . . You froze. I saw it. I kept waiting for you to whale him one, but you didn't. And when Starrett told me about Admiral Tucker—"

"Oh, God." She sank down onto his bed, eyes closed, defeated. "You must think I'm such a loser."

Stan sat down next to her, making sure there was a good three feet between them. "I think you're one of the best helo pilots I've ever worked with. I think you're an extremely beautiful woman—for whom that's probably been more of a curse than a blessing." He also thought she'd probably been sexually abused as a child, but Christ, how the hell did you ask someone about that? "And I think all you need to do is to learn how to be a little less nonconfrontational when it comes to unwanted attention from men."

She laughed then, but it was shaky. "You make it sound like I just have to enroll in a class," she said. "Confrontational Behavior 101. God, I wish it were that easy. All I ever wanted to do was fly. Why can't I just fly?" She finally looked over at him, something akin to misery in her eyes. "I hate it when they win. And they always win." She shook her head. "I don't belong here. That's why I went into the Reserves, into the civilian sector, but I didn't belong there either."

Stan tried not to let her see how her quiet words had affected him. *I hate it when they win.* He blew out a burst of exasperated air. "Well, *that's* bullshit I never expected to hear from you. You don't belong? Who does? They always win? Fuck that. Learn how to beat 'em."

The harshness of his language had done what he'd hoped it would. It had surprised her. Brought her a little bit out of her misery. "It's not that easy."

"Yeah? Tell me one thing that's easy that's worth having or doing."

She wouldn't look at him as she stood up. "Look, you don't understand. And I just . . . I don't want to argue with you."

He got up, too, blocking her path to the door. "No," he said. "No running away. You run away a lot, don't you?"

She didn't answer. She just stood there looking at him as if he'd stabbed her in the heart.

He steeled himself. "You do. You run from confrontation. Not when you're flying though. But the rest of the time. You were running away from Hogan when he caught up to you in the parking lot. But right now, you have to stick," he told her. "You wouldn't run if you were in a helo."

"I'm safe there," she whispered.

"You're safe here, too," he said, and her eyes filled with new tears.

Please, God, don't let her start to cry. If she started to cry, he'd have to put his arms around her, and that would probably kill him. Not him holding her—that wouldn't hurt at all. What would kill him was having to let her go.

Besides, if he pulled her into his arms, and she didn't want him to touch her, he probably wouldn't know it.

She certainly wouldn't tell him, that was for sure.

What the hell was he going to do with her?

And suddenly—just like that—he knew. He looked at his watch. Seventeen minutes to ten. There'd just been a surveillance shift change. Perfect.

"You ever have allergies?" he asked her.

She blinked at his apparent change of subject. "No."

"Neither have I," he said. "But my sister had hay fever really bad, and she took allergy shots. What they did was inject a little bit of the pollens she was allergic to into her system. It worked to desensitize her. That's what we've got to do for you."

She wasn't following him.

"You tired?" he asked.

"No."

Yeah, right. "Are you lying?"

She looked at him and laughed. It was a real life laugh, not one of those forced, fake ones that she sometimes made. "No. I'm not tired—I'm exhausted."

Stan grabbed his key and opened the door. "Well, tough nuggies, Lieutenant. You're with SEAL Team Sixteen's Troubleshooters now, and *exhausted* is no longer part of your working vocabulary. On your feet, grab your flack jacket, and follow me."

"Did you really just say tough *nuggies*?" she asked as she grabbed her jacket and followed him out the door.

"You want me to *what*?" The SEAL nicknamed Izzy was looking at the senior chief as if he'd asked him to set explosives and blow up the local orphanage.

Teri had to admit that everything about this was surreal.

Both Gilligan—Petty Officer Dan Gillman—and Izzy— she had no idea of *his* real name—had just come in from the swampy fields around runway two, where they'd laid low and watched the activity on the hijacked plane for the past two hours. Their faces were streaked with camouflage greasepaint and their uniforms were soaked with a malodorous mix of seawater and briny mud.

"Harass her," Stan said, nudging Teri toward them, right there in the hotel stairwell, his hand at the small of her back. "Hit on her. Have at her. Try to intimidate her. She needs to practice being assertive."

Oh, God.

"If you say so, Senior." Dan Gillman couldn't have been more than twenty-three years old. He was good-looking beneath his greasepaint, with dark hair and melting chocolate brown eyes, a square jaw, and a physique that could have been featured in a six-page spread in *Men's Fitness* magazine. He took a halfhearted step toward Teri. "Um . . ."

"Come on, Dan," Stan said. He'd stopped touching her, and she missed the heat of his hand against her back. "Pretend you're in the Ladybug Lounge. Crowd her up against the wall. Invade her personal space. Get much too close and say, *Hey, babe, come here often?* Give it your obnoxious best."

Gilligan took one step and then another toward her, rather ineffectively attempting to herd her back toward the wall through his sheer size. But he stopped short. He didn't touch her and his eyes were apologetic as he towered over her. "Hey, babe." His voice cracked and he cleared his throat. "Sorry, Lieutenant."

"Ah, Christ." Stan pulled him away from her. "You're about as threatening as little Cindy Lou Who."

"I have a sister," Gilligan protested.

"So do I," Stan said, moving closer and closer, until Teri had to back up to keep him from bumping into her. "Watch me."

Her back hit the wall, and still he kept coming, his eyes hard and colorless in the dim stairwell light.

As he put an arm up on either side of her, pinning her in, his muscles strained the sleeves of his snugly fitting T-shirt. She found herself hypnotized, thinking about his underwear.

The senior chief wore plain white, no-frills briefs.

That fit about as snugly as this T-shirt he was wearing.

It was an image that Teri was going to carry with her to her grave—Senior Chief Stan Wolchonok, all hard muscles and tanned skin and blue eyes and form-fitting white briefs.

Oh, God.

She felt him touch her, his chest brushing her breasts as he got yet even closer. It was exactly the kind of intimidating crowding that she hated, and yet he was being careful, she knew, to keep the lower half of his body away from her.

He leaned forward and she felt his breath hot against her as he spoke, his voice a rough whisper in her ear. "You know you want me." They were the same words Joel Hogan had said to her in the parking lot.

He pulled back slightly to look down at her, and Teri stared up at him, unable to speak or move. Unable to breathe.

For a half second, he froze, too.

But then he pushed himself away from the wall, away from

her. "That's what I mean, Gillman. As stupidly obnoxious as you can imagine. Come on, do what I just did, and Teri . . ." He looked at her. "Don't just stand there. What are you going to do when he says that to you? What are you going to say? Have something prepared. Pretend you're in your helo—that you've got that kind of control of this situation, that kind of confidence."

Gilligan got close, still dubious. God, he smelled bad, kind of like rotting fish, and Teri started to laugh. This was just too absurd.

"Okay, good," Stan said. "Getting laughed at by the woman you're pursuing is an instant soft-on." He caught himself. "Pardon the expression." He cleared his throat. "Now, look him in the eye and tell him to get lost."

"Get lost," Teri said to Dan Gillman. It was easy to sound heartfelt. She wanted both him and Izzy to disappear. She wanted to be alone in this stairwell with Stan. *You know you want me.* He hadn't been serious when he'd said that. He was only trying to be . . . what had he called it? Stupidly obnoxious. But his words were so true. She wanted him.

"My turn," Izzy announced.

Teri turned to him, forced herself to meet his gaze. "Get lost," she said, and Stan grinned, his smile lighting him from within.

You know you want me.
Yeah, she did.
Badly.

"Got a minute?" Sam Starrett asked.

"Sure. What's up?" Max Bhagat looked up from the conference table that had been pulled off to the side of the negotiators' room.

He was pretending to be cool and calm in his three-thousand-dollar suit, but rumor had it the laid-back control was just an act. Rumor had it that Bhagat's true nature would be revealed within a day or two. He'd wear a hole in this cheap wall-to-wall carpet from his pacing. He'd stop eating, stop sleeping, that jacket would come off, and his sleeves would get rolled up.

Rumor had it that Bhagat rarely lost his temper, but when he did—look out! It wasn't a rumor but a fact that the man was the best negotiator in all of the FBI. He'd do whatever it took to buy the SEALs the time they needed to be as prepared as possible for the takedown of the plane.

Starrett could appreciate that. He had the utmost respect for the men and women who worked hard to support his team.

But so far the tangos—terrorists—on the hijacked plane hadn't responded to any of Bhagat's radio messages. Every fifteen minutes the man had broadcast a message to the plane. Down the hall, his team of assistants were placing bets as to when he'd get fed up enough to go out on the concrete runway with a bullhorn.

The silence was unnerving. It was a technique the negotiators themselves frequently used. *Now we'll just sit here and you can listen to yourself breathe and think about all the ways you're probably going to die. . . .*

"Your FBI observers," Starrett said, trying not to sound as hostile as he'd felt just a few hours ago, out on the airstrip, and a half hour ago in the hotel restaurant when he'd gone to get dinner and found that Alyssa Locke was there, too. Everywhere he fucking went, she was watching him. "They're distracting the hell out of my men. Me," he amended. "Me and my men."

Bhagat just sat there, looking at him coolly, letting him sputter and make noise. Kind of like what the tangos were doing.

He could imagine what Bhagat was thinking. Was it Alyssa Locke that Starrett had a problem with, or was it her gay partner, Jules Cassidy?

But Starrett couldn't explain. As pissed off as he was at her, he'd promised Alyssa he'd never breathe a word to anyone about the night they'd spent together. It was a secret he was going to carry with him to his grave. His very cold and lonely grave.

"Do you mind if I ask them to observe from a slightly closer proximity?" he asked, and had the satisfaction of knowing he'd surprised Bhagat with his request. "I want to start working with warm bodies on the mock-up—people playing the parts of both passengers and hijackers. You have any objection to Locke and Cassidy getting involved?"

"None at all," Bhagat said. "Watch out, though, Alyssa Locke is an extremely accurate shot."

Understatement of the century. Along with being drop dead gorgeous and amazing in bed, Alyssa was an expert marksman, a world class sharpshooter.

"We're working on getting you an actual World Airlines 747 to use for practice," Bhagat said.

"We should've had it here this afternoon," Starrett countered.

"Hello?" The voice came from the radio, and Bhagat jumped out of his seat.

"Radio contact!" one of the aides shouted as Bhagat reached for the microphone.

"Get the senator," he ordered.

Another of the aides who'd been dozing in front of the surveillance equipment vanished down the hall.

"This is World Airlines flight 232," the voice from the radio announced. Whoever it was, she was young, female, and American. No doubt about it, that voice was pure New York.

"Flight 232, my name is Max," Bhagat said, sounding cool and unruffled. "Who am I talking to?"

As Sam stood there, the room came to life fast. All the empty chairs filled up and the bright overhead lights were switched on.

"I'm Karen," the voice said. "Karen Crawford?"

"Hi, Karen. Are you all right?"

"Max, you're not, like, the airport janitor or something, are you? Because that was a really stupid question."

The entire room stopped breathing. All of the members of Bhagat's team of agents turned to look at him. Sam guessed he'd been called a lot of things in his life, but stupid obviously wasn't one of them.

He didn't seem particularly perturbed, but then again, he never did.

"I'm trapped on a plane with five angry men," the girl's voice continued, "who are armed with seven different automatic weapons. Seven. Believe me, I know. I've counted them."

Max Bhagat smiled. "Make a note, please—we've got eye-witness verification that there are five hijackers on the plane, all fully armed," he said to his team. He was already pacing. "Good job, Karen. Tell us as much as you possibly can, but do it without putting yourself into additional danger." He thumbed the key to the radio microphone, opening the frequency.

"I'm an FBI negotiator, Karen," he said into the mike with his accentless, smooth, FM radio voice. "I apologize for the stupid question. I was hoping you could assure me that you and everyone else on board—including our hostile friends and the pilots and crew—are all in good health."

"Two of the passengers have been injured," her voice came back, loud and clear. "But I'm okay. They want me to talk to my, well, my *father*."

Senator Crawford must've been sleeping on a couch in one of the other rooms. He came in as if on cue, with his hair a mess, Yale sweatshirt on in place of his suit jacket, blinking in the bright overhead light.

"They know who she is," Bhagat told the senator, getting right to the point, no niceties. "They're using her to speak for them. Remember, no promises at this point, sir." He thumbed the mike. "Karen, we've got him right here. He's anxious to talk to you, too."

As Starrett watched, Senator Crawford nearly grabbed the microphone from Bhagat's hands. "Karen, honey, are you all right?"

"I'm fine, Daddy. You know, I almost didn't make this flight. In fact, my friend . . . my friend *Gina*, she didn't make it on board. Someone picked her pocket and stole her pass-port and they wouldn't let her on the plane. I know her parents must be really worried about her, but they don't have to be, because she's not on the flight. She's still back in Athens and—"

The look on the senator's face was almost comical. "Who the hell—?"

Bhagat almost knocked the man over in his haste to get the mike away from him. For a guy in a suit, he could move pretty fast.

"Hey! I don't goddamn know who that is," Crawford continued hotly, "but she's not Karen. She's not my daughter. And I would appreciate a little more consideration—"

"Peggy, notify the American consulate in Athens," Bhagat barked orders right over him. It seemed as if the rumors of Bhagat's legendary temper were all true. "Karen Crawford's probably there right now, trying to get a replacement passport. Get her to safety, quickly and quietly—no media. Not one reporter finds out about this. If she shows up on CNN, I will go there myself after this is over and personally escort everyone in the Athens office to hell, is that understood?"

It clearly was. "Yes, sir." Peggy hauled ass out of the room.

Max Bhagat turned his glare back onto Crawford. "Another outburst like that, and senator or president or God—I don't give a gleaming goddamn who or what you are—you will be out of this room."

That, too, was understood.

Still, Crawford bristled. "Are you threatening me?"

"Do you really care?" Bhagat shot back at him. "This young woman—and I believe she just told us her name was Gina. George, get me the passenger manifest from World Airlines, fast—she just managed to inform us that your daughter's not on that plane. Glory alleluia, it's your lucky day. *Your* daughter is safe. But whoever the hell Gina is, she's someone else's daughter, and she's taking a real risk here. If the hijackers find out she's not Karen, they'll kill her. I don't doubt that. Now, when you get back on this radio, sir, you remember that. And you keep her the hell alive."

Nine

"BACK OFF," TERI said, but this time Izzy kept coming. The SEAL was built like a professional linebacker, and with the streaks of black camouflage still on his face, he looked faintly savage.

At the senior chief's request, he'd been playing it as skeevy as possible, leering, grabbing at her ass, and muttering faintly obscene suggestions for a solid ten minutes now.

Frankly, she wasn't well enough acquainted with him to know whether or not he was a genuine creep or just a really good actor.

With Gilligan, Stan had been standing right behind her, close enough so that she couldn't back up without bumping into him. Close enough so that she couldn't get caught up in the make-believe and actually start feeling afraid.

But now he'd moved away, and when Izzy came toward her, she felt a swift tug of real fear. Rationally, logically, she knew she wasn't in any danger. Stan was six feet away, tops. Still, the look in Izzy's eyes made the hair on the back of her neck go up. *This* was why she didn't hang out in bars.

"Okay, so what do you do now, Teri?" Stan asked.

Get louder. Sound like she really meant it. Stand her ground, don't back away, chin high, eyes hard.

Izzy reached for her, and she smacked his hand. "Back off!" she said again, and this time her voice rang out, echoing in the hotel stairwell.

And Izzy retreated. "Ouch."

"Good," Stan said, briefly touching her shoulder with approval.

"Yeah, like this has anything to do with real life," she countered, her elation fading as quickly as the warmth from his hand. She sank down to sit on the stairs.

He turned to Izzy and Gilligan. "Thank you, gentlemen, for your help."

"Any time, Senior Chief."

"See you later, Teri." Gilligan gave her a smile and Izzy winked as the two men headed down the stairs.

Teri sighed. Clearly she'd intimidated them. Not a bit.

Stan came over and sat beside her on the same step. He was careful to keep a lot of space between them, same as when he'd sat next to her on his bed. Sometimes it seemed as if every guy in the world crowded her—except the one she wanted to get close to.

"When it's real, I freeze," she told him.

"I thought I saw you do that a couple of times," Stan said easily. "But then you snapped out of it. That was good. That's what you have to practice doing."

She *had* frozen at least once. When Stan had used his body to push her back against the wall. When he'd stood so close that she was pressed against the solid muscles of his chest. Her own body temperature had gone up several degrees simply from the proximity of his heat.

It wasn't fear that had frozen her in place.

She'd been speechless as well as unable to move. Dry mouthed from desire.

"It's not that I don't appreciate your help," Teri told him now, "because I do. It's just . . . different when it's real."

"So you'll practice," he said matter-of-factly. "Until it's *not* different when it's real. Until it's no big deal—just another jerk to put in his place."

He was tired. He tried to pretend he wasn't, but he reached up with one hand to work out the stiffness in his neck and shoulders.

If she weren't such a coward, she'd offer to give him a backrub. Instead she just sat there, watching him, admiring his eyes and his arms and the way his T-shirt clung to the muscles in his chest. Thinking that even though he wasn't conventionally handsome, he was possibly the most attractive man she'd ever met. Thinking about his underwear. Wishing she had the nerve to touch him.

But he'd tried to set her up with his best friend. Surely that was a sign he wasn't interested in her in a touching kind of way.

He met her gaze, looking at her as intently as she was looking at him. What did he see?

An exhausted coward with messy hair and tired eyes. And yet Teri didn't want to stand up and call it a night. She wanted to stay right here, on this step, next to this man, for as long as she possibly could.

"Can I ask you a personal question?" Stan asked her.

Her heart tripped, yet she managed to sound normal as she answered. "Okay."

If there were a God, Stan would ask her to go back to his room with him. But, really, she knew he wasn't going to ask that. The way he was sitting—his body language—couldn't scream *friend* any louder if he tried.

"What's your goal in the Navy?" Stan asked. "What do you want from your career?"

That wasn't personal. That was easy. "To fly. I just want to fly."

He nodded, his eyes narrowing slightly. "Just to fly. Yeah, you told me that was a priority for you since you were a kid. You went after it, and you got it pretty quickly. No fear. But there's really more to your goal than that, isn't there? If you really just wanted to fly, you'd still be a pilot for Harmony Airlines."

He was right.

"Okay, I guess I want to fly for missions like this one," she said slowly, thinking aloud, "where I get to work with people I respect. With people who respect me."

He nodded, seeming to think that was a good answer. "How about your personal life?" he asked. "What are your goals there?"

Teri didn't know how to answer that.

"Do you want a family?" he went on. "And it's okay if you don't—not everyone does. I mean, I don't. What would I do with a wife and kids? Christ. How do you sustain that kind of relationship if you're gone all the time, you know?"

"But your house is perfect for . . ." *Kids*. She tried again. "You have such a great house." God, that was a stupid thing to say.

He laughed. Apparently he thought it was pretty stupid, too, but his laughter was teasing and warm. Inclusive. "Yeah, but last time I checked, having a great house—and it's a bungalow, by the way—wasn't one of *Navy Life* magazine's top ten reasons to get married."

"It needs furniture," she found herself saying. God, she was embarrassed she'd brought it up in the first place, but she was unable to stop sounding stupid. What was wrong with her?

She wanted him to kiss her. She always got stupid when she was with a man she liked enough to want to kiss.

This was too weird. She couldn't get up the nerve to call this man by his first name, yet she wanted . . . Maybe it was hero worship, like the crushes she'd occasionally had on her teachers in school. Maybe it was all part of her ongoing quest to find approval. Maybe she was misinterpreting her emotional need to connect with a father figure for . . .

She snuck another glance at Stan's near-perfect body. Long legs, lean hips, trim waist, big shoulders and arms.

No, what she was feeling was in no way daughterly.

Stan was still smiling, the lines around his eyes crinkling, making him more than merely attractive, making him decidedly handsome. Drop dead gorgeous with those warm blue eyes and those straight white teeth and those lips . . .

"Yeah, you noticed the lack of furniture, huh?" he was saying. "I'm waiting to win the lottery so I can fill it with Stickley pieces." At her blank look, he explained. "Oak furniture—antiques from the Arts and Crafts period. Same era as the bungalow—early 1900s. Currently it's out of my price range and it just seems, I don't know, *wrong* to fill a place I've worked so hard to restore with stuff from IKEA."

Stan Wolchonok's hobby was restoring old houses and collecting antiques. Teri couldn't keep from smiling, and he was comfortable enough with himself to laugh, too.

"Yeah, don't spread it around, all right?" he continued.

"All I need is for my men to find out I'm into antiques. I'll never hear the end of it—forget about the fact that Stickley used nice, clean, simple, masculine lines. It's really gorgeous stuff and . . . I'm just digging myself in deeper here, aren't I?"

She found herself leaning toward him. "How could they not know? Don't they wonder why you don't have furniture in your house?"

"Yeah, well . . ." He rubbed his face, cleared his throat. "They don't come over," he admitted. "My house is off-limits to U.S. Navy personnel, no exception. I decided early on in my career that I didn't want to live in a halfway house for wayward SEALs. See, some of the other chiefs always find themselves followed home by whichever of their enlisted men has the problem of the week, and . . ." He shook his head. "The few hours that I'm off the base and home are *my* hours—and it's usually only about six a day, sometimes fewer, so it's not like I'm being overly selfish here. And they can reach me by phone, twenty-four/seven, I've made that clear. I'll come rescue 'em if they need rescuing, but they can't sleep on my couch. They can't even come inside."

"You don't have a couch," she pointed out. He'd let her into his house. What did that mean?

He gave her another of those amazing smiles. "Yeah, maybe that's another reason why I'm not in such a hurry to get one. There's never any temptation to let anyone come over and sleep on it."

Why did you let me come inside? The question was burning the inside of her mouth, the inside of her very stomach.

He looked at his watch, and she knew it was just a matter of seconds, maybe less, before he stood up. Then this conversation would be over.

"Stan." Oh, God. She'd done it. She'd actually used his name.

He didn't seem aware of the momentousness of the occasion, though he stopped looking at his watch and waited for her to continue.

"I owe you an apology," she said in a rush. "I didn't know I was breaking the rules by coming over to your house."

He was already shaking his head. "Please, don't worry about it. You're an exception—"

"You said no exceptions."

"Yeah, well, I guess that makes me a liar. It's really no big deal."

But it *was* a big deal. He might've been unable to shut the door in her face because he was attracted to her. Or he might've let her in out of pity. Teri wanted to know which it had been.

"I'm glad I was home." Stan stood up. "Come on. Tomorrow'll be here far too soon. I'll walk you to your room."

Stan, why did you let me come inside?

She could do it. All she had to do to start the question was to say his name again. How hard could that be? She took a deep breath.

"Hey," he said, turning back to look at her as she followed him up the stairs. "I meant to ask—what'd you think of Mike Muldoon? Good guy, huh?"

Pity. It had no doubt been nothing more than pity.

Teri forced a smile. "Yeah," she said. "He's a really good guy."

"Hello?" Gina said again into the microphone, aware that Handsome Bob and Snarly Al were watching her closely. Bob and Al, Backstreet Bob had said they were called, after Al had backhanded her hard enough to split her lip. They were clearly Americanizations of more complicated Kazbekistani names. "Are you still there? Daddy?"

Please, *Daddy*, don't say something stupid and give her away. Please, Max of the relaxed, matter-of-fact, soothingly rich baritone voice, understand all that she had told him. Karen Crawford wasn't on this plane. But God help Gina if Bob and Al found that out.

Would they shoot her or club her to death?

Please, *some*one answer or she was going to puke.

"Hey, Karen, this is Max again." The voice came over the speaker, the answer to her prayers. "We can't talk while you've got the thumb key pressed on the microphone. It would be a big help if you would say 'over' or 'go ahead' so we know when you're finished speaking, and then lift your

thumb, okay? And we'll do the same. Here's Senator Crawford again. Over."

Senator Crawford, he'd said. Not your father. He knew.
Now she nearly threw up from relief.

"Uh, Karen? I'm . . . I'm here, honey. Over." Thank God,
Crawford was playing along, too.

"They've told me they've already given you their list of demands," she said. There was silence until she added, "Over."

And then there was more silence. Too much silence.

Handsome Bob shifted in the pilot's seat. Just the slightest
show of impatience. Gina forced herself not to look at him.

She pressed the button on the side of the microphone.
"Daddy?" she said, trying not to sound as desperate as she
felt. "Please go ahead."

"We're . . . we're working on that," Crawford finally said.
"On their demands. I'm going to Washington, uh, Karen, to,
uh, speak to the president and, uh . . ."

God, this guy was a royal loser. To think she'd voted for
him. But okay, to give him credit, he probably wasn't thinking
very clearly. He'd just found out that his daughter wasn't
being held at gunpoint by terrorists.

Lucky bastard. Much luckier than Gina's father.

Well, if the senator didn't have anything important to say,
she sure as hell *did*.

Gina hit the button on her mike and the radio squealed.
There was silence then. At least she'd managed to shut him up.

"Go ahead, Karen," the other voice, Max's voice—dear,
wonderful Max's voice—cut in.

"I love you, Daddy," she said, knowing that somewhere
over in the airport terminal building recorders were running,
taping every word she uttered. Someday, her real father
would hear this. She hoped.

Her throat ached from trying not to cry. "I'm so sorry—I
know you didn't want me to take this trip," she continued.
"You tried to talk me out of it, but there really was nothing
you could have said. I wanted to go. And you can't live your
life expecting to be hijacked. I *still* believe that. Whatever
happens here, it's not my fault, okay? But it's also not your
fault."

Silence. Crap, she forgot to say *over*. But it was just as well, she wasn't done.

"Tell Mommy I love her, too," Gina said. "Tell her I'm thinking about her. Tell her she was . . . God, she was right about Trent Engelman. Tell her I should have listened to her more. That she was probably right about a lot of things. Over."

"Hey, Karen, it's Max." Just from his voice, she could picture him, sitting with his feet up on a table in front of him, lazing back in a chair propped back on two legs. He probably wore his shirtsleeves rolled up and his hair long and pulled back in a ponytail and was twenty pounds overweight. Mr. Don't-Sweat-the-Small-Stuff. "Don't give your farewell speech just yet, okay? We've got a lot to talk about—me and the men who have control of the plane. Are they in there with you right now? Over."

"Yes. Over."

"Do they speak English or should I use a translator—I have someone on my staff who speaks the language and is standing next to me right now. Although, look, your father wants to say something really quick, and then he's heading back to DC. Hang on."

There was about five seconds of silence, and then Senator Crawford's voice came back on. "Karen, honey, I love you." He sounded as if he were reading lines from a bad script. "Tell the men who have control of the plane that I'll be speaking directly with the president, but that these things take time. We'll need a few days at least to—"

A female voice cut in. "I'm sorry, Senator, you really must leave now if you intend to make that flight."

"Karen, do whatever they say," Crawford said. "Be safe. And remember that . . . that your father loves you."

That one almost made her tears escape.

"Hey, Karen. It's me again." Max was back. "I'd really like a chance to speak directly with the men who are holding the guns. Can I do that now? Go ahead."

Bob was shaking his head. No.

"Bob doesn't want to talk to you. Over."

"Bob? Over."

"That's what he says his name is. And his English is probably better than mine. Over." Terrorist Bob had told her he'd learned his nearly perfect English from watching television and reading American books.

"Bob," Max said. "This would be a whole lot easier, sir, if you and I could talk directly. Over."

But Bob was still shaking his head. He took a piece of paper from his jacket pocket and unfolded it.

Handing it to Gina, he said, "Read." He gestured to the microphone. "Aloud."

"He wants me to read something. Over," Gina said into the microphone. The light in the cockpit wasn't the greatest. She angled the loose-leaf paper, trying to see it in the dimness. It was covered with small, slanty handwriting—front and back. Dear God, this was going to take a while.

"I'm here and I'm listening," Max said. "Take as long as you need. Go ahead."

Take as long as you need. These things take time. Maybe Max and the senator had been trying to tell her something, too.

She held the microphone's talk button down with her thumb. "We are the People's Party of Kazbekistan," she read aloud, as slowly as she possibly could. "Our requests are but two. . . ."

Stan came face-to-face with Lt. Tom Paoletti in the stairwell, heading up to the hotel roof where a helo was standing by to take them back to the Kazabek airport.

The phone call from XO Jazz Jacquette had come just as he was sliding into bed.

Just as he was about to close his eyes and slip into blessed unconsciousness.

But then the phone rang. And Stan had his clothes back on inside of fifteen seconds.

Because the terrorists on flight 232 had broken their radio silence. They were talking with FBI negotiator Max Bhagat. And Tom and his top officers—Jazz and Starrett—and his senior chief—Stan—were needed over there, pronto.

Bhagat's FBI team would be making an evaluation of the tangos' state of mind. Were they pushed close to the edge and ready to snap? Ready to start discharging their weapons and killing their innocent hostages?

If so, the SEALs had to gear up and take down the plane, immediately. Ready or not, here they very well might come.

Truth was, it *could've* been worse. The call might've come in before he'd had a chance to eat that dinner Teri Howe had gone to such lengths to provide.

He laughed softly, still amazed that she'd gone to that trouble for him.

"Share it, Senior," Tom Paoletti ordered. "I could use a good joke right about now."

"I had a nice dinner tonight, sir," Stan told his CO. "I was just thinking how glad I was that I'm not hungry. That because of it, I could easily go for another twenty-four hours without sleep. That's all."

Tom shot him a look as they climbed the endless flights of stairs. "Isn't it a little early in the op to be punchy, Senior Chief?"

"Definitely, sir."

"Does this have something to do with Teri Howe?" Tom asked.

Um . . . "Only very remotely."

"How remotely?"

Stan looked at Tom. "Very. Sir."

He was well aware that Tom spoke fluent senior chief, and therefore he knew Stan's real message was a polite variation of "Stay out of my goddamn business. Sir."

But Tom chose to play the friend card. "Stan," he said, laying it out on the table, face up. "I've seen you around this girl."

"You've seen what, sir?" Stan tried to bring it back to CO and senior chief.

"Jazz told me that you sat with her on the plane."

"Next time, sir, I'll be sure to stand all the way to Kazbekistan."

Tom laughed. "Lighten up. It's just . . . You must be aware of potential problems. Fraternizing issues, for one."

Teri was an officer, Stan was enlisted. "The rules are archaic," he told Tom.

"I'm the first to agree with that," Tom said. "But—"

"And they also don't apply," Stan said. "She's Reserve. There's no issue."

"Ah," Tom said. "So you've, uh, already checked into this?"

Meaning Stan had anticipated all the potential problems that came with a romantic relationship with Teri Howe.

God damn, he was tired. Otherwise he would've seen that coming a mile away.

"I meant there's no issue with my *friendship* with her," he told Tom.

"Does *she* know it's just a friendship?"

"Yes, sir." Despite the odd mix of signals he'd picked up from Teri tonight, despite the fact that he'd come into his room to find her sleeping on his bed, he'd seen her holding Mike Muldoon's hand, smiling into the ensign's eyes. "She had dinner with Muldoon last night. They hit it off."

Tom looked at him. "I'm sorry. I didn't know."

"Don't be sorry. I set them up. What's the word from Jazz?" Stan deliberately changed the subject.

Jazz's three-man team had run into some problems in their attempt to wire the hijacked plane with microphones and minicams. Hours earlier, Big Mac, Scooter, and Steve had approached from the aircraft's rear under cover of darkness, with the intention of penetrating the luggage compartment. But everything had to be done silently, and they'd run into an obstacle or two that was really slowing them down.

Once the sun came up, the SEALs would be stuck there, under the plane, in the blazing heat.

"He's going to keep 'em out there for as long as it takes," Tom told him.

"Good," Stan said. MacInnough would glower for a full month if he were—in his estimation—pulled off an assignment too soon. Stan knew that the brawny redheaded ensign would spend two weeks underneath that plane with only MREs to eat and no sanitary facilities before he would willingly quit.

The plane would get wired. Big Mac would see to it. It was just a matter of when.

They went up another flight of stairs before Tom broke the silence again.

"You know, I had to leave San Diego without saying good-bye to Kelly," he said. "She must've been making rounds at the hospital, so I had to do the voice mail thing. The real bitch of it is that I left before I had the chance to ask her if you were right—if she really wants me to resign my commission."

Stan's feet kept moving, but his brain was standing stone still. "Tom. You can't seriously be thinking—"

"You'd be surprised what I'm capable of thinking when it comes to Kelly," his CO said grimly.

And then they were on the roof, running for the helo.

Shit. Stan knew that sooner or later Tom would leave Team Sixteen. He'd either be promoted up, or he'd reach the point where he didn't want to play anymore. Being a SEAL, after all, was a young man's game.

Stan had always figured that when that time came, *years* from now, he'd go, too. Up or out. With Tom Paoletti.

But he wasn't ready for that yet. Not even close.

The helo was in the air before his butt was in the seat, and he checked, out of habit, to see if the pilot was Teri.

It wasn't.

Of course it wasn't. He'd walked her to her door and beat a rapid retreat back down the stairs to his own room. She was in bed right now, her body warm and soft with sleep and . . .

Christ. He shouldn't be thinking about her like that.

But it was a much more pleasant thought than that of Tom Paoletti leaving the team. So Stan closed his eyes and let himself drift back into Teri's room, Teri's bed, Teri's arms.

Ten

LT. ROGER STARRETT was good.

Alyssa Locke sat in the shade of a tent that had been provided for the K-stani officials and other observers, and watched him run his team of SEALs through their drill, entering the mock-up of the hijacked plane again and again.

Negotiator Max Bhagat had been on the radio all night, talking to the terrorists through a young American passenger who was pretending to be Senator Crawford's daughter Karen. The *real* Karen Crawford had been picked up and whisked away to safety in Athens late last night.

Despite the fact that there was still no direct audio and video from the plane, a team of FBI psychologists had come to the conclusion that the situation on board flight 232 was stable. Still, the SEALs were drilling as if they could be called in to take down the plane at any moment.

As she watched, the SEALs burst inside of the wooden plane using grenades that delivered both a loud noise and a blinding flash of light.

Their timing was even better this go around.

Yes, Starrett was good. Of course, the entire team he was leading was first-rate. They worked as a unit, practically thinking and breathing as one. But to give Roger Starrett credit, he was a good leader. Direct and self-assured. And capable of letting each of his teammates do what they did best without his interference.

Yeah, Roger was excellent.

It helped if Alyssa thought of him as Roger, rather than by his nickname, Sam. Sam Starrett was the impossibly sexy man with the wide smile, brilliant blue eyes, and lean body who showed up in her dreams and had steamy, pulse-pounding sex with her atop her kitchen table.

As she watched him now, his long, tanned legs were covered by BDUs—Battle Dress Uniform pants—in the traditional olive drab favored by the Army. It was hot out, and he'd taken off his shirt, and his tan-colored T-shirt was stained with sweat, hugging his well-built chest and shoulders. He looked unbearably good.

"Oh, God," she said.

Sometimes, though, it wasn't sex. Sometimes he made love to her in her dreams. Slowly. Sweetly. Tenderly. As if he were joining more than their bodies—more, even, than their two hearts.

The kitchen table was part of a drunken memory. Alyssa knew it had happened at least once that way, that night when she'd made such an error in judgment. The other, though, had to be sheer wishful thinking.

"You okay?" Jules asked. Her partner was wearing sunglasses identical to the ones Keanu Reeves had worn in *The Matrix*. Alyssa kept expecting him to start hanging in the air and moving in slow motion.

They were the only ones sitting there under the tent, so she answered him honestly. "This sucks. Look at him."

Jules looked. "How does he get away with not cutting his hair? I thought the Navy had all those anal rules about officers and appearances."

"He's what's known as a long-hair," Alyssa told him. "An operative who can blend in in places where a military haircut would stand out."

"He's shaved since last time. Since DC," Jules realized.

"That means he's probably been doing a lot of diving. He told me it's hard for someone with a beard to get an airtight seal around a face mask." He'd also told her his close friends could always tell what he'd been up to—to some degree—over the past few months by the length of his hair and the presence or absence of his mustache and goatee. Other than that and the fact that he looked as if he'd been working out like a maniac, she had absolutely no clue what he'd been up to.

Had he thought about her at all?

Probably not.

"If it's any consolation," Jules told her, "he hates this, too. He's looked over here only four thousand times this morning. And did you see his face last night when he came into the hotel restaurant and saw you?"

"I've handled this badly," Alyssa admitted to herself. "I should have been friendly."

"Friendly would've put you right back into his bed."

"Distant and cool," she countered, "but still friendly."

"If you want to get with him, then get with him." Jules believed in being direct and to the point.

"I don't want to—"

He took off his sunglasses and really looked at her. "Sweetie, I'm not going to judge you."

"Really." She took off her sunglasses, too. "I don't even remotely want to—"

"I just don't want you to get hurt."

"Jules. Hello. I am not going to get hurt. I am not going to 'get with' this man. I would never make that kind of mistake again."

"Okay, good, because he's coming over here right now—"

Oh, *shit*. He was. Alyssa hurriedly put her sunglasses back on.

"—with that kind of caveman walk," Jules continued. "You know, the kind that announces he's the alpha male around here, so if you don't want him to grab you by the hair and pull you into his cave, you better run."

Sam Starrett was at twelve o'clock, heading straight for the observers' tent, his boots scuffing up a small cloud of dust as he came. He was drinking a bottle of water, and try as she might to focus on the fact that, behind him, the rest of his team was taking a break, Senior Chief Wolchonok making sure everyone had water and PowerBars, her eyes were drawn back to Starrett.

With the sun slightly behind him, with the muscles in his arms and chest actually rippling enticingly as he moved— dammit!—he looked like some kind of action hero, despite the baseball cap on his head. Or maybe because of it, she wasn't sure.

"Maybe I should disappear," Jules murmured.

"Don't you dare." Alyssa stood up, unwilling to let Sam loom over her more than he had to.

And then he was there. Standing directly in front of her.

There was sex in his eyes as he gazed down at her. A silent reminder that they'd once shared bodily fluids, that he'd taken her places she hadn't even dreamed possible. A reminder that, try as she might not to be, she was flesh and blood. Human—with human failings.

And human needs.

"You want to make yourselves useful?" Starrett asked in his infuriating Texas drawl, no greeting, no pretense of niceties. "Instead of sitting around wasting taxpayers' hard-earned dollars?"

"You bet we do," Jules answered before she could spit out a scathing retort.

Starrett looked at her, one eyebrow slightly raised, and she knew that he expected her to protest. He *wanted* her to protest.

So she didn't. "What would you like us to do, Lieutenant?" she asked as nicely as she could manage, trying to sound friendly. Friendly, yet still cool.

"I need more people to play the part of the terrorists," he said. "I've got two SAS guys coming in, but I'm still three bodies short." He gestured to Jules with his head. "Can he shoot?"

"He *is* an FBI agent," Alyssa countered. She took a deep breath before calling him a less than flattering name. Don't get mad. Stay cool. And friendly. She forced what she hoped was a friendly smile.

"Yeah, well, in my experience, that means shit," Starrett said.

"Mine, too," Jules said easily. "But, yeah, he can shoot. Is he as good as Alyssa Locke? No. Because no one, my friend, is as good as Alyssa Locke."

Starrett looked at her again, and this time there was something different in his eyes. Something that looked an awful lot like . . . regret?

But then it was gone and he was walking away.

"In fifteen minutes, check in with the senior chief," he

tossed back over his shoulder. "He'll get you the gear you need. Don't bother him before then—he's taking a nap. Hope you brought a hat—you're going to need it. It's fucking hot out here."

Alyssa pulled her gaze away from Sam Starrett's perfect rear end.

"This is going to be fun," Jules said. "Watching you kick ass."

Fun wasn't quite the word she would have used.

Stan was asleep.

He'd found a narrow bit of shade behind the wooden mock-up of the plane and had curled up, right on the dusty ground.

Except the sun had moved and now half of his face was subject to its harsh rays.

He slept on his side, one arm under his head, the other hand open and resting on his chest. It was strange to see him so relaxed, without that high voltage current of electricity that seemed to surge through him at all times.

Teri sat down next to him as quietly as she could, letting her shadow cover his face.

God, it was hot. And dry as hell.

She set down the last of the bags she'd brought from the hotel. Taking a sip of lukewarm water from her bottle, she looked down to find Stan's eyes open and watching her.

"God!" she said, startled. He hadn't moved at all. He'd just opened his eyes and was instantly alert.

"Where's your flack jacket?" he asked.

"In the helo."

"Hell of a lot of good it'll do you there."

"It's hot," she tried to explain. "And I figured I was safe enough out here, surrounded by a SEAL team."

He pushed himself up into a sitting position, brushing the dust from his arm and shirt.

"I didn't mean to wake you," she continued.

"It's all right." He checked his watch. "I got ten minutes. That's better than some days."

Ten minutes? Now she really felt awful. She'd heard through the grapevine that the senior chief hadn't managed to

make it back to his hotel room at all last night. He'd gone
from his session with her in the stairwell to a meeting at the
airport, to a meeting with Adm. Chip Crowley, who'd arrived
in K-stan late last night.

And he'd been back here, with Sam Starrett's team of
SEALs, hard at work at 0400.

The lines of fatigue around his eyes and mouth were more
pronounced than they'd been last night.

"I would've just left you to sleep," she told him, "but the
sun was right on your face. I was trying to, you know, pretend
I was a tree or something."

He stared at her as if she'd just spoken in Greek. "A tree?"
He wasn't quite glowering, but it was close.

"For shade," she explained. "You know, from the sun?"
Great, she was babbling. "I didn't want you to get burned."

Stan touched his peeling nose. "Too late."

"You should really use sunblock." What was she doing?
She should really just stand up and walk away. He obviously
didn't want to deal with her right now.

"Why bother? With *this* face?" He pretended to laugh, but
he was serious. And a little embarrassed by the topic. He actually thought he was . . .

"You have a wonderful face," she said before she stopped
to think. "When you smile . . . You should smile more."

Great, now she'd completely embarrassed him. Or maybe
she'd just totally embarrassed herself. Again. It was definitely
time to run away. She shifted her weight, intending to push
herself up and off the ground.

"My father looks like Marlon Brando," Stan told her. He
didn't sound at all embarrassed. He sounded like Stan. "You
know, before he got fat. Brando, I mean. Not Stan Senior.
He's not fat. He can still run an eight-minute mile."

Despite being tired, despite wanting her gone, he was
talking her down from the ledge again in that easygoing way
he had.

"And no, I don't look anything like him," Stan continued,
as if he knew that she'd glanced at him to try to see if there
was any resemblance. "Aside from basic body type—height
and weight, you know, standard gorilla build. Lots of upper

body strength with twigs for legs. I got that direct from Stan Senior."

Twigs for legs. He actually thought . . . Teri kept her mouth tightly shut, afraid to tell him that she thought his legs were as perfect as the rest of him.

"As far as looks go, though, I don't take after my mother either—except for the fair skin. And I certainly didn't inherit her patience, that's for damn sure." Something in his voice had changed. It was almost imperceptible, but Teri heard it. He was telling her things he didn't usually tell people. Or maybe she just wished he was.

"She was really something," Stan said, with that same little trace of . . . wistfulness? Yes, wistfulness in his voice. Teri *wasn't* imagining it. Big, bad Senior Chief Wolchonok had loved his mother deeply. "She was from Denmark—she lived there as a kid, came over after the war with her older sister. Do you know, the envoy from Israel—Helga Shuler—she knew my mother in Denmark. It's the weirdest thing—she has the same accent when she speaks English that my mother did. It's nice, you know? After this is over, I'm going to sit down with her and talk."

This man wanted to be friends with her, Teri realized. Nothing more than friends. Stan couldn't have been more clear about that if he'd taken out a full page ad in the *New York Times* to accompany his body language. But he didn't have to. She could take a hint.

Stan liked her. He'd said so. But when he'd said it, he was using the adult definition of the word *liked*, not the seventh grade definition. In fact, he probably thought of her the same way he thought of Mike Muldoon—she was just another young clueless kid to watch out for, to take under his badass protective wing. And Stan had one hell of a protective wing, there was no doubt about that.

He'd continuously gone way out of his way to be kind to her. Helping her get away from San Diego and Joel Hogan. His attempts last night to start desensitizing her to confrontations.

He'd spent over an hour and a half with her last night— time he could have been sleeping. He'd made sure she wasn't alone by sitting with her on the airplane, and then arranging for her to have dinner with Mike Muldoon.

Teri owed him, big time. And since he'd made it rather clear that his interest in her was nothing more than that of mentor or some variation of Sea Daddy, he certainly wouldn't appreciate the complications of a full body massage leading to a night of blazing hot sex. Which would lead to shared quarters for the rest of this operation, which would lead to her moving into his charming little bungalow back in San Diego . . .

Yeah, dream on, Teresa.

What are your goals for your personal life? She hadn't answered Stan's question last night because in truth, she didn't know the answer.

She knew she wanted to spend more time laughing. She wanted to feel more relaxed and at peace. She wanted to be happy. She wanted to stop being afraid. But what kind of a goal was that?

Stan had stopped talking about his mother. They were sitting there, Teri realized, in silence. But it was a companionable silence. His glower was gone. He was just looking at her, and as she met his eyes, he smiled that smile that made the world seem to shift beneath her feet.

The smile that made her want to kiss him.

Instead she held out the last of the freezer bags she'd brought with her. "I made some iced coffee. I figured you could probably use both the caffeine and something cold to drink."

He had the funniest look in his eyes as he opened the bag.

"There's not really ice in it," she quickly explained. "I put the coffee in the hotel freezer for most of the morning. And I made sure it was brewed with bottled water, so it's definitely safe to drink. You don't have to worry."

He took off the lid, took a sip. "Holy God. It's—"

"More like a Slusheee than an iced coffee, I know. I got lucky—the power didn't go off while it was in the freezer."

"This is . . . I'm . . . Thank you, Lieutenant. Very much."

Oh, my God, the funny look in his eye wasn't because he'd been afraid she'd unknowingly made the iced coffee with tainted hotel ice. It was because he thought she was hitting on him, like this was some kind of Starbucks-style come on—drink my coffee now, hot stud, and do me later.

His response was to call her by her rank, to retreat from their still shaky, newly formed friendship. God, was the thought of a more intimate relationship with her really that repulsive?

"It's good, isn't it?" she said as brightly as she could manage. "The other guys—Mike and WildCard in particular—really liked it, too. I brought, you know, some for everyone." Thank God that she had. Teri stood up, not wanting to see his relief. "Well, I better let you get back to—"

"Did you just finish a shift?"

She'd spent the morning ferrying SEALs and other U.S. personnel back and forth from the airport, to the airfield, to the hotel. The trip from the hotel to this airfield took about fifteen minutes each way. But she could make it from the hotel to the Kazabek airport in about three minutes flat.

"I'm not exactly finished. I'm on standby. I'm here in case you or Lieutenant Starrett need a helo on short order."

"You know, if you don't sit down, I'm going to have to stand, too," he told her. "It's one of those crazy lieutenant–senior chief things. Do you mind? I mean, as long as you're not going anywhere in a hurry . . . ?"

Teri sat down, both glad and resentful as hell that he'd gone back to talking to her as if they were friends. Unless . . .

Maybe he was seeing someone. Maybe he had a girlfriend back in San Diego. Maybe he was attracted to Teri, but he was too honest and loyal, too upstanding and decent even to *think* about being unfaithful.

"You wanna help?" he asked her. "As long as you're not needed to fly anywhere, we need a few more terrorists to shoot."

To . . . shoot?

He smiled at the look she knew was on her face.

"The bullets aren't real. We use training gear. Computer controlled lasers. You'll have a weapon, too. It's fun—you get into the mock-up and wait for us to storm the plane, try to shoot us before we shoot you."

"I'm not a very good shot," she admitted. Sure, she'd had weapons training, but . . .

"You'll have an assault weapon. Point and spray. I'll remind you how to use it. It'll come back to you."

"Still, it's hardly fair. Me against a team of SEALs?"

"It's not going to be a fair fight against the real tangos," Stan told her. "They're amateurs, while we've been training for scenarios like this for years. Come on, at this point we really just need warm bodies."

"Gee, when you put it that way, how can I say no?"

"Terrific." He smiled again.

And she was lost.

Teri discharged her laser weapon gingerly. Stan knew that she'd had weapons training to be a helo pilot, but there was no doubt about it. Teri Howe was not a natural when it came to handling weapons.

But that was okay. To give her credit, she was up for the challenge. And he'd managed to live through reminding her how to hold the weapon. He'd had to touch her, move her arms and hands into a less awkward position. It had been a job and a half making sure his touch came across as impersonal, businesslike. But he'd done it.

"Any other questions?" Stan asked her now.

"When did your mother pass away?"

He stared at her.

"When you spoke of her, you said *was*," she added.

Stan picked up one of the training weapons the team would be using in the next few minutes for this exercise. As he checked it, he sensed more than saw Teri start to back away.

"I'm sorry, it's none of my business. It's just . . . I got the feeling that you had been particularly close and . . . I apologize for overstepping—"

"Twenty-one years ago," he told her quietly. "She died the summer after I graduated high school."

He glanced at her, saw her doing the math. Yeah, that's right. He was only thirty-nine years old. Just a little too young for the father figure she was searching for.

And that's what this was all about—the dinner last night,

the coffee today. All of the elements of a healthy dose of hero worship had fallen neatly into place.

Teri was looking for guidance and approval, but she also wanted more. She wanted more than for him to fill her former SEAL friend Lenny's long-empty shoes.

It was the stupidest thing. Stan had given her Muldoon, in all of his shining, Boy Scout, good-looking glory. And she liked the kid—he knew she did. Stan had seen the two of them together, seen her holding the ensign's hand. There was something between them—or at least there would be if only she'd let it develop.

But she'd been in Stan's room last night, making sure he had something to eat. She'd brought *him* coffee today—and despite what she'd said about bringing some for everyone, he knew the truth. She'd brought it for him. She'd shaded him from the freaking sun, for Christ's sake.

If that wasn't hero worship, he didn't know what was.

Maybe he could twist it to his advantage—this blatant admiration he could see in her eyes. He could touch her again, let his hands linger. Let her know that he'd welcome her showing up in his room again tonight.

And maybe she'd go to bed with him because her own sense of normal was so warped, because she'd been some kind of hideous victim as a child. And he still didn't know of what. God, it was driving him crazy.

Yes sir, he could take advantage of her trust, and wouldn't he be proud of himself then?

"I'm so sorry for your loss," Teri whispered, as if he'd said it had been only twenty-one weeks or even days instead of years since his mother had died. As if the wound were still raw and painful. Her eyes were so soft, he thought he might go blind if he looked directly at her, like looking into the sun.

He focused on the next weapon, its cold weight in his hands centering him. It, too, was in working order. He picked up the next.

"It was lung cancer," he said, more comfortable with the facts. "She made me quit smoking."

"You smoked?"

"In high school, yeah. Told you I've done some stupid things in my life. But both my parents smoked while I was growing up, so . . ." He shrugged. "When she was diagnosed—and it was stage four; there was not a lot of hope that she would survive—she made both me and Stan Senior quit. It was not a fun time to be living in our house, you better believe that, both of us going cold turkey, her so sick. But we did it, you know?"

For her.

"Do you really think of your father as Stan Senior?" Teri asked. "That's the second time you called him that."

"What is this? Interrogate the senior chief day?" he countered with a laugh.

"It's just . . . you know so much about me," she said. "And I know hardly anything about you."

He turned to face her. It had taken him only five weapons—all checked and ready to go—before he'd regained his equilibrium enough to look her in the eye again. Shit, he was in trouble here.

"I grew up in Chicago. Enlisted in the Navy out of high school." After his mother's long illness, there hadn't been enough money to send both him and his sister to college, so he'd gotten his education via the Navy. "It was supposed to be temporary, but I got into the BUD/S program—SEAL training, you know? And it turned into my entire life. It's what I do. It's who I am. What you see is what you get. There's not a whole lot of mystery here, Lieutenant."

"Except for the four nieces and restoring the bungalow and the antiques . . ."

"If you know all that, you know more than most people know about me," he pointed out. He was glowering at her, but she didn't back down. Not one inch. Amazing. Figures she'd choose now to finally start using her backbone.

"Did your father ever remarry?" she asked.

"No."

"What are you going to do after you retire?"

Oh, Christ. "I don't know! Sleep late in the mornings for about five years. Jesus, Teri . . ."

"Hi, Senior, we're two more of your terrorists. Can you

set us up?" Alyssa Locke and her FBI partner approached, saving Stan's ass before he did something stupid like telling Teri about his idea to furnish his house with antiques that he'd then turn around and sell.

Or his equally stupid-ass idea to sell the house to some bungalow lover who wanted the charm without the restoration work. With the money from the sale, he'd buy a sailboat and live like Jimmy Buffett for a year or two, floating around the Caribbean, at one with the ocean. Then he'd find another bungalow in need of serious repair, get a mortgage, and start all over again. Fix it and sell it. Sail around for a while. Again and again.

He could live all over the country, because the Arts and Crafts revival had spread like a weed from California at the turn of the century. He could find a bungalow in virtually any town in any state and restore it to its original simple charm. He could spend some time in Chicago, near his sister and his golden-haired nieces—enough time to finally learn to tell the four little girls apart.

Of course, they'd be in high school before he'd be ready to retire.

But he didn't have to tell her any of that, thank you, Jesus and Alyssa Locke.

Locke and her partner didn't really need more than a hand pointing in the right direction, but Stan stayed with them, scared to death of what Teri Howe's next question for him might be, terrified of turning this game she was playing back around on her and asking her the too-intimate questions he was both dying and dreading to know the answers to.

When she was a child, did someone she trusted—her father, or a teacher or someone in a position of authority—take advantage of the adoration and hero worship they saw in those big brown eyes?

What had happened all those years ago to make her still so afraid?

Stan briefly closed his eyes, remembering the look on her face as she'd given him the coffee. *Accept me. Encourage me.*

He'd seen that look before—usually on the faces of young enlisted men who were just starting to discover themselves as

SEAL candidates in the BUD/S training program. The men who'd been told too many times that they'd never amount to much. The ones who'd been nearly completely brainwashed into believing that was true.

Nearly completely. There was still a spark left, though. The spark that made them push to get into BUD/S even though everyone told them they'd be the first to ring out. A spark of life. A spark of hope.

Love me unconditionally, so I can start learning to love myself, Senior Chief.

Expect only the best from me, and I'll give it to you, Senior Chief.

Give me shit when I slip and deserve shit because that's further proof that I matter to you, Senior Chief.

Be my hero, Senior Chief, and never let me down.

In the past, it had been a burden at times—his role of the infallible hero, the mighty senior chief—but it had never been so heavy as it was right now.

Because he'd seen something else in Teri Howe's eyes, something different, something he'd never seen in all of the hopeful young faces that had come before.

Kiss me, Senior Chief.

So, Stan, are you seeing anyone back in San Diego?

Teri silently cursed herself for not being fast enough, for letting the moment escape without asking the senior chief the question she really wanted answered.

Although that one would've certainly tipped him off as to her feelings, wouldn't it have?

God, she was such a coward. She was actually relieved that she hadn't managed to ask him that.

Teri smiled automatically as Stan introduced her to the two FBI agents and the two SAS men who, with her, would be playing the terrorists while the SEALs ran their drill.

And then he was gone, leaving her holding the unwieldy weapon, wishing she were brave enough to be waiting in Stan's room again tonight.

Naked and lying on his bed.

Yeah, like she'd ever have the guts to do that in a million years.

She could just imagine him gently covering her up with a blanket, gathering up her clothes, and leading her to the bathroom, so she could get dressed in private.

And that would be the likeliest outcome of that scenario. Stan would surely do his best to make sure she wasn't too embarrassed as he kicked her out of his room. And he *would* kick her out instead of flinging off his own clothes as he rushed to join her on the bed. Instead of kissing her mouth, her neck, her breasts, his mouth hot and wet and impossibly sweet, the heavy weight of his body pressing against her as he pushed himself between her thighs, as she lifted her hips to meet him and—

Boom!

Teri was pushed back on her rear end against the wooden deck of the mock-up, more from surprise rather than the force of any explosion. She felt her head smack the wall with a brain-jarring thwack.

Stan had told her there would be something called a flash bang when they entered, but she'd had no idea it would be so loud, that the sudden flash of light would make it nearly impossible to see as the SEALs rushed into the mock-up of the plane.

Point and spray, he'd told her, but she'd bobbled the assault weapon when she fell. It took her several long seconds to find both the gun and the trigger with her vision still filled with the aftereffects of a brightness akin to the surface of the sun.

And then someone was alongside her, appearing in her peripheral vision. She didn't see more than a shadowy shape of a man and a gun, and she turned just as she found the trigger. Point and spray.

She saw through the spots of light still floating across her line of sight that it was Mike Muldoon, and he looked surprised. No, he looked flat-out shocked.

She'd killed him.

Well, mock killed him.

But then her weapon stopped working, and Lieutenant

Starrett was striding toward them, and just like that—it couldn't have lasted more than thirty seconds—it was over.

"What the fuck were you waiting for?" Starrett lit into Muldoon.

"Teri was down, Lieutenant. I thought she was hurt. I thought—" Muldoon shook his head.

"She's not *Teri*, she's a terrorist. You hesitate and *you're* the one we take out of there in a body bag. She fucking *killed* you!"

"I'm sorry, sir—"

"You okay?" It was Stan's voice.

Teri turned to see him crouching on the other side of her, sweat dripping down the side of his face, looking sexy as hell. He touched her, his fingers gentle as he explored the back of her head, where she'd connected with the wall.

"I'm fine." What he was doing felt very nice, but it wasn't necessary. She hadn't been hurt. No more than a slight bruise, anyway.

"I saw you go down." He checked her again, more slowly this time. "You bounced your head off that bulkhead pretty hard."

"I have a thick skull." Her voice came out sounding breathless and odd. It was all she could do not to close her eyes, to lean back into his hands and pretend he was touching her that way, holding her head in place, because he was about to kiss her.

Stan pulled his hands away from her, killing the fantasy. He stood up, helping her to her feet. "Lopez!" he shouted.

"I don't care if one of the terrorists looks like your favorite uncle Frank," Starrett was continuing his tirade. He was still right in Muldoon's face. "I don't care if one of 'em is a seventy-year-old gray-haired lady. Head shots, Muldoon. Double pops. Without hesitation."

SEAL Team Sixteen's medic, Jay Lopez, was already right there, next to the senior chief. He had a flashlight that he used to check Teri's eyes, and then it was his turn to touch the back of her head, feeling for a bump or a bruise.

"She all right, Senior?" Starrett asked Stan.

"I'm fine," Teri said again. "Really."

"She looks good, Lieutenant," Lopez announced.

Stan leaned closer to Starrett. "Next go round, have Muldoon take out Howe again—or Locke. He needs practice eliminating female targets. We might as well take advantage of having Howe and Locke around."

"Good idea, Senior." Starrett raised his voice. "Who's got the details of what just went down?"

Stan looked at Teri, leaned closer to speak directly into her ear. "You don't mind, do you?"

"Letting your team get practice killing women?" she murmured back. "Why ever would I mind?"

"What we do isn't pretty," Stan said, speaking softly enough so that only she could hear him. "But it doesn't do anyone any good to think about terrorists as anything but targets that need eliminating. Some of the men have trouble with the female targets. My personal hell is when children are involved. Twelve-year-olds with Uzis. Babies used as human shields. But if you hesitate, you're dead. Or worse, your teammate's dead."

Babies. Teri looked at him, but he'd already moved slightly away from her and he wouldn't meet her eyes.

"Estimated seventeen passengers would have been killed or injured." WildCard Karmody had access to some kind of Palm Pilot. "One SEAL death—Muldoon—courtesy of the vicious terrorist Teri Howe. The senior chief got Taggett with a double shot, O'Leary got Ian from out in sniperland—right between the eyes, and Starrett took down Howe. Hey, here's a fun fact. Howe's weapon was discharged the most number of times. Congratulations, Teri. You actually took out two of the other tangos—Locke and Cassidy—within two seconds of the flash bang. You're responsible for most of the civilians killed as well. Hoo-yah, girl."

"You scored points for both sides," Lieutenant Starrett told her with a grin. "Way to go."

"I'm sorry," she said, feeling her cheeks heat. God, she didn't ask to do this. "I thought I'd dropped the gun. I didn't even realize I was pulling the trigger. . . ."

Stan was back, standing beside her again. He touched

her—a brief squeeze of her arm. "Hey, you did good. Your re-action was far more realistic than anyone else's. Most tangos have no experience in this kind of thing—chances are they're going to drop their weapons, too. What we've got to do is move faster going in so there's no time for anyone to spray the cabin with bullets." He looked around at the team, landing on Muldoon. "Right?"

"You going to hesitate on me ever again?" Starrett asked Muldoon.

The ensign looked determined, a muscle jumping in his jaw. "No sir, I will not."

"Good, let's do this at least three times more before lunch."

Stan lingered as the other SEALs went back outside. "Now that you know what the flash bang sounds like—"

"I'll manage to stay on my feet next time," Teri reassured him.

"No, I want you to do the same thing—"

Crack!

The sound came from outside, from the port side of the plane, and Stan went to one of the windows to look out. "Ah, Christ!"

Teri looked, too. The port wing had broken clear off. She could see Lieutenant Starrett on the ground, his face grim as he surveyed the damage.

He looked up, directly at Stan. "Will you please fucking go and fucking get me a real fucking World Airlines 747, Senior Chief? Right fucking now?"

Stan looked at Teri. "Looks like I'm going to need a ride to the airport."

"Don't you mean the fucking airport?" she asked, biting the inside of her cheek to keep from smiling.

God, she loved making Stan laugh.

Eleven

THE PRETTY PILOT—the lieutenant with the dark hair and eyes—had said something to make Stanley Wolchonok laugh. And there it was again. Marte's smile.

Helga sat in the shade of the observers' tent and watched as the pair walked toward the waiting helicopter.

Stanley was a gentleman. No doubt about it, Marte had raised her son well. This beautiful young woman was drawn to him. It was obvious in the way she spoke to him, in the way she stood, in the way she looked at him.

She adored him.

And yet he treated her with complete respect.

Most men would strut with a woman like that walking beside them. Most men would want to make sure every other man around knew that a woman like that wanted him. Most men would broadcast the fact loudly and clearly.

Yet there was nothing even remotely possessive or arrogant in Stan Wolchonok's body language.

Sure, it might've been due to the fact that she was an officer and he was enlisted. He *had* to treat her with respect and maintain a distance from her. Fraternizing was still frowned upon in the U.S. Armed Forces—a throwback to the British army, when officers were peers of the realm or some such nonsense.

Helga would have thought the Americans—those bold, loud, outrageous Americans—would have tossed aside such an archaic salute to the masters and servants class system ages ago.

Of course, it was entirely possible that Stanley—unlike wild Marte—simply had the self-control to be discreet. It was possible that as soon as he found a spot of privacy, he would pull the pretty pilot into his arms and kiss her, finally able to express everything he'd worked so hard to hide from the rest of the world.

The way Helga had once seen Hershel kissing Annebet, in the shadows of her mother's garden. The night of a dinner party celebrating her mother's birthday.

It was summer, the days long and warm, with an evening light that went on and on forever.

Fru Gunvald was cooking in the hot kitchen. Marte had come to help her, and Annebet was one of three girls hired to serve the food to the guests.

Despite the fact that Hershel had been seated next to the extremely buxom Ebba Gersfelt, he spent the entire meal distracted and restless, watching the door to the kitchen for any sign of Annebet.

When she was in the room, serving the soup or clearing the dishes, Hershel breathed differently. It seemed remarkable to Helga that no one else—not even Annebet—seemed to notice.

No one except Ebba Gersfelt, that is.

Helga watched Ebba watch Hershel watch Annebet, who kept her eyes carefully down as she placed more of Fru Gunvald's freshly baked rolls on the table.

Helga saw it all through the open French doors into the dining room, from her perch on the stairs. She was too young to attend the grown-ups' party but old enough to escape the confines of the nursery to watch the glitter below.

With Annebet's hair up under her cap, with her eyes properly downcast, it was difficult to tell her apart from the other two serving girls. Unless Helga watched Hershel.

Or Ebba, who either seethed or leaned closer to whisper into Hershel's ear whenever Annebet came into the dining room.

Once she leaned so close that her enormous bazoombas—as Marte called them—pressed against Hershel's arm.

Only then did Annebet look up, with a flash of her usual fire in her eyes. But it was directed at Hershel, not Ebba.

And fifteen minutes later, as the party was moving out into the other room, as Helga was heading for a better position in the tree right outside the open parlor window, Hershel caught her by the back of her dress.

"Mouse, you've got to help me." His face was pale and his mouth was as grim as she'd ever seen it. "I need a message delivered. It's of the utmost importance, do you understand?"

Helga nodded, her blood turned to ice in her veins. Although her brother had never said as much, she knew he was part of the Danish resistance. Would the Nazis hang a ten-year-old for delivering a message? Of course they would. They were Nazis.

Still, she squared her shoulders, forcing herself to think like Marte. That was only if she were caught. She would not be caught.

Hershel quickly folded a piece of paper into quarters and then quarters again.

No, *Marte* would not be caught. Helga would no doubt trip and fall and . . .

"Give this to Annebet in the kitchen," Hershel commanded. "Only to Annebet, not Fru Gunvald, not anyone else. Do you understand?"

The *kitchen*. Helga's dangerous and death-defying mission was to go to the kitchen with a note for *Annebet*.

The relief made her light-headed and clumsy, and she caught her shoe on the threshold of the kitchen door and tripped. She landed hard on the wooden floor, banging her knees and her hands and even her chin. The note flew out of her grasp and skittered across the floor, next to the sink.

Marte helped her up. "No wonder your parents don't let you go to their fancy parties, you stupid ox. I get to go to all my parents' parties, you know."

Helga knew. Marte had told her that, many times before. The Gunvalds' parties were loud, friendly, casual affairs filled with laughter and music and dancing that went on into the wee hours of the night.

Marte's insulting words stung worse than Helga's bruised knees, but Annebet had explained to her in the past that her little sister sometimes said hurtful things because she was embarrassed to work as a servant in her best friend's house. Marte was envious of the Rosens' wealth.

And it had been a long time since the Gunvalds had been able to afford to have any kind of a party.

Marte pulled Helga over to the sink to run cool water on the smarting heels of her hands. "You tore your dress," she informed Helga, not without some satisfaction.

She *had*. Her mother would send her to her room to mend it. And although Helga was good at reading and writing and mathematics, when it came to needle and thread, she was all thumbs.

"I'll help you fix it," Marte said. "She'll never know."

"I'll help you wash the dishes tonight," Helga promised her friend. Of course, she would have helped anyway. Marte had the ability to make anything fun. Even scrubbing pots.

"What's this?" Marte asked, bending down to pick up the folded note.

Oh, no. "That's for Annebet." Helga reached for it.

Marte snatched it back, out of her reach. "From Hershel?" she asked, delight dancing in her eyes, the last of her jealousy instantly evaporated.

"Marte, give it!"

"Annebet's clearing the table. Quick, into the pantry! It's our big chance to find out if they've fallen in love!"

Helga followed. "Marte, *don't!*"

But Marte had already unfolded Hershel's note. "How will we know how best to help them if we don't read this—oh!"

Helga couldn't help herself. "What does it say?"

" 'Meet me by the roses in the garden in ten minutes,' " Marte read. Her face glowed. "I knew it! A lovers' tryst." She refolded the paper. "Quick, bring this to Annebet. Tell her . . . Tell her Hershel was *trembling* when he gave it to you—just to make sure that she shows up. I've read some of the books she likes, and the lovers are always trembling about something or another. Then meet me in the garden."

"Why?" Helga asked, dreading the answer.

Marte didn't answer. She just pushed Helga toward the door.

"Why," Helga said, five minutes later, in the garden, behind the thick tangle of rosebushes, "are we here? I don't want to spy on them again. It's not right."

"We aren't here to spy," Marte informed her. "We're here to make sure no one else tries to spy on them. What did Annebet say?"

"Nothing." She'd turned away to read Hershel's note. She'd frowned slightly. "She thanked me."

"What did you tell her?"

"That Hershel asked me to give it to her. That he said it was important," Helga reported.

Marte nodded. "Important is good. Not as good as *trembling*, but— Shh! Someone's coming."

It was Hershel. His face was shadowy in the twilight, but it was definitely Helga's brother. He paced for a moment, then sat down on the marble bench across from the roses and lit a cigarette.

The evening air was warm and still, and the scent of the tobacco soon mixed oddly with the sweet smell of the roses. Still, it wasn't unpleasant, sitting there with the night closing in. The whirring and clicking and buzzing of insects made it seem as if they were in the jungle instead of Helga's family garden, not far from the village street.

"You sent for me, Herr Rosen?"

Hershel leapt to his feet. He hadn't heard Annebet approach either.

"Was there something you needed, sir?" she said again, in that same impersonal, emotionless voice.

He reached for her. "Annebet—"

She stepped back, her movements jerky, and Helga knew that, like Hershel, she could hide her anger well but she couldn't hide it forever. "Those services aren't included this evening, sir. But perhaps Herr Rosen would like another glass of wine to accompany his disgusting smoking habit."

Hershel dropped his cigarette and ground it out under his shoe. "Anna, I'm so sorry," he said. "I swear to you, this wasn't my idea. My mother arranged for me to escort Ebba tonight—I didn't even know until this evening. Don't you think I would've at least warned you if I'd known?"

"Do you know how awful it made me feel to see you sitting there with her?" Annebet's voice shook. Annebet—who was descended from Vikings, who didn't fear even the Gestapo.

"I'm sorry."

"She would give you everything you want. I don't know why you're sending notes to me when it's obvious that you could have her with just a—"

"Ebba Gersfelt can't give me what I want," Hershel cut her off, his voice quiet but absolute. "Because all I want is you."

Annebet turned and looked at him. Helga would never forget the look on her beautiful face, the way her eyes were luminous with unshed tears, the way she breathed his name.

They both moved at once. Toward each other. Fast. And then Annebet was in Hershel's arms, and he was kissing her. Not the way Poppi kissed Mother. Oh, no. Hershel kissed Annebet the way men kissed women in those wonderful movies from Hollywood, with their bodies pressed as close as possible, with their hands and arms reaching to pull each other even more tightly together, with their mouths wide open.

Marte had told her all about kissing and mouths and tongues, and Helga hadn't quite believed it—until now.

Annebet had told Marte all about men, and Marte had told Helga. About the way men always wanted to kiss women, and how a woman must decide which of the men she would kiss back. You only kiss the men you think you could fall in love with, Annebet had said, and you only make love with the one you *know* that you love—the one with whom you know you could happily spend the rest of your life.

Marte's eyes were wide as she watched her sister and Helga's brother kiss for what seemed like an eternity. For once, she had nothing to say. They were stuck here behind the roses until Hershel and Annebet stopped kissing. But it seemed obvious to Helga that they were simply never going to stop.

But then Annebet pulled back. Her cap had fallen off, and her dress was askew. She was breathing as if she'd just run all the way from Copenhagen, as if she was about to cry. "This can't work!"

Hershel was breathing hard, too. "Why not?"

Annebet laughed in disbelief. "Look at me!"

"I am," he told her. "You're so beautiful, I can't keep my eyes off you."

"This dress is *ugly*," she told him. "It's a *servant's* dress. Compared to Ebba's gown—"

"There's no comparison. Do you really think I care what you wear?"

"I think your parents care," she countered. "And yes, I think you would care. Maybe not right away. But for the life you want to lead, you need someone like Ebba beside you, not some serving girl who will embarrass you—"

"When I look at you," Hershel said, his voice low but filled with emotion, "I see the future chief surgeon of the Copenhagen Children's Clinic. I would be proud to stand beside you in whatever you choose to wear."

"And yet you didn't invite me to this party tonight," Annebet said quietly.

"The guest list was my mother's."

She just looked at him.

Hershel took off his glasses, rubbed his eyes. "I should have invited you," he admitted. "I didn't think—I made a mistake. Forgive me. This is all new to me. I'm bound to make some mistakes along the way."

"The way to where, Hershel?" Annebet asked, still in that quiet voice. "Where are we going with this?"

"Hershel!" Ebba's voice floated down from the patio. "Are you out here?"

Annebet turned and walked away. Toward the back of the garden. Toward the gate that led to the street.

Hershel followed her. "Where are you going?"

Marte scrambled after them, pulling Helga with her. They both tried not to yelp as the thorns caught their arms and legs.

"Home," Annebet said. She raised her voice slightly. "Marte, tell Momma I'm sorry, but I went home early."

"Pig crap," Marte said. "She knows we're here."

"I'll see you safely home," Hershel said, following her out the gate and onto the cobblestone street.

"Please don't."

"Anna—"

She yanked her arm away from him and her voice rose. "Just leave me alone!"

"America, Anna," Hershel called after her. "That's where we could go with this."

She stopped running away. Slowly turned around.

Marte and Helga didn't bother to hide. They hung on the fence, hung on every word.

"This is better than the radio," Marte whispered.

"Now I know you're crazy," Annebet said to Hershel. But there was something in her eyes. Something bright, something hopeful.

"I am," he said. "Crazy in love with you. Marry me."

Helga looked at Marte. Victory! They were going to be sisters! But it was short-lived.

The light in Annebet's eyes went out. "No," she said. "I can't."

"Wise answer, Fräulein."

Oh, *merde*! It was Wilhelm Gruber, the German soldier. He'd been in the shadows across the street, sitting on the stone wall that surrounded the Fraenkels' house and smoking a cigarette. Helga could smell the smoke now as he stood up and walked toward them.

His voice was tight. "In the Fatherland, to marry a Jew you would risk being tarred and feathered. You'd have your head shaved at the very least."

"What are *you* doing here?" Annebet was horrified. Gruber was in uniform, with his gun over his shoulder.

"I heard you were working tonight. And since it's a dangerous neighborhood, I came to make sure you made it home safely."

A *dangerous* neighborhood? A *Jewish* neighborhood, he meant.

Annebet had stepped in front of Hershel, her eye on Gruber's gun. The German was furious, his jealousy glittering in his eyes and all but fogging up his glasses. Helga had never seen him this upset before.

"Of course, a shaved head is nothing compared to the penalties a Jew would receive for defiling such a beautiful Aryan girl in Germany." His lip curled as he looked at Hershel. "We'd slice off your balls, Juden, and hang you by the neck from a lamppost in the center of town, so everyone could watch you rot."

"And you're *proud* to be a German?" Annebet spat at the ground, barely missing Gruber's boots. "Pig!"

Hershel yanked her back toward the gate, pushing her into the garden. "Go back inside," he ordered. "Marte and Helga, you too. *Now.*"

Helga's feet were leaden as Marte suddenly turned and dashed toward the house. She couldn't follow her friend. She couldn't move. She just kept picturing Hershel, swinging from that lamppost, birds circling. . . .

"I'm not going anywhere without you." Annebet held tightly to Hershel's arm.

"Did you really think she would go with you to America?" Gruber mocked, his hands on his gun, threatening their very lives. He would be in trouble for shooting them—Denmark didn't put up with German soldiers killing civilians in the street, but that wouldn't matter much to Annebet, Hershel, and Helga. In the blink of an eye, they'd be dead. "It won't be long before we invade and it becomes the United States of Germany."

"This isn't the way to win her affection," Hershel said quietly. "With such ugliness and threats . . ."

"Herr Gruber!" Marte came running back from the house. She was carrying a plate covered with a huge slice of chocolate cake, held in place with her thumbs. "I saved you a piece of birthday cake. I was going to give it to you tomorrow, but as long as you're here . . ."

"Marte!" Annebet was furious. "I *told* you—"

Hershel looked at her and she closed her mouth.

"Herr Gruber always shares his chocolate with me," Marte said, her voice trembling. "I thought it was only fair to bring him a treat for a change."

Marte and Gruber were friends of sorts. Friends through a mutual love of chocolate, combined with Gruber's deep admiration for her beautiful sister.

Their friendship had nothing to do with politics or terrible prejudices or with the fact that they were enemies—invader and conquered. It was more simple than that. He had been kind to her, and she was kind to him in return.

Her hands were shaking as she held out the plate. "That wasn't very nice—what you said about Hershel," Marte told the German soldier reproachfully. "He's a friend of mine."

Gruber looked down at the cake, looked at Marte's blue-green eyes, at her worn dress that was a size too small, and backed away, lowering his gun, thank God.

"I thank you, but . . . you'll have to eat it for me, little one," he said. "My appetite is gone."

And with that he turned and walked away. He broke into a jog before he'd reached the Jakobsons' house and quickly vanished in the twilight's shadows.

Annebet drew in a shaky breath. "Dear God. He's a monster."

Hershel looked at her. "He's in love with you." He laughed, but there was no humor in his eyes. "We're more alike, he and I, than I think he'd ever want to admit."

"What do *you* think?" Max Bhagat stopped pacing to turn and face Lt. Tom Paoletti.

As Stan watched, the SEAL lieutenant met the FBI chief negotiator's eyes. "I think you need to be careful."

"So you agree with Helga Shuler. You think I'm getting emotionally involved."

Paoletti laughed softly. "Max, I know you. You always get emotionally involved. But when the time comes to detach, I don't know how, but you do it."

"How about you, Senior Chief?" Bhagat had spotted him standing there, just outside the open door to the small conference room near the negotiators' HQ, ready to knock before he came in. "Do you think it's bad form to become emotionally attached?"

To a female helo pilot ten years his junior? Definitely.

"To the tangos you're negotiating with?" Stan came inside the room. "Absolutely—considering they're going to be dead in a matter of days."

"I'm not negotiating directly with the terrorists this time," Bhagat told him. "I've been talking to them through this

American girl who's on board. Gina Vitagliano. She's a twenty-one-year-old SUNY student, a percussion player—a drummer—with her college jazz band. The hijackers think she's Senator Crawford's daughter Karen. I think we'd have a planeful of dead passengers right now if she hadn't stepped forward when she did. She's bright and courageous and . . . I'll be the first to admit that I'm awed by her tenacity. If awe and respect counts as emotional attachment, then okay, fine. I'm definitely emotionally attached."

"Mrs. Shuler took the morning shift on the radio, talking to this girl," Paoletti told Stan. "Max didn't leave the room the entire time and she dared to wonder aloud if maybe he was just a tad emotionally involved."

"Are you going to be able to do your job, sir, if the tangos start beating her over an open radio frequency?" Stan asked Max Bhagat. "Once MacInnough and his team get those microphones and video cameras up and working, we'll be able to hear and see everything they say and do." Would *he* be able to do *his* job if Teri were suddenly in danger? Please, God, don't let him find out the hard way. . . .

Bhagat didn't hesitate. "Yes."

"Are you going to go in search of this girl after we take down the plane and take advantage of the fact that you've been her lifeline throughout this ordeal?" Stan asked. The kid was already probably more than half in love with Bhagat. Stan had seen it happen before in hostage rescues and negotiations.

It was a lot like hero worship.

"Hell, no. What kind of scumbag do you think I am?"

The human kind. The kind who might give in to temptation if he didn't actively work to take temptation out of the picture.

Stan made a mental note to talk to Muldoon. To push him to ask Teri to have dinner with him again tonight. To take temptation out of Stan's picture.

"You're the kind of scumbag who hasn't delivered a World Airlines 747 for my team to practice on," Stan told Bhagat, deftly changing the subject to the reason for his visit.

"It's on its way, Senior," Lieutenant Paoletti told him. "It's scheduled to land on the practice airstrip in just under ninety minutes. I've already notified Sam Starrett—told him to get the team back to the hotel for lunch and a rest. This afternoon you'll drill on the real thing."

Thank you, Jesus and Tom Paoletti.

A redheaded woman appeared in the open doorway. "Excuse me, Max, Gina's back on the radio."

Bhagat flew out of the room. "Karen," he said, his voice echoing in the hallway. "We have to call her Karen, *all* the time. No way are we going to foul this up by slipping and calling her Gina while the tangos are listening in."

"Slept lately?" Tom Paoletti asked as they went more slowly out into the hall.

Stan just laughed. Dream on. "Need a lift back to the hotel?"

"Hi, Karen." Bhagat was on the radio, his voice carrying into the hall. "It's me, Max. Over."

"Yeah, I think I do," Tom said. "I'm going to take a short nap, then check out the 747 before the team gets back out there."

"Max, I've been talking to Bob and Al over here." The girl's voice was husky and young and brimming with an undercurrent of intensity. Stan found himself stopping to listen. "They've agreed to let Gerhund and Ray and a girl named Casey off the plane. Both Gerhund and Ray have head injuries; Ray's having trouble breathing. Casey's diabetic and she's gone into insulin shock. All three of these people are going to need immediate medical attention, do you hear me? I tried to talk 'em into letting the mothers with babies off, too. There are three babies on board—two have been crying nonstop—but they won't let the babies leave. One of 'em hasn't made a sound, Max, and I'm a little bit worried about that baby, but they won't let any of them go."

Stan followed Tom into the negotiators' room, where Max's staff was scrambling around. Someone pushed past them, sent to give Helga Shuler the news that some of the passengers would be deplaning.

Bhagat was pacing, his team psychologist beside him,

murmuring comments. "There's quite a bit of stress in her voice."

"I hear it, Doc."

The girl continued. "Bob and Al have agreed to accept a shipment of water and food—"

The room erupted with a cheer. This was great news. Permission to deliver supplies meant that they wouldn't have to wait until oh-dark-hundred to bring additional microphones and minicams out to Ensign MacInnough and his team, who'd overcome a jammed luggage compartment hatch only to experience equipment failure.

But now they could send an additional team in, beneath the chassis of the supply truck, without the tangos seeing them. They wouldn't have to wait until dark to give the negotiating and take-down teams twenty-twenty vision and perfect hearing.

"Quiet!" Bhagat shouted.

"—including infant formula and food for the babies. They're opening the doors right now—"

"We have activity on runway two," someone reported in a low voice. "Doors opening!"

"Other passengers will be helping the injured off the plane," Gina continued. "Do not, I repeat, do not approach the runway until they have gone back on board and locked the doors. At that point, you'll have only twenty minutes to bring out water and food and to collect the injured. *Twenty minutes.* Do you copy, Max?"

Twenty minutes wasn't a lot of time, but they could definitely get the job done.

Tom Paoletti turned to Stan. "Call Jazz." Stan knew that the XO had an additional three-man team on standby. They were already here at the airport with the equipment in hand, ready to go.

Stan had already punched Jazz's code into his cell phone.

"I copy all that, Karen," Max said calmly as if the room weren't erupting with activity around him. "Well done. Over."

"There's more," she said. "You have to make the delivery by one of those . . . those luggage carts. You know, with the open sides? And you need to stay a hundred meters back from the plane. If you come any closer they'll . . ." She took a deep breath. "They'll kill me. Over."

Silence.

All of the elation was instantly gone from the room.

Stan shut off his phone before Jazz picked up.

"Shit," Max Bhagat said softly. "Options? Anyone." No one spoke. He looked at Tom. "Lieutenant?"

Tom glanced at Stan, who shook his head. If the distance between the truck and the plane were a few meters, sure, they might want to risk it. Or if it were twilight. But for even one man to move the distance of a football field across a concrete runway in broad daylight . . . The urban camouflage gear they used was good, but it didn't make a man invisible.

"I wouldn't want to risk it," Paoletti said. "Let's focus on small victories—bringing those injured people to safety and getting those supplies to the plane within the time limit."

"You heard the man," Bhagat told his team. "Let's *move!*"

Stan was already halfway down the hall.

Once again, lunch and a nap were going to have to wait.

By the time Sam Starrett made it into the hotel restaurant for lunch, by the time he'd filled his tray with pasta and a thick meat sauce, Alyssa Locke was already there.

Oh, man. She was sitting at *his* table. In *his* seat, no less.

Fucking A.

It had to be plain bad luck.

She couldn't have sat there just to piss him off, could she have?

Surely she didn't realize that he sat at that exact same table at every meal. Just because the other men in the team had left it empty for him because they knew he had a stupid superstition about this kind of thing during an op, well, that didn't mean Alyssa knew.

After all, there was no sign on the table: RESERVED FOR THE CRAZY SEAL TEAM LEADER.

Alyssa had been avoiding him like the plague—why would she start seeking him out now?

Unless she was purposely trying to irritate him. That was always a possibility.

And Jesus, if that *was* her goal, it was working.

Sam knew that superstitions were just that—superstitions. It was ridiculous. What, was he really going to get the job done better, with fewer mishaps, by sitting in the same place in this room every time he ate here?

No.

Probably not.

But with 120 lives at stake, it sure as hell didn't hurt to follow some crazy rituals that helped him feel more in control. What could it hurt?

Right now, it could hurt a lot, Sam realized as he carried his tray toward his table and Alyssa Locke. She was sitting there, right in the middle of her lunch break, with her fruit of a partner, reminding Sam of everything in life that he wanted but couldn't have.

Worst case scenario, they wouldn't scram, and Sam would be forced to eat lunch with a woman he'd dreamed about making love to just a few short hours ago when he'd grabbed a quick nap.

And wouldn't that be fun?

Alyssa saw him coming and her eyes widened before she wiped her expression clean. He set his tray down on the table. *May I join you?* He knew he should probably smile—at least pretend to be friendly and polite. "You're at my table," he said instead.

Alyssa looked at her gay partner, Jules, and laughed. "Yeah, right. Nice try, *Roger,* but—"

Jules took one look at Sam and half stood up. "We can move."

Alyssa grabbed his arm and pulled him back down. "No, we most certainly cannot—"

"Suit yourself." Sam picked up her chair with her in it and moved her about two feet to her right.

"Hey!"

He pulled another chair over and sat, pushing her plate, all her utensils, and her bottle of water in front of her, pulling his own tray in front of him.

"What is wrong with you?" Alyssa asked between clenched teeth.

He ignored her, looking up at Jules instead. "Got a pen?"

"Excuse me, Lieutenant, I'm talking to you," Alyssa said hotly as Jules searched his pockets.

"Never mind," Sam said as he remembered the Paper Mate he'd stuck in the back pocket of his pants. "I've got one."

He leaned back and took a napkin from another table and wrote right on the dingy gray of the linen, "Reserved for Lt. Sam Starrett." His name was Sam, not Roger. His own mother didn't call him Roger anymore. Alyssa was the only one who did.

"What gives you the right to come over here like that and—" Alyssa broke off as he set the napkin smack in the middle of the table.

"Oh, my God," she said. "You've got a—" She shut her mouth abruptly and gave all of her attention back to her salad.

"A teeny little superstition," Sam finished for her, feeling his ears heat with embarrassment. Thank God his hair was long and they were covered. "Big fucking deal, all right?"

"I didn't say it was." But she looked at him when she said it, instead of through him. For the first time all day, he didn't feel like the invisible man. That would've been nice, except she was trying—and not very hard either—to hide a smile that was just a little too smug.

"And you don't have a single superstition, right?" he countered. "Of course not, you're Ms. Perfect. You never make any mistakes— oh, wait . . . I can think of four. Or was it five?"

Something flashed behind her eyes. It was very brief and then it was gone. His needling was getting to her— particularly this latest comment that referred to the record number of times they'd made love in that one short night and morning they'd shared.

But his surge of triumph was short-lived, leaving a bad taste in his mouth.

Jules, meanwhile, was focused completely on his sandwich, like a kid caught in the middle of warring parents.

It was time to shut the fuck up and carboload. He had a

long afternoon ahead of him. Sam got down to eating, trying to shut out Alyssa Locke.

Trying not to smell her subtle perfume, trying not to stare at the smoothness of her cheek, at the delicate line of her jaw, her perfect ear, her eyes, her mouth, her breasts.

Great. Fantastic. Now she caught him staring at her breasts.

It was her fault entirely for wearing a shirt that . . . wasn't low cut or too tight or even remotely transparent. It was a button-down shirt, white, cotton. It was like the one Jules was wearing beneath his purple tie, except it was tailored to fit Alyssa's female curves.

Was it really her fault that it fit her so damn well?

Fuck, yes. She should be wearing something loose, something baggy, something completely unflattering in this shit-hole of a country, where women were second-class citizens, arrested for showing the least little bit of their ankles.

"You should have your jacket on," Sam growled.

"It's warm in here."

"Tough shit. You're in public."

"The book says—"

"Screw the book!"

"—nothing about keeping my jacket on. As long as I'm wearing long sleeves—"

"What you're wearing is inappropriate—"

"You don't approve?" she asked. The look she was giving him was meant to skewer, but at least she was still looking at him instead of through him. "Tough shit back at you, *Roger*. I don't answer to you."

"Oh, yeah? Give me five minutes with Max Bhagat."

Jules stood up, muttering something about coffee. Alyssa didn't seem to notice he was gone.

"I spent the morning playing tango for your team in the one hundred degree heat with my required long sleeves and long pants, Lieutenant," she spat back at Sam. "Unlike you and my other male counterparts, while I'm in Kazbekistan, I don't have the option to strip down to my underwear when I start to sweat. I think Max would agree that it's okay for me to have lunch without my jacket on."

"It's dangerous, god damn it," he said through a mouthful of pasta. "You look too good."

Oh, fuck. There it was. Out on the table for Alyssa to see. He'd just given himself away.

She was looking down at her salad, her eyelashes long and dark against her cheeks.

Oh, God. The wave of longing that hit him came in such a rush that he almost choked. Was he ever going to stop wanting her? It was all he could do not to bend his fork in half in frustration.

And then she surprised the hell out of him. "You look really good too, Sam," she said quietly, giving him a glimpse of her ocean-colored eyes as she looked up and too briefly met his gaze. "Let's try to get along. Try to be nice to each other. Okay?"

Yes. The correct response was yes, please, let's. Instead Sam leaned toward her and said, "You want to be nice to me, sugar? Let's go to my room and—"

She sat back in her chair. "You're such an asshole."

No doubt about it—he *was* an asshole. But what was he supposed to say now? Sorry? He couldn't help himself? She brought out the worst in him? Of course, she brought out the best in him, too.

Maybe if he threw himself at her feet, grabbed her around the legs, and wept as he explained that she'd been driving him crazy for months, that he *hadn't* forgotten her, that he needed her . . .

That he was doomed never to forget her.

"You want a war?" Alyssa said coldly as she pushed her chair away from the table. "Fine, Lieutenant. You got it. You've got yourself a war."

Twelve

"WHO IS SHE?" one of the British officials asked.

Teri didn't mean to eavesdrop. But the observers' tent was small. And the sun was scorchingly hot this time of the afternoon, so she, like they, were beneath it, watching the SEALs practicing the takedown of the plane. It was kind of hard not to hear their conversation.

"Alyssa Locke," Lt. Tom Paoletti answered. "Former Navy, currently with the FBI. Counterterrorism unit."

"Ah," said the one who looked like James Bond. Suave and sophisticated, charismatic and handsome with a touch of gray at his temples, he was obviously in command.

All three of the Brits were from the Secret Intelligence Service or SIS, although they'd probably never admit it.

"She's quite good," said the one who looked like a younger version of Q.

The SEALs had just completed another practice run, and, second time in a row, Alyssa Locke had killed one of the SEALs before being killed herself.

"This isn't even her real strength. She's one of the best snipers I've ever worked with," Tom Paoletti said easily. "But her instincts are excellent across the board. It was a lucky day for the Teams when she went into the Bureau. I know I sleep easier knowing she's part of the FBI unit backing up my men."

All four of them were silent for a moment, watching as Alyssa and the others who'd been recruited to play mock terrorists came out of the plane—the real World Airlines 747 that had finally arrived.

As hot as it was out here, there was no doubt it was really heating up on board the aircraft.

And what it must be like on the *hijacked* plane with the doors locked shut and no working sanitary facilities was too terrible to try to imagine.

"Lieutenant Starrett's still working the kinks out," Paoletti continued. "Having Locke play tango would be a challenge for anyone. He'll get her next time."

As they watched, Alyssa Locke accepted a bottle of water from the senior chief with a smile. She opened it and drank deeply, nodding as he spoke to her.

"Lovely woman," commented James Bond.

Alyssa Locke *was* lovely to look at. She'd changed her clothes since this morning when Teri had first officially met her. She'd put on some kind of lightweight jumpsuit that covered her from her ankles to her wrists as per the customs of K-stan. But the suit was belted, which accentuated her trim figure. She wasn't a voluptuous woman by any definition, but in that outfit, surrounded by a crowd of testosterone, she was unquestionably, strikingly female.

It was more than obvious that Alyssa was old friends with Stan Wolchonok. But how old and how friendly Teri didn't know.

She walked toward them, wishing that she didn't have to check in with Lieutenant Starrett, knowing that it would look strange if she walked past Stan without saying anything, hoping it wouldn't look as if she were checking out the competition if she stopped to say hello while he was talking to Alyssa Locke.

"Hey, Lieutenant." Stan greeted her first, and her heart leapt at his welcoming smile. "Where's your flack jacket?"

She rolled her eyes in exasperation. "Up by the observers' tent."

"Better than in the helo but not by much. It belongs *on* your body. Hey, Mike Muldoon's looking for you."

Great. So much for leaping hearts. She didn't stop walking. "Thanks, Stan."

She headed away from him, toward Sam Starrett, who was deep in discussion with two other men.

"Hey, Lieutenant, how's the head?" Jay Lopez asked as she walked past. He was sprawled in the shade of the wing, next to Cosmo and Silverman, but now he sat up.

"The head . . . ?" She was clueless.

"The bump," he reminded her. "Uh-oh," Silverman teased. "Amnesia strikes. That's not a good sign."

"No," she said. "No, I'm fine. I just . . . It was so not a big deal, I didn't even . . ."

Silverman was grinning at her. "Maybe Lopez should, you know, check you out again, as the team's medical corpsman, huh? Like maybe during dinner tonight?"

Jay Lopez was a handsome man with heavily lidded brown eyes and exotic cheekbones that were flushing with embarrassment.

"You're Reserve, Lieutenant, right?" Silverman continued. "Which means in a few weeks you'll be a civilian again. Which means the fact that Lopez here is enlisted won't matter. Which means—"

"Stop," Lopez said. "Sorry, Lieutenant." He met her eyes briefly, then glanced past her.

Teri turned to see that Stan had come up behind her. He wasn't close enough to be part of the conversation, yet it was more than clear that he was there if she needed him.

But there was nothing threatening in either Silverman's or Lopez's eyes. Silverman was teasing, claiming that Lopez was interested in her. Although . . . was it possible this was just another exercise Stan had set up in advance?

But then Silverman suddenly looked as if he'd swallowed a pincushion as Cosmo said something into his ear. "I beg your pardon, Lieutenant," he said. "I didn't realize you and the senior were, uh, special friends."

She glanced behind her again, uncertain how to reply to that with Stan listening in, but the senior chief was gone.

She murmured some nonsense—"Don't worry about it"—and went to find Starrett.

A quick "I'm here if you need me, sir," and she was heading back toward the observers' tent, trying not to be too obvious as she looked around for Stan.

But then there he was. Maneuvering Muldoon to an intercept point directly in her path.

"Hey, Teri." Mike Muldoon really was remarkably good-looking. Even with a smudge of dirt on his face.

"Hey, Mike." She forced a smile as Stan all but pushed Muldoon toward her. Dammit, Stan, don't do this. "Sorry about this morning."

Muldoon shook his head. "It's not your fault that I choked."

"Let's go," Lieutenant Starrett called. "Time out's over. Let's do this again, and let's do it right this time."

Muldoon looked about as relieved as she felt. *Saved.*

"See you later," she said.

"Sure," Muldoon said. "Ouch! I mean, do you, um, have plans for dinner?"

Teri hadn't seen it, but she was pretty sure that Stan had stepped on the back of Muldoon's boot. Hard.

"My only plan is to eat in the glorious basement of the hotel as usual," Teri said. She included Stan in her reply, looking directly at him. "Maybe I'll see you guys down there."

"Great," Muldoon said.

Stan said nothing. But he glanced at her. Just briefly.

She couldn't begin to guess what he was thinking.

Which was probably just as well, since she wasn't sure she really wanted to know.

". . . let the passengers go?" Max was saying as Gina started awake. "Over."

She was exhausted, it was hotter than hell with the sun pounding down on the plane, and the stench of humanity was close to unbearable. She couldn't remember the last time she'd slept.

"Over," Max said again, his rich baritone voice coming through clearly over the radio's speakers. He'd been talking to her—and through her to the hijackers—nearly nonstop for more hours than she could count.

It was almost funny. She had talked more with Max than

she'd talked to any other man—including the ones she'd slept with.

Trent Engelman was not the master of conversation, *that* was for sure, unless, maybe, he was talking about his new car or his microbrewery or his plans to get work as a musician with Wynton Marsalis's touring band after graduation.

Yeah, right.

When Trent did talk, it was without listening. Gina got the feeling that when she spoke, Max listened with every cell in his body.

"Max, how old are you?" she asked now. Bob was dozing, anyway. And Max didn't have to convince *her* to let the passengers go. "Over."

He didn't hesitate, the way some people might've at her non sequitur. "I'm forty. Over."

Oh, man. Her own father wasn't even forty-five.

"Are you married?" she asked.

His answer came back as quickly. "Nope."

"Why not?"

"Because no one in their right mind would ever marry me."

"Why? Are you hideous looking?"

He laughed. "Yeah."

She smiled. "Warts and long, greasy hair?"

"Mostly it's the fangs that keep the women away," he told her.

She glanced at Bob. He was definitely asleep. Al was awake and glowering but he didn't speak English. "Helga told me you're really good-looking. I think the phrase she used was *blindingly handsome*."

"Yeah, well, she's good at telling people what they want to hear."

"I didn't want to hear that," Gina told him, trying to get comfortable in her spot on the floor. She had to keep her legs crossed, tailor style, or her knees tucked in against her chest.

It wasn't just that there was no room in the tiny cockpit. It was mostly the way creepy Al started drooling when she stretched out her legs. She alternated between wishing she were wearing jeans and being grateful as hell—because of the heat—that she had on her shorts. "I wanted you to be short and rumpled. Kind of like—you know, if they made a movie of this?—Richard Dreyfus would play you."

She'd always had a major thing for Richard Dreyfus. Ever since she saw *Close Encounters* when she was ten.

"We're getting a little off track here," he said, his FM radio announcer's voice like velvet in her ears.

"Bob's asleep," she said. "Will you meet me for a drink after this is over?"

That one made him pause.

And Gina knew. There wasn't going to be an *after*, at least not for her. Max thought the hijackers were going to kill her. The senator's daughter would certainly be the first person they'd shoot if commandos stormed the plane, that was for sure.

"They're going to kill me, aren't they?" She'd suspected it all along. She knew that her fate had been sealed from the moment she'd first stood up and told the hijackers she was Karen Crawford.

When Bob and Al and their buddies decided it was time to play hardball, she was going to be the ball. They were going to kill her, but first they were going to hurt her. Badly.

"No," Max said now, "they're not."

She didn't believe him. "I'm scared," she whispered.

"I'll meet you," he told her, something different in his voice, something rough, something no longer so cool and collected. "All right? I will. It may not be until you're back in New York, but I'll meet you for a drink. No, for coffee. It has to be a cup of coffee. God *damn* it."

Yeah, she was definitely going to die. He, like Helga, was good at telling people what they wanted to hear. "Max, after this is over, will you go see my parents?"

Another pause. When he spoke, his voice was relaxed again, but she knew he was working hard to get it to sound that way. "Hey, I really need you to stop thinking in terms of worst case scenarios."

"Tell them it wasn't as bad as they probably imagined. Tell them I wasn't alone, that you were with me the whole time. Tell them because of that, I was okay."

There was another long pause. Then, "How about you tell

them that yourself? Because I'm going to get you out of there. Alive. In one piece. Trust me on that, all right?"

"Sure," she lied. He could try to convince her all he wanted, but his hesitation earlier had told her all she'd needed to know. "But just in case . . . Thank you. For everything." Gina cleared her throat, forced away her fear and self-pity. She wasn't dead yet. "As long as Bob's asleep, why don't you give me a crash course in negotiating. Teach me how to talk these assholes into letting the women with babies get off this plane."

The emergency exit over the starboard wing silently popped ajar under Muldoon's expert touch, and Stan gave the hand signal to the surveillance team hidden among the dust and rocks a hundred yards away.

Two clicks over his radio headset was the ready signal, meaning Starrett and Jenk, WildCard and Lopez, and Cosmo and Silverman had all succeeded in quietly unlocking their various egresses onto the practice 747. They were set to rock and roll.

When they did this for real, Lt. Tom Paoletti would be the voice of God. He'd give the go command, his omnipotence coming from the surveillance teams' reports of the tangos' exact locations on the plane and from the information from the video cameras. Provided, of course, MacInnough had the cameras up and running by then.

Tonight. The cameras should be in place and working by tonight.

Tom Paoletti would give that go command from the negotiators' HQ, where Max Bhagat would be helping out. The chief negotiator would request that as many of the terrorists as possible gather in the cockpit to discuss some outrageous proposition that he had absolutely no intention of following up on. But he'd use his powers of persuasion and make it sound really good.

Then, on Paoletti's go, the team's snipers would take those tangos out, shooting right through the glass, as the SEALs in Starrett's team burst into the passenger compartment with a flash and a bang and took out the rest.

It would all be over in a matter of seconds.

Go, go, go!

Stan went through their door with Muldoon in choreographed precision, adrenaline surging, his focus sharp. A target. In his kill zone. He eliminated it, clean and clear.

And then, just that quickly, they were secure.

"Karmody!" Sam Starrett yelled.

"Passenger casualties." WildCard Karmody consulted his computer. He looked up and grinned. "Zero."

"Okay," Starrett said grimly. "Let's do it again."

"What, perfect's not good enough for you?" WildCard asked. "Jesus, Sam, we've been going practically nonstop since 0400."

"What, doing it right once is good enough for *you*?" Starrett countered, his usually warm drawl clipped and cold. "And it's *Lieutenant*, Chief. Next time you question my authority, at least make the effort to address me by rank."

"Excuse *me*, Lieutenant Asshole," WildCard shot back. "Maybe I didn't go to officer's school and take a class in how to be a hard-on 101, but it sure as hell seems to me that something needs to be said here besides fucking *okay*."

Stan pushed his way forward. The look on Starrett's face left him little doubt as to his lack of patience. They were all strung pretty tight here, Sam Starrett more than usual. On top of that, stress plus adrenaline plus a whole hell of a lot of testosterone made for some pretty aggressive and uncomfortable physical pressures.

WildCard put that thought exactly into words. "Man, you need to relax." He laughed. "You need to get laid."

"Shut the fuck up," Stan ordered him. He turned to Starrett. "You want him off the team, Lieutenant?"

"Whoa," WildCard said. "Senior Chief, I—"

Stan silenced him with a single dark look, then turned back to Sam Starrett. Come on, Lieutenant, you know what you have to do to be the kind of leader that Tom Paoletti was.

It was possible that every man there—and woman, because Alyssa Locke was standing there, too; she and her partner and the SAS guys were trying their best to be invisible—understood why Starrett had to get WildCard off his team.

Everyone but WildCard, that is.

"Yeah," Starrett ground out. It wasn't easy to kick your best friend off your team. But the man *had* called him an asshole in front of an audience. How could he do anything else? "Replace him with Knox."

For the briefest split second, Stan was almost certain that WildCard was going to start to cry. But he didn't. He also wisely swallowed whatever knee-jerk and probably profane exclamation had been on the tip of his tongue—the kind of expression a man could say to a friend, but not a commanding officer.

Instead he stood at attention, eyes straight ahead. "Lieutenant Starrett, sir," he said in his best imitation of a real military man. "My sincerest apologies, sir. Request permission, sir, to stand in for Knox until he can be brought out here and up to speed."

Starrett nodded curtly. "Fine. Let's run this drill again."

"How about we do it five more times, just the way we did it this last time, starting with the doors already popped, and then we head in for a rest." Stan looked at Starrett, knowing that if he had his way, they'd run it fifty more times. "That okay with you, Lieutenant?"

Starrett nodded grudgingly. "Tonight we'll do it again—in the dark."

It would be easier across the board under the cover of darkness. If they could do this in broad daylight the way they'd just done, taking down the plane at night would be a walk in the park.

As Stan watched, Starrett moved farther away from the group, away from WildCard Karmody. Up until today he'd managed to be both leader and friend to this group of men, many of whom he'd gone through BUD/S training with as an enlisted man. But in truth, he'd left them—left WildCard—behind a long time ago, when he'd crossed over into officer territory.

And today reality had caught up with them both.

"Chief Karmody." Starrett gestured with his head for WildCard to step aside, to speak to him privately. He lowered his voice, but Stan knew what he was saying. "You want to stay? Then you continue to address me only with respect."

"Jesus, Sam—"

"That's *Jesus, Lieutenant Starrett*," Starrett corrected him coldly.

WildCard exhaled a disbelieving burst of air. "Even now? No one can fucking hear us—"

"You better put a *sir* on that, Chief, or I'll have Knox out here so fast your head will spin."

"No one can fucking hear us, *sir*."

"*I* can hear you, Chief," Starrett told him. "Let me give you a refresher course in the way this team works. I give orders, you follow them. This is not a democracy, there is no discussion unless I ask for one. You keep the wiseass comments to yourself or you'll be off my team. And on report."

"Well, *that's* fucking lovely. *Sir.* Some fucking friend you are. *Sir.*"

"I am your friend," Starrett said tightly. "But I'm also your commanding officer. If you can't learn to separate the two and treat me with the same respect you give to Lieutenant Nilsson and Lieutenant Paoletti in a command situation, then I'm going to have to choose for you. And you better believe I'll choose to be your CO."

"Yes, sir," WildCard said. "It's more than obvious that you already have. Sir."

"Get the fuck out of here," Starrett growled. "Don't make me sorry that I'm letting you stay."

But it was Starrett who turned and walked away. Separating himself even farther from the rest of the team. Heading farther out into officer's territory. All alone.

"Hey, Senior Chief!" Jenkins pulled Stan's attention back to the rest of the team. "How about a little extra incentive for those five more times?"

Jenk gave him his best choirboy smile. Uh-oh. That was never good. The petty officer was trying, like he always did, to lighten the mood after an emotional storm. Look out. Someone was going to be in trouble. "How about we do each drill in the same number of seconds or less as we did this last time," Jenk suggested, "and you get up during chow and sing karaoke?"

Stan. Stan was going to be in trouble. Sing karaoke. God-damn Jenk. Jesus Christ.

But he looked at the tired and dusty faces of the men around him. With the exception of Starrett and WildCard, who both looked as if their best friend had just died, they all were starting to smile.

"Come on, Senior Chief," Lopez said.

Stan nodded. "I get to pick the song." What were the chances they'd have anything he knew and liked on tape? Slim to none. Still, if he left it to them, he'd be up there singing "Like a Virgin" or that teen pop song that Izzy liked so much.

Help.

"And if our timing's not as tight?" Silverman asked when the whoops and laughter died back down.

Stan looked at them, one at a time. "Then I get to pick *your* songs."

Instant energy. It was the kind of challenge this team couldn't resist. Their timing would be as tight. No, it would be even tighter.

He was so screwed.

No one sat down in the observers' tent. No one but Helga, that is.

The pretty helicopter pilot—Helga was blanking on her name—stood leaning against one of the support poles, watching Stanley Wolchonok, her heart so painfully obviously on her sleeve. Oh, to be that young again . . .

The commander of SEAL Team Sixteen—his name was Lt. Tom Paoletti, Helga knew from consulting her memo pad—stood on the other side of the tent in that feet planted, legs widespread stance of the alpha male. It was an international phenomenon. Avi, her own husband, had stood the very same way as Tom.

Tom. Helga liked to think of the military men by which she was often surrounded by their first names. It was a great equalizer in a world filled with ranks and rates and big egos.

Tom stood talking to three men, all British. Helga flipped repeatedly through her pad, searching for who they might be.

No, they weren't listed there. There was no mention of any involvement by Great Britain. She hadn't met these men. Of that she was certain.

Almost certain.

Almost. Dammit.

Out by the plane, the SEALs prepared for another practice run of the hostage rescue. She could see Marte's Stanley, smack in the middle of a group of strapping young men. They were laughing now.

He'd been right in the middle of things, too, a few minutes ago when they *hadn't* been laughing. The observers' tent was too far away for them to have heard the conversation, but it had been pretty obvious there was a huge amount of tension out there.

And why shouldn't there be? These few brave men were directly responsible for the lives of the 120 innocent people aboard the hijacked plane.

Helga had glanced at Tom Paoletti as the tension among the SEALs built, but he hadn't moved an inch, hadn't unplanted his big feet. He'd kept one eye on his men, sure, but it was obvious that he trusted them to solve whatever problems had come up between them.

Someone's cell phone rang.

It was the tallest of the Englishmen. The too-good-looking one who fancied himself James Bond's smarter, more handsome brother. Yes, she'd seen his type plenty of times before.

He answered his phone with a businesslike, "Pierce." His name, no doubt. After that he just listened, and finally ended the call with an equally brief, "Right. I'm on my way."

"Trouble?" Tom asked.

Mr. Pierce deposited his phone back into the inside pocket of his jacket. "I'm needed at the airport immediately. Might I talk you into a chopper ride? That way Hawking and Franz can stay here with the car, continue to observe."

Tom took out his own cell phone, considered it for a half second, then stepped out from under the tent, repocketing the thing. "Yo, Jenk!" he shouted over to the SEALs.

Helga had to smile. He *was* an awful lot like her husband.

One of the SEALs, freckle faced and adorable, impossibly young-looking, came running. "Yes, sir?"

"Check with Starrett and the senior chief. See if it's okay with them if Lieutenant Howe makes a quick trip to the airport. Rob Pierce needs to get there pronto."

"Aye aye, sir!" The baby SEAL toddled off.

Teri Howe—that was her name—had stopped leaning and stood up. As Helga watched, she eyed Rob Pierce, surreptitiously checking him out.

Yes, indeed, young lady—definitely beware. Robbie was the sort who would manage to put his hands all over her as he got into the helicopter, unless she made a point to keep her distance.

Over by the plane, Jenk spoke earnestly, first to the cowboy—Helga checked her memo pad: Lt. Roger Starrett—and then to Marte's Stanley.

Stanley turned, shielding his eyes against the glare, and gazed over toward the tent. He looked at them all—Teri, Helga, Tom, and Robbie and Co.—then spoke briefly to Jenk, who came running back.

"No problem, L.T.," Jenk reported. "Senior just wanted to let you know that we were going to be finishing up within the next thirty minutes, so Lieutenant Howe should make an immediate return trip." He grinned. "I think he's in a hurry to get dinner over with. We've got a wager going, and if he loses—which he's gonna—he's going to have to get up and sing with the karaoke machine."

"Thanks for the warning," Tom told the younger man with a laugh. "Although I'm not sure whether to be there or to stay far away. Lieutenant Howe." He gestured for her to approach. "Have you met Robert Pierce?"

"No, sir."

Robbie held her hand just a little too long, gazed into her eyes just a little too deeply. When Helga glanced over, Stanley was watching. Intently.

Okay, maybe this attraction wasn't so one-sided after all. In fact, if looks could kill, old Robbie would've been a smoldering pile of ash.

"Pierce is with the SIS," Tom said to Teri. "He needs a lift to the airport, but then we'll need you right back here for transport to the hotel."

"Aye aye, sir."

"How long have you been flying choppers?" Helga heard Robbie ask Teri as they walked away. Come here often, babe?

Stanley watched them all the way to the helicopter. Watched them lift into the sky. He would've kept on watching, but the cowboy—she consulted her pad: Lt. Roger Starrett—called him.

Stanley glanced at Helga briefly, as if suddenly aware that she was watching him. Glanced at her again as he was walking back to the plane.

Ah, yes, she'd caught him doing something he didn't want anyone to see. There was something going on between him and Teri Howe, of that she was now certain.

But was it love or was it merely sex?

Helga suspected the answer to that question was something Stanley didn't even know himself.

It was a tough one, all right.

Almost as tough as the question she'd first asked as a ten-year-old. *How do you know when you're in love?*

She'd asked Annebet Gunvald one morning, after she'd gone to visit Marte, only to find that her friend had left to tend to an ailing aunt with her mother.

Annebet had been heading to the barn to do her chores and Helga had tagged along, willing as always to help. She would have done anything—even muck out the horse's stall—to remain in Annebet's golden, glowing company.

"How do you know when you're in love?"

Annebet didn't laugh, didn't tease. She just kept on sweeping the floor by her father's workbench. And when she answered, it was slowly. Carefully. As if she were giving Helga's question great thought and consideration.

"When you look into his eyes, and you're more alive than you've ever felt," Annebet said. "When the very breath you take sends both fear and joy rushing through you, and you feel as if you might die if you can't see him again—right *now*. When you want to shout and laugh and cry and curse all at once, when you burn for him to touch you, to make love to you, even though all your life you've been told that you mustn't, that you shouldn't, that you can't. It's when you feel yourself on the verge of becoming everything you've ever dreamed of being, when you can nearly *touch* your own potential because this other person gives you all of his strength and his power and you know he'd give you the very breath from his lungs if you asked. And you realize that you'll never be alone again because there's a piece of him that you'll carry with you, forever, in your heart. A heart that is infinitely bigger than it was just a week or two ago."

Helga was silent. Wide-eyed. Terrified. She wasn't quite sure she wanted to fall in love if it was going to make her feel all that. Fear as well as joy?

"It's important, mouse," Annebet said quietly, "that the boy you love feels all these things about you, too. Unfortunately, it doesn't always work that way. You must be very sure of his feelings before you let him make love to you."

Make love. Marte had told her all about making love. "Do people really . . . do what dogs and horses do?" Helga dared to ask. "Marte said that men turn into snarling beasts."

Annebet laughed. "She's been talking to crazy old Fru Lillilund again. Can you really picture your father—or mine—acting like a snarling beast? And our mothers letting them get away with it?"

Helga hadn't considered that.

"It's not like that at all, mouse. It's beautiful and tender and the most wonderful, special thing, and . . ." Annebet laughed again. "Listen to me. I hope it's all those things. I've heard that it can be. But the truth is, I have no more experience than you."

She gathered up the sawdust, carrying it to the barrel.

"But you said you love Hershel," Helga blurted. "And you must know that he loves you. He wants to *marry* you."

"If the world were a perfect place," Annebet said as she hung the broom back in its place on the wall, "I would have gladly made love to Hershel many times by now. But I know that—as often as he asks—we're not going to be married.

And as much of a freethinker as I am, I can't compromise myself that way. Someday you'll understand."

"But . . ." Helga had to ask. As dreadful as the words felt coming out of her mouth, she had to know. "Is it because we're . . . because Hershel is Jewish? Is that why you won't marry him?"

Anger flashed in Annebet's eyes. "How *dare* you suggest—" She took a deep breath. "No, don't answer that. And forgive me for shouting. I know why you asked. In this crazy world . . ." She gave Helga a hug, enveloping her in her soft warmth, surrounding her with the marvelous scent of flowers and sweet berries.

"Helga, the prejudices here aren't mine." She pulled back to look at her. "I wouldn't care if Hershel were Muslim or Buddhist or . . . or a pagan sun worshiper. His faith only matters to me in that it's a part of him—a part that I admire. I love his faith. It's so deep and strong. It makes him the kind, thoughtful, gentle, loving man he is. I would marry him in a *heartbeat* if I didn't know for sure that it would put a rift as wide as all of Denmark between him and your parents. *I'm* the one who's lacking here. I'm the one who is less than what they want for him."

How could she say that? "No, you're—"

"They're right," Annebet told her. "I understand them. Hershel has a great future as a doctor, as a researcher at the university in Copenhagen. Marrying me would put that into jeopardy. He would be talked about, looked at sideways, passed over for promotions. He would be *that fool with the fortune-hunting shikseh for a wife*."

"You don't care at all about his money!"

Annebet smiled, pushed Helga's hair back behind her ear. "You know that and Hershel knows that and I know that, but no one else knows. Including your parents. He's rich, I'm not. He's Jewish, I'm not. The world will see it the way they want to see it."

"But . . . Hershel has no future in Copenhagen while the Germans are here. You've said so yourself."

Annebet hugged her again. "You're full of fight today—Mouse the Mighty."

Helga was on the verge of bursting out crying. This wasn't fair. "But you love him!"

"I do," Annebet agreed, tears in her eyes, too. "I love him so very much. Enough not to marry him. Someday, sweet girl, you'll understand that, too."

Thirteen

STAN SPOTTED HER on the hotel stairs. "Lieutenant Howe," he called. "Got a minute?"

"I'm wearing my jacket." She gave him a smile as she turned to greet him. "See?"

The warmth of her smile made him hesitate. Christ, what was he doing? After going to all that trouble to make sure she'd have dinner tonight with Muldoon, he should be keeping his distance.

Still, seeing her with Rob Pierce, the Brit from the SIS, had made Stan realize that last night's little game with Gilligan and Izzy had been off base. Teri wasn't really threatened by guys like Iz and Gilligan. Or Jay Lopez. Guys like them would never be disrespectful to a woman like her. And she didn't hang out in bars where nice guys got drunk and turned into assholes.

What Stan really needed to do was coach her through a confrontation with someone like Pierce. Someone older. Someone in authority. Someone with the power to take advantage of her. Someone she looked up to.

Someone like . . . Stan.

Damn, what a thought *that* had been. But try as he might, he just couldn't shake it.

"Impressive job out there today," she said when he'd caught up to her. "You must be exhausted."

"*Exhausted*'s not in the vocabulary, remember?"

She laughed. "Right. Although I hope *sleep* is on your list of things to do this afternoon."

"Shower, food, sleep," he told her, ticking them off on his

fingers. "Definitely. Then at 0230 we go back and run the drill again until the sun comes up."

"I know," she said. "I volunteered to fly you out there."

He stopped walking. "What, are you nuts? Here's a hot tip, Teri. You're supposed to volunteer for the glory assignments, not the grunt work. Who's your favorite movie star?"

She blinked at his change of subject, but went along with the conversational shift willingly as Stan forced himself to keep moving. As nice as it was to stand in the stairwell with Teri Howe, it wasn't very private. And for what he intended to say and do, he wanted privacy.

God help him.

"I don't know." She scrunched up her face as she considered his question. "I guess . . . Russell Crowe. Yeah."

It was his turn to be surprised. "Really?"

"Uh-huh. Or Tom Hanks."

Wasn't *that* interesting. She didn't go for the pretty-boy actors like Tom Cruise or Mel Gibson or what's-his-name—the guy who married that TV star.

"Here's the deal," he told Teri. "When Russell Crowe gets permission to sit in the observers' tent, *that's* when you should step forward. You volunteer to fly the visiting movie star wherever he wants to go. You *don't* volunteer for the 0230 helo-load of grumpy, sleep-deprived SEALs."

She glanced at him. "I'd rather fly you than Russell Crowe any day."

Oh, baby. The double entendre in that one couldn't have been intentional, could it? Surely that had been a plural *you*.

"Russell Crowe only pretends to rescue the hostages," she continued. "You guys do it for real."

Yes, she'd definitely meant that as a plural. The double entendre was just his dirty mind doing its nasty thang. And the bitch of it was, Stan didn't know whether to be disappointed or relieved.

"Here's my floor," she said.

He opened the door for her. "I'll walk you."

She laughed as she went through to the hallway. "You're stalling aren't you?"

He didn't follow. "Stalling?"

"So that the dining room will clear out before you get down there," she said. He must've looked perplexed because she laughed again. "Does the word *karaoke* mean anything to you?"

"Oh, Jesus." He cringed. He'd forgotten. "You heard about that, huh?"

"Yeah, and I wouldn't miss it for the world."

"Oh, please," Stan said. "Please miss it."

"Not a chance. What are you going to sing?"

"Not 'New York, New York.' That's for damn sure."

She tried not to laugh and failed. "*Can* you sing?"

"I can fake it."

Her eyes were dancing. There was no other way to describe it. Her smile was so beautiful, *she* was so beautiful, she just sparkled with life and amusement. Her hair was a mess of wind-tousled curls, such a rich, dark shade of brown and so soft to the touch. He didn't have to reach for her to know that—he remembered. She had a smudge of something on her cheek, probably grease from running the flight checklist. She was as dusty and hot as he was—hotter probably, since Kazbekistani customs prevented her from rolling up her sleeves even when the temperature broke one hundred.

She had delicate features, elegantly shaped eyes and mouth, eyebrows that were dark and graceful against her skin. But, really, it was her laughter that made her truly beautiful. When she laughed, it was with her whole heart, her whole self.

"So, are you going to shower before dinner?" she asked. "Because if you're not, then I won't either. I really don't want to miss this."

"Yes, I'm going to shower first. I stink. And that's even before I start to sing."

She laughed as he finally came through the stairwell door, and they started walking again. But slowly. As if she wasn't in a particular hurry to get to her room either.

There was no one else in the hallway, so he cut to the chase. To the reason he wanted to talk to her privately, with no chance of someone stumbling over them.

"I was watching you when you left with Rob Pierce earlier today," he told her. "You know, the Brit."

"Yes," she said. "I know."

She was instantly tense, and he wanted to punch the wall. Or Pierce. "What'd he do?"

Teri shook her head. "Nothing."

"Nothing," he repeated, letting his exasperation ring in his voice as they stopped outside of her hotel room door. "You're suddenly tense as hell simply because I mention this guy's name, and you expect me to believe he did or said *nothing*?"

"You didn't say 'what'd he say,' you said 'what'd he *do*.' " Teri searched through her bag for her room key.

Christ. Fine. "What did he say to you?"

The door swung open. "Nothing." She glanced at him. Probably because he was making a choking sound.

"Teri," he managed to grind out.

"All right, all right. I mean, sure, he let me know he was interested in recreational sex, okay? Big deal. And I'm paraphrasing—he was far more smooth and sophisticated, so stop looking as if you want to wring his neck. He wasn't offensive—it was kind of funny and flattering if you want to know the truth."

He just looked at her.

"All right," she admitted, "it wasn't flattering at all because he probably hits on every female under forty that he ever meets, and you're right, it made me angry because there are a lot of women who wouldn't have understood his double-talk. They're out there, and he's going to seduce them because he's handsome and charming, and they're going to end up thinking he wants to start a relationship when all he really wants is a quick screw in the backseat of his car. And I'm sure he's married to some poor woman who fools herself into believing that he's faithful and I find that *incredibly* offensive. Along with the fact that he's practically old enough to be my father—isn't that old enough to know better?"

It was a rhetorical question. Since she was obviously not finished, Stan didn't bother to answer it with the best wisdom he could offer, which was that some men just never stopped thinking with their head that didn't have the brain in it. It was, no doubt, exactly what she didn't want or need to hear right now. If ever.

"But what *really* pisses me off," Teri continued, "is that I didn't say a single thing. I didn't tell him any of that. I wimped out. That's what I do. You were so right about me, Stan. I suck. I just . . . I run away unless I'm cornered. I run away, and then I hate myself for days—*weeks*—after."

She was finally done.

"Can I come in for a minute?" Stan asked.

She stared at him, but then stepped back, giving him access to her room. "Sure."

He took the door from her, closing it behind him with a very definite click.

Her room was cool and dim with the curtains still drawn. Well, it was cooler than it was outside, anyway. It was identical to his, only her room didn't have his dirty laundry tossed into the corner—including a pair of socks he'd worn for two days straight that should have been bagged and labeled BIOHAZARD.

He'd surprised the hell out of her by asking to come in, that much was obvious.

His being there made her nervous. He could practically read her mind as she took off her jacket and hung it over the back of a chair. His asking to come into her room like this was the dead last thing she'd expected. Why was he here? What did he want?

He was already scaring her a little just by being here, and if he did this right, he'd kill two birds with one stone. The hero worship would vanish, and she'd maybe learn a thing or two about standing strong.

Only now that he was in here, he wasn't sure what to do. He was frigging nervous, too.

This felt too real.

Bullshit. It wasn't real. Stop thinking like that. Come on, just do it. He'd seen guys act like assholes plenty of times. He'd even been one himself a time or two.

Or ten.

But not like this. Never like this with a woman like Teri

Howe who looked at him with such warmth and hope and trust in her eyes.

It wasn't real. None of it was real. Stop thinking. Just do it.

She cleared her throat. "Was there something specific you wanted to—"

"Yes," he said. Two steps toward her, and he caught her in his arms. He meant to say something rude, something suggestive, something along the lines of what Izzy had said to her yesterday in the stairwell, but she was staring up at him, her lips slightly parted and . . .

And Stan kissed her instead. No, *kiss* was too nice a word for it. He crushed her mouth with his—that beautiful, delicate mouth—pushing his tongue past her teeth, kissing her as hard and as deeply as he'd ever kissed any woman, with no warm-up, no warning, no sweet words or courtship. Just, bang. His tongue in her mouth, his hands all over her, on her ass, yanking up her shirt, her full breast heavy in the palm of his unwashed hand.

He pushed her back toward the wall, pushed between her legs, trying to convince himself that it was more to protect himself from the knee in the balls that he deserved for doing this than because he desperately wanted to be there, right there, cradled by her soft heat.

Except she didn't fight him at all. She didn't try to push him away. She just kissed him back. Christ, she was kissing him back, pulling him even closer to her and . . .

He was the one who leapt away from her, embarrassed as hell because he was completely aroused and there was no way she could've missed it.

This wasn't real. This was just an exercise, so what the fuck was he doing getting a hard-on? And what the fuck was she doing kissing him back?

Damn, he was a fool. He'd imagined she'd fight him, maybe crack him one across the face. He'd imagined them having a good laugh about it afterward.

But she wasn't laughing. Not even close. She said nothing, did nothing. She just stared at him wide-eyed and breathing hard as she leaned against the wall. Her lips were swollen from the force of his mouth against hers, her shirt untucked from her pants and slightly askew. She looked like his own personal sex dream. Replace some of that confusion in her eyes with a touch more heat. Let her lips curl in the slightest of seductive smiles as she reached up and slowly started unbuttoning her shirt . . .

He backed farther away. "Teri, Christ, at the very least you've got to learn to give out the kind of signals that tell a man you want him to stop!" It was the wrong thing to say, and he knew it the instant the words left his lips. "God damn it, I'm sorry. It was my fault that that went too far. I was trying to—"

"Get out," she whispered, closing her eyes as if she didn't even want to look at him anymore.

"Okay," he said, trying desperately to turn this back into the exercise he'd imagined. "You need to be louder. More aggressive—"

"Get *out!*" She shouted it now. "Get the hell out of here!"

"That's better, but—"

She opened her eyes. "That's *better?* How *dare* you?"

"That's good," he said. "That's right. Tell me off. Come on. Hit me if you want to." God knows he deserved it. And he must've misread her when he was kissing her. Maybe she hadn't really kissed him back. Maybe she'd been . . . what? Trying to fight him off by jamming her tongue in his mouth, too?

Hell, no. She'd *kissed* him. He knew what a kiss was, and that had definitely been one. But it didn't make any sense that she could've been so okay with it a minute ago, and so mad at him now.

"I want you to go!"

"Why? So you can feel bad later because you didn't take the opportunity to tell me to go to hell? It's okay to fight back, Teri, even if the guy is someone who intimidates you, someone you respect. You didn't say anything to Rob Pierce—"

"Rob Pierce didn't . . . he didn't . . ."

"And you didn't get angry enough to tell him off. Instead you internalized it, where it would fester and make you feel even worse. Who the hell needs *that?* You don't! You could've said one thing to Pierce, just one thing—*snowball's chance in hell, pal*—and he would've known you were on to him. So say it now, to me. Don't kick me out. Confront me. Get angry. Tell me to keep my freaking hands to myself."

But she just looked at him with those big wounded eyes.

God *damn*, this was a total goatfuck. He knew she wanted him to leave, but he couldn't. Not now. Not like this. So he took a step toward her. And then another.

"Don't," she said.

"Don't," he repeated, hardening his heart. "*That's* supposed to stop me? Tell me to go to hell."

"Go to hell," she whispered.

"Louder."

"Go to hell."

He made himself laugh at her, still moving closer. "That's not loud. Christ, no wonder Hogan thinks you're a pushover, because you goddamn *are*."

"Go to *hell*! Stay away from me! Keep your fucking hands to yourself!"

Jackpot. She was livid, and she was far from done.

"How *dare* you come in here and play this stupid game? How *dare* you practice your stupid pop psychology on me! Have I entertained you, Senior Chief? Have I amused? Or maybe I'm just this month's charity case—is that it? Well, screw you! *Screw* you! Why don't you just leave me alone? Why doesn't everyone just leave me the hell alone! Just stay out of my house! Stay out of my goddamn room! Stay out of my . . ."

The look on her face broke his heart.

"Bedroom," she whispered. She looked at him, her eyes huge in her face, and she knew that he knew. But she tried to hide it anyway. "Get out of my room, Stan. Please."

It was the *please* that did it. Stan didn't want to leave, but how could he stay when she begged him to go like that?

He went out the door, closing it gently behind him.

As she stepped into the courtyard that surrounded the hotel swimming pool, Alyssa nearly turned around and went back to her room.

Because Sam Starrett was there. In the pool.

If he hadn't chosen that very moment to turn around, she might've run away. But once he saw her, she couldn't retreat. No way. She walked out onto the cracked concrete and put her towel on a dilapidated lounge chair. Took off her sunglasses.

He was alone. Not even his obnoxious friend WildCard Karmody was with him. Of course not. Sam had finally seen the light and kicked Karmody off his team. And probably out of his life for good. He'd also taken him back with a stern warning, but the damage had already been done. And Ken Karmody seemed the kind of moronic idiot who would let hurt feelings ruin a friendship.

For a second, Alyssa actually felt sorry for Sam.

But then he swam to the edge of the pool. "Women's swim's not for another forty minutes," he drawled lazily, his Texas redneck twang set on heavy stun.

She glanced at him as she pulled her hair back into a ponytail. "Do I really look like I care?"

His dark, shaggy hair was wet, slicked back from his face in a way that accentuated his cheekbones and blue eyes. If he ever cut his hair short, he'd be even more devastatingly handsome than he already was. "Nice attitude, Locke. Way to respect the customs and traditions of your host country."

"I called the concierge desk and was told the pool was open all day, with American rules," she reported. "I asked if there were restrictions as to swimming apparel and was told that tank suits were preferred." She shrugged out of the sweatshirt and sweatpants she'd worn—as requested— through the hotel lobby. "Good thing I left my thong bikini at home."

Truth was, she didn't own a thong bikini, but Sam Starrett didn't need to know that.

"You shouldn't be wearing that while I'm out here," he said with a frown, as if her faded red Speedo were something that might've been featured on the cover of the *Sports Illustrated* swimsuit edition. He pointed up toward the windows of the buildings that surrounded them on all sides. "We're not the only ones staying in this hotel. There are locals here, too. If they see us in the pool together—"

"I'll be sentenced to death," Alyssa said, slipping into the water. It felt sensuously cool against her hot skin. "That's another delightful Kazbekistani custom—women being punished by death for being found in a compromising position with a man who's not their husband. Do you think we should follow that one while we're here, too, Roger? Out of respect for our host country? And oh, by the way, compromising positions that women should stay away from include rape, did you know that? Because of course it's a woman's fault if a man forces his way into her home and attacks her, right?"

Starrett pushed himself up and out of the pool, water sheeting off his body. His swim trunks were Navy issue—the same snugly fitting style that divers had worn since World War II.

Don't look at his ass. Whatever she did, she could not look at his ass. If she did, he'd know that she still found him intensely attractive.

Along with infuriating, outrageously arrogant and . . .

And she never would've guessed he'd be one of those guys who used some kind of voodoo to center himself during a high stress operation. Sitting at the same spot at the same table in the dining room at every meal?

Superstitions and rituals weren't uncommon in their line of work. Alyssa just never suspected Sam Starrett would have one of his own.

It almost made him seem human.

"It sucks," he said, following her along the edge of the pool as she did a leisurely breaststroke with her head above the water. "The way they treat women in this country. I'll be the first to agree with you about that. But we're not here to lead a revolution. We're here to get those people out of that airplane—alive. To do that, we need the cooperation of the K-stani government. We—*all* of us, even the FBI observers— need to come across as respectful at all times, so that the next time some fuckhead hijacks a 747, they'll let us come back to save the people on *that* plane, too."

If he had left it at that, she might've gotten out of the pool and gone back to her room.

But he didn't.

"What we don't need is you walking around looking like sex for sale."

Alyssa stopped swimming. "*Excuse* me?"

"*Excuse* me?" he mimicked her as he stood there nearly naked—more naked than *she* was—and dripping on the concrete. "You know damn well what I'm talking about. At lunch this afternoon I get on your case about being in the dining room with your jacket off, so this afternoon you wear something to the airfield that makes you look like a comic book superhero."

She smiled at him sweetly. "You mean, in the dining room when you had to push me out of your way because of some asinine and completely childish superstition—"

"Sure," he said. "Go ahead. Try to put the attention back on me. I guess you had enough of it today, prancing around, looking like—"

"You don't need to worry about me sitting at your special little table tonight," Alyssa spoke right over him. "I'm having dinner with Rob Pierce and the SAS team."

"—some kind of fantasy fuck in that skintight Nazi-bitch jumpsuit."

Nazi-bitch? "Fuck you!" The words escaped before she could bite them back. Why, why, *why* did arguing with Starrett always make her as disgustingly foulmouthed as he was? Why did he have the power to make her so completely lose control? She climbed up the ladder and out of the water, furious with him and unwilling to let him continue to loom over her that way.

"Figures you and Rob Pierce would find each other." Starrett laughed in disgust. "Why am I not surprised about that?"

"I'm the furthest thing from a Nazi that you know, asshole," she told him, jamming her finger in his chest. "And that jumpsuit is *not* skintight. At least get your facts straight before you insult me."

He didn't back down. "You purposely dressed provocatively—"

"There was nothing *provocative*—whatsoever—with what I was wearing out there in the field today, *Roger*," she told him. "It *wasn't* skintight—it wasn't even close. It was made of lightweight, loose fabric designed for athletes to stay cool in severe heat. I bought it after . . ."

After she'd nearly keeled over from the heat in Washington, DC, and Starrett had had to come to her rescue, dousing her with bottles of water from a nearby hotdog stand to cool her down. And mere hours later, she'd heated to a near boiling point all over again. In the man's bed.

Because she'd been drunk, she reminded herself as she found herself inches from his well-muscled, half-naked, sinfully attractive body. Too drunk to know that inside that deliciously wrapped package lived a complete and total jerk.

"If I wanted to piss you off by purposely dressing provocatively," she told him now, "I'd have to come here, to the swimming pool, and wear *this*. It's the closest thing to provocative I have in my wardrobe right now. And this is the only place I could wear it without getting arrested."

And it's a Speedo, you fool. It was the kind of suit Olympic swimmers wore. As far as swimwear went, it couldn't be more utilitarian.

But Starrett was looking at her as if she were wearing tassles and a G-string. As if, if they were alone, he'd peel both of their suits off so fast, she wouldn't have time to kiss him more than once before he'd be inside of her.

Oh, God. She actually wanted him inside of her. But she wanted him the way he came to her in her dreams. Funny and sweet and gentle, with a softness in his eyes and a smile warming his face.

"And here you are, right on schedule. Pissing me off," he drawled. "What do you know?"

She scoffed. "That's assuming I care enough to *want* to piss you off. You know, it's entirely possible, *Roger,* that I simply wanted to go for a swim, that the world *doesn't* revolve around you."

"Okay," he said. "Great. You win this round, babycakes. You've managed to annoy the shit out of me. Now do me a favor. Be a good girl and come back later, so I can finish my swim."

Her answer was a clean surface dive back into the pool.

*   *   *

Teri heard the knock on the door and knew it was Stan even before he spoke. He probably hadn't even made it down a single flight of the stairs before he'd turned around and headed back here.

He'd surprised her completely this afternoon—mostly by leaving when she'd asked him to. She was so sure he'd stay until he somehow made everything all right.

Except he couldn't this time. There was no way to make this right.

"Teri, I know you're still there," he said from the other side of the door. "Let me in, okay?"

She didn't move, didn't answer. God, she couldn't remember the last time she'd been this embarrassed, this . . .

Disappointed.

"Teri, come on."

Devastated. That was a better word for what she was feeling.

"Please open the door."

Stupid. Yes, she definitely felt stupid, too.

What was she thinking? The senior chief had been working overtime to set her up with Mike Muldoon. She should have realized right from the moment he'd asked to come into her room that this was another of his kindhearted lessons in confrontation. Instead, the moment he'd put his arms around her, she'd kissed him.

No, *kiss* was too nice a word for it. She'd inhaled him. Attacked him.

Thrown herself at him.

Oh, God.

The door opened with a click, and Stan came in. Figures he wouldn't need a key.

Teri didn't look up, but she knew he was repocketing whatever tool he'd used to pick the lock. And then he sat down beside her, his back against the wall. The miracle worker to the rescue.

She wanted to cry, but she wouldn't. She couldn't. Not with him here.

"I shouldn't have done that," he said quietly. "And I can't just walk away and assume you're going to be all right now."

"I *am* all right," she lied. No, she wasn't. She wanted to kiss him again. She wanted to wrap her arms around him and . . .

"I honestly didn't intend to kiss you like that," he told her.

"I know." Teri wiped her nose on her sleeve. "Believe me, I know."

He sighed and turned slightly to look at her, but Teri kept her own eyes focused on her boots. *Don't cry.*

"I was watching you today and thinking about what you said about being intimidated by men who were . . . I don't know, older. Authority figures. And I thought if I came in here and acted like some kind of asshole, like Joel Hogan, you could practice standing up to me, and Christ, I hear myself say this and it sounds like the most asinine idea in the world. I mean, it was an asinine idea *before* I lost my freaking mind and kissed you."

He took a deep breath. "I don't know why I did that. I have no real excuses—"

"It's all right," she said. God, he thought he'd kissed her. He didn't realize she was the one who'd jumped him.

"I could give you some bullshit about stress and fatigue and the amount of adrenaline that goes through a man's body during an op like this and what that does to the male anatomy. But that's just crap. Or I could tell you that you're the most attractive woman I've ever known but that's not news to you either." He sighed, rubbing his forehead. "And it doesn't make it any better—as if your being beautiful means you deserve it when other people lose control. *You* know that's not true and *I* know it, too. The best I can do, Teri, is apologize and assure you that it won't ever happen again."

Teri rested her head against her knees and tried not to laugh. Or cry. She wasn't sure what would come out if she made so much as a sound.

"Your turn," he said. "Talk to me. God *damn*, slap me across the face if you want to. Say *something*."

She took a deep breath. "It wasn't your fault."

"The hell it wasn't!"

I kissed you. But she couldn't say it. She couldn't bear the thought of sitting here while Stan gently explained that, yes, although he found her attractive, he wasn't in the market for any kind of emotional attachment, especially not with a complete headcase like her.

She still didn't know if he had a girlfriend back in San Diego. She hadn't managed to ask him, and now wasn't the time to do it.

"I forgive you," she said instead. "I know what you were trying to do. Really. I understand. And it's all right. It is."

She could feel him watching her for several long moments. "Has it occurred to you that you might be a little too understanding?"

She lifted her head at that. "You *want* me to stay mad at you? Fine. I'm mad at you."

He laughed softly. "Yeah, I guess maybe I do want that. I'd feel a whole hell of a lot better if you called me a jerk."

"You're a jerk," she told him obediently, her voice muffled. He *was* a jerk—for not realizing she'd *wanted* him to kiss her, to keep on kissing her. For not being on the verge of falling in love with her, too.

Stan was quiet then, for at least a minute. Maybe longer. But finally he cleared his throat. "At the risk of messing up our friendship even more than I've already messed it up today," he said, "I'm going to ask you something I've been wondering abut for a while, about something that I think happened to you when you were a kid. Because you said something before that made me think—"

"Don't," she said.

He was silent for a moment. Then he asked, "You ever talk about it with anyone?"

"No."

"Not ever?"

"No."

"Not with anyone?"

She lifted her head as anger coursed through her. She didn't want to talk about this. Not now. Not ever. *"No."*

He scratched his ear. "That's not good."

"You ever talk about any of *your* bad shit, Senior Chief?" She purposely used his rank even though it suddenly felt strange for her to call him that instead of Stan. When had that changed for her?

But his eyes were gentle, and she couldn't look at him for long.

"I don't have any bad shit, Teri." His use of her name was intentional. Obviously he'd noted her attempt to bring them back to a place where they were mere colleagues instead of friends, and was rejecting it. "Not like yours."

"Then how come you're not married?" she asked. "How come you're alone?" There, she'd asked. Sort of. If he had a significant other, he'd tell her now.

"I'm alone because I choose to be alone."

In other words, he'd rather be alone than be with her. That stung.

So Teri snorted. "Yeah, right. You're really happy living in that empty house. What, are you afraid if you get married, she'll die like your mother did?" She couldn't believe the harshness of the words that were coming out of her mouth.

But to her surprise, Stan nodded. "Okay," he said. "Fair enough. And yeah, maybe I am afraid of that. Or maybe I saw how hard it was for her every time my father left for another tour in 'Nam. I don't go to war, but I go away, sometimes for months at a time. So it's my choice to be alone. But you didn't choose what happened to you."

Oh, God, she didn't want to talk about that. But he kept coming back to it, relentlessly.

"You didn't choose your mother's dying," she countered.

"That's true," he agreed. "But I was eighteen when that happened." He was silent for a moment. "How old were you?"

Teri shook her head. "No."

"No, you don't remember?" he asked.

She didn't *want* to remember. Huddled in her bed, too scared to move . . .

"Give it a guess," he persisted. "You don't need to be exact."

Hoping, *praying* that tonight he wouldn't come in. *Stay out of my room!* She'd never said those words to him. She'd been too afraid.

"Thirteen?" Stan asked.

Teri shook her head. No.

"Older or younger? And, please, I'm praying that you're not going to say younger."

"I'm sorry," she whispered.

"Oh, god *damn* it. Please tell me how old you were."

She had no intention of telling him. She meant to stand up and walk out of her own hotel room, just to get away from his questions, if she had to. But the word came out of her, almost on its own accord. "Eight."

He made the kind of sound a man might make if he were punched in the gut. His face twisted as if he were in terrible pain, and as she looked at him, she saw tears in his eyes.

There were tears in *his* eyes, but she was the one who suddenly started to cry.

She didn't know where it came from, this sudden storm of emotion, but she couldn't stop it. Maybe it was acknowledging it aloud for the first time. Maybe it was knowing that she was finally going to tell someone. Maybe it was because part of her desperately *wanted* to tell, while part of her desperately wanted to keep it buried, forever.

Teri reached for Stan. Or maybe he reached for her. Same as earlier, when she'd kissed him, she wasn't quite sure who moved first. But then it didn't matter, because she was in his arms, and he was holding her tightly while she cried.

"I'm so sorry," he murmured, as if it were all somehow his fault.

"It's not as bad as you think," she told him when the tears finally eased. Her face was pressed against his shoulder, against the warmth of his neck. He smelled like heat and dust and hard work and coffee. "He never touched me. Not really."

"Not really?" Stan asked. "What does that mean, *not really*?"

"He came into my room at night," she whispered. "And he . . ."

She couldn't say it. At the time, she hadn't even known what he was doing with that furtive movement of his arm, as he stared at her with his robe hanging open. It hadn't been until years later that she'd truly understood how sick that bastard had been. The handkerchief he always took from his pocket after he came into the room and closed the door behind him. The full-body shudder that signaled the fact that it was almost over, that he would soon take his ugly face and his whispers of how much he loved her and leave.

Teri knew Stan was imagining that the bastard hadn't stopped at the edge of her bed, and she knew with a revolting certainty that it had been leading to just that. If she hadn't left for summer camp . . .

Summer camp, the bane of her existence, had saved her from physical abuse. The emotional and psychological damage, however, had already been done.

Teri wiped her eyes, embarrassed that he'd seen her cry. She never let anyone see her cry.

But Stan was barely breathing, his arms still around her. He was as tense as she'd ever seen him, waiting for her to finish her sentence, to explain.

Maybe if she started from the beginning . . .

"He was one of my mother's boyfriends," she whispered, not sure just how much of this she'd really be able to tell him, how much she'd be able to say aloud. "A live-in. They all were, really. She didn't like to be alone. This one was younger than the others, younger than my mother. And he would've been good-looking, except his smile was so . . . I don't know . . . fake, I guess. And his eyes . . ."

She'd been afraid of him from the start, from the moment she'd come down to dinner and found him sitting at the table. He was always watching her with those pale eyes, always sneaking up behind her, always touching her hair, her face, her bottom. Always asking for a kiss good night.

"I came home from school one day, and he was in my mother's bedroom, going through her purse." She'd stopped in the doorway, frozen with shock, just as he was taking twenty dollars from her mother's wallet. "He was stealing from her, and as I watched, he didn't try to hide it. He smiled at me, and put the money in his pocket, and put her wallet back in her purse. And I knew I had him. I knew my mother would kick him out. She wouldn't live with a thief no matter how handsome she thought he was.

"But then he told me I couldn't tell. He told me if I told anyone, anyone at all, he'd kill my mother."

"And you believed him," Stan said. "Oh, Teri."

"I was eight," she said. "He told me . . ."

"What?"

"That he'd make it look like an accident, and then he'd get custody of me. He said then it would be just him and me."

She'd gone from the euphoria of knowing that he would soon be out of her house for good to the hot fear that came with the thought of losing her mother. Her mother was far from perfect, but Teri loved her. And the threat of spending the rest of her life with *him* . . .

"So you didn't tell." Stan held her even more tightly. "And, Christ, he was testing you, wasn't he? He probably figured if you wouldn't tell about *that*, then you wouldn't tell if he . . ."

She nodded. "A few days later, he came into my room for the first time."

"Jesus," he said, his voice tight. "It happened more than once?"

"It happened nearly every night for I don't know how long. Months."

Stan made a strangled sound. "And your mother never thought that was strange? Him going into your room like that?"

"My mother passed out around eight-thirty every night."

"God damn her!"

She pulled back so that she could look at him. "It wasn't her fault—"

"God *damn* her!" He was crying. Senior Chief Wolchonok was *crying*. "She drinks so much that she can't protect her own child from being abused, and it's not her goddamn *fault*? Who's fault was it, Teri? *Yours?*"

"I never told anyone," she whispered. He was *crying*. "I should have told."

"You were a baby!" He wiped his eyes with the heel of one hand, still holding her with the other. "Your mother should have protected you. This asshole—what was his name? Because I swear to God, I'm going to find him and I'm going to f— I'm going to kill him."

He was dead serious. This man who was so careful not to use the f-word in front of her had killed before, in the line of duty. He knew what it meant to leave a body lying lifeless. This was no idle threat.

"Tell me his name," he said again.

"I don't know it," Teri told him. "Honestly, I don't think I ever knew. My mother called him *darling*. I thought of him as *him* or *he*. I don't think I wanted to give him a real name."

"*He's* the one at fault," Stan told her, pushing her hair back from her face. "*He's* the one who was sick. Your mother should have protected you, and he . . . He shouldn't have let himself get near you."

He was silent for a moment, and then he sighed. "Teri, you've got to have mercy on me and tell me what he did when he came into your room, because what I'm imagining is pretty hideous."

She tucked her head back into his shoulder. Maybe she could say it if she didn't look at him. Maybe she could say it without actually saying it. "He exposed himself and he touched himself and he . . ."

"Jerked off?" Stan said it for her, and she nodded. "In front of an eight-year-old. My God, how sick is that?"

"I didn't know what he was doing," she told him. "I'd never even seen a naked man before, but I knew whatever it was that he was doing, him doing it there, in my room, was wrong. I tried closing my eyes, but he made me watch. He told me he'd kill my mother if I didn't keep my eyes open and—"

Her voice was shaking so hard, she had to stop and take a breath. But once she'd started, it seemed to tumble out of her, this awful thing she'd never told anyone before.

"After dinner every night, when my mother was still awake, he started making me sit on his lap so he could read me a story. My mother thought it was cute, that he liked reading to me so much, but all the time he was . . . God, he was rubbing himself against me with his . . ." His thing. At the time, as an eight-year-old, she'd thought of it as a *thing*. A hideous thing.

Stan, too, had to work hard to keep his voice level. "And this went on for *months*?"

"I can't remember exactly when it started. I remember he was around for the Easter party at Professor Bartley's house, though. He hid jelly beans in his pants pockets and he got Connie and Mattie Bartley to reach in, looking for them, but I wouldn't go near him." She knew what he was really hiding in there. "It ended when I went away to summer camp in July. He and my mother broke up while I was away." She laughed, but it came out very shaky. "I'd always hated camp, but that year I was packed and ready to go three weeks early."

"How long were you gone?" Stan asked.

"Six glorious weeks."

"Did you find out that this guy and your mom had split while you were there? I mean, did she call you and tell you so at least you knew you were finally safe?"

Teri shook her head no. "I found out when I got home." *Darling, come say hello. Teresa's back,* her mother had called out as they'd walked into the house, and Teri had braced herself, nearly sick with fear, ready to come face-to-face with *him* again.

"So you spent the whole six weeks thinking you were going to have to go home to this monster? Thinking he was waiting there for you."

She nodded. Yes.

"So it wasn't just three or four months," Stan said. "It was more like six. Six months this fucker terrorized you. Excuse me."

She laughed shakily. "It's okay with me if you call him that. You know, the night I left for camp, he tried to . . ." She still couldn't say it. "He came into my room and told me that I had to . . ." She had to clear her throat. "Kiss him good-bye."

Stan knew what she meant and he was horrified. She could feel tension in his arms again. "But you said that he didn't—"

"He didn't," she said quickly. "He didn't get close enough because I, well, I threw up. On myself, on my bed. And he told me he'd see me when I got back from camp, and he left my room."

She was talking now simply because she wanted to stay here like this for as long as possible, with his arms around her. She knew when she stopped talking, Stan would be that much closer to leaving her room. And despite what she'd said to him earlier, she didn't want him to go.

"I made friends with Penny Stolz, one of the twelve-year-olds at camp, and I found out, well, if not *all* about sex, at least certainly more than the nothing I'd known. I didn't tell her about *him*, but I think she knew. Because she set up a trade between me and Stacy Juliani—my radio for the switchblade Stacy stole from her brother."

"You came home from camp with a switchblade knife?" Stan made a noise that sounded a lot like laughter. "Ah, Teri, I think I love you."

He didn't mean it. Not the way she wanted him to mean it.

"I don't know if I would've had the guts to use it," she told him, near tears all over again. Dammit, she wanted him to mean it. "I was lucky—I didn't ever have to find out. Because when I went inside my house, *he* wasn't there." It was a new man, a giant stranger who'd walked out of the kitchen at her mother's request. *Darling, come say hello. . . . "He'd* moved out and Lenny had moved in."

Lenny, who had loved her the way an eight-year-old was supposed to be loved.

Lenny, who'd taken the time and made the effort to gain her trust. Lenny, without whose gentle help she might not have healed enough to have ever had a normal sexual relationship with any man. Lenny, who'd given her back her self-confidence—at least enough of it so that she wasn't a *total* basket case.

Without Lenny, she wouldn't be a helo pilot. She wouldn't be in the Navy. She wouldn't be even half as strong as she was.

She'd still be hiding somewhere, probably under her bedcovers, all the time. Still afraid to come out and face the world.

"I think you're amazing," Stan told her. "To have lived through all that."

"I still sleep with the light on," she told him.

"I sometimes sleep with the light on myself," he admitted.

Teri lifted her head to look at him. "You do not."

"You'd be surprised how often I do." He touched her still wet cheek, brushing it dry with his thumb.

Now was the time to say it, while she was gazing at him, while he was looking back at her with such soft kindness in his beautiful eyes. *I kissed you, Stan. I didn't tell you to stop because I didn't want you to stop.*

But she couldn't form the words. They were wedged too tightly in her throat. Part of her was still hiding in her bed, too scared to move.

And then the phone rang, breaking the spell.

"That's probably Mike Muldoon," Stan said, shifting away from her. "Wondering if you're ready to go to dinner."

Teri shivered, suddenly cold without his warmth.

"Come on," he said, pushing himself to his feet, then reaching down and hauling her up beside him. "Take a quick shower. I'll run to my room and do the same. Then I'll come back here and walk you down to the restaurant."

God, she was exhausted. "I don't know. . . ."

"I'm not going to take no for an answer," he told her. "I'll be back in ten minutes. Be ready to go. And don't forget your jacket."

Fourteen

SAM STARRETT WAS *not* going to be the first to leave the pool.

He was hungry, he was tired, but until Alyssa Locke walked her perfect ass out of there, he was staying right where he was.

If he worked really hard at it, he could pretend that it had nothing to do with the fact that she was wearing a bathing suit or his realization that this was the closest to her being naked that he was going to get, probably for the rest of his life.

Damn, she was gorgeous.

And she was going to dinner tonight with Rob Pierce. The British motherfucker.

Alyssa came out of the pool, adjusting her bathing suit in a way that made him want to scream. Sam let himself watch her from his lounge chair, wishing he weren't so goddamn tired. He was too tired to be angry with her, too tired to feel much but sorry for himself for being the pathetic loser she'd had sex with and then rejected.

"Congratulations on being sent out here as an observer," Sam told her as she dried her face on her towel.

She looked at him suspiciously, as if waiting for him to add a *but* and an insult.

"That's all," he said. "Just congratulations."

"Yeah," she said, "it's been kind of obvious that you're thrilled for me."

He deserved that one. "Actually, I am. Your career's going great. I'm . . . I *am* thrilled for you. I just wish I could be thrilled for you while you observed someone else's takedown of a plane in some other country."

She sat down on the edge of the chair next to his, where

she'd tossed her sweats and sunglasses. "Word in my office is that this observation thing is the precursor to a permanent transfer to Max Bhagat's A-team."

Sam knew what she was telling him. The SEALs in Team Sixteen's Troubleshooters Squad worked with Bhagat's top team all the time. "Gee," he said. "Maybe we should just go steady. I mean, since we're going to be seeing each other so often . . ."

"Right." She stood up. "Excuse me for thinking you were capable of carrying on a serious conversation."

Sam stood up, too. "How am I *supposed* to react to that news, Alyssa?" God, he'd thought it was bad when he didn't see her—he thought he'd go crazy from missing her so fucking much. But it turned out that was nothing—*nothing*—compared to being around her and not being able to touch her, not being able to talk to her, to make her laugh, to make love to her. Another few days of this and they'd have to cart him off in a straitjacket. "Are *you* going to be happy about working with me around most of the time? Can you really be around me and not—"

Want me. He stopped himself from saying it, aware of how egotistical it sounded. But he didn't mean it that way.

She didn't answer. Instead she jumped him.

It was the dead last thing he'd ever expected. He was completely unprepared, and she hit him, hard, in a way that pushed him back and down, as if she'd meant to tackle him instead of leaping into his arms.

It was as he hit the concrete, with Alyssa Locke on top of him, that he realized she *had* meant to tackle him. She was shouting. "Get down!"

Something hit right where they'd been standing, the force of the explosion throwing them even farther back as flames erupted, igniting his towel and her sweats.

It was some kind of Molotov cocktail, tossed down from one of the windows in the building above them.

Alyssa Locke didn't want to jump his bones. She just wanted to save his life. He almost wished she'd just let him die.

He rolled back with her, moving away from the flames and

a second explosion. She dragged him back, too, behind a low concrete wall beneath the overhang, until they were sheltered from further attack.

Holy shit, that had been close.

Sam felt more than heard pounding feet as the Marines ran out from the lobby to investigate. Through the ringing in his ears, he heard an order to put out the fire, another sending squads of men up into each of the towers of the hotel to search for whoever might've thrown those makeshift bombs.

Good. Someone else was going to play Superman. He didn't have to move. He could just lie here for a minute, waiting for his head to clear.

Alyssa made a sound that pretty much summed up the way he felt. "Sam. *Sam!*" She shook his shoulder. "Oh, God, please don't be dead."

Sam. Now he was Sam, not Roger. "I'm alive," he managed. "Thank God!"

He lifted his head and looked down at her, suddenly intensely aware that he was on top of her. Their bare legs were intertwined. His thigh was pressed tight between hers and her body was soft and warm beneath his.

Beneath his very, very undead body.

"Are *you* all right?" he asked.

She nodded as she looked up at him, something unreadable in her eyes. "Yes. Get off me."

If she'd said please, he might've done it. But probably not. Her face was mere inches from his and he found himself staring at the softness of her mouth. All he'd have to do to kiss her was lean forward.

"I don't know," Sam said, trying to look as regretful and in pain as he possibly could. "I think I might have some kind of serious back injury and it's probably imperative that I don't move at all."

"You are *such* an asshole," she said, but she laughed as she said it, and something inside of him snapped.

"God, I missed you, Lys," he breathed, and then, Jesus, he was kissing her.

He'd meant to kiss her sweetly. Gently. Carefully. But like every interaction with this woman, he couldn't do it without

completely combusting. And touching his lips with hers just
wasn't enough. He had to taste her, so he swept his tongue
into her mouth.

And it was all over. Instant meltdown.

He couldn't have stopped kissing her if someone had held
a gun to his head. Her mouth was hot and sweetly spicy. She
tasted faintly of cinnamon gum and the cola they'd all been
practically shotgunning all day, both for the caffeine and to
replenish fluids lost out in the hot sun.

She tasted like hope and laughter and a future in which he
didn't wake up from his dreams of her drenched with sweat—
heart pounding and desperately alone.

Because she was kissing him back, just as fiercely as he
was kissing her.

She. Was kissing. Him. Back.

Holy God.

Her hands were in his hair, her legs tight around his thigh
as she kissed him as if she'd missed him as much as he'd
missed her.

Jesus, he was a fool for having waited so long to see her
again. He shouldn't have listened to her when she'd told him
they had to pretend that nothing had happened between them.
He should have gone after her. He should have dogged her
every hour of every day.

But that didn't matter now. Because she was kissing him.

She was kissing him in the shadows of the overhang by the
swimming pool in the hotel's center courtyard—which was
now crawling with Marines. It was only a matter of time before someone saw them. And he knew it mattered to her that
she not be seen kissing him, at least not in public like this.

So he lifted his head. "Lys, please, let's go to my room."

She looked dazed—far more than she had right after that
bomb had nearly killed them both. "I can't."

"We can go up separately if you want. I'm in 812 and—"

"No." She struggled to get out from underneath him,
pushing at him as if she were suddenly panicked, and he let
her up.

She'd scraped her shoulder and one of her knees, and he

couldn't believe she was just going to kiss him like that and then run away. "Lys—"

But she was. She was backing away from him as if he were a dangerous rabid animal that she shouldn't turn her back on.

"I can't do this again," she told him, and her voice actually shook. "I can't. I don't even *like* you. So just stay the hell *away* from me!" And with that, she turned and ran.

"Fuck!" If there were a wall nearby to punch, Sam would've put his fist through it. But there was only that low concrete divider that would've broken his foot if he tried to kick it.

And there was WildCard Karmody, too, standing silently about twelve feet away, even farther in the shadows, watching him. Jesus, how much of that had he seen?

"Lys as in Alyssa, huh?" WildCard said as Sam met his dark scowl. "As in Alyssa Locke."

"Aw, fuck," Sam said again, sitting down on the concrete divider, utterly defeated.

WildCard came closer. "So you were just never going to tell me that you scored with Alyssa Locke, were you, *Lieutenant*? When was it? In DC probably, right? That was six *months* ago."

"Fuck," Sam whispered. How could things have gone from so perfect to so completely fucked in a matter of minutes? Two minutes ago, he was euphoric. Two minutes ago, he'd been all but deciding who to invite to his wedding. Two minutes ago, he knew—*knew*—that he was going to spend the entire rest of the afternoon and evening making love to Alyssa, and that from now on, he was going to do it right. He was going to treat her so good, she was never going to leave him again.

But two minutes later, the truth emerged—kind of like the sewage that floated up and out into the streets of this stinking city whenever there was a heavy rain.

Alyssa didn't even like him.

And to make things worse, WildCard had seen Sam kissing her. Within hours, the entire team would know. And when the news got back to her, Alyssa would never believe that Sam hadn't been the one to tell.

"Six months," WildCard said again, with that self-righteous indignation that only he could do so fucking well. "It's eye-opening, *sir,* to realize that you thought so little of our friendship six *months* ago that you didn't *bother* to tell me that you'd shagged the Ice Bitch."

Sam exploded. He launched up off the concrete wall and hit WildCard at a dead run. He pushed him back, slamming him against the bricks of the hotel.

"Don't you fucking talk about her like that! Don't you fucking dare! I'll fucking *kill* you!" He was ready to pound the shit out of the asshole, ready to make *some*one bleed.

"Whoa," WildCard said, holding his hands in front of him in a gesture of surrender. "Whoa, whoa, Starrett. I didn't know! Time-out here! Time-out! You used to talk about her like that yourself."

He was seconds from throttling Karmody. "You breathe a word of what you saw to *any*one and I will fucking kill you! Do you understand me?"

WildCard stared at Sam, realization and a deep perception in his dark eyes. "Jesus, man, I had no idea you're in love with her! This is what's been making you act like a lunatic, isn't it? You're freaking out because she's here, but she doesn't want you. And the shit *I've* been giving you—that's just making it worse. God, I'm sorry, buddy. Where you're at right now, I've been there, done that, and it wasn't fun, that's for damn sure."

Sam stared back at his friend. *You're in love with her.* Oh, Holy Christ, WildCard was right. He was completely in love with Alyssa Locke. That's what these feelings were, this achingly awful sense of misery. The nearly bipolar mood swings to joy when Alyssa so much as smiled at him.

"What do I do?" he asked, barely able to believe he was asking WildCard Karmody for romantic advice. "Do I follow her? Should I—"

"Shit, no, Sammy," WildCard told him, the afternoon's altercation by the plane totally forgiven and forgotten. "You stay the hell away from her before she completely breaks your heart."

* * *

Helga made it into the hotel dining room just in time to hear the tail end of Stanley's song.

He actually did it. He got up on the makeshift stage, took the microphone in hand, and sang.

His voice was better than merely good, his intonation uncommonly accurate, but it was his choice of song that made Helga laugh aloud. "(You Make Me Feel Like) A Natural Woman."

He sang the words with a completely straight face, really delivering the soulful melody and tender words. *Your love's the key to my peace of mind . . .*

The pretty helo pilot was there, sitting at a table, but she wasn't alone. She was with a glaringly handsome young officer. What was *that* about? The young man was grinning, as were most of the other SEALs—and the room was packed with them. They'd turned out en masse to see their senior chief make good on the bet he'd made.

The bet Helga had made a note of on the pad that she'd glanced at as she approached the restaurant. She was having a Swiss cheese night. Lots of holes, lots of confusion. She'd be lost without her notepad.

Across the room, the helo pilot looked exhausted. Still, she sat watching Stanley, completely transfixed. What was she doing, sitting with that young officer as if they were out on a dinner date?

The song ended, and the room erupted into a roar even louder than the poolside explosions that had woken her from an afternoon nap. Helga clapped and whistled, too, as Stanley executed a very dignified bow.

"Hey, Senior!" one of the men from the back of the room yelled. "Is there anything you *can't* do?"

"If there is," he said into the microphone, "I'm not telling."

There was more laughter. As he put the microphone back into its stand, his eyes caught those of the helo pilot, who was still watching him from across the room. He gave her a look just a little bit longer than a typical casual glance. No one else in the room probably noticed it.

But Helga did. And when Stanley purposely moved away

from the pilot and the handsome officer, heading instead toward the bar, Helga cut him off at the pass.

"Very nice," she said to him. "You have your mother's gift of music."

"Thank you," he said.

"Do you dance as well? She loved to dance."

"I'm afraid I inherited my father's two left feet."

"Oh dear, your father didn't dance?"

He smiled at her dismay. "I didn't say he didn't, ma'am. He just wasn't very graceful. But if you knew my mother at all, then you know he danced. She had the master chief doing the polka with her in the kitchen every night he was home."

Helga laughed. "That sounds like the Marte I knew."

"He would do anything for her. Except . . ."

"Except stay home from Vietnam?" she asked gently. "I'd bet she didn't ask him to do that, though."

Stanley looked at her closely. "No," he said. "She didn't."

"Do you have a few minutes?" she asked him. "Can you sit?"

He glanced over at the helo pilot. She and the handsome officer had just been brought their dinners. She wasn't going anywhere for a while.

"Yes, ma'am," he said. "I'd like that. Grab a table. Can I get you something from the bar?"

"What are you having?" she asked.

"Just a can of soda."

"Not beer?"

"I'm operational. But I'd be glad to get you a brew, if you like."

"Operational?"

"Lieutenant Paoletti and Max Bhagat could give the order to take down the plane at any moment," he explained. "Until that happens, until those passengers are safe, no one on my team will have so much as a sip of beer."

There was a burst of laughter from a table in the corner of the room. A waiter carried a tray of nearly overflowing beer mugs in its direction.

"They're not operational?" Helga asked.

Stanley glanced at them. "No, ma'am. They're the SAS,

SIS, and FBI observers." He smiled. "They're allowed to have a hangover in the morning."

Ah, yes. She recognized the tall man at the table. It was that James Bond wannabe from the UK. And the female FBI agent sat next to him. Someone Locke—and Helga was lucky she remembered that much.

"Can I get you something to drink?" Stanley asked her again.

"Just a bottle of water," she told him. "Thanks."

As he headed to the bar, she turned to look around the room.

There weren't any open tables. But at the sound of more gales of laughter from the table in the corner, the SEAL she recognized as being the cowboy in charge of the takedown of the plane threw his napkin onto his half-finished dinner in disgust. He pushed his chair back from his table so forcefully, it nearly toppled over. With another grim look at the revelers, he strode out of the hotel restaurant.

There was quite a bit of pressure on that young man. Helga could imagine that she'd have little appetite—or patience for people having a party—if she were responsible for a team of men who were planning to force their way onto a locked aircraft to try to kill five hostile terrorists without injuring any of the innocent passengers on board.

Either that or he was miffed because what's-her-name Locke was drinking without him.

Helga smiled at her tendency to find a budding romance under every rock. Avi used to tease her about it all the time.

She took the cowboy's still warm seat as a busboy quickly cleared the table, stopping him from taking a linen napkin that had been placed in the middle of the table. "Reserved for Lt. Sam Starrett," it said in messy blue ink.

That was right—the cowboy's name was Starrett. Just like the character from the book *Shane*, about the gunslinger and the farmer's family in the old American West. How fitting.

And how ridiculously odd that Helga should be able to remember that—the name of a fictional character from a book she'd read at least four decades ago—when there were times she couldn't remember the name of the person she was talking to.

Or—worse yet—when there were times she didn't *recognize* the person she was with. Such as the man sitting down across from her at her table, giving her a bottle of water and a smile.

It was frightening beyond belief when her world gave a sideways slip and she found herself here. Completely at a loss.

"You okay?" he asked, whoever he was who had sat down across from her, concern in his eyes. Eyes that she'd seen before. Eyes . . .

Annebet, her eyes filled with concern as she pulled Marte off of Helga. "Why are you fighting? What's this about? Helga, are you okay?"

"Just . . . just a little warm," Helga managed to say.

The man with the blue eyes so like Annebet's reached across the table and took back the bottle of water. He opened the top, put it into her hand.

"Tak."

He smiled. "My mother used to say that. You sound so much like her, it's a little unnerving sometimes."

His mother. Marte. This was Marte's son, Stanley. The world slipped back into place. Thank God. "It's a little unnerving for me, too," she told him. "You have Marte's smile and Annebet's beautiful eyes. Did she become a doctor, Annebet?"

"Yes, she did," Stanley told her. "She was a pediatrician—ran a children's clinic in Chicago."

Helga put her hand to her mouth, suddenly afraid she was going to cry. "Did she ever . . . marry?" She had to know.

"No. She always said she was married to her career. She passed on just two years ago. The winter after she retired."

"That must've been hard for Marte."

Stan looked at her. "My mother passed twenty years ago."

Merde. "Forgive me," Helga said. "Of course. I'm . . . tired, and . . ."

"It's all right. Really."

"She was my best friend during a time when I couldn't have survived without a best friend. Quite literally," she told him. "In my heart, she'll always be twelve years old. In my heart, she'll never be gone."

"In mine, too," he told her quietly, a completely unexpected admission of deep love from this big, rough warrior.

"The first time I defied my father," Helga told him, "the first time I stood up to him and told him he was wrong, I pretended I was Marte. She was so brave, so ferocious."

He smiled. Damn, she'd lost his name again. The more she tried to force herself to remember, the more it eluded her.

"That's a good word for her," he said.

"She beat me up once," Helga told him.

He laughed. "Why doesn't that surprise me?"

"She thought I'd told my parents . . . about something we'd been hiding from them. She was furious with me. Annebet had to pull her off. She felt just awful when she found out she was wrong. Marte," she qualified. "It turned out another girl, Ebba Gersfelt, was the one who told."

Ebba Gersfelt had been jealous. She'd seen Hershel and Annebet meeting in the park, and she'd told her parents, who had called the Rosens.

Marte's son glanced across the room, trying not to be obvious about the fact that he was more interested in watching the pretty dark-haired helo pilot than in what Helga was saying. The pretty pilot was finishing up her dinner with an outrageously handsome young officer. What was *that* about? Why didn't Marte's son go and talk to her, join them?

Maybe it was because he was sitting here with her.

Helga might not be able to remember a name, but after being a diplomatic envoy for over forty years, she knew how to end a conversation.

"I've kept you here for long enough," she told the man with a smile. "I know you have things to take care of. But perhaps we can find another time to talk."

He was enough of a professional soldier to recognize a dismissal when he heard one. He stood up, pushed in his chair. "Your assistant mentioned something about sharing a flight back to London. I'd like that."

She had no idea what he was talking about. Was she going

to London? Still, she kept her smile intact. "Wonderful. It was nice talking to you."

"Likewise, ma'am."

As he walked away, Helga dug through her purse for her notepad. *Stanley.* His name was Stanley. And the helo pilot was Lt. Teri Howe.

But as she watched, Stanley gave Lieutenant Howe a wide berth, passing the young woman without even giving her a glance.

It didn't make sense. But too often these days, nothing made sense.

Of course, that was really nothing new. Nothing had made sense back when she was ten years old, either.

"You've continued to see this girl, despite our objections," her father had roared at Hershel on that awful day that had started with Marte's fists and her angry accusations that Helga had betrayed them. The accusations had hurt far more than the fists.

Hershel had looked at their father, his anger evident only by the tightening of his jaw. "I've asked her to marry me."

Poppi exploded. "Over my dead body! I forbid it! I forbid you to see her *ever* again!" He caught sight of Helga cowering in the doorway. "And you—I forbid you to play with the other Gunvald girl! From now on you will come straight home from school! You will not *talk* to either of them, am I understood? If you live in my house, under my roof—"

Forbid her to see Marte . . . ? Helga couldn't breathe.

But Hershel just laughed. "I'll pack my things."

Mother was aghast. "And go where?"

"Anywhere but here," Hershel told her. "If my friends in the resistance don't have room for me, I'll stay in the Gunvalds' barn. They've never been anything but welcoming to me."

"Because they're fortune hunters—all of them," Poppi stormed. "If you walk out of this house, I'll cut you from my will. Go and tell this Annebet that—that you have no more money. See if she'll marry you then."

"You're wrong!" Helga stepped into the room, and her father turned to look at her, incredulousness and anger on his big face. She'd never dared to speak back to him before.

She nearly faltered, nearly backed away and scrambled up the stairs to the safety of her bedroom. But Marte wouldn't have run, and she closed her eyes for a second, trying to imagine what Marte would say next.

She'd call him a fat pig and tell him to eat horse droppings.

Helga tempered Marte's fight with her own gentle reasoning. "Poppi, you don't really know the Gunvalds. You don't know Annebet. If you took the time to meet her, you'd see that she doesn't want Hershel's money. She cares nothing for that, and *everything* for him. She loves him more than she loves herself, more than she loves her own comfort and happiness. The only reason she won't marry him is because she can't bear to be the cause of a rift between you."

"She told you that?" Hershel's face was filled with emotion. For an instant, Helga wasn't sure if he was going to laugh or cry. "Mouse, my God, she said that to you? That she loves me that much?"

Helga nodded.

Hershel laughed as he kissed her. "She loves me *that* much! Thank you, God! I've got to go find her." He started for the front door.

Poppi was still furious. "If you leave this house, you'll get no money from me!"

Mother was crying. "Hershel, don't do this!"

Hershel stopped, looked back. "I don't want your money— take it, please."

"If you walk out that door, you will be my son no more!"

Helga gasped, but Hershel just shook his head. "How does that work, Poppi? You proclaim it and make it so? You can shut me out of your heart, but you can't shut yourself out of mine. I may not be your son, but you'll always be my father, in my eyes and in the eyes of God. Unless you think He listens to your pronouncements, too?"

For once her father was speechless.

"Won't you wish me luck and long life?" Hershel asked quietly. "Because tonight will be my wedding night."

Poppi pointedly turned away.

"Luck, Hershel," Helga said. "Luck, and prosperity and—"

"To your room, miss," her father raged, as Hershel quietly shut the door. "To bed without supper!"

And Helga escaped, only too glad to take the stairs to the second floor two at a time. She closed her bedroom door behind her. Locked it. And went out the window and into the softness of the late summer twilight, down the drainpipe, just the way Marte had shown her.

Hershel had seemed so convinced that Annebet would marry him—tonight.

And Helga wouldn't have missed their wedding for the world.

"The best we could figure, it was some kind of equipment error," Mike Muldoon told her as they sat over coffee in the hotel restaurant.

Teri was exhausted. She was having what had to be very close to what people described as an out-of-body experience. She was still partly numb from the afternoon's emotional roller-coaster ride. She still couldn't quite believe that, after over twenty years of silence, she'd finally told someone about those awful months when she was eight.

She'd told Stan.

And he hadn't blamed her and he hadn't hated her. And, probably most important, he hadn't pitied her. He'd listened and held her. He'd cried, but it hadn't been from pity. It had been because he cared.

Yeah, he cared—enough to bully her into coming downstairs for dinner and then virtually delivering her to Mike Muldoon.

Teri had been stunned. Again. Stan wasn't going to join them. Again. She'd thought . . .

Obviously she'd thought wrong. Her whole world had gone through some major gyrations, yet nothing had changed for Stan. He was still working overtime to set her up with his friend.

And she'd sat down at Muldoon's table, even more exhausted than ever, figuring, Why not? Why fight this? Stan wanted it so much—one of them deserved to get exactly what they wanted.

It had been awkward again at first, sitting there alone with Muldoon. The ensign was remarkably bad at small talk. Still, she'd managed to get him going by asking him questions about Stan.

Muldoon admired the senior chief possibly even more than she did. And he was full of some pretty wild stories—wild enough to keep her from begging exhaustion and crawling back to her room the minute she'd finished her dinner.

She glanced at her watch. It was only 1700. It felt closer to midnight.

"But there was no doubt about it," Muldoon was telling her now. "We were dropped so far from the LZ—the landing zone—we were in a completely different country."

"I know what an LZ is," Teri told him.

"Right. Sorry." He made a face. "I keep forgetting you're a pilot. You're . . ." He cleared his throat, fiddled with his glass of water. Glanced at her. "Too pretty to be a pilot."

"You're too pretty to be a SEAL," she countered, and he laughed.

"I had a good time tonight," he told her. "Stan was right. You're great."

It took every ounce of willpower she had not to pounce on that statement, to ask if Stan really said that about her in those exact words. But she knew she really didn't need to ask. Of course Stan had said that. He said it while trying to talk Muldoon into going out with her. It meant nothing.

"So you missed the LZ by a few dozen miles," she said, wanting to hear the rest of Muldoon's story before she went up to bed. She had fewer than nine hours before she had to report for duty, and she was determined to spend every one of them sleeping.

"Try a few hundred," he told her. "Like, three hundred."

What? "How could that have happened?"

"We didn't spend a lot of time speculating," he said with an adorable smile. There was no doubt about it, Muldoon was gorgeous with that chiseled face—a nose that was the closest thing to perfection she'd ever seen, those cheekbones, that sensitive mouth and strong jawline and chin. It was not a hardship to sit here and watch him tell his story, watch his eyes light with amusement, watch emotion and candlelight play across his face.

"We were in the middle of the jungle, near this mountain road. It was raining so hard visibility was down to eight inches, communications had crashed, our team leader was missing, and we had four hours to travel three hundred miles to meet L.T.—Lieutenant Paoletti—and his squad for an op that was . . . Well, let's just say we *needed* to be there. But the senior chief is undaunted. He goes out to find us a truck. We need wheels because we're running out of time—so he's going to get us wheels. Our job is to find Lieutenant O'Brien, our missing CO.

"Stan set up a rendezvous point where we're all supposed to meet—him with a vehicle and us with O'Brien. And then we start search patterns. It was a big jungle—I'm talking a needle in a haystack situation.

"But Izzy and I found him. He'd hit his head and was way out of it. I remember thinking, thank God—because the last thing I wanted to do was show up at that rendezvous point empty-handed." He laughed softly. "I also remember thinking, thank God he's unconscious. Now the senior chief will remain in command, and he'll get us out of here. I mean, I outrank the senior, sure, but I didn't have the experience, so . . ."

"Let me guess," Teri said, her chin in her hand as she watched him. "While you found O'Brien, Stan managed to find a truck."

"He did." Muldoon grinned. "It just so happened that it was filled with cocaine and being pursued rather relentlessly by the angry drug runners he'd stolen it from. So suddenly we're in a firefight, and the senior chief's like, 'Well, I couldn't just leave the drugs behind, could I?' As calm and matter-of-fact as could be."

Teri had to smile. She could just picture Stan. . . .

"Did I mention the volcano?" Mike said.

She laughed. "You're making this up, aren't you?"

"I swear to God, I'm not. This really happened on my first op with the team."

"A volcano," she said. "Where did you say you were?"

"I didn't. But you can probably guess."

"I'd bet it wasn't Hawaii."

He laughed—a flash of white teeth. "You'd win. Anyway, there we are. We're being chased by forty angry men with automatic weapons, and Mount Kumquat or whatever the heck it was called chooses that moment to erupt. Now, it's not quite in our neighborhood, but it's close enough for some pretty intense earthquakes as we're zooming down this mountain, heading for some little one-hut town in the valley. The road is crumbling beneath our wheels and Senior's like, 'Oh, good. This way security'll be down on the airfield.' Turns out there was a map in the truck—he's pinpointed where we are and where we need to be, and there's a nearby airport where we're going to steal a plane so we can get there."

"Of course," Teri said with a laugh. "I should have guessed."

"Yeah," Muldoon said, grinning back at her. "It won't be easy, but we're SEALs. We can do it. At least that's what the senior chief tells us. He has me and Jimmy rig enough C-4 to blow the truck and the drugs to Kingdom Come. Turns out—oops—the airport is a military air base, but Senior turns *that* snafu to our advantage, too. We drive that truck right through the locked gate and trigger the explosives—and we've got ourselves a nifty little diversion. We get off the ground in a military transport, complete with jump gear.

"By now O'Brien is awake and pretty embarrassed that he missed most of the action. He swears he's feeling up to making another jump, so Senior tells Cosmo to set the plane on autopilot—it's got just enough fuel so that it'll go down over the ocean—and we get ready to make our second jump of the day.

"Visibility sucks because of the ash and dust from the volcano, but the senior chief says he knows where we are. He says jump, so we jump."

"And . . . ?" Teri said. This entire story was pure Stan.

Missed LZs. Rainstorms, volcanos, earthquakes, drug runners, trucks filled with cocaine. He would glower about the PITA factor, but then he'd go about taking it all in stride—and making things right.

"And he was right. He knew where we were," Muldoon told her with another smile. "This time we hit the ground an eighth of a mile from the LZ. We made it to the rendezvous point with Lieutenant Paoletti with ten minutes to spare.

"And L.T. says, 'We expected you here sooner. Did you have any problems, Senior?' And the senior chief doesn't bat an eye. He kind of shrugs and says, 'Nothing the team couldn't handle, sir.' "

Nothing *he* couldn't handle was more like it. And it was true. There was nothing that Stan couldn't deal with. Nothing he couldn't fix.

Except maybe for the fact that Teri couldn't stop thinking about him—couldn't stop wanting him. Even when she was sitting here with Muldoon, who was undeniably gorgeous and incredibly sweet.

"You okay?" he asked.

She looked up to find concern in his pretty eyes. What was wrong with her? It was obvious that this man was interested in taking their budding friendship and tweaking it up a level. Or ten. But when she looked at him, she felt . . .

Exhausted.

And maybe a little flattered.

That was the best she could do. Maybe after a good night's sleep . . .

"You look beat," Muldoon said gently. "We should get out of here so you can get some rest."

Teri didn't argue. She let him lead her out of the restaurant, let him carry her heavy flack jacket. Together they went up the endless stairs and into the dimly lit hotel lobby.

"Which tower are you in?" he asked.

"West. You?"

He rolled his eyes. "South. But it's not that far—I'll walk you up anyway."

"That's okay," Teri told him, shaking her head no. She didn't want him to. She didn't want to stand awkwardly with him outside of her room, praying that he wouldn't try to kiss her good night.

She didn't want to kiss him. Not after kissing Stan earlier this afternoon.

God, she'd never been kissed quite like that before. With so much passion and power and ferociousness. She gazed up at Muldoon, watching his mouth as he said something to her, something she couldn't hear over the memory-induced roaring in her ears.

No, although he had a very nice mouth, Teri didn't want to . . .

He kissed her.

Muldoon kissed her. Right there in the lobby, where anyone could see them. Shock made her just stand there, so he kissed her again, settling his mouth against hers. As far as kisses went, it was nice—warm and soft and sweet.

And Teri realized that she'd asked for this. By looking at his mouth the way she had, he'd no doubt assumed that she *wanted* him to kiss her.

Oh, damn.

She stepped back, away from him, pulling out of his arms.

They were standing in the gloom of a lobby that was more shadows than light, thanks to the current brownout. And it was an empty lobby, too, thank goodness. No one had seen them.

Muldoon was looking at her as if he were thinking about kissing her again, so she quickly held out her hand to him. "Good night."

He laughed as he shook her hand and opened his mouth to speak. "Teri, I—"

Teri didn't want to hear it. So she did what she did best. She took her jacket from him and ran away.

Fifteen

TERI NEARLY SPRINTED to the stairs, leaving Mike Muldoon gazing after her.

Stan sat down in one of the hotel lobby's battered easy chairs, suddenly exhausted.

He eased himself farther back into the gloom as Muldoon crossed to the south stairwell, praying that the ensign wouldn't see him, wouldn't stop to say hello.

Stan didn't think he could stand exchanging pleasantries with anyone while he was so goddamn tired.

Yeah, right. That was it. His sudden aversion to Mike Muldoon had nothing to do with the fact that he'd just watched the guy kissing Teri Howe.

What the hell was wrong with Stan? He wanted Mike and Teri to hook up.

But he didn't want to have to watch them kissing.

Have to? Yeah, he really *had to* stand here and watch. He couldn't possibly have slipped deeper into the shadows and silently walked away. He couldn't possibly have used another stairwell to get up to his room.

No, instead he had to stay and watch and freaking torture himself. Because the sad truth was that he wanted this woman for himself. He wanted to take advantage of her trust, of the way she looked to him for advice and help. Screw the fact that a guy like Mike would be good for her. Screw what she needed, because Stan *burned* for her.

That kiss Muldoon had given her—that was no real kind of kiss. Teri hadn't leaned into it, hadn't leaned into him. She hadn't reached for him at all. She'd backed away, shaken Muldoon's hand. And he'd just stood there when she walked away.

Christ.

Wasn't the fact that Stan had gotten the two of them together enough? Did he have to teach Muldoon how to kiss the woman, too?

That kiss had been nothing like the way she'd kissed Stan just hours earlier.

God damn it, he should just give up. He should just go to her room. He should knock on her door on the pretense of making sure she was okay after all that she'd told him that afternoon.

It wouldn't take much effort on his part to get her clothes off, to get her naked and eager beneath him. And that wasn't ego talking—it was years of experience, of coming to conclusions after gathering evidence and facts.

All he had to do was stand up, walk the few extra flights of stairs up to her room instead of his.

That was all he had to do.

That, and throw away his belief of what was right, of what it meant to be a man of honor.

God *damn*, he still couldn't believe what she'd told him, what had happened to her when she was only eight. It wasn't as terrible as it might have been, thank God for that. But it was still awful. And it still made her vulnerable, that was for damn sure.

Knowing that made him more convinced than ever that someone like Mike Muldoon—sweet, funny, sensitive Mike— was exactly what Teri needed.

Stan put his head back and closed his eyes, trying to figure out the best way to approach Muldoon and offer him advice without offending him.

Helga couldn't find her room.

She knew the number—it was written in her notepad: 808. She'd climbed all the way up to the eighth floor. She'd followed the numbers all the way down to 805, but then the hallway ended. There was a door, but it was locked. She couldn't go any farther.

She'd almost sat down right there in the corridor and cried. Instead she'd retraced her steps. She'd come back here.

All those stairs—both up and down—had been too much for her, and she sat now in a corner of the dimly lit lobby, disoriented, exhausted, and upset.

A group of military men, dressed for battle, went past her. She didn't recognize any of them, but she knew she should. She should know their faces, know their names.

But she didn't even know where she was. What city, what *country* even. What was wrong with her, that she didn't know something so basic, so simple?

She shrank back into the shadows, her heart pounding, praying that the men didn't see her. She was uncertain as to why she should hide her confusion, her disorientation. She only knew it was something that *should* be concealed from everyone.

She'd hidden in shadows from soldiers plenty of times before. She'd held her breath as she'd ducked behind the Gunvalds' henhouse, afraid he'd hear her gasping after she'd run all that way. She was careful to keep her eyes down as she listened for him—for Wilhelm Gruber—to march off down the street.

But he'd be back. The German soldier never patrolled far from Annebet's house.

Helga scurried to the barn, where she knew she'd find Annebet and Marte, and maybe even Hershel, too. He'd left the house before she had, walking away from Poppi's threats. But Helga had run as fast as she could, taking shortcuts through yards and muddy alleys that Hershel wouldn't—not dressed the way he was in his good suit.

She burst into the barn. Just as she'd known, Marte was playing with the puppies, Annebet was . . . Helga didn't know what Annebet was doing—she'd leapt up from her seat on a barrel and was concealing whatever she'd been holding behind her back.

"Helga, you scared me!" Annebet scolded. "What are you doing here at this time of evening?"

"Hershel," she gasped, and Annebet dropped what she'd been holding. It fell with a thump onto the floor—a deadly looking gun. Helga stared at it, but Annebet knelt in front of her.

"Please tell me he's all right." Her face was pale, her voice shaky.

"I'm all right." Hershel closed the door tightly behind him as Annebet sprang up with a cry of relief.

"Thank God!" She ran to him, threw herself into his arms. Helga's brother closed his eyes as he held her tightly.

It seemed such a private moment, Helga looked away. And found herself staring, once again, at the gun Annebet had been cleaning. Marte inched back, her eyes on her sister and Hershel as she pushed the gun behind the barrel Annebet had been using as a seat, hiding it.

"I thought you don't believe in God." Hershel pulled back to look into Annebet's eyes.

"I think I might now," she told him. "I was sure Helga was coming to tell me you'd been taken. Or killed."

He touched her cheek. "I'm not the one who's started carrying a gun." He pulled away from her, crossed to the barrel, and nudged the gun out from behind it with his foot.

"Maybe if you did, I'd worry about you less," Annebet countered.

"What I worry about are all those kids in the resistance, walking around armed and dangerous. Someone's going to get hurt—there's going to be an accident. Bjorn Linden is *fifteen* years old. He carries a Luger wherever he goes—" Hershel broke off, shaking his head. "I didn't come here to argue with you, Anna. I came here to . . ."

"He came here to marry you," Helga said.

Annebet laughed, but then realized that Hershel didn't deny it.

"You fought with your parents," she guessed correctly. "They forbid you to see me." She turned away from him in frustration. "I'm not going to *marry* you in some kind of reaction to their anger. I'm not going to marry you, period. We've been through this before."

"No, we haven't," Hershel said. "We haven't been through all of it. You forgot to mention the part where you love me more than your own happiness. You forgot to say that you'd marry me in a heartbeat if you weren't convinced that doing so would cause a rift between my parents and me."

As Helga watched wide-eyed, Annebet steeled herself. She turned to face Hershel, to meet his gaze.

"That's right," she said. "I would. As much as I would hate it, I could live with the talk, the whispers from strangers. I could even live with you never getting that position at the university. I could live in America, as long as you were with me. But I can't live with knowing that I came between you and your parents. I can't—"

"But you haven't," he told her, stepping toward her, holding her by the elbows and all but shaking her. "Don't you see? You haven't done anything but love me, too. God, I love you, and I will until the day I die! Whether you marry me or not, my heart is yours."

Annebet had tears in her eyes, and Marte was flat out crying.

But Hershel wasn't finished. "He told me if I left the house, he'd disown me. I don't want his money—that part of his threat meant nothing to me. As for his love . . ." He shook his head. "I don't want that either, if having it means I've got to let him control me. This isn't about you. Not really. It's about me not living my life the way my father wants me to."

"It's just that he wants what's best for you."

"He wants what's best for *himself*," Hershel countered. "Love should be unconditional. He should have said congratulations, not—" His voice shook. "*—you will be my son no more.*"

"Oh, Hershel." Annebet wept for him.

Hershel was crying, too. They all were. Helga could feel her own tears, wet on her cheeks.

"He's at fault," Hershel persisted. "Don't you see? You didn't cause this problem—my father did."

"But if it weren't for me—"

"I wouldn't be the happiest man on earth," he told her. "So marry me. You've *got* to marry me, because this *isn't* your fault. Please, Anna. I won't care so much about not being Eli Rosen's son anymore if I can be Annebet Gunvald's husband."

Helga was watching Annebet's face, and she saw the battle

being fought within her, saw the moment Hershel—and her heart—won.

Annebet kissed him. "Yes," she whispered. "I'll marry you."

"Helga? My God, what happened? Are you all right?"

It was Des.

She wasn't sitting in the Gunvalds' barn. She was in the run-down lobby of some hotel in . . . in . . .

It didn't matter that she didn't know, because *Des* she knew. His face was familiar.

His eyes were filled with concern as he gave her his handkerchief, and she realized she had been crying.

"I was remembering the night Annebet told Hershel she would marry him," she explained as she dried her face.

"You know better than to sit in the lobby," he told her. "Particularly after that incident by the pool this afternoon. Security's been increased, but it's by no means safe down here."

"I was just resting my feet for a minute. This place is so big—"

"You got lost," Des interpreted.

She pretended to laugh. "Don't be ridiculous."

"We've got to talk about this. We *will* talk about this. Just not right now. If we don't get moving, I'm going to be late for a meeting."

A meeting. At this hour? Helga realized that Des was dressed all in black.

"Come on," he said, helping her up. "I have just enough time—I'll walk you to your room."

Sam Starrett wasn't sleeping when the phone rang. He was wide awake and staring at the ceiling even though he damn well should have been completely unconscious and refueling for the 0230 practice session that was approaching far too soon.

When the phone rang, he knew it wasn't Lieutenant Paoletti calling to bring the team in early. The phones in the hotel were way too unreliable.

That meant it was WildCard, calling in to report that Alyssa Locke had made it safely back to her room after partying with that asshole Rob Pierce and the SAS observers. Sam would've gone prowling through the hotel himself, looking for her, but WildCard had advised against it. Unless he *wanted* Locke to know that he was ... Jesus, he couldn't even *think* it without cringing. But it was true. Seeing her again—*kissing* her again—had clarified it for him.

He was in love with her.

The phone rang a second time, and Sam was tempted not to pick it up. WildCard's news might not be so good. He might be calling to tell him that Alyssa had gone back to Pierce's room, that she was there right now.

With him.

That was not news Sam wanted to hear on a night when drowning his sorrows in a bottle of Jack Daniel's wasn't an option.

He rolled onto his stomach and picked up the phone, bracing himself for the worst. "Where the fuck is she?"

There was the sound of distant laughter and talking, glass and silverware clinking on the open line. And then a soft laugh that wasn't WildCard's. "So you *did* send Karmody down to check on me. I thought so."

Holy Jesus, it was Alyssa herself.

"We're having a discussion about nicknames down here," she told him, "and yours came up."

She'd been drinking. He could hear the alcohol in her voice, relaxing her consonants, messing with her vowels.

"Rob wanted to know the story behind you being called Sam, and I remembered that *Sam* came from *Houston*, but that you weren't nicknamed Houston because you were from Texas, because you *weren't* from Houston, but I couldn't remember what . . ." She laughed. Covered the mouthpiece of the phone badly as she spoke to someone else. "No, no. Really, I don't want—" It was muffled, but he heard her. Heard her laugh, too. "No, *I* want to talk to him. Wait—"

"Lieutenant, I'm extremely sorry. I hope we didn't wake you." It was that British fuck, Rob Pierce.

Sam was grinding his teeth so hard, he could almost feel little pieces breaking off. "No," he said, somehow managing not to sound as if he wanted to kill the bastard. "I was still awake."

"We're dreadfully confused about the origin of your nickname. Would you mind running it past me? Just quickly. I don't want to take up too much of your time. And I'm a little more coherent than, well, than just about everyone else, so once I've got it figured out, I'm sure I can explain it to the lot of them. Right?"

Right ho, you stupid fuck. "My given name is Roger Starrett," Sam explained tightly. "I got the nickname Houston because of Roger. Like NASA. Mission Control? Roger, Houston, got it?"

"Ah."

"Then, after months of being called Houston, someone who thought it was my real name started calling me Sam. Because of Sam Houston."

"Because of . . . ?"

"A famous Texan. American historical figure." You stupid fuck.

"Right then. I've got it. I'll let you get back to—"

"Put Alyssa back on the phone," Sam ordered.

Pierce made some British-sounding noise that Sam ignored.

"Now, Double-oh-seven," Sam said over him. "Put her on the fucking phone *now*. Unless you're afraid she's going to hang up the phone and ditch you for me. Is that what it is, you dumb fuck?"

Pierce laughed. "You Americans are so ill-mannered." But then he heard, "He'd like to talk to you, darling."

Then Alyssa's voice. "Yes?"

You gonna fuck him, *darling*? The words were on the tip of his tongue. Instead he closed his mouth, took a deep breath, exhaled, and said, "Lys, what are you doing?"

He could almost hear her surprise.

"This guy doesn't give a shit about you," he continued. "Come tomorrow, he won't even remember your name."

She pretended to laugh, but it was fake. "Great advice, coming from a guy who—"

"Remembers your name. Real well. Alyssa."

Silence. Sam tried to count to ten but only made it to seven. "Look, is WildCard still down there?"

"Glowering at me from the other side of the room," she said. "Yes. My hostile little guardian angel."

The idea of WildCard Karmody as anyone's guardian angel would've made him laugh if this hadn't been so fucking important to him.

"Let him walk you to your room," Sam said, still in that reasonable, almost gentle voice, praying that she'd listen to him. "Get out of there right now, okay, Lys? If you don't want to do it for me, then do it for yourself. Please. This guy Pierce is one of the biggest assholes in the world, and you're going to hate yourself tomorrow. And I don't want you to have to go through that again. Once was enough, don't you think?"

There was another long pause, then, "Sam?"

"Yeah?"

"How come you're only nice to me when I'm drunk?"

Sam laughed tiredly. "That's just an alcohol-induced illusion. I'm still the same son of a bitch I always am. You interpret me differently when you drink, that's all."

"I don't think so."

"Yeah, well, you're skunked. What the fuck do you know?"

"I know that I miss you."

Jesus. Her soft words all but knocked the very breath out of him. "Yeah," he managed to say, "well, that makes two of us."

"May I . . ." She cleared her throat. "Would you mind if I . . ." A cough this time. "I'd really like to continue this conversation someplace more private." A deep breath. "Can I come up? To talk," she added quickly.

"812," he said.

"Right," she said, and hung up the phone.

Teri had a bottle of nonaspirin painkillers in her toilet kit and a headache that needed at least three of the caplets. But nothing to wash them down with.

She ran the water in the bathroom sink, remembering Stan's warning. Drink only bottled water.

She needed those pills, but she needed whatever lousy,

stomach-turning, intestine-infesting bacteria that was in that water even less.

Resigned to her fate, she put her boots and her flack jacket back on then headed back down to the restaurant. There was bottled water there, free for the taking. Her fault completely for not thinking to bring a bottle up with her after her dinner with Mike Muldoon.

Mike Muldoon, who had kissed her good night.

She grabbed several bottles of water, then headed up the stairs and back across the lobby, trying not to think of Muldoon or Stan.

Except there he was. Right in front of her. Stan Wolchonok. Her personal hero.

He was sleeping on a beat-up couch in the hotel lobby, his hands tucked up in his armpits because the night air had a sudden sharp coolness to it.

Teri stood and watched him, afraid to leave him there to catch a chill, afraid to wake him. If she woke him, he'd just find something else urgent that had to be done before they all met at the heliport at 0230. No, it was far better to let him sleep.

She went to the front desk. But the drowsy clerk didn't speak much English, and she didn't know how to say *blanket* in Kazbekistani. So she just went up to her room and took the blanket off her bed.

When she got back to the lobby, Stan hadn't moved an inch. She covered him carefully, silently, resisting the temptation to lean down and kiss his forehead or touch the softness of his hair.

She stood there for a moment, allowing herself a small fantasy. He would open his eyes and smile at her. She'd need to do no more than hold out her hand for him, and he'd follow her upstairs, to her room. . . .

But he didn't wake up, and she went back to her room alone and fell into a deep, dreamless sleep, her headache forgotten.

The door to room 812 swung open, even before Alyssa had a chance to knock.

And then there he was. Sam Starrett. Long hair down around his shoulders. Five o'clock shadow on his lean face. Neon blue eyes. Long legs and broad shoulders.

She'd pulled him out of bed. She could see it, rumpled behind him. He'd attempted to pull up the bedspread, same as he'd attempted to put on a T-shirt. Both attempts were pretty laughable.

His shirt was inside out.

But even with the seams of his shirt showing, with the ratty shorts he was wearing, with that almost-but-not-quite beard on his face and the slight red of fatigue rimming his eyes, he was still the most physically attractive man Alyssa had ever met.

He stepped back to let her in, and she moved past him, aware of how good he smelled, aware of how easy it would be just to reach for him and . . .

He closed the door, still not saying a word, just looking at her with those eyes.

He'd kissed her just a few hours ago, down by the swimming pool. Then, she'd run away. Now she couldn't wait for him to kiss her again. Funny what a few glasses of the local spirits could do to even the most steadfast resolve.

Only Sam didn't kiss her, didn't move, didn't even speak. He just watched her, almost warily.

So Alyssa did it. She dropped her fanny pack on the floor and reached for him.

And *she* kissed *him*.

At first it was like kissing a statue. He didn't move, didn't respond. But then he exploded, yanking her hard against him, forcefully deepening the kiss as she clung to him, his tongue sweeping into her mouth.

Yes. *Yes.* This was what she wanted.

His hands were rough against her breasts, against her rear end, and she could feel him, hard and hot beneath his shorts as he pressed himself against her. She opened to him, wanting him now, right *now*. Quick, get rid of their clothes. . . .

But just as quickly as he'd started kissing her, he pushed her away. "I thought you came here to talk."

She was breathing hard—he was, too. He didn't want to

talk any more than she did. She took a step toward him. "Sam—"

She was right. He didn't back away. He kissed her again, just as fiercely as before. She slid her hands up beneath the edge of his shirt, touching the smoothness of his back, angling her head so he could kiss her deeper, deeper, and he groaned.

But again he pushed her away. "Jesus, I'm going to get drunk myself, just from kissing you. You taste like a fucking distillery. What the hell were you drinking?"

"Shots of the local moonshine," she admitted. "It was stronger than I thought. But Ian from the SAS started making cracks about Americans not being able to hold their liquor and—"

"You can't hold your liquor worth shit," Sam told her. "All you did was prove them right."

She didn't want to talk. She didn't want him angry with her. She wanted him gentle—the way he'd been on the phone. Or she wanted him laughing. Naked and laughing and in her arms. She took a step toward him but this time he took a step back, reaching up to run his hands through his hair, his movement jerky with anger.

"So here you are. Shit-faced and in my room again," he said. "What's that about, Alyssa? Do you really have to get trashed to be with me?"

She took a step toward him, and again he took a step back. He was serious. He wasn't going to let her touch him until she answered his question.

So she answered it. Honestly. "Unless I've been drinking, I can't . . ." Alyssa struggled with the words, suddenly wanting him to understand. "I can't admit—to myself—that I want you."

She'd taken that first drink tonight, knowing full well that she could end up right here. *Hoping* that she'd end up right here.

When Sam had kissed her by the swimming pool, when he'd asked her to go to his room in that low voice roughened with desire, she'd been scared out of her mind. She'd wanted him, too. Desperately. But if she'd gone with him then—cold sober—she would have had to acknowledge everything she was feeling.

Alyssa searched his eyes, praying she'd see him soften, but again he was like a statue. Hard and cold and unrelenting.

Uncertainty hit her. After the way he'd kissed her by the pool, she hadn't considered that he might change his mind. That he might not want her here tonight.

But she'd said some harsh things to him. *I don't even like you.*

She nervously wet her lips. "Do you want me to go?"

Did he want her to go?

No. There was no fucking way Sam was letting Alyssa walk away from him. He'd take her however he damn well could get her. So what if she was drunk. So what if most men—honorable men—would walk her back to her room and gently put her to bed, alone, because they wouldn't want to take advantage of her in this condition.

He'd taken advantage of her before. Why the hell should he stop now?

Besides, he wanted her too much. There was just no fucking way she was leaving here, not after she'd told him that she wanted him, too.

But, shit, he was angry. At her, at himself, at the world.

Three steps brought him threateningly close to her.

There was a flare of surprise, of uncertainty—and Jesus—of hope in her eyes.

So he pulled her toward him harder than he should have, and kissed her, harder than he should have, too. But she melted in his arms, molded herself to him, as if she wanted whatever he could give her and would still be ready to beg for more.

So he kissed her harder, pushing her so that her back bumped the wall with no small amount of force. He yanked her shirt up and over her head and unfastened her pants, all the while still kissing her.

Still being kissed by her. She was kissing him as if she'd been starved without his mouth to feast on.

Dammit, it felt too real. Too much like a reunion with a real lover, not just someone who wanted to fuck him only when she was drunk enough not to care.

Anger burned in his stomach. Tomorrow she would wake up, and this would have turned into another bad idea. Another lousy mistake. And she'd leave him. Again. Raw and bleeding and alone.

Again.

But it wasn't tomorrow yet.

He roughly pushed his hand down her pants, down inside her panties, and then, God, he was inside of her.

She made a sound that might've been pain, and he started to pull back, angrier than ever at himself. What the hell was he trying to do? Did he *want* to hurt her?

But she caught his hand and, looking into his eyes, she pushed him even more deeply into her.

That sound had been pleasure. She was slick and wet and completely ready for him.

She gazed up at him as she unfastened his shorts, as she, too, reached down into his briefs and touched him. It felt so good, he almost started to cry.

"Please," she breathed. "Sam, I need you so badly."

Need.

He knew all about need.

He moved fast then, pushing down her pants, pulling them off her long, perfect legs. He tried to unfasten her bra, but got distracted by her breasts, pushing away the stretch lace so he could taste her, loving the way the tautness of her nipples rasped against his tongue.

She climbed on top of him, her arms around his neck, her legs around his waist and—

"Whoa." He held her perfect derriere with both hands to keep her from pushing him hard and deep inside of her.

But she was ahead of him. She had a condom already open in her hands.

"Sorry," she said, as she reached between them to cover him. "I meant to do this first. You make it hard for me to think straight."

No, it was the fifteen shots of the local rotgut that made it hard for her to think straight. But apparently it hadn't made her forget to grab a condom on her way up to his room.

Or maybe she'd brought it with her when she'd left her room to meet Rob Pierce for dinner.

The thought made him crazy.

Jesus, he had to stop thinking. He had to lose the jealousy, the gut-churning anger. He had to just feel. Experience. Enjoy this for what it was—not for what it couldn't be.

It might well be another six months before he had this chance again. And that was thinking optimistically. It might never happen again.

So he slowed himself down and watched Alyssa's face as she finished covering him with the condom, as she looked up at him with those sea green eyes and smiled.

That almost-shy smile was the one from his dreams. It was the one she gave him before she kissed him and told him that she loved him.

But that wasn't going to happen here. She didn't even *like* him. She'd made that more than clear. This was pure sex for her.

Sam couldn't smile back at her. He was probably never going to smile again. But he held her gaze and slowly pushed himself inside of her, pushed himself home.

She . . .

Don't think, you stupid shit! Just *feel*.

Was . . .

Bring it down to pure pleasure. Sensation. Alyssa surrounding him with her sweet heat. Alyssa's mouth there to kiss as he slowly pulled out of her, slowly thrust back in. Pure sex.

What . . .

The bite of alcohol blended with the sweet, familiar taste of Alyssa, as if he were having an exotic bar drink. An intake of breath. Her legs, tight around him. Smooth skin beneath his hands. A ragged exhale.

He'd . . .

"Oh, Sam," she breathed, and he couldn't keep himself from thinking anymore.

She was what he'd been missing all those months.

It wasn't just great sex that he'd been longing for, as much as he'd tried to tell himself otherwise. It was Alyssa. Her voice in his ear. Her smile lighting up his world. Her take no shit, take no prisoners attitude. Her ability to take what he dished out and give it back to him in large quantities.

He didn't just want her, he loved her. And he didn't just love her, he liked her. The world was fifty-two thousand times a better, more interesting, more exciting place to be when he was with her. And that was when they *weren't* having sex.

"Please," she said. "Oh, please . . ."

He knew what she wanted, knew she liked sex hard and fast, but he didn't change his rhythm. He wasn't in control of very much here, but he *was* in control of that. And he was damned if he was going to give up what could well be the only opportunity he'd ever get to tell her that he loved her.

To anyone looking in from outside, it might seem as if he was nailing her. With her back to the wall, his shorts around his ankles, they were the very definition of carnal lust and pure desire.

But he'd slowed them down. He kissed her tenderly, thoroughly, taking his time. From the outside, it might look like pure sex, but god damn it, in reality, he was making love to her.

He pulled back from the sweetness of her mouth, willing her to look at him, to meet his eyes as he slowly pushed himself impossibly deep inside of her, as he slowly drew himself out.

"Alyssa."

She opened eyes that were glazed and heavy lidded with pleasure. "You're killing me," she breathed. "I'm going to die, this is so good."

Her soft words combined with her soft body pushed him closer to the edge. He didn't know what gave him away, but he could see in her eyes that she knew damn well what she did to him.

She started to close her eyes as he began the slow slide back. Shifting all of her weight to his left arm, he reached between them and touched her, gently at first, excruciatingly lightly. He knew just where to touch her. He remembered.

Even if he lived to be four hundred, that was something he would never forget.

"Alyssa, look at me," he commanded.

She was seconds from climaxing—he was, too. When it happened, he wanted to be right there, watching her face, gazing into her eyes. And he wanted her to do the same, to see him come, to see the love in his eyes, love that he wouldn't be able to hide while his body shook and his world blew apart.

Because there was no way he could ever say the words aloud. *I love you.* Yeah, right.

Courage wasn't usually something he lacked, but he didn't have even half the courage he needed to do that.

"Sam—"

She exploded around him, and he hung on for what seemed like forever, desperately fighting his own release until her eyelids fluttered, until she was coming back to earth.

"Look at me," he growled through clenched teeth.

The instant she did, the instant her eyes met his again, he came with a rush of pleasure that was blindingly intense. It was physical pleasure and emotion intertwined, each heightening the other so much that death seemed a real possibility. How could he feel this and continue to breathe? Still, he forced his eyes open, holding her gaze.

Then, Jesus, there they were. Face-to-face. With their eyes wide open. Both spent and breathing hard.

The silence was terrifying, so Sam said the first thing that popped into his head. The first thing that wasn't a declaration of undying love, that was. "Well, happy fucking birthday to me."

Surprise and confusion flitted across her beautiful face. "It's your birthday?"

"No, but it should be. It sure as hell feels like it."

She nodded. "Happy birthday to me, too."

Still looking into his eyes, she smiled.

Sam somehow managed to smile, too. And he kissed her. Because he knew that tonight wasn't over. Not yet, anyway.

Sixteen

GINA WAS GETTING frustrated. "It just doesn't make sense." She could hear an echo of Max's warning. Whatever you do, don't insult them. Don't make them angry. Don't give them any excuses to lash out at you.

But Bob the terrorist wasn't insulted. He smiled. Shrugged. He looked exactly like the guys who came to her dorm room to hang out, maybe listen to music. Easygoing. Too cool to get angry about anything.

"Not much in this life makes sense," he pointed out.

She tried another tack. "What could it hurt," she asked, "to let the women and children off the plane?"

She was holding the radio microphone on her lap, and the send button was pressed. Somewhere, in one of those ugly buildings that she could see out the windows, Max was listening to every word they said.

Bob scratched his neck. Yawned. Gestured to her bare legs. "Do you know the police would arrest you for wearing that in my town?" His smile seemed apologetic. "That's if the . . ." He muttered something in his own language, searching for the word. "People," he said. "The regular people, not the army or the police—"

"Civilians?" she offered.

"Yes." He gave her a brilliant smile. "Thank you. Civilians." He pronounced it with four distinct syllables. "That's if the civilians didn't beat you to death, first."

Nice.

"Well, these shorts are acceptable in America," she told him. "They're even considered conservative."

"I know what's acceptable in America. I watch TV. I watch *Dawson's Creek* and *Buffy*. I watched *Survivor* and MTV."

Gina couldn't believe it. "They have MTV in Kazbekistan? Where women are killed for wearing shorts in public?"

"Of course not," he said. "But I have some friends who have access to a satellite dish. We watch what we want. Purely in an attempt to understand the evils of Western thinking, of course."

He was making a joke, wasn't he? He'd all but winked. Gina laughed despite the tension that was increasing hourly throughout the plane. Snarly Al had been about ready to jump out of his own skin just a short time ago, and Bob had banished him from the cockpit.

Bob was official barometer of the hijackers. As long as he was relaxed, there was no reason to be more afraid than usual. And as long as Al stayed away from her, she was safe. If someone was going to hurt her, it wasn't going to be Bob.

He liked her. She knew he did. If they'd met on campus, they would have been friends.

"Why are you doing this?" she asked him. "How did you end up here? Holding a gun on innocent people. I don't understand."

He gazed at her silently for a moment, but then he shook his head. "You know, I watched *Survivor*."

"Yeah," Gina said impatiently. "You said." She didn't want to talk about TV shows. She wanted to get some of these people off the plane. "You and ninety percent of the free world's population."

"The whole time I watched it," he told her, "I was thinking, they wouldn't last a day here. Susan and Gervase and Richard. What they survived was nothing."

When he looked over at her, she could have sworn there were tears in his eyes.

Gina's heart lodged in her throat. What atrocities had he lived through? What horrors had he witnessed on a daily basis? She waited for him to say more, but he was silent.

"Please," she whispered. "Let the women and children off the plane. Let everyone off the plane. You've got me as a hostage—you don't need them."

Bob gazed at her, his expression unreadable.

But then the radio squealed, and she quickly released the talk button on the microphone.

And Max's voice came over the speaker, strong and clear. "Flight 232, come in. Over."

Bob wiped his eyes. Squared his shoulders. "Ask him if our demands are being met," he instructed her.

Crap, she had been on the verge of some kind of break-through with him. She knew it. And yet she knew why Max had interrupted them. Never offer anything that you aren't immediately prepared to deliver. And never make it personal.

Gina thumbed the mike. "Bob would like to know the status of their demands, please. Over."

"The senator—your father—is in a meeting with the presi-dent," Max said. She knew it was total bullshit. The United States didn't negotiate with terrorists. The end. This guy they wanted released from prison? He wasn't going anywhere. Not a chance. The senator could meet with the man in the moon and it wouldn't change a thing.

"Bob," Max spoke directly to the hijacker. "It's time for a good faith gesture. Something big, something generous. Something that will tell the U.S. government that you're se-rious about keeping the people on that plane safe and alive. Something like—send Karen off the plane. Let her walk off, Bob. Let her just walk away. That'll send a positive message, I guarantee it. Over."

"Ask him if he thinks we're stupid, Karen," Bob countered.

"Max," Gina said. "You don't think Bob is stupid, do you? Over."

What was Max doing? He'd heard her conversation with Bob, heard her connect with him. He knew the hijacker was vulnerable right now because of that connection. She knew Max knew it—he'd taught it to her himself—told her all about negotiating with someone who was under stress—just hours ago. And yet he was trying to use this opportunity to get Gina free. Just Gina, no one else.

He must really think she was going to be killed. And soon.

"Why don't you want to release her?" Max asked. "Be-cause she's the senator's daughter? Over."

Gina looked at Bob, who nodded. "Yes. Over."

"You want an important hostage?" Max asked. "You can have an important hostage. You can have *me*. I'm one of the United States' top negotiators, Bob. There are a lot of people who would be having heart attacks if they knew I was offering to put myself in your hands. But I am offering. She comes off, I'll come on. Let's do it. Right now. I'm walking out of terminal A, heading right for you, Bob. So let's do it. Send her off the plane. Over."

Bob scrambled for the window. Gina looked, too, out into the night.

And then she could see him. Max. A distant, shadowy figure backlit by the lights from the terminal. For the first time, he was more than just a disembodied voice. He was a real man, and he was walking toward them. Ready to trade himself for her. She didn't know whether to laugh or cry.

"Tell him to stop," Bob ordered.

"Max, stop. Please."

The distant figure stopped moving. He raised what had to be some kind of wireless walkie-talkie to his mouth. "Come on, Bob. Doing this will show your willingness to work toward mutual satisfaction. It's a goodwill gesture, *and* it puts you into an even better bargaining position. You are not losing here. Over."

"Tell him no," Bob said. "Tell him he's the one who needs to make a goodwill gesture. Tell him meeting the first of our demands and freeing our leader from prison is the kind of goodwill we're looking for."

Gina took a deep breath and gave it another try. "It doesn't have to be me going off the plane," she told Bob. "Freeing the women and children would be a gesture of—"

He turned to her swiftly, his voice sharp, his face suddenly angry. "I said *no*."

For a moment, Gina was certain he was going to hit her. Right in the face with the butt of his gun.

"Tell him if he comes any closer," he said, "we'll shoot him and then we'll shoot you."

That was no idle threat. Gina keyed the microphone. "Max, go back inside. Now."

* * *

Stan woke up right before his watch alarm went off.

He wasn't certain if it was his internal alarm clock that was so accurate or if his watch made some kind of small, almost indiscernible noise or click—something that he'd learned to listen for in his sleep—right before it beeped.

He sat up, switching it off and rubbing his stiff neck, momentarily surprised to find himself on a couch in the hotel lobby. But then he remembered stopping to sit because he was too exhausted and too much of a pouty baby to come face-to-face with Mike Muldoon right after he'd seen the ensign kissing Teri Howe.

Yeah, he remembered that a little too well.

What he *didn't* remember was this blanket. It was chilly tonight—the desert effect—and he'd have had a whole lot more than a stiff neck without it.

Who the hell had gone to the trouble to cover him?

He caught a whiff of a familiar scent, and he brought the blanket to his nose. It smelled like . . .

No. That was crazy. Besides, he'd seen Teri Howe go up to her room. She'd looked tired, not as if she were about to start wandering the hotel lobby, handing out blankets to sleeping SEALs.

But he smelled it again. No, he definitely wasn't imagining it. It smelled like Teri's hair. As crazy as it seemed, he would bet his life that she'd used this very blanket in the not-too-distant past.

Maybe she'd been too tired to sleep. He knew all about that—he'd been there too many times to count.

Maybe she'd been too tired to sleep, so she'd left her room, looking for him.

Oh, yeah, right. That must be it.

Except, *damn,* maybe that *was* it. Maybe she'd wanted to talk more about everything she'd told him that afternoon. He still couldn't believe she'd never told anyone—that she'd been carrying that terrible secret around inside of her since she was eight years old.

That was a real possibility. Maybe she'd come looking for

him to tell him something else that she'd remembered or, Christ, maybe just to get a little comfort after stirring up the past, and what had he done? He'd been unavailable. He'd been unconscious and drooling on this sofa.

Way to go, Stanley.

He took the blanket with him and headed up to his room. He'd return it to her later. With an apology.

Right now he had just enough time to grab a shower and some food before he had to report to the roof.

Sam Starrett slapped the off button on the clock radio before it woke Alyssa.

0200. He had just enough time to shower and get something to eat before he had to report to the roof.

He'd slept maybe two hours, max. Yet he felt far more refreshed, far more energized than he had in months.

Because Alyssa was in his bed.

She stirred, burrowing against him, all smooth, warm skin and soft breasts and taut thighs. He kissed her—how could he not?—and she roused.

"Mmmm," she said, smiling at him sleepily. Reaching down between them, she found him hard again—big surprise. She drew her leg up over his hip, pulling him toward her as she moved closer, too.

Damn, the woman was insatiable. But then again, he couldn't get enough of her either.

He was starting to hope that she would still want him, come the morning. That she'd wake up just like this—smiling and still hot for him.

Sam looked at the clock: 0202. He could get dressed in a minute. Another minute to take a leak and splash cold water on his face. And if he ran all the way, he could get to the roof in two minutes. That left twenty-four.

He grabbed a condom from the pile Alyssa had put on the bedside table and covered himself. Showers were overrated anyway. And he could always call WildCard—his friend once again—and ask him to bring something to eat and lots of coffee for the helo ride.

Alyssa was barely awake but waiting for him, warm and wet from wanting him—even in her sleep. He slipped into her tight heat and she clung to him, moaning his name.

Oh yeah, showers were way overrated.

By 0215 Teri had run the helo's checklist. She was ready to fly.

Standing on the roof was no longer as hazardous as it had been when they'd first arrived in this city. Marines were posted everywhere, their presence obvious in the buildings that surrounded the hotel. Still, she was more comfortable waiting just inside the door.

At 0216 there were footsteps heading up the stairs. It was Stan. Had to be. No one else walked like that, with such steady confidence.

"Hey," he said, when he caught sight of her. It was hard to tell if he looked less tired than last night—he had black greasepaint smeared on his face.

"Hi, Stan," she said, using the opportunity to practice saying his name.

"Aren't you sorry you volunteered for this now? This is the time of night I always regret that I didn't take my mother's advice to get a job as a plumber."

She laughed at that. "You do not."

He didn't even hesitate. "You're right, I don't. Sleep okay?"

"Yeah. Thanks." Actually, she'd slept better than she had in a long time.

"Really?" he said. "No nocturnal wanderings?"

He was standing right beside her now, and for half an instant, she could have sworn he was leaning closer to smell her still damp hair.

"It *was* you," he said. "I thought so. The blanket," he explained. "It smelled like . . . well, like you."

He *had* been smelling her hair.

Teri didn't know what to say. "Should I apologize?" she asked. "I guess it really depends on whether the next thing you say is *Teri, you smell great,* or *Teri, you smell like a barnyard.*"

He laughed. "Trust me, you smell great." He caught himself and began to backpedal. "I don't mean that with anything other than the utmost respect and—"

"Stop." Teri let her annoyance show. "I know how you meant it." As a friend. As in no, she didn't smell like a barnyard, so yes, that meant, by default, that she smelled great. God forbid he slip and let himself be attracted to her.

He surprised her by holding her gaze. "Okay," he said. "Good. This isn't the time or place to talk about this, but after what you told me yesterday, you'll forgive me if I bend over backward a little to reestablish whatever amount of trust I lost when—"

"How could you think I don't trust you?" she asked. "After what I told you?"

His gaze softened. "You know, I thought about it all night. What you told me. Christ, I even dreamed about it. I just keep picturing the way you must've looked when you were eight and I . . ." He shook his head, the muscle jumping in the side of his jaw. "Teri, God help me, I still want to hunt this son of a bitch down and kill him. I have a feeling I'm going to be ninety, and I'll think about him, and I'll *still* want to find him and tear out his throat with my bare hands."

Teri didn't let herself think. She just reached for him, and God, he didn't push her away. He just held her. She wasn't quite sure who was comforting whom.

"I'm so sorry," she whispered.

"For who?" Stan asked with a forced-sounding laugh. "Him or me?"

He was trying to keep this from being too heavy, too intense.

She didn't feel like answering. She didn't feel like doing much of anything—besides standing there in the warm circle of Stan's arms.

God, she was pathetic. One friendly, comforting hug, and she was ready to melt. Mike Muldoon had *kissed* her last night, and it hadn't made her heart race even a quarter of the way it did when Stan so much as *looked* at her.

What would Stan say if she asked him to have breakfast with her? When the sun came up and they returned to the hotel after running the drill on the practice plane a few million times? What would he do if that breakfast was a private one, in her hotel room with room service and the curtains drawn and the bed right there—the centerpiece of the room.

He would eat his eggs, be polite and gentle as he explained why the two of them getting naked would be a particularly bad idea.

And then he'd try to set her up with Muldoon again.

God, maybe she should just do it. Get with Mike Muldoon. He seemed to want her. *Stan* sure wanted them together, that was clear. She wanted Stan, she really did, but if she couldn't have him, Muldoon was certainly a good second choice. He was a nice enough guy. And he seemed to have no problem talking about one of her favorite subjects—Stan.

"If you ever need to talk," Stan told her now, "just wake me, okay? I woke up with your blanket on me, and I immediately pictured you wandering the lobby all night long, dying for someone to talk to, while I snored."

"You weren't snoring. And I was in the lobby for only a few minutes."

"I'm serious," Stan said, pulling back to look at her. "Day or night, Teri. If you need someone . . ."

Gently he extracted himself even further from her arms, and she realized someone was coming up the stairs. Lots of someones. It was 0225 and the team was finally on its way.

"Did I thank you yet?" Stan asked her, his voice low. "For the blanket?"

She shook her head, wishing he hadn't let go of her so soon. Wishing he hadn't let go of her at all.

"Thanks," he said. "Really. I don't think anyone's tucked me in like that since my mother died."

Great, now she reminded him of his mother.

"Yo, Senior Chief!" It was Mark Jenkins, far too enthusiastic than he had a right to be, considering the hour.

Cosmo, Silverman, Jefferson, O'Leary, and Jay Lopez were with him, all considerably less thrilled. WildCard was next, dragging himself up the stairs, looking like death warmed over—which was pretty standard for him any time of day, come to think of it.

Mike Muldoon was last and then they were all there—except they weren't. Stan noticed the same time she did.

"Where's Starrett?"

Their team leader was missing. Sam Starrett, usually fifteen minutes early and tapping his foot for the others to show, had yet to arrive.

They heard him before they saw him, with the slam of a door as it was pushed open echoing in the stairwell. Then pounding feet—he must've been taking the stairs two at a time and running full speed.

"Everyone here?" he asked, when he was still a half flight away.

Teri stared. They *all* stared.

His was hair was down around his shoulders and he was only half dressed. He was barefoot, carrying his boots and socks, with his shirt unbuttoned and his belt undone.

Starrett glanced at his watch. "Oh-two-thirty," he said. "On the nose. Let's do it. Let's go."

Helga awoke to the sound of someone running.

Hard and fast down a long length of something—a hallway.

It was a sound that signaled danger, the need for flight, and she was up and out of her bed, heart pounding, before she realized she wasn't sleeping in the Gunvalds' kitchen, on a pallet that Herr Gunvald had made, between her mother and father.

There was a crash—the sound of a door being smashed open, and she jumped, nearly diving beneath the bed.

But it wasn't her door being forced. There were no voices shouting in harsh German, no dogs barking, no more noise at all.

Of course not. She wasn't ten years old. She was a grown woman. No, she was an *old* woman.

And she was in a hotel room, with generic hotel furnishings and curtains. Generic and shabby. She'd come down in the world from . . . from . . .

From she didn't know where. She didn't even know if it was safe to turn on the light—if she were someplace where there was a nightly blackout to prevent bombers in the skies overhead from targeting them here below.

She listened hard, but she could hear nothing. No sound of distant fighting. No drone of aircraft.

Nothing but the ticking of the wind-up alarm clock she'd brought and set next to the electric clock radio on the hotel bedside table—so that she'd be sure to wake up even if the power went out.

There were Post-it notes all over the room. They were stuck on every available surface. On the dresser, on the bedside table, on the lamp next to the bed, on the light switch, on the door.

Helga could see light through the crack under the door to the hallway. Keeping the chain on, she opened the door. Peeled one of the sticky notes that was posted right there by the lock and angled it to the light.

Don't leave without your room key, notepad, and purse.

She plucked the note from the light switch by the door. It, too, was written in her own neat handwriting.

It's safe to turn on the lights.

That was good to know. Helga closed the door and flipped the switch.

Welcome to Kazbekistan, said another. Thank you. Maybe. She hoped she wasn't here on her vacation. Kazbekistan wasn't the kind of country one went to relax.

World Airlines Flight 232 has been hijacked by terrorists. Possible GIK connections? 120 passengers on board. Oh, dear. And oh, yes. She remembered. She and Des had come here to make the terrorists believe there was hope of negotiating a settlement. But there wasn't. U.S. Navy SEALs were preparing—probably right now—to take down the plane, although she couldn't for the life of her remember the name of the CO or even the number of the SEAL Team. It wasn't Six, was it?

List of major players in notepad. Thank you, dear self. That would help.

It would almost be funny if it weren't so damned pathetic. Clearly she'd been having these little lapses in memory with some frequency, hence all the Post-it notes to aid her in moments just like this one.

She climbed back in bed.

Ah, here was an interesting one, right on the headboard. *Senior Chief Stanley Wolchonock is Marte Gunvald's son.*

If she closed her eyes and focused, she could picture him. Light hair, broad shoulders, craggy features. Not exactly handsome, but not exactly *not*. He didn't smile all that often, but when he did, his face became wonderfully warm and tremendously appealing.

And he had eyes just like Annebet's.

Helga's notepad was right there on the bedside table, and Annebet's name seemed to jump out at her from the page.

"Annebet Gunvald," she read, also in her own familiar hand. "Went to America after the war. Became pediatrician, died two years ago. Never married."

Stanley had told her this late this afternoon. She remembered that now.

Annebet had never married.

Again.

She'd married once, though. To Helga's brother, Hershel. Helga had attended the ceremony.

It had been a strange one, although possibly the nicest Helga had ever witnessed, both before and after. The rabbi— no doubt heeding Poppi's grim wishes—claimed he couldn't find the time to marry Hershel and Annebet until the following spring. And the pastor of the Gunvalds' church had been ready to perform the ceremony right then and there, until he heard Hershel's name. Then, suddenly, he was also unavailable for a great many months. Anti-Semitic, Annebet had muttered angrily, but Hershel had merely moved on to the next possibility. But every church they approached, they were turned away.

The justice of the peace had been rounded up with a group of known communists five months earlier. No one had heard from him in nearly that long.

By then it was after midnight. Annebet, in true fashion, suggested she and Hershel simply jump over a broom—the way she'd read that slaves had done in the 1800s in America, when they wanted to be married. What did it matter what the government thought—since their government was currently based on a weird amalgamation of Danish beliefs and harsher Nazi rules. What did it matter what *any*one thought, as long as Annebet and Hershel believed they were married?

In frustration, Hershel called upon a friend, a woman, a divinity student despite the fact that women were not permitted to be clergy.

This girl—a little slip of a thing—performed the ceremony. It was a beautiful mix of both Jewish and Christian traditions, ending with a crushed glass *and* a leap over a broom.

It satisfied the elder Gunvalds, as well. They welcomed Hershel into their home with open arms.

Helga's parents, however, were livid when they found out.

"It's not legal," Poppi stormed. "They are not legally wed!"

Hershel and Annebet had gotten a tiny, drafty, one-room apartment in the city. They'd lived there together for a week, and Helga had never seen Hershel happier.

They'd returned to the Gunvalds to pick up the rest of Annebet's clothes, and somehow the Rosens had found out that they would be there.

Helga's parents had shown up in the horse-drawn wagon from the store—gasoline being so scarce by the summer of '43 that few besides the Germans could drive.

Helga and Marte had watched from the barn's hayloft as their two fathers met, face-to-face, looking as if they were about to have a tug-of-war with Hershel in the Gunvalds' yard. Or at least Poppi had looked that way. Herr Gunvald was calm. He was smiling, even.

Helga's mother had sat stiff-backed on the wagon, and Inge Gunvald stood on the porch, wisely holding Annebet back, keeping her from the fray.

"How could you condone such a thing?" Poppi asked Herr Gunvald.

The bigger man smiled again. "Such a thing as love, you mean? Have you even stopped to look at them when they're together—your son and my daughter?"

Hershel refused to let his father speak over him, ignoring him as if he were nothing more then a naughty child.

"This is not your business anymore," he told Poppi. "You can't kick me out of your house and then pretend you have any say in my life."

"This is killing your mother." Poppi spoke directly to him for the first time. "It's not too late to forsake this folly and come home."

Hershel laughed. "What, you mean desert my wife and the child she might already be carrying?"

In the loft, Marte turned to Helga, glee lighting her face. "They're going to have a baby! We're going to be aunts!"

"Dear God in heaven," Poppi's face turned from pink to purple. "You got the girl pregnant. *That's* what this is about."

Hershel got very quiet. "That's not what I said. If you bothered to listen—"

Poppi turned to Herr Gunvald. "How much?"

Herr Gunvald shook his head and glanced back at his wife in confusion, as if she might know what Poppi had meant. She didn't. "How much what?"

"Money," Poppi said.

Out of all of them, it was only Hershel who seemed to understand. "Stop," he ordered his father. "Don't say another word."

But Poppi was furious. He wasn't thinking at all—that was the excuse Helga gave him. It was the only way she could keep from hating him for what he'd then said.

"How much money do you want," he asked Annebet's father, "to make this problem—the girl and the baby—go away?"

Herr Gunvald's reaction was to laugh in disbelief.

Annebet was not quite so easily amused. "How dare you!" She escaped her mother's grasp and launched herself toward Poppi. Or maybe Fru Gunvald pushed her into the yard. She looked pretty angry, too.

"How *dare* you come here and say such things!" Annebet was outraged. "You . . . you . . ."

"Vile Jew?" Wilhelm Gruber suggested from the gate.

Helga hadn't seen him approach, and they all turned, almost as one, to stare at the German soldier.

He held his gun loosely in his hands, not over his shoulder, his position definitely threatening.

Fru Rosen was still sitting in the carriage, on the same side of the gate as Gruber, within a few short feet of the man. The way he was holding his gun, the barrel was pointing directly at her. She looked as if she were about to faint.

Annebet alone had the presence of mind to cross the yard to her. "Get your ugly thoughts and your ugly face away from my parents' house!" she said, leveling her anger at Gruber as she went past him. "Fru Rosen, won't you come inside for a cup of tea? You must be thirsty after your ride over here."

It was absurd, the ride over had been a five-minute nothing. But Annebet practically lifted her new mother-in-law out of the wagon and nearly carried her past Gruber and up the path, away from him.

Fru Gunvald took over, bringing Helga's mother into the house. It wasn't really that much safer, but it had the illusion of being so.

Annebet turned back to Wilhelm Gruber. "Leave. Now!"

Her father stepped up beside her, as if creating a wall between Gruber and the Rosens. It was a very big, very strong, very angry wall.

"There was a commotion," Gruber explained, "and I came to investigate. In Germany, nine times out of ten, if there are angry voices, there are Jews involved."

"He's furious," Marte whispered to Helga, "at Annebet for marrying Hershel. He's even more furious at Hershel."

"In Germany, it's hard for Jewish civilians *not* to be involved when thugs break the windows of their stores or attack them on the streets," Annebet countered hotly.

Gruber addressed Herr Gunvald, Aryan man to Aryan man. "You have to admit, your troubles didn't start until she married that kike."

Herr Gunvald got large. "We don't use that kind of language here. We don't believe in Dark Age thinking—that race or religion makes one man different from another. We don't believe in a God who commands us to destroy anyone and everyone who doesn't think the way we do. Before you Germans closed the borders, people came to Denmark for freedom of religion and we welcomed them. The Rosens are Danish citizens now and while you are in Denmark, when you are in *my* yard, you will address them with respect!"

"This *commotion* has nothing to do with anyone's belief in God," Annebet added. "It's about a father who doesn't realize his son has become a man with a will of his own."

"It's about a wealthy man who's forgotten that there's far more to make a man rich than money in the bank," Hershel said.

"Leave my yard," Herr Gunvald ordered Gruber sternly, "before I call the Danish police."

Gruber looked at Annebet, all of the fight and anger gone from his eyes, leaving only perplexed sorrow. "You could have had me," he said. "It won't be long until he's rounded up—him and the others. You have to know it's coming. So why would you choose him over me?"

"I love him," Annebet said.

"I love *you*," Gruber said, tears in his eyes.

"I'm sorry," Annebet whispered.

"And I'm sorry for you." With one last look at Hershel, Gruber turned and walked away.

For several long moments, no one moved, no one spoke.

Then Poppi started toward the wagon. "Get your mother," he commanded Hershel.

That was it. No words of apology. No mention of thanks. Helga burned with shame, fighting tears, while Poppi loaded her mother onto the wagon and they silently pulled away.

"Anna, I'm so sorry," she heard Hershel say to Annebet.

She pulled him into her arms, held him close. "It *is* coming, you know," she said. "God help us all."

And up in the loft, Marte put her arm, warm and heavy, around Helga's shoulders. "He'll come around," she whispered. "Your poppi. Right now he's scared. My father says he has every right to be frightened, but that he shouldn't be. Because we won't let them take you anywhere."

Helga looked into her best friend's fierce blue-green eyes.

"We won't," Marte whispered. "We won't."

Seventeen

THE SUN WAS just starting to come up as Sam Starrett dragged his tired ass back down the hotel corridor. Then there he was. Room 812.

He stood in the hallway, just staring at the numbers on the door, afraid to open the damn thing.

Now, *there* was some real irony. He'd spent the past long hours practicing opening a door to a hijacked airplane and going head-to-head with AK-47-wielding terrorists.

He was pretty much one hundred percent certain that there were no terrorists behind the door to his hotel room.

Only Alyssa Locke.

Of course, he'd rather face the wrath of a thousand religious zealots than deal with her anger as she realized he'd taken advantage of her again. He'd rather face those thousand zealots than live through the disappointment this morning was destined to bring.

Although maybe he could slip back into the room without waking her. Maybe he could shower off the dust and sweat of the past hours and climb back into bed, beside her.

It was that pathetic hope, that he could have even just another half hour—hell, he'd take fifteen minutes—with her sweet warmth next to him, that kept him from turning around and hiding in the hotel restaurant until he was certain she'd returned to her own room.

He unlocked the door silently, careful not to let the latch click.

The room was dim, most of the early morning light kept out by the heavy curtains.

Sam closed the door behind him just as silently as he'd opened it, setting his vest on the floor and letting his eyes adjust to the low levels of light.

The bed was in the shadows. If she was still here, she was silent and unmoving. Still sound asleep.

He took a step farther into the room.

And nearly jumped out of his skin as the bathroom door opened behind him.

"Jesus *Christ!*"

"Starrett! My God!" Her hair was wet from the shower, and she wore only a towel wrapped around her, held in place under her arms. She was awake, she was sober, and if her expression were any indication, she was already angry with him.

God *damn*, she looked good wearing only a towel. Sam wanted to touch her, to run his hands across her smooth shoulders and down the gracefully muscled contours of her arms. He wanted to unwind her from the towel so he could see not just the very tops of her breasts but her entire beautiful body. He wanted to kiss her, to make love to her, to fall asleep exhausted and satisfied beside her. He wanted to wake up to her smile every day for the rest of his life, like some stupid coffee commercial on TV.

He fucking wanted to marry her.

He almost kissed her. He almost figured what the hell. She was already mad, already getting ready to leave. How much worse could it be if he kissed her and dropped to his knees and started begging. *Don't leave, Lys. Please don't ever leave. . . .*

"What are you doing sneaking in here like that?" she asked sharply. "You nearly scared me to death."

"It's my fucking room," he said, and she flinched as if he'd hit her.

Jesus, what did she expect? That he wouldn't respond hostilely to her hostility? He sat down on the bed and started taking off his boots, praying that she would just throw on her clothes and leave before he did something really stupid. Like start to cry.

But she didn't pick up her clothes from where they'd

landed last night. She just stood there. As if she had something important to say.

And with the kind of realization that hit like a knife blade to the heart, Sam knew exactly what was coming. He fired one of his boots across the room. It smacked the wall with a bang and a shower of dirt.

"Don't worry, I won't tell a soul," he said flatly. "I remember the fucking drill, Alyssa. Last night never even happened as far as I'm concerned. Does that make you happy?"

"Ecstatic." She moved then. Picking up her pants and her bra. Her shirt. A pair of satin and lace panties that made him get hard just from remembering what they'd looked like on her.

She managed to gather her clothes with chilly dignity—how the hell did she do that while wearing only a towel?—and headed toward the bathroom.

"Make it snappy," Sam told her as he launched his second boot at the wall.

"Hey, Muldoon. Got a sec?"

Stan caught up with Mike Muldoon on the stairs heading down to the restaurant.

"Sure, Senior. What's up?"

First things first. "Good job tonight."

Muldoon smiled ruefully. "Yeah, well, I seem to have overcome my fear of female terrorists."

He'd successfully "killed" Teri Howe close to a dozen times in a row during the night's drill. And she'd been looking particularly adorable and feminine, wearing one of Stan's extra Navy-issue sweaters under her flack jacket to fight the chill. It had hung on her, nearly to her knees.

"If Teri ever decides to start her own terrorist cell, you'll be the man we'll call to hunt her down," Stan said with a grin.

"Yeah, right," Muldoon said. "She's a likely candidate for terrorist activity. She's got to be one of the nicest women I've ever met."

Nice? After having dinner with her two nights in a row, the best Muldoon could come up with to describe Teri Howe was *nice*? What the hell was wrong with him?

"How'd it go last night?" Stan asked, even though he knew damn well how it had gone. Muldoon had kissed Teri good night in the frickin' hotel lobby, where anyone could see them. No wonder she'd run away. Or maybe she hadn't run away. Maybe she'd intended for Muldoon to give chase.

But he hadn't.

Muldoon shrugged. "I don't know, Senior. She's, uh . . ."

Don't say *nice*.

"Great," he said instead. But *great* wasn't much better.

Teri Howe was poetry, she was song, she was sunshine. She was all those corny song lyrics Stan had always rolled his eyes over. She was amazing, astounding, spectacular, phenomenal. She was fabulous. Stunning. Wonderful. She wasn't merely *nice*, merely *great*. Come *on*, man.

Stan pulled Muldoon to the side to let O'Leary and Nilsson pass them on the stairs.

"But . . ." Muldoon was saying.

"But what?" Stan said in total disbelief after the two SEALs had gone out the door. "What's there to say *but* about? This woman is incredible. She's incomparable. I can guarantee it, Muldoon, you will never meet anyone like her again in your entire life."

Muldoon nodded. "Yeah. Yeah, I know. I'm . . . I just . . . You see, women come to *me*, Senior. I've never had to, you know, go after them."

"So?"

"So, she's not exactly jumping into my bed," Muldoon admitted. "I mean, last night, I kissed her, but she didn't invite me up. I mean, everywhere I go, women usually just, you know, invite me up. So then I go to their room or their apartment or their house, and they take off my clothes and I can pretty much handle it from there. But . . ."

The kid was serious. Women invited him home and then they took off his clothes. Of course he was serious. He was standing there with a body that made grown women get tongue-tied and a face that could've made a fortune in Hollywood, even when it was covered with muddy, sweated-through camouflage paint, the way it was right now.

Stan wasn't sure whether he wanted to laugh or cry. To hit the kid or high five him.

"I don't know how to do it this way," Muldoon continued. "I suck at this. I don't even think Teri's interested in me."

"Okay," Stan said, somehow managing to keep a completely straight face. "All right. Just relax. So you don't have much experience pursuing women. That's okay. I think most men would kill to be in your shoes, if you want to know the truth. But for right now, you just need . . . Okay. You need an operational plan. That's all you need. First thing you're going to do is find her and ask her to have lunch with you, provided, of course, that we're not called out between now and then."

Muldoon wasn't convinced, his handsome face dubious. "Senior, I don't—"

"Then," Stan bulldozed over him, "after lunch, you walk her back to her room. All the way, Muldoon. Right to her door. You don't give her a choice about it."

"But—"

"And you get inside her room by telling her that you're concerned for her safety, what with the explosions by the swimming pool and all. You just want to check to make sure everything's all right. That's how you get your ass in there."

Muldoon laughed in disbelief. "Does that really work?"

Stan's hair was matted with sweat and dust. Muldoon's was charmingly tousled. It would work for him.

"If she's interested, she'll let you in, yes. You've just got to remember—if she says no at any point, you turn around and you leave. You understand?"

"Well, yeah," Muldoon said, all injured blue eyes. "You don't think I'd . . . I mean, God, Senior Chief, it's not like I'd ever force myself on a woman. What kind of jerk do you think I am?"

"The kind of jerk who has no experience in inviting himself into a woman's room," Stan replied.

Muldoon laughed, but it was definitely halfhearted. "I'm not sure I can do this," he said. "I mean, Teri Howe? She's . . ."

"Great?" Stan volunteered.

"Yeah, but . . . I don't know, Senior. She's not a particularly good kisser so . . ."

* * *

They were talking about her.

She was the *not a particularly good kisser* that they were talking about.

At first Teri had refused to believe they were talking about her, when she'd started to go up the stairs that led from the restaurant to the lobby, cup of coffee and some kind of local Danish-type thing in hand. She'd thought she'd heard Stan and Mike Muldoon's voices.

She didn't really mean to eavesdrop.

Okay, that was a lie. She *did* mean to eavesdrop. She'd heard Stan asking, "How'd it go last night?" and she'd stopped walking.

O'Leary and Nilsson had gone past her, and she'd pretended to tie her boot laces. And then she'd stood there and eavesdropped shamelessly.

And she was *so* a great kisser. *Muldoon* was the one who needed work.

"What do you mean, she's not a great—?" Stan laughed. "How the fuck do you know, Muldoon? I saw you kiss her last night, and it was definitely uninspired on *your* end."

Stan had seen her last night. Kissing Mike Muldoon. Oh, God. But of course. He'd been in the lobby. He'd fallen asleep there.

"And if you tell me, jeez," Stan continued, imitating the younger man's voice, "you don't have much experience kissing women because all you have to do is lean toward them and *they're* the ones jamming their tongues down your throat . . . Holy Christ!"

"It's true!" Muldoon laughed, but it sounded defensive. "I can't help it if it's true! When I'm with a woman, I let her set the pace, the mood—it's all up to her. Is that so wrong?"

"No," Stan said. "No, it's great. It's . . . actually exactly what Teri needs right now."

What *Teri* needs . . . ? To use what appeared to be one of Stan's favorite expressions, how the fuck did *Stan* know what Teri needed?

"It's just, some women need . . . a little encouragement,"

Stan continued. "A little obvious pursuit. They need . . . Look, don't you ever picture her naked?"

Teri nearly spilled her coffee down the front of her shirt. *What?*

"I don't know," Muldoon said.

"How could you not know?" Stan countered with a laugh. "I mean, either you picture her naked or you don't, Mike. That's not a real tough question."

Teri couldn't believe what she was hearing.

"I do, but I don't want to admit it," Muldoon admitted. "It's not very nice to—"

"Are you a man?" Stan asked.

"Yes."

"Are you straight?"

"Well, *yeah*. Jeez—"

"Don't you find her attractive?"

"Of course. She's beautiful. And she's nice—"

"Fuck nice," Stan said. "The woman is fucking hot, Muldoon. There's not a single heterosexual man in the Troubleshooters Squad who hasn't pictured her naked. Well, okay, maybe Nilsson because he's a newlywed. But everyone else . . . And I'm not saying anyone should tell her this. She doesn't need to know. Because it's not a disrespectful thing. No one's undressing her with their eyes. At least they better not be. It's just, you know, you're a guy, you're daydreaming, and whoops, there she is. Naked."

"Senior, I think I'm too tired for this conversation right now."

"Give me just a few more minutes, Muldoon. Please."

Teri held her breath, about to bolt for the door.

Mike sighed. "All right."

"Look, sometimes that's what a woman needs," Stan said. "She needs to know that the guy *she's* attracted to is out there picturing her naked—you know, that he wants her, too. So that's what you do."

"You want me to picture her naked."

"For a genius, you're one hell of an idiot."

"Yeah, I'm kidding. I'm following you, Senior. I need to

let her know that I want her. I got it. Except . . . I mean, I *like* her and all. I like her an awful lot. It's just . . ."

"It's just what?" Stan was completely exasperated. "How could you not be head over heels in love with this woman? She's incredible, Muldoon. She's got a body to die for, a face like an angel. Her eyes are . . . Have you even looked into her eyes? She has eyes that make you just want to, I don't know, Christ, *die* for her if she asked you to."

Teri's heart was in her throat. The way Stan was talking, it sounded as if . . .

"I don't understand why the hell you are hesitating here," he continued. "Why are you not with her right now? What are you doing standing here talking to *me*? You should be outside her room this very instant, knocking on her door, asking if she needs help scrubbing her back while she's in the shower."

Silence.

"Is it okay if I get some coffee first?" Muldoon asked.

Stan said a string of words Teri had never heard quite in that order before.

And then he completely killed any hope that had started growing inside of her with his poetic description of her eyes. Then he delivered the final death blow to her already tattered pride.

"Mike. Please," he said. "I'm asking you to do me this favor. This girl—"

Girl. Oh, God, he called her a *girl*, and he was asking Muldoon to do him a *favor*.

"—needs someone like you in her life, someone willing to spend the extra effort both physically and emotionally to—"

Teri couldn't stand to listen to another second of this. Stan—the senior chief—was virtually begging Muldoon to be with Teri. To *be* with Teri. He was trying to talk Muldoon into being her boyfriend, into sleeping with her. As a favor to him.

God, did he really think she was that completely desperate? How hideously mortifying.

"Just ask her to lunch," Stan was saying. "Just start there and see where it goes. Okay?"

Teri ducked out the door and into the lower lobby, just outside the restaurant doors. She could hear Stan and Mike coming down the stairs.

Shit. She had to hide.

One look at her and Stan would know that she'd overheard all of that. And the only thing more mortifying than overhearing that conversation would be having Stan know that she'd overheard.

There was a ladies' room across the faded red carpeting, and Teri ran for it, bursting through the door.

It was like the rest of the hotel. Tacky and faded, with broken tile and stalls that had out-of-order signs taped to the them. The single fluorescent bulb that still worked flickered.

She counted to a hundred. Splashed water on her face. Counted to a hundred again.

She tried to drink her coffee, but her hands were shaking too badly.

Stan asked Mike Muldoon to do him a *favor*, no doubt to get her off his back. Except what had all that been last night before they'd flown out to the airfield? Night or day, he'd told her. She should come to him night or day—if she wanted to talk.

Apparently if she wanted anything else, she should go to Mike Muldoon, who would take care of her as a *favor* for the senior chief.

God damn it.

Teri stared at her face flickering palely in the cracked bathroom mirror, willing herself not to cry.

At least she wasn't throwing up.

Alyssa looked at herself in the mirror of Sam's bathroom. She actually had tears brimming in her eyes, caught on her eyelashes, ready to spill over the edge and down her cheeks.

How pathetic was that? How pathetic was *she*?

She wiped them away with the heel of her hand.

Look on the bright side. At least she wasn't throwing up and handcuffed—naked—to the asshole, the way she'd been the last time she'd spent the night with him.

This time, she was barely even hungover. Her head ached, but that was it.

Because, despite what Sam thought, she'd barely even been drunk last night.

Oh, she'd had a buzz on, that was for sure. She never would have had the courage—or the foolishness—to come to his room if she hadn't.

Alyssa hung her towel on the rack and put on her clothes, cursing herself out soundly all the while.

What was wrong with her? Why on God's green earth did she find herself so attracted to a man who didn't give a damn about her? Sam Starrett was selfish and rude—shockingly so at times. The mouth on that man should have been—alone—enough to keep her far away from him. Forget about the fact that he was infuriating and egotistical and overbearing.

He was also the best lover she'd ever had.

He was funny and capable of being incredibly, impossibly tender.

And the way he'd kissed her good-bye this morning, as if he loved her with all his heart and soul, still took her breath away.

But it didn't serve her well to remember that. What she should remember was the look on his face as he sat on his bed, taking off his boots. *It's my fucking room.* Like he was an eight-year-old with a trash mouth—yeah, he was about as attractive as that. *That's* what she should remember.

The heartless son of a bitch.

She opened the bathroom door, and Sam was standing there, holding her sandals. As if he wanted her to leave, fast. As if, now that it was morning, now that they were no longer going at it, he didn't want anything more to do with her.

Anger burned her throat, her eyes, her chest, but she said nothing. Anger was better than the hurt, than the self-disgust. She took her sandals from him silently and slipped them onto her feet.

He stood there watching her, big and grimy, his face smudged with the remains of camouflage paint, most of it sweated into a grayish mud. As she straightened back up, he cleared his throat. "So. If you ever want to do this again—"

Yeah, right. "I don't," she said coldly. "Trust me, I won't be back."

"Well, that's kind of what I thought last time, sweet thing, but—"

Sweet thing. He was purposely trying to get her angry. Purposely baiting her, the asshole. She kept her voice cool and controlled. "Believe me, next time I'll save myself the aggravation. I'll just hook up with Rob Pierce."

He took a step back as if she'd punched him in the stomach. Good. She was glad.

"Jesus," he said. "That's just great, Locke. That's just . . . fucking perfect. You do that, babe. A married man is just your speed." He turned and walked toward the window, standing there with his back to her, looking down through a crack in the curtains at the swimming pool below.

Rob Pierce was *married*? And what about "Don't do it, Alyssa. You'll feel awful in the morning"? Sam had sure changed his tune now that it was the morning.

Some of the hurt and misery leaked through Alyssa's anger.

He'd been right. She *did* feel awful.

She should have taken his advice and applied it to all of the men she knew, Sam Starrett included. Sam Starrett *especially*. She should have gone back to her room alone last night.

Because lonely and restless was a hell of a lot better than this empty hurt she was feeling right now.

She went out the door without another word, closing it gently and permanently behind her, not even giving the bastard the satisfaction of hearing her slam it shut.

Sooner or later, Helga had to leave her room. She couldn't hide here forever simply because she didn't know what was waiting for her on the other side of that door.

Besides, she knew what was waiting for her—a bunch of Americans and Kazbekistanis, working together to bring those civilians safely off of that hijacked plane. World Airlines Flight 232—it said on one of her Post-it notes.

She had the names of all the major players in her notepad.

The problem was, she wasn't sure she'd recognize any of them even if she tripped over them in the lobby.

I know your secret.

She'd found the words in her notepad, written in Des's strong handwriting.

It's time to quit. Call Des and tell him.

That was written in her own hand, on a Post-it note that she'd put directly on the telephone at some point—probably last night.

She'd picked up the phone, but there was no dial tone.

Phone system sucks, said another of her notes, the word *sucks* underlined three times, with three exclamation points following it. *Phone lines are not secure.*

The Gunvalds had had no telephone.

Helga had hidden with her parents in their house, sleeping on the floor of their kitchen for nearly two weeks in late September and early October of 1943. It was after the terrifying news had come out that the Gestapo was going to round up the Danish Jews. After a hot summer filled with acts of sabotage and Danish resistance, the "peaceful occupation" was peaceful no longer. Everything had turned upside down.

Mother and Poppi hadn't believed it at first. This was Denmark! That couldn't happen here! But Herr Gunvald had come to the house and had managed to convince them to pack their valuables and hide.

Herr Gunvald had brought them here.

Fru Gunvald had offered the Rosens their bed, but Poppi had refused to put them out that way. "You're already risking so much, just having us here," he'd said, humbled by their generosity. Poppi—humbled. It was a day, a moment, Helga would never forget.

Annebet and Hershel had gone to Copenhagen despite the curfew to see what they could do about getting the Rosens passage on a fishing boat that would take them—illegally, and at great risk to all involved—across the sound to Sweden.

Fru Gunvald had served Helga and her parents big bowls of her delicious peasant's soup. "This is nothing we wouldn't do for any of our neighbors," she said matter-of-factly. "It's wrong, what they're doing, and we won't let those Nazis do it."

Herr Gunvald lowered his big-boned frame into the seat at the head of their kitchen table. He smiled at Marte as he passed the basket of brown bread to her, and he winked at Helga. "Herr Rosen, may we trouble you for a prayer of thanks for what we're about to receive?"

Helga sat there while her father spoke, aware that her mother was crying, and that Fru Gunvald had reached over and taken her hand.

"It's an awful thing," Marte's mother had murmured to hers, "to have to leave your home."

Under the table, Marte took her hand and squeezed it. "You can stay with us forever," she whispered.

They ate in silence then, for several minutes.

And then Poppi cleared his throat. "We'll pay you," he said. "Of course. For our room and board."

Both Herr and Fru Gunvald stopped eating, their spoons almost comically poised halfway to their mouths. Fru Gunvald looked at Herr Gunvald and then kept on eating. Herr Gunvald put down his spoon.

"A few coins now and then to help pay for food would be appreciated," he said easily. "Because we all know that Helga eats like a horse." He gave Helga another wink. He was kidding. He was turning Poppi's insult into a joke. "But other than that," he added quietly, "it's best you save your money. Who knows what expenses you'll run into in Sweden."

Poppi nodded. He kept eating his soup. But he'd started to cry, too, just like Mother.

"And what do you girls have planned for this evening?" Herr Gunvald purposely drew their attention away from Poppi. Helga had been terrified. Poppi—crying!

"I think a wonderful feast like this and good company calls for some music," Herr Gunvald proclaimed. "Marte, go with Helga and fetch your recorder. I think a concert is just the thing."

Helga never knew what her father said to the Gunvalds after she and Marte had left the room.

She could only guess.

* * *

She'd left her fanny pack in Starrett's room.

Shit.

Alyssa stood in the stairwell and tried not to cry as she cursed her stupidity and bad luck.

So much for vowing never to look at, think about, or talk to the man again.

Her room key was in that pack. Her wallet. And the painkiller she was planning to take to try to soften the edge of this headache that was throbbing inside of her skull.

You'd think she'd've learned after last time. You'd think she would've never touched a drop of alcohol ever again.

Well, she hadn't had a drink in six months. Not until last night.

She also hadn't been with a man, hadn't taken another lover, since she'd last been with Sam. No, she just got by on six-month-old memories and dreams and wishful thinking. On focusing all of her energy into her work.

Which had caught Max Bhagat's attention and brought her here to K-stan where she found herself face-to-face with Sam Starrett and his amazing eyes and mouth and hands. Face-to-face with her inability to forget about him, the way she'd told herself she had to do.

Alyssa retraced her steps back to his room more slowly, rehearsing what she was going to say. She'd knock on the door and be cool and businesslike when he answered. "Sorry to bother you, Lieutenant." Yeah, she'd address him by rank. "But I left my bag in your room."

And then there she was. Standing in front of his door. Forced to face her folly one more dreadful time this morning. Come on, just get it over with. She squared her shoulders and knocked. Softly.

And the door popped open.

Apparently it hadn't quite latched when she'd left. She knocked gently again, holding it open, but again there was no answer. No Sam striding toward her, the devil in his eyes as he smirked at her humiliation, holding her fanny pack out to her, dangling it off of one elegantly long finger.

Damn, the man had nice hands.

For a son of a bitch.

He was probably in the bathroom, about to get into the shower.

And there was her fanny pack. On the floor where she'd dropped it—apparently along with her brain—when she'd first come in last night.

Alyssa stepped quietly into the room. Praise the Lord for small favors. Sam didn't even have to know she'd been here.

But then she heard it. A soft sound. Like something an animal might make. Snuffling. Sniffing. Unsteady breathing.

And then she saw it.

Everything on the dresser had been swept onto the rug. The desk chair was knocked over and the big gilt-edged mirror on the wall was askew and cracked—as if there had been some terrible struggle in here in the ten minutes since she'd left the room.

Was it possible that someone—like the as-yet-unapprehended terrorists who'd thrown those homemade bombs down toward the pool just yesterday afternoon—had come in here after she'd left and overpowered Sam and . . .

Heart pounding, terrified that he was lying there dead or dying, she went past the wall that separated the entryway and closet and bathroom from the rest of the room.

The mattress was off the bedframe. The blankets and sheets had been hurled to the corner of the room. And Sam Starrett sat on the floor, shoulders bent, head bowed and . . .

He was crying.

The man was sitting on the floor and *crying*.

Alyssa stared, frozen in place.

She must've made some sort of sound, because he turned toward her with a look of sheer horror in his eyes. His still-muddy face was streaked clean in places from his tears.

And she understood. He'd made this mess. This was the aftermath of some kind of temper tantrum, some kind of fit of anger that . . . *she'd* caused?

Was it possible that Sam Starrett was crying—*crying*—over . . .

Her?

But that hadn't been anger she'd seen in the bend of his shoulders. That had been hurt. Misery.

Heartache.

"Get out!" He pushed himself to his feet in one smooth movement.

But she was stuck there. Hypnotized by the sight of those eyes filled with tears, by the very idea that this tough, unbreakable man was capable of crying over anything.

He took a threatening step toward her. Shouted. "Get the fuck out of my room!"

Alyssa turned and ran, scooping up her fanny pack on the way out the door.

Eighteen

TERI FORCED HERSELF to wait in the basement lobby.

She could see Mike Muldoon inside the restaurant, carrying a hot cup of coffee, getting himself a pastry—or four—from the self-serve line.

She couldn't see Stan at all, but if he'd come in with Muldoon, it was likely that he'd leave with him, too.

After what seemed an eternity, Muldoon headed for the door. Directly toward her.

She knew he wasn't really attracted to her. He'd said that he didn't think she was a very good kisser.

It was all she could do not to run and hide.

But Teri steeled herself. She wanted this confrontation. She needed this. She could do this. She was mad at this loser who was willing to ask her out and even sleep with her merely because his senior chief had asked him to.

"Hey, Teri." Muldoon greeted her cautiously, no doubt leery of the steam coming out of her ears. "Everything all right?"

"Great." God, what was she saying? And through clenched teeth, no less? "No," she said instead. "No, Mike, actually, everything's not great. I need to see Stan right away. Didn't he come down here with you?"

"Oh," he said. "No. He went upstairs. He wanted to shower before he got something to eat."

Muldoon was the lousy kisser. If he'd kissed even *half* as good as Stan did, maybe she would have bothered to kiss him back. As it was, she hadn't wanted to waste her energy. She started for the stairs.

"Hey, I was wondering . . ." Muldoon followed her.

287

"You want to have lunch?" she said shortly, taking the stairs two at a time, forcing him to rush to keep up. "Sure. Why the hell not? How's noon?"

"Uh, fine," he said.

"Great," she said. "Lunch at noon, and then what do you say we have sex afterward, say, at 1300?"

Muldoon dropped two of his pastries. They went bouncing down the stairs, and he hesitated, having to choose between going after them or following the woman who'd just suggested having postlunch sex with him.

His hesitation didn't last too long. He followed Teri.

"Glad to know I'm more appealing than a prune-filled Danish," she told him.

"Teri, what's going on?" he asked. "Are you all right?"

She was angry as hell. At Stan. At Mike. Mostly at Stan.

You didn't get angry enough, his voice echoed in her head. *Instead you internalized it, where it would fester and make you feel even worse. Who the hell needs that? You don't! So say it to me. Confront me. Get angry.*

"I'm great," she told Muldoon, and this time it wasn't a lie. She did feel great. She was angry. No. She was *furious.* But that was okay. Because she was heading upstairs to go pound on Stan's door and tell him a thing or two about playing God, about messing with her life, thank you very much.

She *wasn't* going to jam it all inside, the way she'd done so many times before. She was going to blast Stan.

Come on, hit me.

Yeah, maybe she would. Maybe she'd give him a solid knee to the balls. Son of a bitch.

And as for Muldoon . . .

Teri stopped on the landing right before the doors to the main hotel lobby and grabbed him by the shirt. He was juggling his paper cup of coffee, the remaining pastries, and her outrageously bold suggestion that they follow lunch by taking off their clothes and getting busy, but she didn't give a damn. She just pulled his mouth down to hers and kissed him.

It was a no-holds-barred kind of kiss. A soul sucking, total tongue, teeth clicking, going for the tonsils kind of kiss. The kind that promised hot, deep, total penetration, a bed rocking, sweat slickened, gasping for air, and screaming for more kind of sex.

It was a Hall of Famer as far as kisses went, and Muldoon, brave SEAL that he was, was completely up for the challenge. He tossed his remaining pastries and coffee onto the floor, where they hit with a splash. He was solid and warm and he tasted like sweetened coffee.

But he wasn't Stan.

Teri pulled away before he got his arms around her.

"Gotta go."

He followed her into the lobby. "Hey, whoa, why wait till noon—Teri, I'm not busy now."

"Yeah, but I am."

"Noon, then," he said, still following her. He nodded as they went past Lieutenant Paoletti and Jazz Jacquette, waiting until they were out of earshot, but then still lowering his voice, "I'll come to your room."

"You know," she said, stopping short, "on second thought, I can't have lunch with you. And as for having sex . . . ?" She pretended to think about it. "Nope, can't do that either. Not in *this* lifetime."

She started for the stairs up to the west tower where both she and Stan had rooms. But Muldoon grabbed her arm.

"Wait a minute," he said. "You just . . ." He was completely confused and she almost felt sorry for him.

Almost.

"You're just going to kiss me like that and then . . ." He shook his head in disbelief. "That's it?"

"You know, Muldoon," she said, making a very sympathetic face, "you're just not a particularly good kisser."

And with that, he instantly understood. "Oh, shit," he said. It was the first four-letter word she'd ever heard him use. "You *heard* that?"

Teri nodded. "Let go of me."

He dropped her arm. "I'm sorry. I'm . . . really sorry."

"Great. That makes it all better." She started for the stairs again, and again he followed her.

"Teri, I don't know what I can say—"

She stopped. "Don't say anything. Just leave me alone."

He stood in front of her, blocking her path. "If you won't let me try to explain now, then why don't you meet me for lunch."

Teri laughed in his face. "Oh, *there's* an original idea."

But he persisted. "You've got to eat, right? I've got to eat. Let's sit at the same table, and please, let me try to—"

"Mike. Don't you get it? You're off the hook. You don't have to have lunch with me. I know Stan set you up to—"

"But I *want* to have lunch with you. I *need* to have lunch with you. Please? Come on. Give me a break. I really like you, Teri. I don't want to lose you as a friend."

She looked at him. And she knew. The man was a Navy SEAL. He had pitbull-like tenacity. He was going to dog her every step until she agreed to meet him for lunch.

"Noon," she said through gritted teeth. "Lunch and only lunch. As friends."

"Absolutely." He nodded. "If that's the way you want to play it, that's the way we'll play it."

For now. He didn't say the words aloud, but they hung there as he walked away.

Teri knew that kissing him that way had been a stupid mistake.

And it was all Stanley Wolchonok's fault.

"We got video!"

The negotiators' HQ room—mission control, so to speak—erupted in quiet cheers.

Quiet, because after three days of hemming and hawing and buying the SEALs in the Troubleshooters Squad time to rehearse the takedown of the plane, everyone in Max Bhagat's team was exhausted.

Desmond Nyland stood in the doorway, watching Max watch the screen. Max himself looked fresh as a daisy. He was too much of a son of a bitch to let anyone know he was running on caffeine and nerves strung way too tight.

The man shaved two or three times a day so that his team never saw him looking anything but completely in control.

Although rumor had it he'd nearly broken Senator Crawford's nose. *And* rumor had it that last night he'd actually gone out onto the runway in an attempt to trade himself for this Gina girl who'd been brave enough to step forward and say she was Karen Crawford when the tangos were about to start killing the other passengers.

That sure as hell didn't sound like the Max Bhagat *he* knew.

The miniature cameras had finally been put into place, and the equipment was finally up and running. Two days those SEALs had spent there in the scorching heat and the chill of the nights, refusing to give up.

And now they had video.

Out of the three cameras Ensign MacInnough and his men had managed to get placed and working, two gave a snake's eye view of the cabin—from the floor, of course. It was limited, but they were lucky they had that much. The third was in the cockpit.

Max stared at that screen, both hands on the table in front of him, leaning closer.

"Oh, God," he breathed, more to himself than anyone standing around him. "She's just a girl."

Des moved into the room to look over Max's shoulder at the screen.

The picture was amazingly clear despite the fact that, again, the camera was angled up from the floor to the ceiling. But there was a young woman sitting on the floor, knees in close to her chest. She had long dark hair and big dark eyes and a face that was more than merely pretty. She was striking looking—with cheekbones and a nose that announced her Mediterranean heritage.

And Max was right. She *was* little more than a girl. In a few years she was going to be a gorgeous woman. A real Sophia Loren-type beauty.

Of course, right now her life expectancy wasn't more than a few days. Hours even.

Especially if what Des suspected was true—that this was a suicide mission for the hijackers, and had been right from the start.

"How old is she?" Des asked.

"Twenty-one—going on thirty-five. She's been cooler

under pressure than some of my agents who've been on the job for five years."

"You might want to send over a skirt or pants or *some*thing so that girl can cover those legs." Des tapped the screen. Not that *he* had any problem with it. She had legs like a movie star. Five miles long and gorgeously shaped.

"Yeah, and how do we do *that* without letting them know that we can hear and see what's going on in there?" Max asked.

"Details, details," Des said. "I'm surprised she hasn't been hassled by the tangos for indecent exposure."

"One of 'em, calls himself Bob—we've IDed him as Babur Haiyan—" Max told him, "was talking to her about it last night. But it didn't seem exceedingly threatening."

Des tapped on the screen again. "Lookee here. Whoever this is, he's just waiting for the order to play rough so he can have at this girl. Look at him watching her. He's going to be first in line for the gang bang."

Max raised his voice. "I need a visual ID. Tango on screen three. Anyone match a name to that face, call it out!"

As he waited, a muscle jumped in his jaw. Now, wasn't that interesting? Our man Max had let little Gina Vitagliano under his incredibly thick skin. Under what Des had always believed was impenetrably thick skin.

"Helga all right?" Max asked, still watching the tango watching Gina on the video screen.

Oh, *damn*. "She's not here?" Des countered.

"I haven't seen her."

Max never missed anything, but right now it was possible he wasn't up to his usual speed, glued the way he was to the video screen. Des quickly scanned the room, looking for that familiar head of gray hair, that beautiful round face that was always smiling.

Double damn. Helga was supposed to be here. She was scheduled to be.

But she wasn't.

"She didn't call in?" Des tried to sound casual. As if he weren't picturing Helga wandering the streets of K-stan, confused and disoriented and in terrible danger.

"She didn't call me," Max replied.

"Alojzije Nabulsi"—the name he'd been waiting for—rang out.

"You stay the hell away from her," Max said to the video screen. "She's just a kid."

When the power and air conditioning kicked back on, Stan closed the curtains in his room, shutting out the hot sun. It would take a minute or two for the air coming through the vent to turn cool, but at least it was moving again.

He was tempted to take another shower—to stand there under the water until the room cooled down, until the terrorists surrendered, until the team was on its way back to California, where he could return to his regularly scheduled life and not have to think or worry about Teri Howe ever again.

He was giving in to the urge and had just stepped out of his pants when someone started pounding on his door.

Holy Christ, whoever it was wanted him to open up in a hurry. He grabbed for a towel and lunged for the door. With that kind of lead fist, it had to be WildCard or Cosmo or . . .

"Is there a problem?" he asked as he yanked the door open. Or Teri Howe. Oh, *shit.*

"You bet your ass there's a problem." She pushed past him, into his room, as he scrambled to pull the towel more completely around himself.

She was willing to bet his ass—she didn't necessarily want to see it flapping in the breeze.

He knew exactly what this was about. Mike Muldoon had called on the hotel phone just minutes ago with the bad news of the hour. It seemed that Teri had overheard their entire conversation in the stairwell.

She turned to face him. "Close the goddamn door."

Muldoon had told him that she was angry, but Stan had imagined that meant that she'd avoid him, maybe give him the cold shoulder until the end of time. Be passive aggressive at best.

But, damn, here she was. Ms. Nonconfrontation, getting right in his face about something he'd done to upset her. As bad as this was, it was also good. It was beyond good. It was amazing.

He was so fucking proud of her, he wanted to cry.

Christ, she was livid. And gorgeous. Her eyes were hot and bright, her delicate mouth a tight line in her flushed face. She was breathing hard, as if she'd sprinted five miles. Or gone up eight flights of stairs at a dead run.

She didn't seem to notice—or care—that he was wearing only a towel.

Stan didn't shut the door. "How about we just leave this open until I get some clothes on? I'm not comfortable being alone like this without—"

Teri interrupted him. Loudly. Loudly enough so that anyone standing in the hall would have no problem hearing her. "*I'm* not comfortable with *you* asking your friend to *do* me as a favor to you!"

O-kay. Stan closed the door. "Teri, look—"

"What is *wrong* with you?" Her voice shook. "Really, Stan, I want to know. Why would you spend all that time trying to set me up with Mike Muldoon when he's not even remotely interested in me?"

"Well, that's just it," Stan told her. "He is interested."

"Bull*shit*!"

"Teri, he *is*—"

"I heard you trying to talk him into—"

"He's interested now, all right?" He took a step toward her. "Look, I thought he'd be good for you. He's a sweet kid. I thought *he* could use some help, too, you know, getting—"

"Laid? From what I heard, I think he's probably got that handled."

Stan fought to keep his own temper from rising. "That's not what I was going to say. That's not what this is about."

"Yeah, right," she said, with a laugh that sounded an awful lot like a sob. "I *heard* you, Stan. I heard *every*thing you said. You wanted him to go up to my room with me after lunch, and I don't think you imagined we'd play cards when he got there. Why don't you just admit it? You were trying to talk Muldoon into throwing me a—God—a pity fuck!"

Oh, dear Christ, did she really think that? Stan couldn't decide whether to laugh or be insulted.

He took another step toward her. "That's not true. Come on, Teri, you look me in the eye and just goddamn *try* to accuse me of *ever* treating you with anything remotely resembling pity—"

She wasn't listening, she was talking right over him. "Poor Teri Howe. She hasn't gotten laid in years because she's too much of a loser to be able to hook up with any nice guys. She only attracts the scum of the earth like Joel Hogan and Rob Pierce. So come on, Mike, you're a nice guy. Do the senior chief a *big* favor and throw her a bang. You don't really mind, do you?"

Wildly she threw off her jacket and grabbed her shirt, pulling it out of her pants and over her head.

Stan couldn't move. He was taken totally by surprise, completely stunned by the sight of her standing there in her bra. It was a sports bra—the kind she could have worn out for a jog in almost any Western nation without a shirt over it. But still, the sight of all that smooth, bare skin was unnerving after days of long-sleeved shirts and collars buttoned to her throat. Just the sight of her bare arms seemed erotic and impossibly daring.

What the hell was she doing?

As he stood there and gaped like an idiot, she unfastened her belt. Defiantly she kicked off her boots and shucked her pants down her legs.

And then, Christ, she was standing there, six feet away from him, in only her underwear.

"If you think I need a pity fuck so bad, then I want it to come from *you*." Her voice shook with anger and emotion. "Come on, Senior Chief. Don't you have some kind of rule about never asking your men to do something that you wouldn't do yourself?"

For one wild second, Stan considered calling her bluff. He considered throwing down his towel and striding toward her and picking her up and carrying her to his bed.

What would she do then?

Beg him not to stop, never to stop.

Jesus, he tried not to look at her long, gorgeous legs, her stomach with its perfect belly button and . . . He cleared his throat, made himself look into her eyes. "I didn't think you'd really want me," he admitted.

"Yeah, well, you were wrong."

Oh, God. "It's a bad idea. You know it." When did his voice get so hoarse, his mouth so damn dry?

"You're wrong about that, too." She took a step toward him. He took a step back.

And she took off her bra.

Teri caught sight of herself in the mirror that hung on the wall of Stan's hotel room.

For an instant, she flashed hot and then cold. She was standing in only her underpants in the senior chief's room, having just told him that she wanted to have sex with him.

Oh, God, maybe coming here like this wasn't such a good idea.

What on earth was she doing?

Pretend you're in your helo—that you've got that kind of control of this situation, that kind of confidence.

She'd come up here angry as hell at this man. Intensely, passionately, furiously angry. She'd wanted to yell at him. She'd wanted to lash out at him, to kick him where he'd feel it, to bring him to his knees.

She also wanted to make love to him.

And maybe that was what she was the angriest about.

She wanted him. She'd done everything but tell him so in plain English. And he'd done everything in return to keep his distance.

But the truth was, he wanted her, too.

She knew that now for a fact.

How could you not be head over heels in love with this woman? She's incredible, Muldoon. She's got a body to die for, a face like an angel. Her eyes are . . . Have you even looked into her eyes? She has eyes that make you just want to, I don't know, Christ, die for her if she asked you to. . . .

Those weren't just words of hype, meant to spark Mike

Muldoon's interest. Those words were straight from Stan's heart. She would bet her life on it.

Her life, and her pride.

Yeah, Teri was betting her pride that he wanted her, but for some reason she didn't understand, he'd worked overtime to keep from getting too close.

Even now he was standing there, trying not to look at her. Trying—and failing. His gaze skimmed her bare breasts, nearly as palpable as a touch before he forced himself to look up and into her eyes.

He was breathing hard, as if he'd just run a mile at top speed. He was also hanging on to the towel he had wrapped around his waist with both hands.

And Teri let herself look at him, really look at him.

He was all hard, lean, artfully sculpted muscles—the kind that came from real hard work rather than machines in a gym. He had powerful-looking legs—one with a mean-looking scar on the knee—and big feet. Wide feet. Solid-looking, dependable feet. The kind that would keep him upright and standing tall forever, if need be. His shoulders looked broad enough to hold the weight of the entire world, his arms strong enough to carry the moon. He had a faded tattoo high on his left arm—a simple anchor, a sailor's classic. Thick blond hair covered his chest, swirling down to nothing before it reached the perfect six-pack of tight muscles at his waist. He didn't have an extra ounce of fat anywhere on his body— probably because he never had time to eat.

There was a line of slightly darker hair that started at his belly button and disappeared beneath his towel. Teri followed it with her eyes, lingering a long time—way long enough for him to know without a doubt that she was thinking about what that towel was hiding.

She was following Stan's own advice—letting him know that she wanted him—that she pictured him naked, too.

She knew he'd thought about her that way.

The woman is fucking hot. He'd said that. About her. *There's not a single heterosexual man in the Troubleshooters Squad who hasn't pictured her naked.*

Including—she was betting—Senior Chief Stan Wolchonok.

With nothing left to lose, going for all or nothing—the way she would've if she were flying her helo—Teri pushed her panties down her legs. And then she knew he didn't have to rely on his imagination anymore, because there she was. Naked.

He gave up trying not to look, gave up trying to hide the heat in his eyes. But he still didn't move toward her.

"Come on, Stan," she whispered, fighting the self-doubt that threatened to make her throw her clothes back on and run from the room. "How much of a green light do you need?"

"I'm toast," he admitted, which helped a great deal. But he still didn't reach for her. "Damn, I was toast the minute you walked in here. If you're going to leave, you're going to have to do it yourself now because I am no longer capable of asking you to go. I mean, come on, Teri, put your clothes back on—see, I can say it, but not with any kind of real conviction."

She took a step toward him, and this time he didn't back away. But she wanted more than that from him. She wanted him to reach for her. Only then would she really know that she'd won.

"I'm dying to kiss you," she told him.

"Bad idea." Stan moistened his lips. "But, you know, don't let that stop you."

She did stop, though. Inches away from Stan. Close enough for him to feel her body heat. Tantalizingly close, yet still far enough away not to touch him.

And he couldn't resist. He was powerless. He watched himself reach out and touch her. Her hair. God, he loved her hair. Her cheek.

Lightly, with just one or two fingers.

The delicate bones at the base of her throat. Her breast.

After days of resisting, Mike Muldoon had finally come to the realization that Teri was all he could possibly want in a woman. He'd called Stan, elated and terrified. *You were right, Senior, she's incredible. . . .*

And you, my friend, came to that conclusion too late.

But Jesus, did Teri really know what she was getting into

here? Did she have any clue at all? Stan was lousy relationship material. Couldn't she see that?

Apparently not.

Apparently she wasn't thinking clearly.

"Bad idea," he whispered again, but he didn't pull his
hand away. He couldn't. To hell with Muldoon. To hell with
everything.

Because Teri was gazing up at him with such an expression
on her face—as if he was everything she'd ever needed. How
could that be? And yet . . .

"Please," she whispered.

Stan didn't know what she wanted, not precisely, but he
was damned if he wasn't going to try to give it to her.

He moved to kiss her, but she was already there, her arms
already around his neck, her mouth against his, her body soft
against his chest.

Skin on skin. It was a mind-blowing sensation, even more
mind-blowing when his towel fell to the ground and the softness of her stomach was against him.

He froze, suddenly uncertain. He was completely aroused—
there was no way she could avoid knowing that. He was a big
man, and that was a fact.

For the first time in his life, Stan wished he were a little less
well-endowed. He didn't have a clue what was okay with her
and what wasn't. He pulled free from her kiss, tried to pull
slightly back from her. "Teri—"

But she pressed herself even more closely to him, shifting
her hips to rub herself against him, moaning her approval as
she kissed him again, as she ran her hands up his neck, raking
her fingers through his hair.

God damn, it felt too good. He skimmed his hands across
her impossibly smooth skin, too, filling his palms with the
soft weight of her breasts as he kissed her.

Still, he had to ask. "Will you tell me if I do something you
don't like?"

"I don't like it when you stop kissing me."

He had to laugh at that. "Teri, I'm serious."

"I am, too." She pulled his head down and kissed him,

sliding her hands down his back, across his buttocks, pulling him even more tightly against her.

She was hot and deliciously spicy, and Stan kissed her deeper, longer, sweeping his tongue into her mouth as his hands explored her body, as her hands explored his. God, the way she touched him was amazing—like she couldn't get enough of him either.

Teri was exhilarated.

It was working.

She'd never dared to be so aggressive about sex before. She'd always hung back and waited for her lover to take charge.

It had never occurred to her that a man might like to get pushed around a little bit. To be controlled. To be told, Do me, *now*. To be the one to be made love to for a change.

It was something she'd overheard Mike Muldoon say to Stan. *When I'm with a woman, I let her set the pace, the mood—it's all up to her.*

And Stan had replied by saying he thought that was exactly what Teri needed right now.

He'd been more right than he knew.

Pretend you're in your helo—that you've got that kind of control of this situation, that kind of confidence. He'd said that to her, too.

Although she was pretty sure when he said it he didn't dream she'd apply it to *this* particular situation.

She could feel him against her, hard and male. She could feel his restraint, too, his worry that she was fragile, that she needed to be treated with extra care.

Teri wanted that gone.

She was strong, she was in control, and she wanted him more than she'd ever wanted anyone—no holds barred.

She tried to tell him all that with her kiss and by looping her leg around his, by boldly reaching between them to touch him. He was hot and heavy, so hard and smooth and utterly male and . . .

Teri pulled back and found herself looking directly at Stan.

He was still worried about her, damn it. She could see it in his eyes.

So she smiled as she caressed him. "Oh, boy."

He smiled, intense pleasure on his face. But he couldn't let his worries rest. "Look, Teri—"

"What happened to me when I was eight wasn't about sex," she told him, trying to make him stop thinking about it once and for all. "It was about intimidation. It was about some sick pervert getting pleasure from a little girl's pain and fear. It wasn't about sex—the same way rape isn't about sex—it's about violence, you know? That was emotional violence. It has nothing at all to do with what we're doing here. It's not as if the sight of a penis makes me faint." She looked pointedly down at him. "At least not usually."

He laughed at that. But try as she might, he wasn't done being serious. "What *are* we doing here?"

"We're about to have the most incredible sex either one of us has ever had in our lives," she told him. "That is, if you would stop talking and kiss me."

And still, he hesitated.

"This whole thing is a bad idea," she said. "Yes, I know. Screw it! I want you *now*. So *kiss* me."

Stan kissed her.

With her fingers wrapped tightly around him and her tongue in his mouth, with her breast in one hand while his other held her close, he was having trouble remembering his own name, let alone the myriad of reasons he had for trying to slow her down.

Teri was okay with this. She'd made that more than clear. She was smiling, she was laughing.

She wanted him. *Now.*

As if she could read his mind, as if to prove the point, she took his hand from her breast and brought it between her legs. It was the kind of invitation he didn't need repeated. He touched her, lightly at first, then more deeply, more intimately. She was smooth and soft and utterly female. She was also wet and hot.

For him. Because she wanted *him*.

Now.

She pulled him toward the bed and he hit the mattress with the backs of his legs. She pushed him down and he dragged her along. As his shoulders hit the bed, she landed on top of him.

She laughed as he rolled her over, as he kissed and licked her throat, her collarbone, her neck. She was so unbelievably delicious, so outrageously perfect. He licked her nipple into his mouth and her laughter turned to a moan as she arched her back and opened her legs to him.

He could feel her, hot and slick against him, and his entire world exploded out of control. In the blink of an eye—less—she reached down to guide him as she lifted her hips and then, with a burst of pleasure that was blindingly intense, he was buried inside of her, surrounded by her heat.

Her legs were around him, and she kissed him as deliriously as he kissed her as he began to move, as she met him, matched him, set a pace that was wild.

There was a reason he shouldn't be doing this. He knew it—it was back there, lurking at the edges of the haze of pleasure. But he couldn't think, couldn't focus on anything but Teri and the incredibly sexy little sounds of desire she was making way back in her throat.

He could feel the sharp bite of her fingernails on his shoulders as she gripped him as tightly as she possibly could. He could've written a book about the sweet sensation of her tongue against his, about the familiar scent of her hair, about the grip of her thighs or the softness of her breasts as he crushed her to him.

She pulled her mouth away from him. "Stan, oh, God, don't stop! I'm gonna . . ."

"Come on, Teri," he said. "Come on, I'm right behind you."

"Oh, my God," she gasped. "Don't we need a condom?"

Condom. *Shit!* Stan pulled himself out of her, off of her so quickly, he fell off the bed.

"Holy shit," he said. "Holy, holy, holy *shit.* What the hell am I doing?"

"Quick," she said, scrambling off the bed and searching

through the pockets of her pants. She slapped a foil wrapped little package into his hand.

"You carry condoms?" he asked inanely, still stunned that he'd even been inside her without protection. Christ, he didn't have to come inside of her to get her pregnant. They only had to do what they'd just done.

"Yes," she said. "I do. Are you going to put it on, or am I going to do it for you?"

He ripped open the package, but he wasn't fast enough for her. She snatched it out of his hand, pushing him back on the bed and straddling his legs.

"God, is this even going to fit?"

"Yeah." He sat up to help. "Teri, Jesus, I might've already gotten you pregnant."

"Are you sure you want to talk about this now?" she asked. "I'm going to come in about five seconds whether you're inside of me or not."

And with that stunning announcement, she finished covering him, shifted her weight, and slid down, directly on top of him.

Yes, that was his voice crying out. Mr. Much Too Easily Distractible. He, who prided himself on never making mistakes, had just broken the biggest rule in the book. Sex without protection.

But it suddenly didn't matter because her breasts were in his face. He kissed her, suckled her—hard—and she moaned his name, moving on top of him as if she couldn't get enough of him, as if she wanted more.

The woman knew exactly what she wanted. She pushed his shoulders down, back toward the bed, so that he was lying flat. So that he was pressed fully inside of her, as deeply as he possibly could be.

Time stopped for Stan as she held herself there, just looking down at him. The sight of her like that—dark curls tousled, full breasts tightly peaked, her skin slick with perspiration, pleasure shining in her beautiful brown eyes—was something he would carry with him to his grave.

"I don't want this to end," she whispered. "But if I move, even just a little, I'm going to come."

He laughed in amazement. "If you keep saying things like that to me, *I'm* going to come. You won't even have to move."

She smiled. "Really?"

It was her smile that did it. That beautiful, beautiful smile of pure delight lighting her incredible face . . .

He had to move. He had to . . .

"Teri," he gasped.

He bucked beneath her, and she moved, too. And she was right there, with him, true to her word. She fell forward to cling to him as she shattered, as his release rocketed through him in an explosion of color and light, sensation and sound.

Teri's sweet face. The taste of her mouth, the softness of her lips. Her voice, thick with pleasure, calling his name. Her storm of tears as he'd held her. His vision of her at eight years old. Her eyes filled with anger. With fear. With desire. With trust.

With *trust*.

Stan opened his eyes as Teri lay on top of him, breathing hard. He could feel her heart still pounding. His was still going at quadruple time, too.

He was still inside of her and he didn't want to move, even though he knew he had to. He wanted to stay like this, right here, forever. But used condoms could leak. He'd learned that back in Birth Control 101, in junior high school. And this one had already leaked in a very major way. Condoms were susceptible to that—particularly when you failed to put them on prior to penetration.

Ah, Christ. Welcome back to reality.

It was an ugly place to be right now—particularly after the sheer perfection of the place he'd just been.

He gently lifted her off of him, tucking her alongside him, her head on his shoulder, under his chin, as he held her close.

She sighed, running her fingers through the hair on his chest, intertwining their legs despite the heat.

And making him want her again, already, despite the harshness of a reality in which she could be pregnant, a reality in which Muldoon, a kid who looked up to him, who trusted him, was definitely going to wind up hurt.

Nineteen

MAYBE COFFEE WOULD save her.

Alyssa headed through the lobby, careful not to jar her head. She'd showered and changed and tried to lie down for a while, but failed to sleep.

Her head was pounding and she couldn't shake free from that image of Sam Starrett with his head bowed as he cried. It was haunting her even more than this infernal headache.

"Hey, Alyssa!"

The dead last person she wanted to see was heading toward her across the lobby. Well, okay, maybe the *second* to the dead last person.

"Are you okay?" Jules asked. "Where were you last night?"

Resolutely she turned to face her partner.

"Whoa," he said, taking in the bags she knew were under her eyes, the death-warmed-over color of her skin. "You look like hell."

He, on the other hand, looked adorable with his perfect hair and his perfect face and his trim little body clad in impeccable army wear—a very clean T-shirt and neatly creased camouflage pants. He looked like GI Joe's gay little brother.

"At least I'm consistent," she told him. "Because I *feel* like hell."

His concern was immediate and genuine. "Oh, no, did you eat or drink something you shouldn't have? One of the SAS guys ate some kind of stew and—"

"I had too much to drink last night."

Jules closed his mouth. And looked at her closely. And just

like that, he knew where she'd gone, who she'd been with. "Oh, shit," he said.

To her horror, tears welled in her eyes.

Jules hugged her. "Okay, sweetie. No recriminations. No blame. You did it. Let's deal with it. Let's get you to your room. The last thing you need is for him—or anyone—to see you crying in the lobby."

Stan was too quiet.

Teri lifted her head to look up at him, and even though he smiled at her, she knew.

He was having regrets.

Her heart sank and all of her newfound self-confidence shrank to a little shriveled ball of lead in her stomach. Maybe he'd never really wanted her in the first place. After all, she'd made it impossible for him to turn her down, coming in here the way she had and taking off her clothes like that. Oh, God.

She sat up, her back to him, wanting nothing more than to find her clothes and leave.

"You all right?" He touched her on the arm as he sat up, too, his hand as warm as his voice.

"I don't know," Teri admitted.

He sighed. "We need to talk about this."

The last of her hope died.

God, she was so stupid. She had been actually lying there mere seconds ago, completely content, thinking what they'd just shared was more than a morning of casual sex. She'd done it again. She'd jumped to the conclusion that this was the start of something big, of a relationship that would build and grow and last, maybe even forever.

But it wasn't.

It was just what she'd claimed it would be when she first stormed into the room.

A pity fuck. She'd felt bad, so he made her feel better. The end.

And now that it was over, Stan was sitting there, trying to figure out the best way to repair their friendship. He was in mop-up mode. Mr. Fix-It to the rescue.

"Where are you in your cycle?" he asked, and his words didn't make any sense.

She looked at him. "What?"

"Do you know when you're due to get your period?"

Oh, damn, he actually thought he might've gotten her pregnant. Well, if he had, *that* was going to be a hard one to fix, wasn't it?

"I don't know exactly," she told him. "Maybe a couple of weeks?"

He nodded. Exhaled a laugh that had nothing to do with humor. "That couldn't be more perfectly worse, could it? Christ. Okay." He took a deep breath. Mr. Calm-and-in-Control. "All right. We're just going to have to wait it out. And if you *are* pregnant—"

"Don't worry, I won't make you marry me." Teri said it more sharply than she'd intended as she crossed the room. Her underwear was right in the middle of the floor, right where she'd dropped it.

Stan didn't move. "That's just one option," he said evenly as she pulled up her panties, wrestled herself into her bra. "But, you know, if you don't want to consider—"

"I don't. Why are we even talking about this?" She pulled on her shirt.

"I thought it might be reassuring for you to know—"

"That you'd ruin your life over an hour of sex? Great sex, but still . . ."

"That I take responsibility for my mistakes," he countered quietly.

Teri was glad her back was to him as she pulled on her pants, glad he couldn't see the effect that word had on her.

Mistake.

"What happened here was my fault," she said just as quietly. She turned to face him and even managed to smile. "You kept saying it was a bad idea. I guess you were right."

"Teri, don't run away," he said, but it was too late.

She'd grabbed her jacket and was already out the door.

Jules Cassidy was walking toward Sam Starrett like a man on a mission.

Okay. Perfect. Here we fucking go. The shittiest day in the world—round two.

Sam didn't stop eating. He just sat there, at his special table. In his special seat. Shoveling pasta that tasted like crap into his mouth. Giving the world a great big *go away* message with his glower and his body language.

But Jules didn't go anywhere. He stood there, obviously waiting for Sam to look up at him. Well, fuck it. Sam wasn't going to.

So Jules sat down. Sam had to give him credit—the little fruit had balls.

"This has got to stop," Jules said quietly. "Wasn't Washington enough for you?"

Well now, wasn't *that* the ultimate in irony? Alyssa Locke had warned Sam not to tell anyone about the night they'd spent together in Washington, DC. She'd nearly threatened him with bodily harm over it. And he hadn't told a soul.

But apparently *she'd* turned around and spilled the whole sorry-assed tale to her swishy little partner.

"Starrett, you can't play Neanderthal with me. I know that you care about her," Jules continued.

Sam finally looked up. Two weeks after he'd seen Alyssa last, after Washington, DC, he'd called Jules. Just to make sure she was really all right. He'd made up some stupid reason why he was calling, but he knew that Jules had seen right through it. He hadn't asked him any questions then, not even when Sam had asked him not to tell Alyssa.

"I never told her you called," Jules said softly.

Sam couldn't hold his gaze. But he managed a nod, a gruff "Thanks."

"You can't take advantage of her whenever you feel the urge," Jules told him gently. "She doesn't need this. She needs someone who's going to be there for her, someone willing to commit." He paused. "Someone who loves her."

Sam laughed at that—a burst of disparaging air. "Who? You?"

Jules just smiled. "Well, I *do* love her, but Adam might get a little upset if I tried to bring her home."

Jules had a live-in lover named Adam. Now, that was more information than Sam had wanted to know. Ever.

Jules sighed. "I know you probably think I'm the last person to judge anyone in terms of what turns them on, but this sadomasochistic thing you've got going with Alyssa is killing her. Now, maybe that's part of the game to you, but—"

Sam put down his fork. "You think I *like* it? Hooking up with her once every six *months*? Only to have her hate me again in the morning? Fuck you—she's the fucking masochist!"

Jules was startled. "But she said . . ."

Sam lowered his voice. "She gets drunk so she's got an excuse to get down with me. Then she comes to my door and it's *my* fault when I don't turn her away? Fuck you twice."

Jules narrowed his eyes. "You know, the bad language might be part of the problem. I can see how that might be off-putting for someone like—"

"Yeah, how well do you know her anyway?" Sam said. "It makes her laugh, if you want to know the truth. Jesus, when she's drunk, she relaxes enough to let herself like me. It's the rest of the time that . . ." He shook his head. "Fuck."

"What?" Jules persisted.

"Just leave me the fuck alone."

"It's the rest of the time that what?" Jules asked.

Sam tried to eat. Now it tasted like cold crap.

"She likes you when she's drunk, but it's the rest of the time that what?" Jules would not let go of it. "The rest of the time, as in when she's sober?"

Sam set down the fork very carefully, instead of throwing it across the room. Or at Jules, who simply would not let this rest. "Look, she sobers up, and it's like she . . . she . . . fuck! She instantly forgets who I am. Sobered up, she can't see past her own fucking expectations, all right? She thinks I'm some rednecked asshole, so, yeah, okay, I play the part. Jesus." He glared at Jules. "She thinks she knows me, but she doesn't have a clue. She's prejudged, prelabeled, and prerejected me. How the fuck do you fight that?"

Jules laughed. "Well, gee, I couldn't *possibly* know what that's like."

Sam realized what he'd just said and who he'd just said it to.

As a gay man, Jules had spent most of his life prejudged, prelabeled, and prerejected by most of society.

Including Sam.

"Ah, fuck." He couldn't hold the other man's gaze.

"*Fuck* is kind of like your *aloha*, right?" Jules said. "It means *hello* and *good-bye* and *thank you* and—in this case—*I'm sorry*?"

Sam had to laugh at that. "I am sorry," he managed to say. "You're . . . okay."

"Whew," Jules said. "I was worried about myself for a minute there."

"Just don't get too close."

Jules grinned. "Sweetie, you're hot, but my heart belongs to Adam." His smile faded. "And something tells me your heart belongs to Alyssa."

Sam looked at him. "Does she . . ." God, he couldn't believe he was actually asking this. "Ever say anything about me?"

Jules looked uncomfortable.

"Forget it," Sam said. "Don't answer that. That's not fair. Whatever she said, she probably said it in confidence."

"She thinks you're great in bed."

Sam laughed. "She told you that?"

"Well, sure. We compare notes. *Kidding!* No, the past few days, she's been doing this kind of *hold me back*, you know, *keep me away from him* thing." Jules sighed and shifted in his seat, as if deciding how much to tell him. "Between you and me, Alyssa doesn't get out much. I'm pretty much a hundred percent certain that she hasn't been with anyone between you and you. No, I'm a hundred and ten percent certain. She would've told me if she had."

"She talks to you about private stuff, huh?" Sam asked. He shook his head and had to laugh. "You and me, together we're the perfect man for Alyssa Locke. She tells you her secrets, and you love her unconditionally—and you've got no problem telling her that. And me . . ."

Jules nodded. He knew what Sam gave her. There was no need to say it aloud.

Sam made her come.

"I think she's the one who's been using me," he told Jules.

Jules nodded again. "Maybe you should tell her it's not enough."

Sam nodded, too. He closed his eyes, remembering the way she'd walked in on him crying. Jesus. It was possible that she already knew.

"Mrs. Shuler, remember me? I'm Senior Chief Stan Wolchonok. Marte Gunvald's son."

Helga peered out from behind the chain lock on her hotel room door at the large man standing there. Marte's son. "Of course," she said with a smile to hide her lie. Had they met? Yes, obviously they had.

"Desmond Nyland called me, ma'am. He thought you might appreciate some company for lunch."

"Oh, is it that time already?"

"Yes, ma'am. If you're not ready, I don't mind waiting out here."

Don't leave without your room key, notepad, and purse. The note was right there, right in front of Helga's nose. "Let me just get my purse," she told him. Stanley. Stanley, Stanley, Stanley.

She closed the door and went to the dresser, quickly leafing to a fresh page in her notebook. "Stanley," she wrote, and stuffed her pad into her purse, along with the room key. On second thought, she took the pen and wrote the name on the palm of her left hand. "Stanley."

She checked her hair and her lipstick in the mirror and went out the door.

"Got your key?" Stanley asked, holding the door open a crack.

Helga opened her purse. There it was. Good. She held it up for him to see and he closed the door tightly.

"Don't you have better things to do with your afternoon?" she asked.

"Actually, ma'am, I *do* have to eat and . . ." He smiled tightly. "Let's just say I welcome the distraction."

Hmmm. "Do I know you well enough to comment that that sounds as if you've got woman trouble?"

He laughed. "I don't think anyone knows me well enough to say that to me."

"Not even your mother?"

"With the sole exception of my mother. You're right. But she's been gone a long time."

"She helped save my life," Helga told him. "Did I already tell you that? She and Annebet and your grandparents, too. When the Nazis began rounding up the Danish Jews, they took us in. Hid us. For weeks. It was doubly dangerous because Hershel—my brother—and Annebet were working for the resistance." She pushed the down button for the elevator. "Did your mother ever tell you about that time?"

"Not a lot. And I'm sorry, ma'am," he said. "We can't take the elevator. If the power goes out . . ."

"Of course," she said. "What was I thinking?" She followed him to the stairs.

He held the door for her. "Did you say your brother's name was Hershel?"

"Yes." She held tightly to the bannister as she started down the stairs.

"Hershel *Rosen*?"

"Yes."

"My aunt Anna told me about him," Stanley said.

"Really?" Helga stopped on the landing between flights of stairs, and Stanley courteously let her pretend that it wasn't because she was out of breath. "Did she tell you they had been married?"

"Well, considering she called herself Anna Rosen, I guess I'd always just known—"

"Anna? Not Annebet?"

"My mother sometimes called her by her full name, you know, when they were arguing, but her prescription pad said Dr. Anna Rosen."

Helga wasn't sure whether she wanted to laugh or cry. Anna had been Hershel's sweet name for her. She started down the stairs again. "No wonder I could never find her. I searched for a Dr. Annebet Gunvald."

"I'm sorry."

"I should have known," Helga said. "Anna Rosen. What did she tell you? About Hershel."

"That she'd married him when they were both pretty young," Stanley told her. "That they didn't have your parents' approval. That he was Jewish. When I was a kid I used to go with her to synagogue. She claimed she was an atheist, but . . . She liked to go. She told me she and Hershel worked for the resistance, that it was pretty unorganized, even after the Germans came looking for the Jews, but that everyone in town stepped forward to hide their neighbors."

"Seventy-eight hundred Jews in Denmark," Helga told him, "and all but four hundred seventy-four escaped to Sweden, thanks to people like your mother and her family." She smiled. "Do you know when your father—no, your *grand*father—came to warn us that the order had come to remove the Jews from Denmark, my father and mother didn't believe him. They argued for so long that your grandfather was still there when the Germans came pounding on the door. We hid in the basement, and Herr Gunvald went out the back. He came around the front of the house and told the Germans that we weren't home, that we were vacationing up north. He told them to go away, that he'd been asked to keep the property safe, and he was determined to do so. He threatened to call the police. And do you know, they actually left?"

"I can't imagine what that must've been like to live through," he told her as he ushered her into the dank restaurant in the basement. She snuck a look at her left palm. *Stanley.*

"We stayed with Marte's family for weeks while Annebet and Hershel used their contacts to try to arrange passage to Sweden," she told him, thanking him as he held out a chair for her at a nearby table.

He glanced around the room as if he were looking for someone before he sat down, too. He was trying not to let it show, but she could read frustration in his body language.

"She's not here, is she?" Helga said.

He looked startled for a moment, but then he laughed. "No, she's not."

"You want to talk about it?"

His smile was beautiful. "The situation is a little, um . . . Well, let's just say it's not something I'd share even with my mother."

"Ah," Helga said. "You slept with her. That pretty pilot, right? What happened? Didn't you tell her you're in love with her? Of course not. Men always leave out the most important details."

Stanley didn't blink. "Might I recommend the curried vegetables over noodles? There's a buffet line, I can get us both plates. It's quicker than ordering."

"Don't worry," Helga said. "I won't tell."

She probably wouldn't even remember by the time he came back with their lunch.

By 1220, Alyssa was feeling solid enough to give lunch a try.

But the sight of Sam Starrett and Jules Cassidy sitting together in the hotel restaurant, deep in discussion, made her blood run cold.

What was Starrett up to? God, he was probably setting Jules up for something. This had to be some kind of cruel con, some kind of payback or revenge trick—all because she'd seen him cry.

Didn't it?

Except she was watching Starrett's eyes as she walked toward him. She saw when he first noticed her. He looked up and a myriad of emotions crossed his face. Apprehension and embarrassment, anger and even fear—she saw it all before he quickly looked away.

He actually thought she was going to walk up to him and rub in his face the fact that she'd seen him crying.

She knew better than to do something like that.

Didn't she?

Confused, she made a sharp detour and went to the table where piles of wrapped sandwiches were on ice.

She couldn't deal with this. She couldn't deal with Starrett looking that nervous at the sight of her, couldn't deal with not knowing for certain if she *had* been about to fling his tears right back in his face.

Dear God, she could actually imagine herself doing it. All Starrett would have had to do was greet her with some stupid-ass comment about the clothes she was wearing, and she would've lashed out without thinking. "Poor baby, are you going to cry over that now, too?"

When had she become such an insensitive monster?

Whatever had made Sam cry, that was none of her business. It was off-limits. Using it to try to hurt him was going too far. *He* didn't seem to know where to draw the line in the war they had going between them, but damn it, that didn't mean *she* had to sink to new depths.

Yes, his tears were none of her business.

Unless, of course, he'd been crying over her.

Kind of the way she'd cried over him just this morning.

"You, um, getting that to go?"

He was standing right behind her.

Alyssa braced herself before she turned to face him.

"I, uh, wanted to apologize for, um, shouting at you that way in my room," he said, not quite able to meet her eyes. "You caught me at, um, you know, a disadvantage there, and I, uh, I kind of freaked out." He cleared his throat. "I know you thought I was going to hit you, but, Jesus, I would never do that, Lys." He looked directly into her eyes. "I would never hit you. Never."

"Oh," she said, surprised. "No, I didn't think that. Not at all. I didn't . . ."

He nodded. Forced a smile. "Well, good."

"Why were you sitting with Jules?" She wanted to know, and she figured what the hell, she might as well ask. Especially when he was standing right in front of her, completely stripped of his arrogance and his cock-of-the-walk attitude.

Well, maybe not *completely* stripped. He had enough in him to bristle slightly. "Don't get any ideas. I'm not crossing over to the other side or anything."

She tried to swallow a laugh and failed. "Sorry," she said

quickly. "It's just, out of all the men I've met in my life, you're about the most unflinchingly heterosexual."

He laughed softly. "Thank you. I know you don't mean that as a compliment, but thank you anyway." He looked down at the sandwich she was holding, gestured toward it with his chin. "*Are* you taking that with you? Do you mind if I, uh, walk with you?"

Alyssa nodded, unable to trust her voice.

"You want a soda to go with that?"

"Water," she said, and he grabbed two bottles from a bin of ice as they headed out of the restaurant.

"It's good and cold," he said, bracing open the door to the stairs for her with his shoulder. He held both bottles of water in one hand. He had big hands with long, graceful fingers. Strong hands that always bore some kind of cut or bruise—a fingernail turning colors from getting jammed, or a scraped knuckle. She tried not to look at his hands, tried not to think about the way he'd touched her with those beautiful hands just last night.

"You might want to drink one now," he continued. "Two minutes out of the ice and it'll be tepid, like everything else around here. This f—" He stopped himself, cleared his throat. "This, uh, damned heat, you know?"

She looked at him. "Are we actually talking about the weather?"

"Yes," he said. "Yes, we are. I thought I'd start with the fucking weather, maybe touch on what you've been up to the past six months, and, shit, work my way up to the conversation I just had with Jules over lunch. See, I had it all figured out that we'd talk for a while, and then I'd bring up your partner. And I'd tell you that I got a chance to talk to him a little and he's an okay guy, and you'd be like 'Jules and *you*? Wow, *Roger,* there's a friendship I never dreamed would happen in a million years.' "

Alyssa had to laugh at his imitation of her. It was pretty accurate, down to her habit of using his given name.

"And I'd say," he continued, "kind of casually, that Jules and I actually have a whole hell of a lot in common because, you know, we're, um . . ." He took a deep breath. "See, we're both in love with you."

Alyssa bounced her sandwich on the landing and scrambled to pick it up again. She looked at Sam, and she knew that he'd said exactly what she thought she'd heard him say.

"Of course, you had to go and ask why I was sitting with Jules, which made me have to deliver the . . . the . . . punchline, I guess you'd call it, earlier than I wanted to."

"I'm sorry," she said, hardly able to breathe.

"You're sorry that I'm in love with you, or—"

"I'm sorry I blew your timing," she said.

She could see hope in Sam's eyes. It was growing with each second that went past.

"So you're *not* sorry that I'm in love with you?" he asked. "Sorry if I'm getting obnoxious about this, but I want to make sure I understand what you—"

"How could you love me?" Alyssa asked. "You barely know me."

Sam shook his head. "No," he said. "I know you. I know enough. And I want to know more. I want you to get to know me, too. And I know what you're thinking—this is just me wanting you back in my bed tonight, but it's not that. I want to spend the night with you, but I want to spend it talking." He cut himself off. "Okay. Right. That's a fucking lie. I'm dying to make love to you again, but I want to do it when you're sober. When you know exactly what you're doing. And if it's a choice between spending an hour talking or spending an hour making love, I'd pick the talking. Of course, I'd rather spend *two* hours with you and—"

Someone was coming. Sam must've heard the door open. It was Gilligan and Izzy coming up from the restaurant, arguing about baseball.

He took her hand and pulled her up the stairs with him, careful to stay ahead of the two SEALs and out of their line of sight.

He let go of her as he opened the door to the lobby, as he led her across to the stairs heading up to her room. His room, too. They were in the same tower.

He took her hand again as he took the stairs at a pace that

was extremely aerobic. But she was damned if she was going to let him see she was struggling to keep up. And he knew it, too, the jerk.

He *loved* her. Alyssa didn't know what to think, what to say, what to do. She wasn't quite sure how to *feel*—if she even *wanted* Sam Starrett to love her.

If she even believed him.

"Sam," she said as he pulled her out into her hallway. Her room was three doors down, and he stopped in front of it.

He didn't let her speak. He kissed her. But it was completely different from the Sam plus Alyssa equals nuclear meltdown type kisses he'd given her in the past.

It was the sweetest, most devastatingly gentle kiss she'd ever shared with anyone. He brushed his lips across hers in a way that could only be described as tender. He coaxed her mouth open, and . . .

It was over much too soon.

"I love you," he whispered. "I want as much from you as you're willing to give. So if you have any desire at all to turn this thing—I don't know, what do you call it, this get trashed and go slumming thing you do with me every six months?—into something more regular, I'm right here. I'm ready. I want to have dinner with you after this is over. I think the situation here is coming to a boil within the next twenty-four hours. And by the way, I could use your help with the practice—we're going to be back at it in three hours."

She nodded. "I'll be there." That was the easiest of his questions to answer.

He smiled ruefully as if he could read her mind. "I'll let you think about dinner," he said. "It doesn't have to be in public, if you don't want anyone to know you're seeing me—I don't give a damn about that. We can keep it completely backdoor. We could get room service. You just have to promise to dress for dinner. And promise not to let me take your clothes off—at least not until the second course."

Sam kissed her again, deeper this time, but just as slowly and thoroughly.

"Thanks for hearing me out," he said, handing her one of the bottles of water.

And he turned and walked away.

Alyssa couldn't believe it as the door to the stairs closed behind him with a very solid thunk.

He had three hours before he had to report, and he'd just *walked away*?

She stood there for a moment, waiting. Certain he was going to come back.

But he didn't.

She went as far as the stairs and even opened the door, but he was definitely gone.

Alyssa laughed in disbelief. One more kiss like that, and she would've invited him into her room.

She'd all but decided that this *was* just another ploy to get back into bed with her. *I love you.* Yeah, right.

Except it was working. He had to know it was working. He was on the other end of those kisses. There was no way he couldn't have known that by kissing her that way he'd made her melt.

But he'd walked away.

I love you.

Oh, my God.

"He's getting impatient," Bob told her apologetically.

Gina wiped her face. Jeez, she hadn't even realized she'd started crying. Her heart was pounding, drumming in her ears. "It scares me to death when he does that."

Snarly Al had been kicked out of the cockpit and into the main cabin of the plane. She could hear him still shouting, hear the babies and some of the passengers start to cry.

"I'm sorry," Bob said as if he really meant it.

"His shouting at me isn't going to help," Gina said. "I have no clue what he's saying. I mean, I don't even speak his language."

"Of course you don't," Bob said. "You're American."

He was smiling despite the accusation in his words. But his voice wasn't even slightly hostile. Or maybe it was. Maybe everything he said was hostile, and she just couldn't see it that way.

She'd been so convinced he was kind. Gentle. Her friend, even.

The way they'd talked . . .

But the look in his eyes when he threatened to kill Max and then kill her . . .

Maybe he was only bluffing. Maybe not.

Gina didn't know anything anymore. She was losing it, big time.

"Do you want me to get on the radio and see if there's any news?" she asked, praying that he'd say yes. Al had taken his gun and stuck the barrel right up to her head during his latest rant. She'd been certain this was it, that even if he didn't mean to kill her that his finger would slip in his rage, and her brains would be sprayed across the cabin.

In the aftermath of her fear, she desperately wanted to hear Max's soothing voice.

She knew he was listening in all the time. He'd dropped hints to let her know they'd managed to plant cameras and microphones on the plane. He could see and hear what was going on. Even right now when the microphone switch wasn't pressed down.

She could feel Max watching her. She knew with a certainty that he never left that room over in the terminal. He was with her 24/7, and would be until this ended. Or until Al pulled that trigger, whichever came first.

Bob shrugged, so she keyed the microphone. "This is flight 232. Is there any news? Over."

Max's voice came back, warm and thick and easygoing, like a security blanket. "This is Max, 232. We're checking the status of that." It was his usual I'm-stalling response, designed to keep the channel open and the conversation going. "I don't suppose our friend Bob is willing to talk to me directly yet. How 'bout it, Bob? Over."

Bob shook his head. He stood up and went out of the cockpit and into the cabin, no doubt to try to rein Al in.

"Please, God, don't bring him back in here with you," Gina said, under her breath. "Al's strung pretty tightly," she said into the microphone. "You might want to give them that guy they want released from jail—Razeen. Or something. *Soon.* Over."

"Or something," Max repeated. "Roger that, 232. We're working as quickly as we can, but it still might take some time." There was an edge to his voice. Yes, he definitely knew Bob had left the cockpit. Still, he was being careful, in case they were being overheard. "I bet you're tired, huh, Karen? I bet you're glad you're sitting *down* on the floor. Over."

"Yeah," Gina said, her heart pounding for an entirely different reason now. "I'll just stay right down here, as long as they let me. Go ahead."

Please, *please* go ahead.

"It was two weeks to the day after we went into hiding at the Gunvalds," Helga said as she stirred sugar into her coffee. "I remember it as if it were yesterday. We were just sitting down to breakfast and Annebet burst in."

Helga's whole amazing story had been leading to this. But Stan wasn't sure he wanted to hear any more. He took a sip of his own coffee. Bracing himself.

"Hershel had been shot," she told him, just as he'd expected. "In his and Annebet's search to find passage for us on a boat to Sweden, he'd found a fisherman willing to take the risk. But he'd needed a crew, and they made a trade—they'd be his crew for a fortnight in return for passage for the five of us to Sweden."

She fell silent for a moment, just gazing into her coffee, momentarily transported back to that day all those years ago.

Stan had been surprised when Desmond Nyland had called him, even more surprised when the man had taken him into his confidence, telling him that he believed Helga Shuler was suffering from some kind of age-related mental deterioration, perhaps even Alzheimer's.

She had no problem at all keeping track of this story she was telling him. She seemed clear about the details and didn't repeat anything. She was actually a very good storyteller. Stan was intrigued by her description of his mother and aunt as young girls, by this glimpse into the lives of the grandparents he'd never known.

It was almost enough to keep him from thinking about Teri. About the way it had felt to be inside of her.

About the scratches from her fingernails that she'd left on his back. She'd wanted him, *needed* him so badly that she'd marked him.

But possibly not as permanently as he'd marked her.

Christ, how could he have let himself get so out of control that he'd forgotten to put on a condom?

And what the hell was wrong with him that despite the fact that he should be worried about whether or not he'd gotten Teri pregnant, what he *really* couldn't stop thinking about was when he'd get to see her again. When he'd get another chance to drive himself inside of her, to feel her clinging to him so desperately and gasping his name and—holy fuck, it made him so hot just to think about it—making more of those welts on his back.

The sweet little old lady sitting across the table smiled at him.

"Where was I?" she asked.

Um . . . "Annebet," he said, struggling to remember. "She and Hershel had been working as crew in trade for passage for your family."

"Ah, yes. Hershel and Annebet both had been spending their nights making the crossing with this fisherman and another student, Johan, that they knew from the resistance. It was very dangerous.

"That night they'd arrived safely back in port and were making their way to shelter when they were stopped by the Germans. Hershel heard them coming, and he pushed Annebet into the brush by the side of the path. He knew the Germans had seen them, but it was dark—they couldn't know how many of them there were.

"It was probably just a regular patrol, stopping them for breaking curfew, but Johan panicked. He had a gun and he opened fire." Helga smiled sadly. "Of course, the Germans fired back. Johan was killed, Hershel badly wounded.

"The Germans took him to the hospital in Copenhagen. They didn't know it, but by doing that, they handed him right back to the resistance. The hospital was being used to hide hundreds of Jews. Everyone who worked there either did their part or looked the other way. Hershel was instantly declared dead on arrival—oh, he was still alive. But he was put into a bed under the name Olaf Svensen. A nice, non-Jewish name.

"Annebet told us she had seen him, spoken to him at the hospital," Helga told him. "His biggest concern was to get us—my parents and myself—to safety in Sweden. One of the nurses at the hospital knew of a ship that was leaving that night. But Poppi wouldn't leave Denmark without Hershel.

"Annebet begged and argued and cajoled and even cried. She finally ordered me and Marte to the barn to play, and I knew then that Hershel was dying. I wouldn't stay and eavesdrop even though Marte wanted me to—I didn't want to hear it. I remember sitting in the barn and Marte telling me that it was going to be all right, but knowing that it wasn't. Not for me, not for Mother and Poppi, and especially not for Annebet. It was never going to be all right again."

Helga sighed heavily. "Poor Annebet. She felt to blame. It was her gun—she'd sold it to Johan just that evening. Hershel had been bugging her to get rid of it, for fear something just like that would happen. If she'd never had the gun in the first place . . ."

"Johan probably would've gotten one from someone else," Stan pointed out.

"Yes, that's what Hershel told her. Still, she felt to blame."

"Excuse me, Senior Chief."

Stan glanced up to see Jenk making a beeline for him. "Excuse me," he said to Helga as he got to his feet. "Trouble?"

"Lieutenant Paoletti wants us to do a few more rounds of practice runs a little earlier than scheduled," Jenk reported. He lowered his voice, leaned closer. "Apparently things are getting tense aboard the aircraft. They want us together and ready to go."

"Mrs. Shuler, I'm afraid you're going to have to tell me the rest of this story at another time," Stan said.

"Of course," she said. She glanced at her hand—she had his name written there. "Stanley."

Damn. He couldn't just leave her here. He looked around

the room. "Yo, Gilligan!" The petty officer had just finished lunch.

"Yes, Senior Chief?"

"I need you to escort Mrs. Shuler to her room. 808. Don't let her take the elevator. Take her all the way to her door, see that she gets inside. Do I make myself clear?"

"Aye aye, Senior Chief."

"Mrs. Shuler, this is Petty Officer Third Class Daniel Gillman. He'll take you back to your room, ma'am."

"That's really not necessary," she said.

"Ma'am," Stan said as politely and as respectfully as he could manage, considering he had to stop at his room and change his clothes before heading up to the helo on the double, "I think you know that it is."

Twenty

STAN HIT THE roof at a run.

Most of the team was already there, along with the two FBI observers, Locke and Cassidy.

Sam Starrett was on a landline, a hotel phone. "Tell O'Leary to catch another helo over because we're ready to— *Fuck.* These fucking phones." He redialed on his cell phone.

"Power's gone out in the hotel again," Jenk reported. "Possibly this entire sector of the city."

"We got a pilot?" Stan asked Jenk, who was carrying a clipboard.

He flipped through the papers there. "Yeah. Howe. No, wait. Edwards. Yeah, they switched assignments at the last minute. L.T. okayed it."

Shit. Stan was unaware that he'd spoken aloud until Mike Muldoon spoke.

"That's probably my fault, Senior." Muldoon pulled on his vest and lowered his voice. "I think she's avoiding me. She canceled lunch on me, too. She left a message saying she thought we should talk when we get back to San Diego. I think I'm getting dumped before I even got attached."

"Yeah, I'd like to talk to you, too," Stan said. "I'm pretty sure I steered you in the wrong direction, and I owe you an apology. After this is over. Maybe on the flight home?"

Muldoon shook his head. "Senior, you don't owe me anything."

"Yes, I do." He owed Teri an apology, too. She'd come to him for help, and he was such a pompous prick, so goddamn full of himself, he'd assumed he could fix all her problems. Of course he could. He was Mr. Fix-It, the Miracle Man. He could make things right for her. And the fact that he'd been hot for her from day one? Well, he could just ignore that. He was stronger than that, tougher than a mere mortal man. Things like lust and desire—the mighty senior chief was above all that.

Except when she came into his room and took off her clothes. That was something he hadn't planned on happening. Yeah, that was well outside of his projected possible scenarios.

Then, after completely losing his mind over her, he didn't even have the balls to come clean and tell her. He didn't say a single word about how crazy he was for her, how much he liked her and respected her, how beautiful he thought she was. He hadn't told her that making love to her had been completely beyond his wildest imaginings—and he had one hell of an imagination.

He hadn't admitted that he was scared to death because he was falling in love with her. Yeah, he couldn't come clean even with *himself* about that one. Falling. Right. As if he hadn't already fallen. As if there was still a chance that he wasn't going down and going down hard.

And while "Teri, I love you," may not have been the words she particularly wanted to hear either, he could have gone for something more along the lines of "God, you're incredible."

Instead he'd asked where she was in her menstrual cycle.

Yeah, he'd messed this up but good. Teri had gone into run and hide mode again—because of *him. He* was the asshole she was hiding from now.

"Let's go!" Starrett shouted. "Let's do this right!"

It sure would be nice to do *some*thing right today.

Helga sat in her hotel room, surrounded by Post-it notes.

Never forget. It was the cry of all Holocaust survivors. Never forget.

She'd told her story so many times. To classrooms full of children. To women's clubs. To religious groups. At cocktail parties and diplomatic functions.

"I lived in Denmark as a child—during World War II. I was but one of seventy-eight hundred Danish Jews living near Copenhagen when Hitler invaded. Did you know Denmark was the only country that said, No, you will not take our Jewish citizens. Denmark was the only country in Europe where Jews weren't required to wear a yellow star on the front and on the back of all their clothing.

"Did you know that in February 1942, in Nazi-occupied Denmark, a man who tried to burn down the Copenhagen Synagogue was tried and convicted—and sentenced to three years in prison? For a crime against Jews.

"Did you know that of the seventy-eight hundred Danish Jews, all but four hundred seventy-four escaped to Sweden? And of those unlucky four-hundred seventy-four who were rounded up by the Nazis and sent to Theresienstadt, all but fifty-four survived because the Danish king sent word to the Germans saying, We are watching you. Those fifty-four died from sickness and old age.

"Denmark said no. You cannot do this to our citizens. Denmark said *no*, and her people rose up, at great risk to themselves, and thousands of lives were saved. In other countries, they shrugged. What could we do? If we tried to help, they'd have killed us, too.

"Maybe so. But maybe all they really had to do was just . . . say no."

She would write a book. About Annebet and Hershel. About Marte and her parents. She would do it soon. While she still could. Surrounded by Post-it notes, if necessary. She'd finally put her story onto paper. Then, when her voice was finally silent, when she could no longer remember her own name, her words would still ring out. Her story would not be forgotten.

Helga had faced challenges before. With the grace of God, she could face this one, too.

The hotel's fire alarm went off.

Teri quit pretending she was sleeping and just lay on her bed, staring at the ceiling, listening to the braying of the horns.

When she'd switched assignments with Jeff Edwards, she'd told herself it was because she was tired. She needed to sleep.

She'd come back here and climbed into bed and pretended she hadn't switched assignments because she was hiding from Stan.

But the truth was, she was hiding from Stan.

And Stan, being a highly intelligent man, had probably figured that out.

What she didn't know was, once he knew she was hiding from him, would he steer clear of her or would he make an effort to seek her out?

If he came knocking on her door, looking to talk seriously about the possibilities of her being pregnant, she would scream.

But really, what were the odds he'd come knocking on her door only to step inside, lock it behind him, and give her one of his knockout smiles? What were the odds he'd admit that the sex they'd shared was the best sex he'd ever had in his entire life, and that he wanted to do it again—right now?

And what were the odds that, afterward, still tangled together on her bed, he'd kiss her. Softly. Tenderly. And he'd tell her . . .

What?

Teri sat up and put on her boots. She shrugged into her hated flack jacket and grabbed her key from the top of the TV that didn't work and went out into the hallway. The sirens were louder out here, and she covered her ears as she jogged toward the stairwell, heading down to the lobby.

The power was out in the hotel and emergency lights were on in the stairwell, giving it a creepy, otherworldly feel.

There weren't as many people heading down the stairs as she'd imagined there'd be. And she even passed a maid carrying an armload of towels and going *up*. That was probably a large clue that this was just a false alarm, but she was more than halfway to the lobby, so she kept going.

Besides, maybe she'd run into Stan.

And then what? He'd drop to his knees and tell her that he loved her? That he wanted to marry her?

The man didn't even have furniture in his house. He'd told her he had no intention of getting married—ever.

And she—when the hell had she turned into Snow White? Lying around praying that someday her prince would come?

So what if Stan didn't want to get married. So what if he didn't love her. So what if he considered their lovemaking to be a mistake.

He liked her. Teri knew he did. And he was attracted to her, too. She knew that as well.

She'd gone to him this morning, and he'd been unable to resist her. Maybe if she did that enough times, he'd get used to the idea, get used to having her around—having someone take care of him for a change.

God, she just wanted to be with him.

And she was damned if she was going to let him get away without a fight.

Someday my prince will come, indeed.

How about tonight? Tonight she'd find her prince. She'd go to him. And tonight, yeah, if she did it right, her prince would definitely come.

Teri laughed aloud at the rudeness of that particular double entendre as she pushed through the door to the lobby.

Sirens.

There should have been sirens when the Germans finally came for the Jews, but there weren't. It was silent and the sky was very blue. It was just another October day.

Helga was in the Gunvalds' barn with Marte when they heard voices in the street.

They went to the door, thinking it was the vegetable cart.

But it wasn't.

A crowd of neighbors and friends had gathered—and the German officer in charge was warning them to stand back.

"This isn't your business," he said.

Helga saw Wilhelm Gruber standing off to the side, smoking a cigarette, just watching.

And then the German officer, in his gleaming black boots, saw them. "You there," he ordered, pointing to Marte. "Do you live here?"

"Stay here," Marte said to Helga. "Stay hidden."

But the German had already spotted her. "Both of you girls. Come here."

There was nothing to do but go forward. Running would only prove they had something to hide. Helga had heard Annebet say it often enough.

Marte took her hand, holding it tightly. "I won't let them take you," she murmured.

Then Annebet came out of the house, cool as could be. "Is there a problem?"

The German officer stood a little taller at her smile. "We received information that there were Jews hidden here."

From where Helga stood in the yard, she could see Fru Gunvald leading her parents out the back door and through a hole in the fence to the neighbor's house.

"There's no one here but my mother and my sisters," Annebet said, crossing to stand beside Helga, her hand on her shoulder.

Wilhelm Gruber shifted his weight.

And Helga heard Annebet draw in a sharp breath. She hadn't realized Gruber was there. Gruber, who knew Annebet had only one sister. Who knew Helga was not just a Jew, but the sister of the Jew who had married Annebet.

Gruber looked at Helga. He looked at Marte. He looked at Annebet.

And then he looked off down the street, without saying a single word.

And Annebet came to life again. "I'm taking my sisters and going to the market," she told the German officer. "You can search the house if you like. My mother is inside. Mama!"

Fru Gunvald hurried back into her house through the back door and came right out the front, wiping her hands on her apron as if she'd been in the kitchen, cooking all the while.

"Someone has wasted this officer's time," Annebet told her mother, "claiming we're hiding people here."

Fru Gunvald looked so surprised, even Helga found herself believing her. "In this little house?" Fru Gunvald said with a laugh. "There's barely room for us, let alone guests. Come in, come in, and see for yourself."

"Come," Annebet whispered, taking Helga and Marte by the hand. "Keep walking, don't speak, and don't look back."

Helga didn't look back.

And she never saw the Gunvalds' house or brave Fru Gunvald again.

The hotel lobby wasn't as crowded as Teri had expected with the fire alarms still wailing, but then again, the big hotel was barely full—most of the rooms being used by U.S. military personnel, most of whom weren't hiding from their lives, the way she had been.

She spotted the SEAL who was nicknamed Izzy, a sandwich in each of his hands.

"False alarm," he told her. "Someone broke the call box on the second floor. Probably just—"

His T-shirt turned red and he dropped his sandwiches and crumpled to the floor. And Teri realized that that tearing sound she heard was an automatic weapon being fired.

Izzy had been shot. Still, he reached for her, trying to pull her down. But it was too late.

Teri felt the punch of the bullet hit her, the force pushing her back and over the top of a sofa. She landed on something hard as her world went black.

"Get on the radio," Sam Starrett ordered Jenk, "and find out what the fuck is keeping O'Leary."

He turned to find the senior chief standing next to him, washing down some of this infernal dust with a bottle of water.

"You know, we're ready for this," Wolchonok said with that matter-of-fact confidence that only the senior chief could pull off. "When L.T. calls and says go, we're good to go. My guess is it'll be right before sundown. The tangos'll be expecting us to wait until dark, so we'll jump the gun."

Sam nodded. "I wish I had your confidence."

"We can run it again, if you want," the senior said.

"Oh, shit!" Jenk had turned a shade of pale beneath his tan, the radio handset to his ear. "Oh shit, oh *shit*." His voice shook. "Frank O'Leary's dead, Lieutenant."

No one moved, no one spoke, no one breathed.

The senior chief was the first to kick back to life. "Report," he ordered Jenk. "What happened? Did a helo go down?"

O'Leary—dead. It didn't seem possible. The men who'd been resting in the shade stood up, moving closer so they could hear.

Frank O'Leary had been a quiet son of a bitch, but he'd been laid-back and easy to get along with. Although few besides Jenk knew him particularly well, he'd been well liked. And he'd been dearly loved for his skills as a sniper.

"Someone set off the fire alarm back at the hotel," Jenk reported, "waited until everyone got downstairs, then opened fire in the lobby."

"Oh, Christ," the senior chief breathed. "What kind of casualties?"

"At least six Marines killed," Jenk said. "About twenty wounded. Izzy and Gillman were both hit—I don't know how badly, or if they're even alive."

"Find out," Senior ordered him. "I want to know the location and status of every member of the Squad. Get everyone to check in. Support personnel, too. Helo pilots, everyone."

"Everyone's checked in but Big Mac, Steve, and Knox," Jenk reported. "Support personnel's checked in, except for Bob Hendson and—no, Hendson and Howe are both on the casualty list."

The senior chief made the kind of sound a man made when gut punched. It was not the kind of sound anyone there had ever heard coming out of the senior chief before.

Howe. *Teri* Howe. Oh, Jesus. Sam glanced at Alyssa, glad beyond belief that she was standing right there, whole and alive. He couldn't even imagine how crazy he'd be going right now if he'd just been told her name was on that casualty list and that she could well be dead or dying.

"Which list?" the senior asked, swiftly pulling out of whatever he'd almost fallen into.

Jenk was still staring at him, wide-eyed.

"Which casualty list?" The senior seemed to expand, intent on getting this information *now*. He got louder. "Which fucking casualty list are Hendson and Howe on? The question's not that hard, Jenkins."

But Jenk shook his head. "Senior, it's chaos over there—"

Sam stepped in. "Find out. Call Lieutenant Paoletti directly if you have to."

"Aye aye, sir."

The senior chief turned to Sam, the muscle jumping in the side of his jaw. "You want to run this drill again, Lieutenant?" he asked tightly, ready to do his job despite the fact that the woman he cared for—and despite all his protests, Sam knew now for absolute certain that the senior chief cared for this girl—could very well be dead.

Sam shook his head. "No, we're ready. Let's go breathe down Max Bhagat's neck. We'll take a couple hours of rest, but we'll do it over at the airport. Senior Chief, take Jenk and go to the hotel. Find out what the fuck is going on over there and report back in."

The order wasn't even out of his mouth before Wolchonok had grabbed Jenk and headed for the helos at a dead run.

There were tanks out in front of the hotel. Stan could see them as the helo approached. The number of Marines had quadrupled, too.

Christ, they should have gone into siege mode *before* lives had been lost.

Frank O'Leary—God rest his soul. The world was going to be a darker place without him in it.

And Teri Howe . . .

Just before they'd gotten onto the helicopter, Jenk had found out that Navy pilot Bob Hendson was on a list of names of personnel who had been flown via helo to the hospital on board the U.S.S. *Hale*, an aircraft carrier just off the coast, not far from Kazabek. Izzy and Dan Gillman were on that list, too.

But not Teri Howe.

Stan closed his eyes as the helo set down, praying to whatever God was listening that the reason Teri wasn't on that list wasn't because she was on the KIA list with Frank O'Leary.

Please God, don't let her be dead. Please God, I'll be good
for the entire rest of my life. . . .

Jenk touched his arm, gesturing that they'd landed.

Ah, Christ, Stan had tears in his eyes. Jenk pretended not to
see them as he followed him off the helo and across the roof.

He'd heard Jenk shouting on the helo, trying to talk on the
radio despite the noise. He was still plugged in to the damn
thing, still trying to get that information.

"Any word?" Stan asked.

Jenk shook his head, no, his eyes apologetic. "Not on Teri
Howe. Stevie and Knox have both checked in. They were in
their rooms. They slept through the whole frickin' thing."

"Head down to the lobby," Stan ordered. "Find out what
kind of information center has been set up down there. I want
a status report on Izzy, on Gillman, on Hendson. Find out
MacInnough's room number—maybe he's still asleep. I'm
going to check Teri's room."

"Aye aye, Senior Chief." Jenk didn't blink at the news that
Stan already knew Teri Howe's room number.

They went down the stairs together, Stan pushing through
the door that led to Teri's hallway when they reached that
level. He ran down the corridor, not daring to think about the
hope that had sprung to life when he'd heard that two of the
SEALs had slept through the attack. Maybe Teri, as well, had
been too tired or too smart to head down to the lobby when
the fire alarm had gone off. Maybe the alarm didn't work on
her floor. Maybe . . .

He pounded on her door. "Teri!"

Jesus, Jesus, Jesus, please open the door with your hair
messed from sleep, squinting a little at the light, and . . .

Stan pounded and pounded, and even if she'd been in the
bathroom she'd had to have heard. And even if she'd taken her
time, she could've gotten to the door and opened it. He finally
stopped pounding, and he did what he should have done from
the start—unlock the door. It took him four seconds to get inside, another two to see, indeed, that the room was empty.

He stood there, in her empty room, knowing that he didn't
have any time to waste on his own frustration and pain. He

had to find her. He had to go down to the lobby, where she may well have died. He turned around, closing the door behind him. He had to go into the conference room they were using as a temporary morgue and—

Teri was standing in the hallway.

Her clothes were covered with blood, and her eyes were huge in her face as she stared at him.

"Oh, my God," he whispered. "Are you hurt?"

"It's not my blood."

Stan reached for her, needing to see for himself that she truly was unscathed. But he hadn't so much as touched her when she lunged for him, her arms tight around his neck. She was shaking, and he held her tightly, too, his hand slipping up beneath the edge of her jacket and her shirt. His fingers found smooth skin, unbroken skin, unwounded skin, thank you, dear Lord.

"Frank O'Leary's dead," she said, her face against his chest.

"I know." But she wasn't. She was alive and warm and her heart was still beating. He could feel it. She was pressed that tightly against him.

"I held him while he died," she said. "He called me Rosie and he told me that he loved me."

"Oh, Christ—" Oh, Frank.

"I told him I loved him, too, and then he just . . . oh, God, Stan, he *died*."

"Oh, baby, I am so sorry."

She was crying. Thank God she was crying. When he first saw her standing there, she'd looked dazed. Battle shocked. What she'd been through this afternoon had been the closest thing to a battle that she was likely ever to experience. And in many ways it was far worse. It was bad enough getting caught in a firefight when you were fully armed, but to have some asshole open fire into an unarmed crowd . . .

"All I could think was that I didn't know where you were," she told him. "The lobby was filled with people who were hurt or dying, and I didn't know if one of them was you. And then I couldn't stop to look because they needed pilots to fly

the wounded out to the U.S.S. *Hale*, and every time we came
back I was afraid it was going to be you I was carrying to the
hospital there. And I kept trying to find out where you were
and nobody goddamn knew anything. So I just kept flying,
covered with O'Leary's blood. God, it's under my fingernails,
and poor Rosie! Her world has ended and she doesn't even
know. . . ."

He held her tightly, aware as hell that while he'd been
scared out of his mind about her, she'd been worrying about
him, too.

"I'm okay," he said. "Tell me again that you're okay."

"I'm okay," she said. She pulled back to smile at him
through her tears. "I'm so much more than okay, because *my*
world didn't end."

Stan's radio shrieked.

Teri pulled back from him, wiping her eyes. "God, I need a
shower."

She unlocked her door. Held it open for him.

He triggered the radio's switch, refusing to think about
what she'd just told him. "Wolchonok. I found Teri Howe.
She's all right. Come back."

He stepped into her room. Only for a minute. Held the door
open wide with his foot.

"Thank God. I found MacInnough, Senior," Jenk reported.
"You don't want to know where he's been. Let's just say he's
seen a different kind of action. Over."

"Izzy, Gillman, Hendson? Over," Stan asked as Teri
slipped off her jacket and kicked off her boots. She stepped
out of her pants—Christ, what was it with her and taking off
her clothes in front of him?—and he let the door close.

"Izzy's in critical condition, but already out of surgery.
Took a round to the chest," Jenk told him. "Gillman got hit by
flying glass. And Hendson got hit in the knee. He's in surgery
right now. They're trying to save his leg. Over."

Stan turned his back to her as Teri peeled off her shirt.
"Radio Lieutenant Starrett with this information. Over."

"Already have, Senior. Over."

"Good. Get your ass to the airport. I'll join you there
ASAP. Over."

The shower went on.

"Negative, Senior Chief," Jenk came back. "Starrett's already sent the team back to the hotel. Max Bhagat's afraid it'll look like retaliation if we go in with force now. We're back to stalling for as long as we possibly can. Looks like we've got the night off, Senior. Get some sleep, if you can. Over and out."

Stan slipped his radio into his vest pocket, aware that Teri hadn't heard that. For all she knew, he couldn't stick around, which was probably just as well.

Definitely just as well.

"Where are you heading now?" she called from the bathroom. She'd left the door ajar.

"Um," he said.

"Can I come with you? I would really love not to be alone right now. I'll stay out of the way, I promise."

Stan shrugged out of his combat vest, setting it on the floor. It didn't mean he was going to stay. It just meant it was warm in here with it on, that was all.

He picked up her flack jacket from where she'd dropped it. Thank God she'd remembered to wear . . .

"Stan?" she called. "Are you still here?"

"Uh, yeah," he called back.

Holy shit, she'd been hit. The bullet was there, flattened and stopped by the bulletproof mesh.

He pushed the bathroom door open. It hit the wall with a thump. "Why didn't you tell me you were shot, god damn it?"

"I wasn't shot." She turned off the water.

"A bullet connected with the jacket you were wearing. I don't know what *you* call that but—"

"Will you hand me a towel?"

"Teri, you're driving me crazy," Stan said. "How badly were you hurt?"

"It knocked me over," she said, reaching out an arm and grabbing a towel without his help. "Knocked the air out of me. I'm a little bruised. But I wasn't shot." Her voice shook. "Frank O'Leary was shot."

"Okay," he nodded, giving her that. "You're right. There's a definite difference. But you were hit. I know what that can do. I just want to make sure you're okay."

She pulled back the curtain and stepped out of the tub, swathed in a towel. "I'm okay."

She would have breezed right past him but he shifted left, blocking her.

Stan didn't say a word. He just looked at her.

She lifted her chin. "You know, if you really want me out of this towel, you'd get a lot further by kissing me."

He still didn't move.

Teri reached up to loosen the towel, suddenly modest. She pulled it back, just enough to reveal her right side—the whole long expanse of her leg, her hip, the soft curve of her waist, all that skin, still damp from the shower. The effect was far sexier than if she'd simply flashed him. She pulled the towel farther up, and there, just beneath the soft underside of her breast, was a spectacular rainbow-colored bruise about the size of his fist.

Stan winced. "Christ, that must've hurt."

"It hurt a lot less than it would have if I hadn't been wearing my jacket."

She probably would've died. Stan looked at the place where that bullet would've entered her body and drew in a long, shaky breath. "Have I thanked you yet for wearing your jacket?"

She laughed as she pulled the towel back down around her. "Have I thanked *you* yet for making me wear it?"

He shook his head. Damn, he had to get out of here. The way she was looking at him, the way she was standing there with nothing on but a towel, close enough for him to reach out and touch, all that warm, soft skin . . . All he had to do was reach for her. Or say one word. If he whispered her name, she'd drop the towel and be in his arms in a heartbeat. She wanted him that much—he could see it in her eyes.

And he wanted her, too. He wanted her more than he'd ever wanted anything or anyone, more than he wanted to breathe.

"Is there any chance you can stay?" she whispered. "Because I really want you to stay."

"Yeah," he said. "I really want to stay, too, but . . . Teri, I'm good at problem solving, but this . . . this is out of control. I just can't come up with an option where everyone wins."

"I can," she said, and she let go of her towel and kissed him.

Teri kissed him, and Stan swept her up into his arms and carried her to her bed.

She kissed him and, like magic, his clothes seemed to fall away.

She kissed him, and time slowed as he kissed her, as he touched her, loved her.

Slowly this time, with an awareness of every second that ticked past—with their eyes wide open.

He sat on the edge of her bed as he covered himself, as she lay back, waiting and breathless, dying to kiss him again.

He took his sweet time then, looking and touching. Heating her with the gentle touch of his fingers and the desire in his eyes. Kissing her, tasting her. Smiling at her, at the sounds of pleasure she made.

His mouth was soft and warm, his tongue teasing her slowly, sensuously until the sounds she was making became words. His name. She called his name over and over. Please. Stan, please. She wanted . . . She *needed* . . .

Finally, as he held her gaze, he filled her, still moving so deliberately slowly, as if they had all the time in the world.

She wasn't in control. Each time she reached for him, to touch him, to urge him faster, deeper, he gently pushed her back. He finally pinned both of her wrists up above her head, holding her easily in place with one of his hands.

"Please," she gasped, pressing her hips up toward him.

But he pulled back. Every time she tried to move with him, to push him more deeply inside of her, he pulled away.

"I want you to feel what I felt this morning," he told her. "I want you out of control."

It wasn't until she lay back and just opened herself to him that he pushed himself all the way home. "That's right," he murmured. All the time he kept moving slowly. Maddeningly, heart-stoppingly, deliciously slowly.

If she moved at all, he pulled away. It was only when she

relinquished all control that he gave her exactly what she wanted.

She watched his eyes as she gave herself completely over to him. And as her release began, as it built and rolled through her in wave after endless exquisite wave of sensation, pure pleasure and intense satisfaction flashed across his face.

And only then did he release her hands. "Now," he said. "Come on, Teri, take me with you!"

His hoarse words were enough to push her over the edge again, and she clung to him, moved with him, locking her legs around him and driving him harder, more deeply inside of her.

She was in control again, or was she? The sensation of being completely at the whim of another's desire, the feeling of flying without instruments into a fog, completely blind, of losing her sense of which way was up, remained. She held on to Stan as tightly as she could, but still she flew apart, shattering around him as he shouted her name, and she knew without a doubt that she was never going to be in control again.

It was a surprisingly freeing thing—to lie back and give in to everything she was feeling, instead of fighting it, instead of trying to hide it from everyone, from him, and from *herself*. She loved him. Whether he wanted her to love him or not, it was too damn bad. It was out of her hands—she *loved* him.

Her world hadn't ended today.

But maybe, just maybe, it had begun.

Twenty-one

IT WAS NEARLY dawn.

Another night had come and gone, and they were all still here, on this stinking airplane.

Bob had fallen asleep in the pilot's seat, his arms wrapped around his automatic weapon. Al was in the co-pilot's seat, also dozing, thank God. Gina didn't think she could stand another minute sitting here with his eyes on her.

She didn't think she could stand another minute of this, period.

She didn't understand. Max had all but promised that something would happen. Soon, he'd said.

So where was the cavalry, coming to the rescue? All night long she'd sat here, waiting.

If he'd said a week, she could've hung on for another week. But he'd said *soon*, and she'd been so sure *soon* meant before another morning dawned.

And now she didn't think she could bear another day.

"Max," she whispered through her tears, certain that he could hear her. "They're sleeping. Do it now, Max."

Of course he couldn't answer her.

And she knew from the glimmer of light on the horizon that no one was coming. Not for another day. Somewhere, somehow, she'd find the strength to bear it.

She'd have to bear it.

But the hijackers *were* sleeping, and even if Max—for whatever reason—wasn't able to help her right now, maybe she could help him.

She wiped her eyes, wiped her nose on the short sleeve of her shirt.

"Each of the men has an automatic weapon," she whispered, "but I think some of them don't have any ammunition. I've been watching and it looks like only a few of them have clips attached to their guns—I think that's what they're called."

"Magazines," Bob said. "They're called *magazines*."

Oh, shit, he was awake.

He sat up. "Who are you talking to?"

"Myself," Gina said quickly. "I'm just talking to myself. I'm just making mental notes—I'm going to write a book after it's all over, so . . ."

" 'Do it now, Max'?" he repeated. The friendly student was gone, and the cold-eyed man who'd threatened to shoot her if Max didn't go into the terminal was back, and Gina knew with a cold certainty that the game playing was about to come to an end.

She risked everything by reaching up and turning on the radio. Bob had turned it off last night, cutting Max off midsentence, proclaiming himself to be bored. But Bob didn't shout at her now. He just smiled as he stood up and stretched.

It was not a very nice smile.

"This is flight 232," Gina said into the microphone, praying for something, *any*thing to interrupt them. "Is there any news? Over?"

Max came instantly back. "Good morning, flight 232, hope you had a pleasant night. We hope to get the details of when Osman Razeen will be arriving very soon. Come back."

Bob took the microphone from her hand. "We were just talking about you, Max. Although I think I don't need to talk into this microphone for you to hear me, no? Shall we try?"

He dropped the microphone and raised his gun, firing several bullets into the panel inches from Gina's head. She shrieked and cowered. "Stop! Stop! Bob, I'm sorry! Please, don't! Please . . ."

She was an instant waterfall of tears and snot, her ears ringing from the noise of the gunshots. Just like that, all the calm dignity she'd been faking for so long dissolved. And she knew. She wasn't going to die well, with a knowing smile on her lips like Princess Leia facing down Darth Vader. No, she was going to die begging and pleading and sniveling, too scared and desperate even to hate herself for doing it.

"I'm sorry, Bob." Max's voice came back completely unperturbed. "I think I missed most of that. Can you repeat? Come back."

One of the hijackers from the cabin poked his head in. Bob gave a terse order and the man disappeared again, closing the door tightly behind him.

"He's good, huh? This Max," Bob said to her in his nearly perfect English. "Let's see how good."

He picked up the microphone. "I think our hostage is getting a little tired of us. And we're getting tired of her, too."

"That's easy to fix, Bob. Trade her for me. I'm here. I'm ready. You win millions of goodwill points by letting her walk off the plane. Over."

"And how many points do we get for dumping her dead body off the plane?"

Sam awoke to the sound of running feet.

Ah, fuck, he'd fallen asleep, right here in the terminal. He'd sent his team back to the hotel after Max Bhagat had gotten into a shouting match with his superiors in Washington. Bhagat had insisted that they send the SEALs in, that it was time to go, but they'd ordered him to drag this thing out for at least another twelve hours. Which would bring them to morning, which meant they'd probably have to wait *another* twelve hours.

Bhagat had been like a wild man. Starrett had never seen him so upset. He'd actually put his hand through the freaking wall. The timing was right, he kept saying. The hijackers were on the verge of meltdown. They were exhausted, the SEALs were ready. They could do this now and it would all be over by morning. Why did they have him here, if they weren't going to let him run this operation?

But Washington said that the world was now watching. And the world would think the swift and deadly takedown of flight 232 was retaliation for the hotel massacre. Not that *that* was a particular problem, but Washington was afraid something would go wrong and more civilians would die as the world watched. Apparently Washington didn't have the balls to stand behind its own highly trained, highly skilled professionals.

Sam had stuck around, waiting for Bhagat to cool down, hoping to get a chance to talk strategy. When *would* the timing be right? Tomorrow night? Tomorrow afternoon? He wanted to keep drilling his men, keep 'em fresh, but he didn't want to wear them out.

He now followed the sound of voices into the negotiators' room. Lieutenant Paoletti was there, looking like he'd been up all night. God knows he probably had been, dealing with sending O'Leary's body back home and making arrangements for the wounded to be shipped to a real hospital in a country where they believed in the sterilization of surgical instruments.

"Bob, I need you to talk to me," Max was saying. "Pick up the radio microphone and talk to me. No one's dead yet, don't cross that line. Come on back."

Jesus, one of the minicameras was picking up the action in the cockpit of the plane. One of the tangos was standing with his weapon aimed right between the girl's eyes.

"Bob, talk to me, man," Max said as calmly as if he couldn't see what was going on. "Come back."

"But wait," the tango said. "I better not waste the bullet, right? After all, we don't have much ammunition."

On the screen, he shouldered his weapon and turned, saying something to the other tango in the local dialect— something no one but languages expert John Nilsson could've understood.

And what do you know? Nils was there. Leaning over Bhagat's shoulder, murmuring a translation.

Sam didn't need to hear it to know that the first tango had ordered the second to hurt the girl.

Tango Two took off his weapon, obviously preferring to use his fists on anyone female and under thirty.

This was going to be bad.

Max was talking nonstop, trying to get the first bastard to pick up the radio microphone, and the girl was trying her damnedest not to cry, also talking, but in a voice that shook—

"I thought, you know, if we'd met somewhere else that we'd be friends"—and backing away, but she had nowhere to go.

She had nowhere to go, and when Tango Two hit her, when she cried out, her fear and pain rang in the room.

Sam was going to be sick.

Because, oh shit, this guy was going to kill her while they could do nothing but stand here and watch. He hit her again, and Jesus, she must've landed on the microphone because the sound went out. The video was still running, and they could hear faint, ghostly cries from the microphones out in the main cabin—picking up the sounds of her pain from a distance. It was surreal.

The position of the camera on the floor made for a hideous angle as she landed right beside it, her lip bloody, one eye swollen.

She lay there stunned as Max continued to talk, broadcasting over the radio. Somehow he kept his voice steady. Sam didn't know how he did it, how he managed.

Especially when, on the screen, the girl was flipped onto her back. Especially when, on the screen, she began to struggle. The way she was fighting, the intensity, the desperation, meant only one thing. The motherfucker was going to rape her before he killed her. And because Washington had told them to stall, they weren't ready to go in. And because they weren't ready, they were going to have to stand here and watch.

Sam threw up. Right there in the fucking wastebasket.

She thrashed so hard, the picture went out. It was impossible to say if she'd just covered it with her hair, or if she'd actually taken out the camera. Either way, they couldn't see.

They could still hear her, though. Faint crying and pleading. And then, Jesus, just crying.

Max threw his radio against the wall. "Where's Helga Shuler?" he shouted. "Someone fucking find me Helga Shuler!"

The news wasn't good. "Cell phones aren't working. We should have temporary access to landlines in several minutes, sir!"

Max pointed at Lieutenant Paoletti. "I want the SEALs ready to go in. I want them here in five minutes!" He turned around to face his silent staff. "Someone give me a goddamn radio!"

It was there, in his hand, almost instantly.

And as Sam watched, he took a deep breath and blew it out hard, and when he spoke his voice was smooth. Calm. As if he couldn't hear the sounds of that girl being attacked.

"Bob, let me talk to Karen. Will you please let me talk to Karen?"

Something was ringing.

It took Helga several long moments to realize that it was the telephone.

She groped for it in the darkness next to her bed. Found it. "Hello?"

"Helga. I need you here." Whoever it was, he was very upset. "I'm ready to give the order to go in," he said, "fuck Washington, and I'm not sure I'm making an impartial decision. I need your help."

She felt for the light. Switched it on.

And found herself surrounded by a yellow sea of Post-it notes.

"I'm sorry," she said, putting on her glasses and trying to read as many of them as she could. *You are in Kazbekistan. An airplane has been hijacked. Stanley Wolchonok is Marte Gunvald's son.* "Who is this? Stanley?"

"What? No. It's *me*. It's *Max*. Wake up, for Christ's sake! I need all synapses firing."

Max. There was no Max anywhere, on any of the sticky notes.

He was talking to her as if she surely knew what he was saying, as if she could give him the answers he needed. "They've beaten the crap out of Gina," he told her from between clenched teeth. "They raped her, too. We could hear—" His voice broke. "Jesus, we could hear them. They knew we could hear them, the bastards. They know we've got the plane miked."

Dear God, no wonder he was upset. "Breathe," she told him. "Just breathe, dear, and give me a minute here."

She didn't know who this Gina was—not that it mattered,

precisely. And she was still trying to identify Max. Did he work for her? Or did she work for him?

A notepad lay on the bedside table, and she flipped through it.

"Helga, I don't have a minute." Max's voice was strained. "These phone lines are unreliable. I'm lucky I got through to you at all. I want to give the order to go, but I can't step back from this. I don't know if I just want to save this girl, the hell with the other hundred and twenty passengers, the hell with the politics, the hell with the fact that after this, the hijackers are going to be ready and waiting for us to respond with force, and that puts the lives of my SEAL team at risk."

FBI negotiator Max Bhagat, Helga read, and the last name stirred her frozen memory.

"I'm calling on you as a friend," he said to her now. "This is not official, you know that."

She'd first met Max nearly fifteen years ago. He'd been impossibly young, incredibly cocky. One of those young men who was convinced beyond the shadow of a doubt that he was always right. She could remember the situation in which they'd met with a clarity that was astonishing. A Palestinian man had taken hostage a busload of Americans touring Jerusalem.

And Max had talked the man off the bus.

Try as she might, she couldn't remember more than the vaguest specifics of the current situation. Something about an American senator's daughter. But the girl's name was Karen, her notes said. Helga didn't know who this Gina was.

She didn't know even half enough to help Max now.

"I'm sorry," Helga told him, ashamed that it should have come to this. How dare she put herself in a position where others had to rely on her? She had completely blown it. She had let down a friend—by pretending she was okay, when she so obviously was not. Perhaps she could hide the truth from other people, but she couldn't hide it from herself. At least not anymore. "I can't help you." She closed her eyes. "I'm ill. I'll call Desmond, though. Maybe he—"

The phone line was dead.

Helga jiggled the button. Got a dial tone. She pushed zero.

The hotel operator greeted her in the local language.

"This is Helga Shuler," she said. "Can you reconnect me to the party to whom I was just speaking?"

"I'm sorry, ma'am. All outside lines have just gone down."

Merde. "Connect me to Desmond Nyland's room, please."

There was a click and then a buzzing.

Des picked it up on the first ring. "Nyland."

"Des, I'm so sorry, did I wake you?"

He just laughed. "Not a chance. I just got in. Are you all right? Are *you* awake? This is good timing actually. I have something urgent I need to talk to you about."

"I have something I need to tell you first," she said, closing her eyes. And then she said it. Aloud. "I have what I think is Alzheimer's. I think I've had it for a while—of course, I'm not certain—it's like that bad joke. I don't remember. But I do know that I can no longer do my job. I'll be faxing my resignation in the morning." She opened her notebook to a fresh page. "And I'm writing this down—that I've told you all this. I'm sure I'll need to be reminded."

Des laughed softly. "Lady, I'm going to miss you. But we're not done working together yet. I think you're going to be able to help me with one last thing. It's important. Are you dressed?"

"No."

"Get dressed—I'm coming over."

"It's time, Senior," Jenk said over the radio. "Come back."

"Holy shit," Stan said, checking the clock, surprised that it was morning. He'd fallen asleep facedown in Teri's bed, and here he still was, as if he hadn't moved an inch all night long.

Except he had. He definitely had. He distinctly remembered Teri waking him up in the middle of the night with a kiss and . . .

Yeah, he'd definitely come alive for that.

He pushed himself up and off the bed. "I expected to get called hours ago. What the fuck happened? Over." He winced as he looked at Teri. "Excuse me."

She sat up, and the sheet fell away from her as she stretched. Dear God. He was *definitely* not used to the sight of her naked. He suspected he never would be. She got out of bed, and he watched her walk across the room to the dresser, unable to look away.

"L.T. said whoever woke you before the last possible second was going to get their ass kicked, come on."

Man, he'd been trying to pretend that he hadn't woken up aroused, but the male anatomy being what it was, it was going to be hard for her to miss.

"Do we have food and water? Coffee?" Stan asked as he tried to focus his attention on his search for his briefs. "Do we even have a pilot? Over?"

"It's all taken care of, Senior. Just get to the roof, ASAP, come back."

"Yeah, who's our pilot, over?" Found 'em. Two more seconds and he would've given up and just pulled on his pants.

"Green, come back."

Teri was getting clean clothes from where she'd actually unpacked them into the hotel dresser drawers, and she turned to look at him in almost comically outrageous dismay.

"Where's Teri Howe assigned? Do you know, over?" Stan asked, slipping into his briefs and stepping into his pants.

There was a pause while Jenk searched through the paperwork.

"I wanted this assignment," Teri said. "After all this, to not even be there, at the airport, with you . . . ?"

"I'm sorry," Stan said as he pulled on his T-shirt. "But maybe it's just as well—"

"Howe's been assigned to standby at the hotel," Jenk came back.

"Thanks, Jenkins," Stan said. "Over and out."

He went into the bathroom to take a leak, and Teri followed him right in.

"You're happy about this," she said as she quickly brushed her teeth, watching him in the mirror. "Aren't you?"

He couldn't lie to her. "With the increased security, you're probably safest right here," he said as he zipped his pants, flushed, and went to the other sink. He splashed water on his face. "So, yes, I am."

"You said I was the best pilot you know," Teri countered as she handed him a towel and then the still soapy toothbrush.

"You are." This was . . . unique. While he'd had one or two relationships where he'd spent the entire night, he'd never shared bathroom time with a woman before. And he'd never shared a toothbrush. But why the hell not? He'd had his tongue in her mouth last night.

"The reason you don't want me to do my job is . . . ?"

"You are doing your job," he told her as he rinsed his mouth and dried his face. "Someone's got to be here— Look, I've got to go."

"I'm coming with you," she said, following him to the door. "I'm going to see if Green's willing to switch."

He stopped her. "What are you doing?"

She didn't get it. Christ, even after yesterday, she still didn't get it.

"You leave this room," he said sternly, "you wear your flack jacket."

She nodded. Grabbed it from the floor. And looked him dead in the eye. "Where's your flack jacket, Stan?"

He laughed. None of the SEALs wore jackets. There was no way they could maneuver and move quickly with all that extra weight. Forget about the fact that by noon it would be close to 120 degrees in the shade.

But Teri was serious, and laughing was a mistake. She caught his arm. "What is this?" she said. "That we've got going here? Is it just sex or is it something more?"

"Whoa," he said. "Teri, I'm late. Don't do this right now. Please. Just wear your flack jacket and stay safe." He kissed her—it was like kissing a two-by-four. Great. He started for the stairs. "I'll see you later."

The pounding on her door was so persistent, Alyssa was sure it had to be Sam Starrett.

She'd been certain he'd show up sooner or later, but frankly, she'd expected him more on the sooner side. And at nearly 0500, it was definitely later.

She crawled out of bed and opened the door without bothering to find her robe. "If you think I'm just going to let you into my room without so much as a . . ."

She found herself staring at the empty space where Sam Starrett's head should have been.

"Sorry, ma'am." She shifted her gaze down about eight inches and found Mark Jenkins's apologetic face. "But it's urgent. L.T. needs to talk to you, and cell phones are out. There were four different terrorist attacks to satellite receivers last night. Landlines are down, and even if they weren't, the hotel lines are not secure."

He held out a radio.

She took it, aware she was standing there in only an extra large T-shirt and her underpants. Jenkins politely looked the other direction as she thumbed the mike. "Locke."

"Alyssa, it's Tom Paoletti. You know O'Leary was killed yesterday. Over."

"Yes, sir. I was very sorry to hear it. Over."

"I need a second shooter for this takedown, and I want it to be you."

Alyssa nearly dropped the radio.

"I know it's highly irregular," Paoletti continued. "You're supposed to be observing, but I want you in place with Wayne Jefferson as our second sniper. We've got other marksmen in the team, but no one even comes close to your level of skill—hell, O'Leary wasn't as good as you. It's absurd to use anyone else if you're available. I've cleared it with Max Bhagat. Will you do it? Over."

"What's Sam Starrett have to say?" she asked. "Over."

"He generally says Aye aye, sir, when I give him an order," Paoletti came back. "I haven't spoken to him yet. But if he gives you trouble of any kind, tell him to come see me. Over."

"I'll keep that in mind, sir," Alyssa said, wondering if Tom had any clue at all about the kind of trouble Sam Starrett had been giving her lately. "Count me in."

Stan made it all the way to the stairwell door before Teri ran after him.

"No," she said as she followed him up the stairs. "No, Stan, I'm not going to wave good-bye and hope you come back in one piece so that I can then tiptoe around the fact that there's *far* more going on here than you and me having a good time in bed. You're the one who's always telling me to confront people when they piss me off, to get aggressive, to fight back, and god damn it, you just really pissed me off!

"Yes, you're older than me, yes, you're more experienced than me in a lot of ways, there's a lot you can teach me, I'll give you that, but I don't want you to be my teacher or my mentor or—" She shook her head, wishing he would slow down, but knowing that his haste to get to the roof was as much to make her stop talking as it was to reach the helos and the rest of the team.

"When we made love last night, that was just me and you, without any other garbage. It was about . . ." *Love.* Teri wanted to say it, but she couldn't get the word out. "We were equal partners. Fifty-fifty. It wasn't about you telling me to be a good girl and wear my freaking flack jacket. If you want me to wear my flack jacket, if you care about me enough to want me to wear it, then dammit, don't laugh at me when I care about you and ask where yours is."

Stan stopped her. One flight from the roof. "Teri, please, you're turning this into something bigger than it is. I'm telling you to wear your flack jacket because it saved your life yesterday. This is not an unreasonable request. It doesn't have anything to do with . . . with any of this other . . . bullshit."

She stared at him. "This is bullshit?"

"Oh, Christ," he said. "Teri, look, I hear what you're saying, I don't necessarily agree with it. I'm glad you're telling me that you're angry, I'm not so glad it's right this second. Your timing needs a little work."

"When is the right time to get angry?" she asked hotly. "If you want me to do it when it's convenient for you, then maybe you should stop being such a jerk."

He laughed as he took the stairs up two at a time. "God save me from estrogen-induced insanity."

She followed him up the stairs. The entire team was up there. Trying their damnedest not to listen—or maybe trying to listen, she didn't care either way.

"Who's not here yet?" Stan asked.

"Cosmo and Lopez," someone volunteered. "They're coming."

"That was a really assholeish thing to say," Teri lit into Stan, catching his arm and scrambling so that she was in front of him, blocking him. "God save *me* from testosterone-induced assholeishness! I love you, god damn it!" With all the words she'd stumbled over while chasing him in the stairwell, *that's* what she should have said. "I want you and I'm coming after you. I'm not going to let you get away from me. You better get some furniture for that house of yours, because I'm coming over!"

Oh, God. Everyone was looking at her. Sam Starrett. Mike Muldoon. WildCard and Jenk. "That okay with you?" she asked Jenk.

He nodded quickly. "Yes, ma'am."

Teri nodded, too. "Good. Well." She glanced at Muldoon. "Sorry."

He shrugged. "I think I pretty much knew."

She looked at Stan again, but he was looking away. Over toward the helo, as if he wished he were on board and flying away from her forever. Oh, God, what had she just done?

And there, in front of her, was helo pilot Walt Green. "Walt, I don't suppose I can talk you into switching—"

"Not a chance, Teri."

"Right. So. *My* day's going particularly well." She looked at Stan again, and this time he was at least looking back at her. But for the life of her, she couldn't read the expression on his face. God, she loved his face. "Good luck."

She turned and would have walked away with dignity, her head held high—at least until she made it back to her room.

"Lieutenant."

She stopped walking and turned around, resigned to facing the formality in his voice.

"I apologize for being an asshole," Stan said.

It was one of the last things she'd expected him to say. "I apologize, too," she whispered. "For embarrassing you like this."

"Do I look embarrassed?" He laughed. "A little overwhelmed maybe, but I'm sorry, the most beautiful, smartest, sweetest woman that I've ever met announces that she wants me? You've just cemented my reputation for being able to do anything. If you want to embarrass me, Lieutenant, you're going to have to do better than that."

She nodded, relief surging through her. "I'll try harder next time."

He smiled. "Good."

Lopez and Cosmo came bounding up the stairs, and Stan turned away, busy then being the senior chief, loading the team on board the helo. He was the last man on, and as he turned to look at her, she hugged herself, arms across her chest, determined not to stand there and wave good-bye while he went to save the world.

He cupped his hands to his mouth and shouted. "Keep your flack jacket on."

And it occurred to her in a flash of realization that when he said that, maybe it wasn't because he wanted to boss her around, to keep the distancing effects of age and experience prominent in their relationship. When he said that, maybe it was his way of telling her just how desperately he cared.

Teri waved.

Twenty-two

A BODY HAD been kicked down the stairs of the hijacked plane.

Stan went into the terminal building to find the negotiator's room grimly silent.

Lieutenant Paoletti turned to meet him, gesturing with a twist of his head for the two of them to step out in the hall.

"Shots were fired about fifteen minutes ago, and again about ten minutes ago," the lieutenant informed Stan. "The tangos opened the door just now, dumped this body."

"Is it the girl?"

"We don't know yet," L.T. told him. "Scooter and Knox are out there on surveillance, but even with high-powered glasses, they can't give a definite ID. The tangos wrapped some sort of blanket around the girl's body—that's assuming it is the girl. Bhagat is trying to raise them on the radio, trying to negotiate getting a vehicle out there to pick up the body. Meanwhile audio and visual are still out in the cockpit."

"Does Max want to wait till nightfall to send us in?" Stan asked.

"No," L.T. said. "He's got seven different people advising him to wait, but he wants to go now anyway. He knows damn well that that body is a 'come get us' message."

"So let's go and get 'em, sir," Stan said. "Let's be done with it. I want to go home."

The lieutenant sent him a sidelong glance. "To pick out furniture for the house?"

Oh, Christ. "News spreads ridiculously fast around here."

Paoletti held out his hand. "Congratulations, Senior Chief."

"Hold up, Lieutenant. There's a long road between getting laid and getting married."

Paoletti was visibly taken aback. And Stan instantly understood. "No," he said. "Tom—don't get me wrong. That's not what *I'm* . . . that's what *she's* doing. I mean, she thinks she loves me. . . ." The memory of her standing there, telling him so in front of the entire team, still shook him to the core. "Jesus, what's she thinking? Where's it gonna go? At the risk of sounding as if I'm boasting, because you know me—I'm not—I think she's blown away by the, uh, shall we say, the physical nature of the relationship. She's not real experienced, and trust me, in a week or two, she's gonna be—"

"Blowing *you* away," Paoletti finished for him. "Because if she means what she says, she'll prove it. The sex is a great part of the package, believe me, I know, I've been there, but it's just a part of it. It's her face, her smile, her knowing something's wrong and talking to you in bed at night until you cough up the problem, even when she's exhausted. It's her eyes. You look in her eyes and she's not afraid to let you see that you're her world. It's her taking care of you and needing you to take care of her, too." He laughed. "Stan, trust me, your life is never going to be the same."

"I hope so," Stan said quietly. "I'm not convinced she's thought it through and that's really what she wants, but Christ, Tom, I hope so."

"Alyssa!"

Alyssa turned around with a defensive set to her shoulders and a coolness in her voice and face that made his heart sink. "Lieutenant Starrett."

Damn. He'd thought they'd gotten beyond frosty and formal the last time they talked. Unless her response to his declaration of undying love was this cool *get lost.*

But this wasn't about them. This was about getting his team ready to go.

And the gods, in a last-ditch attempt at ultimate irony, had aligned the planets and put O'Leary into the path of a bullet, thus making the impossible happen. Alyssa Locke had become a member—temporary, yes, but still a member—of his, Sam Starrett's, SEAL team.

And maybe there were some devils at work, too, because— and what were the odds of *this* ever happening—Sam was ac- tually glad to have her.

The woman could shoot.

He and his men were going to kick their way onto a plane in which five men were in possession of deadly weapons. And he knew that because Alyssa was one of his two snipers, there were at least two fewer tangos that he and his team were going to have to tango with.

It wasn't as if she was going to be in any danger. It wasn't as if Lieutenant Paoletti had assigned her to muscle her way onto the plane alongside of Sam. If he had, Sam would've fought him, kicking and screaming. *That* he would've flat out refused.

But using Alyssa as a sniper—that was something he could agree with.

No, it wasn't easy to shoot another human being—to shoot to kill. There were people who argued that women weren't up to that task. They claimed a woman would choke in a sniper situation.

But Sam had no doubt that Alyssa would do her job, that she had her own way of coping with the elimination of a human target. Of course, maybe she was like him, and she just threw up afterward and then went out and got drunk.

But probably not.

Right now part of his job as CO was to make sure the other members of the team had as much faith in their snipers as he did. So he spoke loudly and made sure he was overhead. "L.T. told me you volunteered—"

"If you have any problem with it, you need to talk to—"

"I don't." Jesus, would she just relax? "I just wanted to tell you I'm glad you're here and to thank you."

She nervously moistened her lips, clearly surprised. Jenk and Cosmo were surprised, too. In the past, Sam had laughed at Alyssa's desire to be in the action, at the front lines, every chance he could get. "You're welcome," she said.

Sam nodded. Lopez and Muldoon were watching, too. "So

you want the welcome to the team handshake or the welcome to the team kiss? I figure since I've never really had the opportunity to give the welcome kiss before I should take advantage of—"

"I'll take the handshake," she said. Her face was straight, but she was fighting a smile. He saw it lurking at the edges of her mouth.

He took her hand and shook it. He wanted to hold on to it inappropriately long, to kiss her palm or even suck one of her fingers into his mouth, but he didn't because the team was watching.

There was a time when he would have done it *because* the team was watching.

And she knew it.

"I won't let you down, sir," she said.

"I know." He nodded at her. Turned away.

"Sam."

He turned back, surprised she'd used his name.

"Stay safe. Take head shots."

He smiled, touched that she cared. "I will."

She stepped closer. Lowered her voice. But it still wasn't low enough to keep Jenk and Cosmo from overhearing if they really wanted to. "After we're done here . . . Well, I was thinking, um, that, well, that you're someone I'd really like to get to know better. And I was wondering if maybe you'd like to have dinner with me."

Sam glanced at Jenk, who was pointedly not looking at him. He looked back at Alyssa, into the warm swirl of hope in her eyes, and he was afraid to open his mouth because he didn't think he could form any coherent words. He was afraid that a mindless howl of joy would escape, embarrassing her to death.

"In a restaurant," she added, as if he wasn't already aware that she'd fucking invited him to dinner in public.

So he just breathed for several long moments and nodded his head, hoping that she could see the party going on inside of him by looking into his eyes. And when he finally could speak, he uttered the understatement of the fucking millennium. "I'd like that."

"Good." She smiled and headed for the roof.

He did his best to walk away, too, without doing a dance.

And then he stopped dancing, even in his mind, because his radio squawked. It was Lieutenant Paoletti.

"We're done waiting," L.T. said. "There've been more shots fired on the plane. It's time to go in."

Des was more than half expecting Helga to be surprised to see him. But she opened the door quickly at his knock and let him in without a murmur of protest.

He didn't know whether to laugh or cry. The place was covered with sticky notes. Reminders, comments, lists of names.

"Man," he said.

She nodded. "It's a mess."

He pulled her close for a hug. "How bad is it? Do you remember talking to me on the phone?"

"Of course."

"Really?"

She pulled away from him, showed him the page of her notepad.

"Des is coming here. You told him you're losing your marbles. He has something important to tell you," was written on it.

"I figure since I wrote this, I must've spoken to you on the phone," she said. "How else would I have told you?"

"What year is it?" he asked.

She pulled a note from the headboard of her bed. "It's 2001. Most of the answers are here. Of course, if I spend all my time reading them, over and over, I manage never to leave this room."

"I bet it'll be better at home," he said.

Helga nodded. "It makes sense that it would be."

"We'll go to the doctor," Des said past the lump in his throat. "Maybe there's some new medicine."

She nodded. "That's not what you came here to discuss."

"No." He sat down on her bed, rubbed his forehead. God, where to start. "Do you know who I work for?"

There was a gleam in her eye. "You mean, besides me? You're with intelligence, no?"

"Not exactly. I'm part of an organization even more covert than Mossad or . . . But that's not important. What's important is that my immediate superior is a man with political aspirations that have seriously clouded his judgment. And no, I'm not going to tell you his name."

She sat there, watching him, and he had to wonder how much of this she was going to remember. Maybe it didn't matter if he used his superior's name. "Over the past few days, I've discovered some information about our hijackers that raises the stakes." He took her notepad and a pen from the bedside table. "I'm going to write some of this down for you, because I need you to remember. How many hijackers are on that 747?"

Helga looked at her Post-it notes. "Five."

"No," Des said. "There are six. In addition to the five men that we all know about, there's also a woman. She's rigged with explosives under her coat—a suicide bomb."

"Oh, my God," Helga breathed.

The approach to the plane went down exactly as they'd rehearsed.

The SEALs moved in from the rear, from the aircraft's blind spot.

Stan was with Muldoon, leading the way—a relatively easy task despite the fact that it was broad daylight. He knew exactly where the blind spot was, where the tangos could and could not see them. There was no need even to crawl—extra Marines had been brought in during the past twelve hours, and they were guarding the perimeter of the airport, making certain that no one unauthorized could see the movement on the runway.

Yeah, the last thing they needed was the hijackers getting a warning signal via mirrors from someone watching from the brush, tipping them off to the fact there were SEALs crawling around on the outside of the aircraft.

Big Mac and his two-man team were already out there under the plane, having taken advantage of the freedom of movement allowed by those extra Marine guards. They were attempting to get audio and video back up and running.

Once under the aircraft, the take-down team would begin the far more dangerous and painstaking task of gaining access to the front and rear emergency doors.

From here on in, they'd communicate via hand signals only.

Stan looked at Lieutenant Starrett and nodded.

Starrett nodded back, a glitter in his eye, clearly as glad as Stan was finally to be *doing* instead of waiting.

"They're all members of an extremist group," Des told Helga. "Their goal is simple—to die. They don't expect Osman Razeen or anyone to be freed by hijacking this plane. They only want to bring as much attention to their cause as they can. And the best way they know to do that is to take as many American lives with them as possible.

"I've found out that their plan is to wait until the rescue team is on the plane, and then blow it and everyone on board to hell," Des told her grimly. "Apparently the bomb has a fail-safe in the event that the woman wearing it is killed in the takedown. There's a sensor that reads the woman's pulse. If it doesn't pick up that pulse after thirty seconds, it goes into a three-minute countdown. Which isn't even close to the amount of time we'd need to evacuate all those people from that plane. They don't just want this thing to blow up—they want us to know it's going to blow and be unable to stop it."

"How did you find out this kind of detail?"

"I had a little conversation with the designer of the bomb."

"Do . . ." Helga took her notepad back from him and flipped through the pages. "Do Max Bhagat and Tom Paoletti know about this?"

"No."

It was blazing hot on the roof of Terminal A.

A fly buzzed around Alyssa's face, but she ignored it. She watched her target through her scope and breathed, listening to Max Bhagat's voice through her radio headset, hearing what her target could hear in the cockpit of that 747.

Persuasive and smooth, like an FM radio announcer, Bhagat was keeping both her and fellow sniper Wayne Jefferson's targets up by that radio.

Bhagat was talking to them as if they were friends. Fellow caring human beings.

Alyssa wouldn't have been able to do that. Not knowing they were murderers. Rapists.

She'd heard a rumor that Sam had been in the negotiators' room when the girl, Gina, had been attacked. Rumor had it that he'd thrown up. Tossed his cookies right in the wastepaper basket.

Alyssa believed the rumor.

Poor Sam. He pretended to be so tough, but she'd seen him get sick like that before.

She tried to imagine what it must've been like to be Sam and have to stand there and listen to that girl getting beaten. Raped.

And then she thought long and hard about what it must've been like to be the girl.

She kept her crosshairs aimed in the middle of her target's forehead, waiting for the clicks over her headset that signaled the SEALs were in place, waiting for the word from Tom Paoletti: *Go.*

"No one knows but me and now you." Des rubbed his face. "I've been ordered to sit on this information. My superior believes that the destruction of the plane and the death of so many Americans—including a team of Navy SEALs—will make the U.S. and Israel even more strongly united against terrorism. If I come forward with this, my career is over."

"But by leaking the information to me . . ." she said, still a very smart woman despite the disease that was ravaging her brain. "My career has already come to an end." She looked at him. "Order me not to tell."

"I order you not to tell."

"Phooey to you. I'm not going to let those people die." She picked up the phone. "Who do I call with this?"

"Yeah," Des said. "That's where we've got a little problem. Landlines are down and my cell phone's been dead since last night. Short of hitching a ride to the airport and flagging down Max—"

"What are we waiting for?" No-nonsense to the bitter end,

Helga grabbed her purse and her notepad and headed for the door.

Sam Starrett clicked once into his headset microphone as he gave the hand signal—*ready*.

The SEALs on surveillance would be watching him and they'd report to Lieutenant Paoletti in the negotiators' room that Starrett and Karmody were in place and ready to go.

He thought about Alyssa up on the roof, lying there in the hot sun.

He thought about Alyssa in his bed.

In his life.

WildCard was looking at him oddly and Sam realized he was grinning like a stupid-ass fool.

Wouldn't that be just his luck? To be too distracted to do his job, and get his ass killed.

God, don't take me now, he prayed. Don't pull some ironic shit here and have me die today.

And then he helped God out a little by refreshing his grip on his weapon and focusing on the job ahead, waiting for the other members of his team to signal that they were ready, too.

"We need to get to the airport immediately."

Teri turned to see Helga Shuler and her assistant hurrying toward her.

"Can you take us?" Mrs. Shuler asked.

"I'm sorry, ma'am," she said. "Not without proper authorization. I'd need to receive orders to—"

"Do you have a radio?" Mrs. Shuler asked. "Can you get in touch with either . . ." She looked down at a pad of paper she was carrying.

"Lieutenant Paoletti or Max Bhagat," her assistant supplied the names.

"Is there a problem?" Teri asked. "Is this some kind of an emergency?"

"There's a bomb on the hijacked plane," Mrs. Shuler said with a grim certainty. "There's a sixth terrorist on board—a woman. Once the SEALs take the plane, she's going to set the thing to blow. Everyone on board will die."

Teri stared for two or three seconds. Then she leapt for the radio.

Her vision was blurred.

Both of her eyes were swollen, one of them nearly all the way shut.

Her lip was split, her entire mouth cut and bleeding from her own teeth.

Her wrist was broken and each breath she took—both in and out—made her sides burn with pain.

She was bleeding. Her head, her nose, between her legs.

She lay there, beaten and naked from the waist down, her shirt torn, her shorts gone. Her uninjured hand covered what little she could manage to cover, and her knees were pressed tightly together—as if that would keep the next one from pushing her legs apart and pushing himself inside of her.

She'd known what was coming when Bob told Al to hurt her. She'd expected it, braced herself for it. Planned to endure it.

As long as she could keep breathing, as long as she was still alive, she was winning.

And finally it was over. Al had spit in her face and climbed off of her and she knew that she'd won.

Except she hadn't.

Because Bob had dropped his pants. And it wasn't over. And it was worse, far worse because he'd made her believe that he was her friend.

There was blood on the walls. Sprayed in a pattern. Someone—the pilot, she thought—had tried to stop them from hurting her and had died for his efforts. They'd shot him—the pilot—and he'd lain there beside her, half of his head blown away, for countless long minutes until they'd dragged him away.

She didn't want to look at that pattern of blood anymore, and she closed her eyes as she listened to Max's soothing voice over the radio, as she breathed and tried to convince herself that breathing still meant that she'd won.

*   *   *

"Helga Shuler is standing right in front of me," the pretty young helicopter pilot said into the radio, obviously working hard to sound rational and calm. "She has information that it's *imperative* Max Bhagat and Lieutenant Paoletti receive ASAP. Over."

The transmission wasn't very good, and Helga couldn't hear what the person on the other end of the radio had to say, but whatever it was, it didn't make the pilot very happy.

"No, sir, I will *not* keep this channel clear. I'm not going anywhere until I connect with Max Bhagat or Lieutenant Paoletti. I repeat, it is imperative I speak with either of them or with Lieutenant Jacquette or with Senior Chief Wolchonok or with Lieutenant Starrett, or God! Let me speak with Petty Officer Jenkins! I'm not picky here! Over!"

Des touched the girl's arm. "We can be at the airport in three minutes if you fly us."

She looked from Des to Helga, and Helga could see that her career was flashing in front of her eyes. But still, she nodded. "Get in."

Alyssa lay on the roof, watching her target, listening to Max Bhagat.

He was talking about money. An offer, he said, from an outside source. They were willing to pay twenty-five thousand dollars, U.S., he said, for each passenger who walked safely off the plane.

Yeah, he'd caught their attention with that one.

She wasn't listening so much to the words anymore as to the tone of his voice. The rise and fall of the phrases. Every so often he'd say *over* or *come back*, and there'd be a pause.

And then he just paused, without an *over*, and she knew before she heard the word, that it was coming now.

Jefferson shifted slightly, too, as in tune with it as she was.

Tom Paoletti's voice. "Go, go, go!"

She squeezed the trigger.

Go, go, go!

The door opened and Starrett turned his head away as the flash bang exploded.

And then he was inside, facing a tango, weapon in hands, in his kill zone.

He fired.

She heard a crack, heard what sounded like a single loud explosion from the cabin, then Max, shouting, his voice distorting over the radio speakers. "Gina, stay down!"

She opened her eyes to see that she'd been sprayed with blood.

Al, who'd been in the co-pilot's seat, was sitting there still, but he wasn't going to hurt her anymore.

Bob had been pushed back and down, against the door, his eyes sightlessly open, a neat hole in the middle of his handsome forehead.

"If you can hear me, please God, I hope you can hear me," Max was shouting over the sounds of gunfire and screaming from the cabin, "stay down, Gina! Stay down!"

She crawled to the microphone dangling down near the floor and keyed the thumb switch.

"Max," she said through her broken lips, "can you bring me some pants?"

Teri connected with Lieutenant Paoletti as the airport came into view.

Helga was in the co-pilot's seat, radio headset on and ready, and as soon as she heard Paoletti's name, she began to speak. Clearly. Concisely. In her gentle Danish accent. Reading from her notebook.

"This is Helga Shuler. I have sources with Israeli intelligence who have informed me that there is a sixth terrorist on board the hijacked plane. A woman rigged with a suicide bomb. You must abort, repeat abort. Over."

"It's too late to abort," Paoletti said, and Teri's heart clenched. "Please stand by with your information, over."

Too late. They were too late. Stan was already on that plane, and her world was about to end.

She could see the hijacked aircraft out on the runway, see the snipers and other personnel on the terminal roof.

Teri headed for the runway.

* * *

Stan went in fast, Muldoon to his left.

He both heard and saw Muldoon fire, neatly taking out one of the terrorists.

The noise was intense, both in the aircraft's cabin and over his radio headset.

Five tangos had been eliminated within seconds of the flash bangs.

He could hear Sam Starrett's voice shouting for the passengers to stay down, to stay in their seats, nobody move fast, nobody move.

Stan was still in adrenaline mode, his senses relaying information to his brain at warp speed. He caught sight of movement from the corner of his eye, and he turned.

And the world went into slow-mo.

A woman.

Standing up.

Right near the bulkhead, mere feet from where he and Muldoon had come in.

Muldoon's back was to her.

Light glinted on metal.

A handgun—she was pulling it free from her coat.

She was wearing a fucking overcoat while everyone else was stripped down to their T-shirts.

Stan pulled up his weapon.

And saw that—Jesus!—she had a baby in her arms.

He could fire and stop her cold, but not without hitting the baby.

He hesitated, and his hesitation—just those few brief seconds—cost him dearly.

He was dead.

Her handgun was out and up and there was nothing to do but step in the way to prevent her from hitting Muldoon.

He saw her fire, and realized. It was a doll she was holding. He was going to die for a fucking plastic doll. And as she moved, he saw beneath her overcoat that she was rigged to blow, wired with some kind of bomb, loaded down with C-4.

And he pulled his own gun higher even as he felt the impact of her bullet and he fired back a double burst. Head shots. Praying there wasn't some kind of automatic trigger that would take them all instantly to hell.

The woman went down and Stan grabbed her.

Teri landed the helo next to the plane.

"Are you nuts?" Des shouted. "This thing's going to blow!"

"Then you better run away," she told him.

Helga was on the radio, reading aloud her information about the bomb, broadcasting to the SEALs.

To Stan, who was somewhere on that plane with a bomb that could go off any second.

She switched her radio to the channel Paoletti had said the SEALs were using.

Starrett couldn't fucking believe his ears.

"The bomb has a fail-safe," a woman with an accent not entirely unlike the famous Dr. Ruth's was saying over his headset, after Lieutenant Paoletti had dropped the less than welcome news that there was a bomb on board.

"There is a sensor designed to read the pulse of the woman who has the bomb," Dr. Ruth said. "After thirty seconds without reading that pulse, it will go into a three-minute countdown, repeat, three-minute countdown."

"Have we located this woman?" Starrett shouted. God was doing it. He was pulling an ironic on him. Sam never should have agreed to have dinner with Alyssa Locke.

But then, over his headset, he heard the most beautiful words spoken by one of the most beautiful voices in the entire beautiful world.

It was the senior chief, the team's miracle man. "I've got the bomb."

Alyssa Locke stood on the roof of Terminal A, her heart in her throat.

Someone—it looked like Muldoon—had triggered the emergency slide on their side of the plane.

"The woman is dead." Senior Chief Wolchonok's voice

was only one of many coming through her headset, but it was the only one she was paying attention to. "I'm exiting with her out of the port side of the aircraft."

"Let's get these people off the plane! Starboard side!" That was Sam's voice now, his lazy drawl transformed, his voice rapid-fire and nearly accent-free. "Move!"

Three men had come out of the terminal and were running toward the runway. Tom Paoletti, Jazz Jacquette, and Alyssa's boss, Max Bhagat.

Jules Cassidy was down there, too, in a truck, no doubt waiting to give Bhagat a ride to the plane and win brownie points for being there and ready. He pulled alongside of them with a screech of brakes and they all jumped aboard. He zoomed out onto the runway.

Toward the plane and the bomb.

Alyssa looked at Jefferson.

Who nodded. They headed down the stairs and toward the plane as fast as they could run.

"Get Mrs. Shuler out of the helo," Teri shouted at Des. "Move back, move away."

He didn't need to be told twice. He nearly picked the woman up and hustled her off, hurrying in the direction of the terminal.

She could see Stan then. Coming down the slide. Carrying a body.

He was covered in blood—not his, please God.

But he staggered as he reached the ground, staggered again when he shouldn't have staggered, and she knew.

"Stan's been hit," she reported. "I need the hospital corpsman—Jay Lopez!—on the port side of the plane *now*! Stan, how bad is it?"

"Teri? Shit, you're not supposed to be here."

"Glad to see you, too, babe. Muldoon, get your butt down that slide and help the senior chief. He's wounded! And someone get me the new coordinates for the U.S.S. *Hale*. Now!"

* * *

Stan was already dead. He'd known that the moment he'd stepped in front of that gun.

Except he was still moving. Still walking.

It was the adrenaline that kept him going.

He didn't have much of a plan other than getting the bomb off the plane until he saw that helo sitting there on the runway like a gift from God.

Three minutes wasn't a lot of time, but if he could get the bomb and himself onto that helo, he could pilot that thing far enough from the plane and terminal to keep anyone else from getting hurt.

And then it was more than the adrenaline that kept him going. It was the adrenaline and his knowing that he could fix this. It would be his last fix, but it would be a good one.

But then he'd heard Teri's voice, and he knew. She was on board that helo and getting her off wasn't going to be easy. She wasn't going to leave him, and because of that, she was going to die, too.

"Teri, get the hell out of here. I can fly that thing."

"Yeah, you can do a lot, hot stuff," her voice came back, "but I'm the one who wears the wings in this relationship. Lopez, where the *hell* are you? We're counting down and I'm in the air the second Stan is aboard."

Muldoon was beside him, then, helping him carry the body. "Senior, you're wounded."

"Get back!" The timer was running. Two minutes and fifteen seconds and everyone near this thing was dead.

But Muldoon didn't back off. He took most of the woman's weight from Stan and helped him move faster.

And then Tom Paoletti and Jazz Jacquette were there, too. And Lopez. And then Stan wasn't carrying anyone anymore. He was being carried.

Onto the helo.

They were in the air, then, and he was shouting. This wasn't part of his plan. Teri wasn't supposed to be there. Or Muldoon. Or Jacquette. Or Lopez, who was starting an IV on him right there, tearing open his shirt.

"Lieutenant Howe, can you fly this thing a little faster?" That was Jazz Jacquette's sub-bass voice. He was good, but there was no way he was going to defuse a bomb like that one in under three minutes.

"Believe me, sir, I'm doing the best I can. Stan, you still with me?"

"Teri," he said. The adrenaline was wearing off and his whole world was pain. Pain and a bomb that was going to blow in a matter of seconds. "Gotta ditch the bomb! Don't want you to die, too—"

"No one's going to die. Lieutenant Jacquette is watching the timer. What's the countdown, sir?"

Jacquette: "Can you get me over the open ocean in fifteen seconds?"

"You bet." Teri. "I'll be flying nice and low. Let me know the minute the bomb hits the water. I'll take us up and out of here. Stan, no one's going to die, do you hear me? *No one*. We get rid of the bomb and our next stop is the hospital on board the U.S.S. *Hale*."

"Teri," Stan said, having trouble breathing, afraid she was wrong.

"Bombs away," she said. "Any time now!"

"It's in the water," Jacquette shouted. "Go!"

Gina lay on the floor of the cockpit, aware of the door being forced open.

Someone came in. Someone in uniform who took one look at her and began shouting for the lieutenant, shouting for medical assistance.

And then another man came in. He was wearing a white button-down shirt and a tie, and he had a blanket that he used to cover her.

"I'm so sorry," he said, "that we didn't get here sooner," and it was so strange to hear that voice, Max's voice, coming out of a real mouth, in a real face.

It was a good face. Blurry, but good. What she could see was older than she'd pictured, with deep lines of fatigue around his eyes.

He had tears in his eyes, and she knew that seeing her like that, broken and bleeding, hurt him badly.

"At least you got here," she said. "I'm pleased to finally meet you, Max."

He laughed at that, but then started to cry. As she watched, he composed himself, wiping his eyes and even managing to give her a smile. "I'm going to get you off the plane now."

He was ready to pick her up in his arms, but she didn't want him to remember her that way forever. First impressions were important, after all, and she was already at a serious disadvantage.

And dammit, she wanted to see something besides pity in his eyes.

"No," she told him. "I want to walk." And as she said it, she realized it was true. She did. She wanted to walk off that plane. "Will you help me walk out of here?"

"Yeah." He nodded and helped her to her feet, the muscle jumping in his jaw as his repositioning the blanket around her forced him to get another glimpse of her battered body.

He stood on the side of her unbroken wrist, slipping her arm over his shoulders, his arm around her waist, supporting her.

And she walked. Out of the cockpit. Out of the plane. One step at a time.

The force of the explosion pushed them forward and up, and Teri wrestled with the controls.

And then they were home free.

Heading toward the U.S.S. *Hale*.

"What's the status of the patient?" Teri asked.

No one answered her.

"Lopez?" She couldn't keep her voice from sounding sharp.

"Make sure we have a medical team ready," Lopez finally said. "The moment we touch down."

"Teri," Stan whispered.

"No," she said, suddenly terribly afraid. "Don't say it. Look, I've got my flack jacket on. There's nothing you need to tell me now that you can't tell me later."

He said it anyway. "Love you."

"Yeah?" she said. "Well, screw you, Senior Chief. If you love me, dammit, you stay alive!"

And then there it was. The U.S.S. *Hale*. Right where it was supposed to be.

She landed the helo and Stan was taken away, and then there was nothing left to do but pray.

Twenty-three

SAM STARRETT OPENED the door of his hotel room to see John Nilsson and WildCard Karmody standing there, looking like someone had died.

"Oh, shit," he said. "Don't tell me the senior chief—"

"No," WildCard interrupted. "Senior's fine. Well, considering he took a round to the chest and spent three hours in surgery . . ."

"L.T. just got a call," Nils told him. "The senior chief's still in intensive care, but he's looking strong."

WildCard grinned. "If Teri Howe were holding *my* hand, I'd get well soon, too. Damn, this op has been like a fucking *Love Boat* episode."

Nils gave WildCard a look that Sam didn't like the looks of.

"So then what's the bad news?" Sam said.

"Can we come in?" Nils asked, way too seriously.

"Is something wrong with Meg?" Sam asked about Nils's wife as he let them into his room. "Some problem with the baby?"

Nils closed the door behind them. "No, Meg's fine. In fact, I just called home and spoke to her. She's great, the baby's—everything's great. Right on schedule. She had another ultrasound, and . . . But she told me that Mary Lou called, looking for you."

Mary Lou Morrison? "She's got to stop calling," Sam said. "I haven't seen her in months. In fact, I'm having dinner tonight with—"

"You better sit your ass down and cancel your dinner plans, Sammy boy," WildCard said. "We've got some extremely intense news. Mary Lou's preggo, my friend, and she says you're the father—and that she's already had the tests done that prove it."

Sam didn't sit down. "What?"

Nils looked at WildCard in disgust. "You sure broke it to him gently." He sighed. "Sam, you really better sit down. Mary Lou's got a friend who works in some medical lab. She had tests done. It wasn't legal, she didn't have your permission, but that doesn't change the results. She used some old T-shirt that you got blood on when you cut yourself fixing her car and . . . Meg's seen the results, man. Mary Lou's pregnant, and the baby's definitely yours."

Sam sat down.

Gina awoke to find Trent Engelman sitting by the side of her hospital bed.

She'd been flown out of Kazbekistan, here to London, last night.

Her one eye was bandaged, and the other was swollen and her vision still blurred. She'd been stitched and X-rayed and examined, her broken wrist set. She'd had an IV started, and a doctor from the U.S. embassy who'd taken one look at her and had been quite liberal with the dosage of painkillers.

And she'd floated. Out of Kazbekistan, aboard some kind of special hospital plane. She'd floated through the night, but she could have sworn that it had been Max sitting by her bed, holding her hand.

Not Trent Engelman.

He stood up when he saw that she was awake.

Her mouth was fuzzy, and he helped her take a sip from a cup of water, his mouth tightening sympathetically as he put the straw to her swollen lips.

There were coffee cups all around the chair he'd been sitting in.

Imagine that—Trent Engelman sitting by her bed all night.

"Your parents are on their way," he told her. "They should be here in a few hours."

"Oh, God." They were going to take one look at her and . . .

Her mother would be so angry. Not at her. But she'd want to get a gun and kill Bob and Al all over again.

Her father would cry.

"You know, Gina, I, uh, just came by to thank you, you know, for saving my life," Trent told her. "If you hadn't stood up the way you did . . ." He cleared his throat. "I know you must think I'm a coward because I just sat there when they were, you know, and I heard you screaming, but . . . Shit, Gina, they had those *guns*. They killed the pilot."

"Yeah," she said sharply. "I know. I was there."

He looked at the floor.

"I don't think you're a coward, Trent," she told him, knowing that he'd come here not to comfort her, but to comfort himself. God, had she dreamed Max? Was he ever really here with her? "Would you mind going, because I kind of want to be alone right now?"

He inched toward the door. "I promised that guy I'd stay until your parents came."

She looked at him. "What guy?"

"The guy that was sitting here when I got here this morning. He was holding your hand," Trent said. "Some old guy. He left a note for you."

Sure enough, there was a folded piece of paper on the rolling table right beside the bed.

"Gina." It was from Max. He'd signed it at the bottom just Max. His handwriting was as clean and clear as his voice. Or maybe he'd just taken care when writing this note because he knew she'd have trouble reading with her eyes all messed up.

I can't meet you for coffee. I know I promised I would, but . . . The counselors and therapists who are going to be working with you will tell you that you need to move ahead with your life, to let the traumatic events of the past few days fade away. Meeting me for coffee will only make it that much harder for you to forget and move on.

You are without a doubt one of the most amazing people I've ever met in my life. Your inner strength awes and inspires me. I have no doubt that you will come through this.

I'm so sorry for not being there when you needed me the most.

"Trent," Gina said. "When did you get here? When did Max leave?"

"Just a few minutes before you woke up."

"Go out into the hall," she said. "Run down to the lobby. See if he's still here."

Trent made that sound he made that was almost a laugh, but not quite. He made it whenever he was being put out. "Gina . . ."

"Please."

Trent went.

He was gone for close to forever. Gina had nearly given up on both him and Max when he came back. "I didn't see him," he reported. "Who is this guy anyway?"

He was gone. Max was *gone.* Gina closed her good eye. Even with Trent standing right there, she'd never in her life felt more dreadfully alone.

"Thank you," she said. "I need you to go now."

She didn't hear him leave, but she didn't hear him breathing anymore either.

She kept her eyes closed, feeling sick to her stomach. Her parents were going to be here in a few hours. She had to figure out what she was going to tell them. *It wasn't that bad.*

It was a lie, but she suspected it was a lie she was going to have to get used to telling. People were going to know. Back at school, wherever she went, everyone she met was going to have gotten the scoop. *Have you heard about Gina Vitagliano? She was on that hijacked plane. She was beaten and gang raped. Poor thing.*

Maybe if she just said it—*it wasn't that bad*—first thing. She could make it her version of hello. "How are you? Yes, I know you've heard all about me. You don't have to spend another minute thinking about it—it wasn't that bad."

God, she'd survived the hijacking. Now she had to survive being a survivor. It had almost been easier back when she was so certain she was going to die. Now she had to live as a victim, and she already hated that.

She heard a sound by the door. "Trent, I asked you to leave."

"Yeah, he already did."

Max.

Gina opened her good eye. And there he was. His suit was even more rumpled than it had been back when he'd come onto the plane. And he'd taken off his shirt and tie. God, she must've bled on him.

He was standing there in a T-shirt and a suit jacket.

"Going for the *Miami Vice* look today?" she asked him.

He laughed and came farther into the room. "Yeah, you know I normally have about seven assistants all ready to run and get me a clean shirt or even a fresh suit. But I seem to have lost them somewhere between here and Kazbekistan."

"Please stay with me." She couldn't stop herself from saying it.

He sat down. Pulled the chair even closer to her side. Took her good hand in both of his.

"Yeah," he said. "You know, I was out in the parking lot. And I'm standing there and I'm thinking, I don't even have a car here. What the hell am I doing? And I realized that wasn't the only mistake I'd made. I realized—it just kind of occurred to me—that *right now* was probably when you needed me the most."

His eyes were brown. Dark, deep, warm brown.

And Gina knew as she looked at him, looked into his eyes, that with his help, she was going to survive.

Stan woke up.

He hated hospitals, but even he had to admit that he wasn't ready yet to go home.

And as far as hospitals went, this one here in London was okay.

Especially since his room seemed to be equipped with the most beautiful, sexiest, sweetest woman he'd ever met, sitting in a chair by his bedside.

Teri was sleeping, and Stan just watched her, aware as hell that she was the one who had made this entire experience bearable.

She'd found him—somehow—a real blanket for his hospital bed. She'd brought in not just flowers but living plants. Books to read. A real lamp that wasn't glaringly fluorescent. Frickin' aromatherapy—that one had made him laugh, and Christ, that had hurt. A white-noise maker that shut out the sounds of the busy hospital and actually made it possible for him to sleep.

She'd set it to "mountain stream," and it murmured soothingly even now.

She'd held his hand more hours than he could count. Run her fingers through his hair, giving him just a little bit of pleasure in a world that had become ruled by pain.

But every day hurt a little bit less, and it wasn't going to be long before he could go home.

He wanted to go home.

And he wanted Teri to go home with him.

His father had come to see him. He'd been that badly injured; the old man had left Chicago and come all the way to London. And apparently the son of a bitch had spoken to Tom Paoletti—whose ass Stan was going to kick the moment he was able to lift his foot more than a few inches off the bed— who'd told him about Teri.

And his father had jumped the gun just a little by dipping into the Wolchonok family safe-deposit box and bringing along the beautiful diamond ring Aunt Anna had bequeathed to Stan upon her death.

"Thought you might want this," Stan Senior had said when Teri was out of the room. "I like her."

And that was it, thank God. His father had said nothing more, and Stan had locked the ring in his cabinet drawer and let the entire subject drop.

But he hadn't been able to stop thinking about it.

He'd fallen in love with Teri that day she'd first come to his house. Before that, he'd been in lust with her, but on that day . . . He'd liked the way she needed him, he realized now. More than liked it. All his life, he'd been waiting to be needed like that. And all his life, he'd desperately wanted to be loved—he'd had no idea how much he wanted that, too.

And she loved him. There was no doubt about it. It wasn't

just loyalty that kept her by his side all these days. Although she had plenty of that inside her, too.

No, the woman loved him.

But he still couldn't see it. Teri Howe—happy with him for the rest of her life?

And even though he had that ring and plenty of opportunities, he couldn't bring himself to ask her to marry him.

She woke up, saw that his eyes were open, and smiled. "Can I get you anything?"

"I'd like a hot tub, please," he said. "With you in it—naked."

She laughed. "Feeling better?"

"More and more every minute."

"Tom Paoletti came by while you were sleeping," she told him.

"You should have woken me."

"He came to see *me*," Teri said. She was still sitting back in the chair, her position relaxed, but he knew her too well. She was tense.

"What's going on?" he asked.

"I got into a little bit of trouble for, well, unauthorized use of a U.S. Navy helicopter, for one thing. He's been helping me get that ironed out."

"Teri, you should have told me."

"I was waiting until you were feeling a little better."

"And until it all got straightened out," he guessed.

"Lieutenant Paoletti's pretty good at fixing things, too," she told him. "Everything's fine."

But her shoulders were still tight. "What else?" he asked.

She wet her lips. "Tom's been helping me look into, um, a lateral move. San Diego Coast Guard needs a helo pilot. I was looking to get back into the service full-time, but if I stay in the Navy . . ."

If she were regular Navy instead of Reserve, suddenly there'd be fraternizing issues. *Shit.*

"I didn't realize you were hoping to get back in full-time," he said. Suddenly he didn't feel too good. "Teri, I don't want you to screw up your career because of me."

"I want to fly," she said. "I'll actually do more flying for the

Coast Guard. I'm excited about it." She paused. "It'll keep me in San Diego."

There it was. Another perfect opportunity to ask her to stay in San Diego with him forever. Stan nodded, his mouth suddenly dry. "Well, if it's something you really want to—"

"It is," she said, absolutely. "I've been thinking about it, and it is."

When had he become such a coward?

Teri stood up. Stretched. "I'm going to get some coffee. Do you want anything before I go?"

"You," he managed to say. "I want you."

She laughed. "Yeah, in a hot tub, naked. I know. Just keep getting better and I'll deliver."

She went out the door and he nearly stopped her. That's not what he'd meant. But instead he let her go.

Alyssa rarely wore more than just a touch of makeup. She rarely dressed up, and even more rarely went out of her way to look good.

But when she did, look out.

She stood in front of the mirror on the back of her closet door in her Washington, DC, apartment and was glad she'd borrowed this dress and these shoes from her sister.

"Keep the dress," Tyra had said, claiming it was from her pre-pregnancy wardrobe and therefore something she'd never fit into ever again.

It was outrageously clingy. And short. With the heels and the makeup, and her hair down loose around her shoulders instead of pulled back tight in her usual ponytail, it made her look like . . .

Like a woman who was finally getting together with the man she wanted to get together with, in the euphemistic sense of the phrase.

Like a woman who wanted to make damn sure she was going to catch and keep that man's attention, and not just for one night either.

God, was she trying too hard? Would he take one look at her and know she'd been thinking about him nonstop ever since he'd called her in K-stan and told her he had a family emergency. He had to fly back to San Diego, he told her, and that the flight was literally leaving in minutes. He'd said he'd call her in a few days to explain.

It had been weeks since she'd seen him, but he'd called. Repeatedly. Nearly a dozen different times—and always when she was out. He couldn't have done a better job at missing her if he'd tried. He left short messages on her answering machine, telling her he'd call back.

He never left his phone number, but she was in the FBI after all, so she tried calling him and got his machine, too.

Forty minutes ago, that had all changed.

The phone had rung, she'd picked it up, and there Sam Starrett was, live and in person on the other end. The news just kept getting better, too. He was in town. At the airport. Could he come by?

She'd hopped into the shower. Put on this dress.

Alyssa looked at herself in the mirror again. She was breaking every one of her personal rules by doing this. But, hell, she'd started breaking her rules back in K-stan by asking Starrett to dinner in front of his team.

It was a huge mistake to become intimately involved with anyone she worked with, let alone an alpha male cowboy like Roger Starrett. It was a human tendency to define women by the men they were with, and she didn't want her coworkers and her boss to start seeing her as the woman Lieutenant Starrett was screwing.

But maybe it wouldn't be so bad to be defined as the woman Lieutenant Starrett loved.

Still, she was about to take off the dress and put on a pair of jeans and a T-shirt when the doorbell rang.

She nearly tripped in the heels on her way to the door. She caught her breath and composed herself while she buzzed him in.

She heard his footsteps on the stairs, but she waited until he knocked before she opened the door.

And then there he was. Sam Starrett.

Dressed way down in torn jeans and a grease-stained T-shirt, at least three days of beard glistening on his chin, baseball cap on his head, looking as if he'd just climbed out from working underneath his pickup truck.

"Oh, Jesus," he breathed when he saw her. But he didn't smile the way she'd imagined he'd smile. Instead he looked as if he might break down and cry. Or faint.

"Are you all right?" she asked.

"No," he said. "You got some coffee? I could use some coffee."

"Come in," she said. "I'll make a pot."

He followed her silently into the kitchen. He didn't say a word about her apartment. No "nice place" or other comments. It was almost as if he didn't see it. What was going on?

"Are you sick?" she asked. Maybe that was the family emergency. Or maybe his father had died. She remembered he'd mentioned once that he and his father had never gotten along.

"No."

He just stood there in the middle of her kitchen, taller and broader than she'd remembered, making what had always seemed to be a good-sized room feel small. She glanced at him as she got the coffee beans from the freezer. "Why don't you sit?"

He sat.

And Alyssa measured out the water, turned on the coffee-maker. This was a strange experience even without his odd behavior—Sam Starrett sitting in her kitchen, because she'd invited him to her apartment. Who would've thought *that* would ever happen?

She got two mugs down from the cabinet and set them on the counter. And turned around to find him looking at her as if he wanted to eat her alive.

It took her breath away, that look in his eyes.

"You look amazing," he said.

"I thought you might want to go out to dinner," she said. "I guess I jumped the gun."

"I'm getting married," he said. "Probably on Sunday."

She heard the words. They just didn't make any sense. "I'm sorry," she said. "You're getting *married*?"

He nodded, pure misery in his eyes. "Her name's Mary Lou

Morrison. I went out with her for a couple of weeks, back about four months ago. She's pregnant, Lys. And the baby's mine."

Oh, God, he was *serious*. Alyssa sat down across from him at the table. "Are you sure?"

"The test results just came back positive—for the second time." His voice broke. "Jesus, I've got to do the right thing. She's already more than three months' pregnant—I mean, she's *got* to be. It's been at least that long since I've seen her." He leaned toward her, his eyes actually filled with tears. "I swear to you, Alyssa, I broke it off with her months ago. I had no idea she was pregnant. If I knew, I wouldn't have let you into my room back in Kazbekistan."

She nodded. "I believe you."

"You have no idea how sorry I am," he whispered.

"Actually," she said, "I think I might, because I'm pretty sorry, too."

"I have to do right by her," he said, as if, like Alyssa, he wished they weren't separated by the wide expanse of the table. As if he wanted her in his arms as much as she wanted to be there. "I have to do this."

"Do you?" she asked, and then hated herself for asking it. God, she was shocked by her reaction to this news, by how badly she wanted to fall to her knees and ask him—no, *beg* him—not to marry this other woman.

Sam wiped his eyes with the heels of his hands, and she knew if he hadn't, his tears would've escaped. He was crying. "I'm sorry," he said again. "I was working on my truck when the lab called. And they said it was positive. And then, Jesus, I was at the airport, because I knew I had to tell you and I didn't want to do it over the phone and I'm sorry I didn't even shower or change my clothes. I just got on the next flight. And all the way out here I was thinking maybe I shouldn't say anything. Maybe I should just get you drunk and take you to Las Vegas and marry *you*."

Great. Now *she* was crying. But she could pretend she wasn't as well as any man. She wiped her eyes. "God knows I could use a drink."

"I used protection," he told her. "I know you probably

think I'm always careless because I was that one time with you, but I did it right. I didn't lose my head over her, not ever. Nothing broke. Nothing leaked. She shouldn't be pregnant—but she is. And now I have to do what's right."

The coffee was ready, and Alyssa stood up and poured them each a mug, wishing she had something stronger to add to hers.

"Well," she said, because she knew she had to say something, "we're just going to have to pretend that night in Kazbekistan never happened. We've done it before—pretended it never happened. We can do it again. We'll just have to . . . forget that you . . . said what you said to me, forget that I got all dressed up like this because you were coming over, and . . ."

She turned to put the mug on the table and found that he'd gotten to his feet. She set it down in front of him, but he didn't touch it.

He was looking at her, his eyes hungry again. "I love that you got all dressed up for me," he whispered. "I'm not going to forget that. I'm not going to forget you."

Alyssa couldn't stop herself. She took a step toward him and then another, and then, God, she was in his arms and he was kissing her.

He tasted like Sam, like everything she wanted but shouldn't want.

She knocked his baseball cap to the floor as she kissed him, as she tugged his shirt free from his jeans and ran her hands up the smooth, broad expanse of his back. His skin was hot and he groaned at her touch as he pulled her closer to him, her skirt riding up all the way to the tops of her thighs as she opened herself to him, as she wrapped one leg around him and . . .

And he broke away. He stopped kissing her, pulled back, stepped free from her embrace. He was breathing as hard as she was as he held her at arm's length, but he held her there.

"I can't do this," he gasped. "Jesus, I want to. I want you more than I've ever wanted anyone. But I'm getting married on Sunday, and I'm not just going to play at it, Lys. I'm marrying her. I'm going to have a family with her."

Alyssa stepped back from him as she pushed her skirt down, aware that he could see the red silk panties she'd put on just an hour ago with such anticipation and hope in her heart. "Then you better go."

He went.

But he stopped in the kitchen doorway and turned to look back at her. "Thanks for getting dressed up for me, Lys," he said quietly.

And then he was gone.

Alyssa heard her apartment door shut.

She'd wanted to get to know him. Well, she'd just gotten to know him a whole hell of a lot better in the past fifteen minutes.

She'd found out he was the kind of man who could resist temptation, the kind of man so intent upon doing what he considered to be the right thing that his own happiness came last. He was a good man. An honorable man.

An amazing man.

Sam hadn't touched his coffee, and his baseball cap was on the floor. She picked it up, knowing that he wouldn't come back for it.

Knowing that he wouldn't ever come back.

She put on his hat and drank his coffee. And then she sat there at her kitchen table, wearing the dress she'd put on for him, for a good long time.

Helga knocked on the hospital room door. "May I come in?"

"What do you know," said the deep male voice from the room, "someone who actually knocks. Please, by all means, come on in."

She pushed the door open to find a very large, still young-looking man sitting up in a hospital bed. His hair was blond and his face was that of a man who'd lived hard but well, with a nose that had been broken at least once. His eyes were blue and Annebet's, and his smile of greeting was pure Marte.

As soon as she saw him, she remembered meeting him, talking to him about Marte and Annebet. And Hershel.

"How are you, Stanley?" she asked. "I'm Helga Rosen Shuler, remember me?"

"Of course," he said with another of those charming smiles. "Mrs. Shuler. Please come in."

"I'm glad I caught you," she said. "I understand you're getting ready to leave."

"Tomorrow," he said. "I'm flying home to San Diego. Not a minute too soon. Please, won't you sit down?"

Helga sat in a chair by his bedside. He was alone in the room.

"Your young lady's not with you?" she asked, disappointed. She remembered a pretty, dark-haired young woman, a helicopter pilot who had looked at Stanley with love in her eyes. Funny how she should remember that and have trouble with other things. Ah, well, better to remember love.

"No," Stan said. "Teri, uh, she went to San Diego—something she said she had to take care of. She's actually flying back in this afternoon so she can go home with me tomorrow. It seems crazy to come all that way just to go all the way back, but . . ."

"It's not crazy if she loves you," Helga said.

"That in itself is pretty crazy," he said, and changed the subject, as men often did when the topic of love came up in a conversation. "I understand I have you to thank for coming through with that information about the bomb."

"You're welcome, I'm sure," she said, "although I have no idea what you're referring to. And no, don't explain. I'm sure I have a note about it somewhere here. I came all the way to . . . *Merde,* this is annoying."

"London," he supplied.

"Thank you." For crying out loud. She had to look at her notepad. Thank God for her notepad. *Hershel,* it said. "Ah. I wanted to finish telling you about my brother."

"Aunt Anna's husband."

"Annebet," she said. "Yes, that's right. Hershel used to call her Anna. Oh, he loved her so. And she loved him. How far did I get in the story?"

"Hershel was shot," Stanley said, "and taken to Copenhagen Hospital. Annebet came and told you. That's where we were."

"After Hershel was shot, the Germans got a tip that we were hiding in the Gunvalds' house," Helga told him. "My parents were moved to the neighbors, and then to Copenhagen Hospital, where Hershel was being cared for. But he was dying. Annebet knew that and so did my parents when they saw him.

"Marte and I were with Annebet at the time. We walked to the market, quite literally right out from under the Germans' noses. It was quite terrifying. I hadn't been out of your grandparents' house for weeks, and then there I was in the town square where people might recognize me.

"I remember there were German soldiers marching, and I later found this picture in a book." Helga pulled it from her purse. She'd had a reprint made of the old black-and-white photo.

A small crowd of civilians had gathered, sullenly watching the Germans goose-step past. Two little girls stood together, their arms around each other. "That's me—" Helga pointed herself out to Stanley. "—and that's your mother." Then she pointed to the older girl, standing several feet away, a solitary figure, all alone. "There's Annebet."

"This is a wonderful picture," Stan told her.

"Yes," she said. "I was quite pleased to find it. A short while after this must have been taken, Annebet found us a ride into Copenhagen. And we went to the hospital, too.

"The entire place—and it was a rather large facility for the times—was used to hide hundreds of Jews. It was quite miraculous. All those people who believed so completely in saving lives that they felt it was their duty to risk their own. I remember being led down a corridor to Hershel's ward. They had him hidden in plain sight. 'Olaf Svensen' it said on his bed.

"And, oh, I knew when I saw him that he was dying. I may not have wanted to believe it before that, but when I saw him . . ." She cleared her throat. It still made her cry to think of him lying there. "Annebet went to him right away. It was so clear to see that she brought him respite from his pain. But he wanted nothing more than for me and my parents to be taken to safety in Sweden.

"I don't know what Hershel said to my father, but he apparently convinced him to take my mother and me and to leave. Annebet would take us to a contact on the coast and put us aboard a boat that very night.

"It had become quite a dismal day, rainy and dark, and we left the hospital in a funeral procession. Hundreds of Jews were smuggled out of the Copenhagen Hospital in broad daylight either disguised as mourners for real funerals or in completely false processions. It was quite a setup they had going there.

"We left, my parents, Annebet, and me. Marte stayed behind, sitting with Hershel, who lay close to death's door. I remember riding in the black car, the four of us, tears streaming down our faces. We didn't have to pretend to be mourners.

"We traveled some distance and had to wait for quite a while in a fisherman's shack. It was cold. I remember the way the wind blew and the rain came down. And Annebet sat with us, holding my mother's hand even though her heart was so clearly back in that hospital ward.

"And it was then," Helga told Stanley, Marte's precious son, "before we were smuggled into the hold of a fishing boat, on that rainy night in a town called Rungsted, my mother took off her diamond ring. It had been in our family for many years, I heard her tell Annebet. Poppi's mother had worn it, and had given it to her on the occasion of her marriage to Poppi. It was only fitting, Mother said, that this ring should go to Hershel's bride.

"And Annebet, she cried," Helga remembered, "because although she and Hershel weren't married in the eyes of the church or the state, they were married in their own eyes and in the eyes of God. And this blessing from my mother, this acceptance, made it all the more real to Annebet, who was soon to be left with nothing but a memory of Hershel's love.

"Mother asked her to come to Sweden with us—on the chance that she was carrying Hershel's child. And Annebet wept again as she told us she was not so lucky as to have conceived in the short time they'd shared.

"She put on that ring," Helga told him, "and put us on the fishing boat. I remember watching as she hurried away, as she slipped into the woods to rush back to Copenhagen. I knew she hoped to see Hershel one last time, to kiss him once more, to hold him as he left this world."

Helga shook her head. "I never knew. Did she tell you? Did she make it in time?"

Stanley had to clear his throat. "Yes," he said. "She did." He reached for her hand and held it. He had nice hands, strong and warm. "She told me that she was with him at the end. She said the doctors gave him morphine, that he wasn't in pain. That he slipped into sleep as she held him. That he went quietly."

Helga closed her eyes and said a prayer of thanks.

"I have her ring," Stanley said.

Helga looked at him. "I'm sorry?"

"Yeah," he said. "I never understood why Aunt Anna gave it to me instead of my sister. But if it went from mother to son . . . She wrote me a note—it was part of her will. I can't remember exactly what she said, but it was something like, 'If I'd had a son, I would have been proud if he'd been like you,' or something. It makes sense now. I have it here—the ring. It's kind of funny, actually. My father came a week or so ago, and he brought it with him. He kind of got it into his head that, I don't know, that I might want it."

"You were going to give it to your young lady," Helga realized.

"Well." Stanley cleared his throat. He moved carefully, up and out of bed. He held on to the bed railing and moved painfully to the cabinet. "Yeah, I, um, hadn't really got that far. I think it still might be too soon. And besides, it seems only fair that the ring goes back to you. To your family."

There was a drawer that was secured with a combination lock. He opened it with a few quick turns, took a deep blue jeweler's box from inside, and shuffled back to her.

And then Helga was holding it in her hands. Her mother's diamond ring. Annebet's ring. Annebet had worn it all her life.

It was as beautiful as she remembered. Beautiful in its elegant simplicity.

"Annebet was my family," Helga told him. "She was my brother's wife." She closed the box, handed it to Stanley, who'd settled himself carefully back in bed. "She gave it in turn to her sister's son—someone I should like to think of as being part of my family, too."

She wrote in her notepad. *Stanley has Annebet's diamond ring.* "I had a note here," she said. "I wanted to ask you a question. I don't remember this, and it's possible it never happened, but didn't you say something to me once about Annebet selling an heirloom, a ring, for passage to America?"

"Yeah," he said. "That was her mother's ring. It was quite old. My mother was angry with her for selling it because it had been in the family since the time of the Vikings, I think." He grinned. "Or at least that's what my mother liked to believe."

"Tell me about Marte," Helga said. "And forgive me if I've asked this before. Was she happy?"

"She said she was," Stanley told her. "She first met my father when she was very young, when she and Anna first arrived in Chicago. She met him again when she was eighteen. He was on leave from the Navy. He had three weeks before he had to go back, and it took him only five days to convince her to marry him. She said she never regretted it."

Helga had to smile. "I, too, married my husband a very short time after we met. I think maybe we both learned a thing or two from watching Hershel and Annebet. We learned never to waste a single moment when it comes to love."

She sighed as she looked around the room. "Where's your young lady?"

"She had some business to attend to," Stanley told her with a patience that told her she'd asked that question before. "I expect her back sometime this afternoon."

"Is that when you plan to give her Annebet's ring?"

"Um," he said.

"Stanley," she scolded. "What would your mother say?"

He laughed. "She would say, What are you waiting for? A sign from God?"

"What are you waiting for?" Helga said. "A sign from God?"

"I just . . ." He shook his head and laughed again. "You remind me so much of her."

"So what would you say to her?" Helga asked. "You'd say, *Mother . . . what?*"

"I'd say, Ma," Stanley said, "I'm afraid Teri doesn't know what it's really like to be married to a man like me, like Dad. I'm afraid that being with me will make her unhappy in the long run."

"Shame on you," Helga said. "Who are you to decide what is or isn't going to make this young lady happy? Don't you think enough of her to allow her to make that decision for herself?"

Stanley laughed. "Well, yeah, but—"

"But, but, but! There's always a but to be found if you want one. Here's your sign from God," Helga said, holding out her hands. "I am your sign from God. God is telling you to listen to your aunt Helga and learn from Hershel and Annebet. Seize the day, young Stanley. In matters of love, seize the day!"

The ring box was burning a hole in Stan's pocket.

It was amazing, though, how ever since Teri had returned to London, he'd had exactly zero time alone with her.

Back in London, whenever he'd thought they finally had some time to themselves, some nurse had come in with some pain in the ass final test. His blood pressure, for God's sake. How many times did they need to take it to know that yes, he was alive? His temperature, for crying out loud.

Then they needed a urine sample.

Yeah, that one really set the appropriate romantic mood.

It was the same thing on the plane. Nurses checking his pulse. It had been easiest just to close his eyes and go to sleep.

And now he and Teri were being driven to his house from the airport by Mike Muldoon. Yeah, that would be just about perfect. He should ask Teri to marry him in front of Mike Muldoon.

"Need help getting out?" Muldoon asked.

Stan gave him his death glare.

"Right," Muldoon said.

Teri was carrying his seabag and her own little overnight

duffel. She stood back and let him get out by himself. Let him walk up his own goddamn stairs on his own goddamn feet.

Christ, he needed to sit down.

She unlocked the door, but didn't open it. "Don't freak," she said. "If I overstepped the bounds, it can all go back."

She swung the door open.

And his house had furniture. Holy shit, it was filled with original Stickley pieces. It was gorgeous, and it had to cost at least . . .

Now he really had to sit down. And damn, if there wasn't a turn of the century sofa right there, four steps away.

He sat on it.

He had to ask. "Where did you get the money?"

"I had some left over from my inheritance," she told him. "You know, from Lenny? I've been investing. I had a couple of good years and . . ."

"I'll say. Christ, Teri. This furniture's almost worth more than the house."

Teri set his seabag down. Tried to make a joke. "I figured as long as I was planning to spend a lot of time over here . . ."

He tried to make a joke out of it, too. "For that kind of money, you better be planning to stay forever."

"Well," she said. "Yeah. Actually forever sounds about right." She looked him in the eye, squared her shoulders, and he realized suddenly that she was forcing herself to confront him. She didn't realize . . .

"I'm giving you another day or two," she told him staunchly. "But that's all you're going to get. After that, I'm just going to go ahead and ask you. You know. To marry me."

Stan laughed. This must be what Dr. Frankenstein had felt like. Like, holy God, look at this beautiful monster he'd helped create.

His laughter threw her and she looked around the room. "You were right about this furniture," she told him. "It's really beautiful. It turns this house into a real home."

"The furniture's great," he said. "Have I said thank you yet?"

Silently she shook her head.

"Thank you," he said. "I've never been given a gift like this before."

"You really like it?"

He reached for her. Tugged her down so that she was sitting next to him. "I love it," he said. "But what I really love is you. *You* make this house a real home. Please, will you stay forever?"

He put the ring box into her hands.

"Oh, my God," she said. "You already got me a ring?"

"Will you marry me, Teresa?" Stan asked. "I can't promise you that it's going to be a constant ball of fun being a senior chief's wife, but I can promise that I'll love you and be faithful to you until the end of time."

Teri was looking at him with so much love in her eyes, he thought *he* might be the one who was going to start to cry here. "Yes," she breathed. "I'll marry you."

She kissed him and he kissed her, and they both pretended he wasn't crying.

And then she opened the ring box. Stan told her Hershel and Annebet's story in between long, slow kisses, and she didn't bother to pretend not to cry.

And their kisses got longer. Slower. And he pulled her shirt free from her pants. She drew in a long breath as he touched her. "Did the doctor say you could . . . ?"

Stan smiled at her. "The doctor said I should listen to my body. My body says *oh yeah.*"

Teri smiled back at him. "In that case, I have something else to show you."

She slid out of his arms, unbuttoning her shirt and kicking off her boots. Her pants, underwear, and socks followed in record time.

"Very nice," Stan said. "I've noticed that about you. You're very good at getting naked. I think that's an excellent skill for a wife to have."

She laughed. "This isn't what I want to show you."

He laughed, too. "Bad plan, then, because I'm completely unable to look at anything but you. Damn, you're beautiful."

"Follow me," she said.

He stood up. "Is there any doubt in your mind that I won't?"

She laughed as she disappeared into . . . the kitchen?

"Bedroom's upstairs," he called. "I was kind of hoping what you wanted to show me was my beautiful new Stickley bed frame. . . ."

God *damn*, as he got to the kitchen, Teri opened the back door and walked outside. Naked.

He was moving slowly, but he was definitely moving. He pushed open the back screen and . . .

There was a hot tub in his backyard.

Teri'd put up very tall wooden fences on the two sides of his property, providing privacy from his neighbors. The view out to the ocean, however, was still wide open.

"We can probably be seen by someone on the bridge with a telescope," she told him from her perch on the side of the tub. "I figure if they go to that much trouble, they deserve to see us naked."

Stan lowered himself into one of the new lounge chairs that had appeared on his patio, courtesy of his fiancée—who clearly had had more than a few good years with her investments. "My body's telling me no hot tub for me—not yet. But I'm going to sit here and enjoy watching you."

And he did.

And it wasn't too much longer before someone—provided they managed to stop their car on the bridge and set up a telescope—would've gotten quite an eyeful as the senior chief of SEAL Team Sixteen's Troubleshooters Squad and his bride-to-be seized the day.

Read on for a sneak peek at

OUT OF CONTROL
by
Suzanne Brockmann

Available at bookstores everywhere.

AT ABOUT 0530 that very morning, Ken "WildCard" Karmody became a terrorist.

It wasn't a career move he would normally have made, especially on such short notice, with no time properly to prepare. But seeing how it was a direct order, he had no choice but to embrace it completely.

"You believe you'll be rescued in a matter of a few short hours, don't you, Mr. Bond?" he asked his hostage—an SAS enlisted man named Gordon MacKenzie who was sitting, tied up, on the sagging floor of the hut they'd chosen as Tango HQ. "But such an easy escape—no, it is not to be."

"Ah, Christ." Gordie rolled his eyes along with his *R*s, sounding as if he were doing an excellent imitation of Scotty from *Star Trek*, except, hot damn, Jim, the Scottish accent was for real. "Here we go, on the move again, is that what you're trying to tell me?"

Kenny slipped neatly from evil overlord to Yoda. "Try not," he told Gordie solemnly as he untied the rope that held the Scots' feet. "Do. Or do not." He grinned. "And in this case, my friend, what I need you to *do* for me is strip."

Gordon sighed. With his dark hair cut close to his scalp, his dark brown eyes, and his lean build, he looked more like George Clooney than the rather portly chief engineer of the Starship *Enterprise*. "Kenneth. Be reasonable, lad. It's a training op. You're only supposed to *pretend* to be the bad guys. Don't you know if you let my boys catch you and liberate me, you'll be home in your girlfriend's bed before 2230?"

His girlfriend's bed.

The rest of the SEALs who were playing the part of Ken's merry band of nasties got very quiet. Too quiet.

Did they honestly think those three words—*his* and *girl-friend's* and *bed*—would set him off? He could feel their uncertainty bouncing around the rough-hewn walls of the shack.

Yup. No doubt about it.

Jenkins and Gilligan and Silverman and even Lopez were all expecting him to go postal.

Ken laughed. He supposed it served him right. Once upon a time, he *would* have lost it at the merest whisper of Adele's name.

But, come on. That was then, this was now. Hadn't they noticed how fricking serene, how absolutely Buddha-like he'd been lately?

Imperturbable. Oh, yeah. That was him, all the way. In fact, his picture had gone up next to that word in the dictionary.

He unfastened Gordie's hands. "Kinda crowded in my girl-friend's bed these days, considering she got married to some rich dickhead last weekend."

Gordie winced. "Shite. We're in for a night of it then, are we boys? Up till dawn's early light?" He glanced at Jenk, at Lopez, at Gilligan, at Silverman, sending them each a silent individual apology for having said the wrong thing. As if Kenny were some kind of special-needs child who had to be handled with extra care—instead of the imperturbable son of a bitch he'd worked hard to become.

He let the flash of annoyance roll off him as he shook his head. "Naw, it won't take until dawn. We'll take 'em out long before midnight."

The Scot laughed aloud. "*You'll* take *them* out? Is that what I heard ye say?"

"You bet your pointy ass. Now strip," Ken ordered.

"No focking way." Gordie was still chuckling to himself. "A fully outfitted SAS team—they're youngsters, true, and fresh out of . . . No, I won't bet any body parts, but I *will* wager a crisp hundred dollar bill that if there's any taking out to be done, my boys will be the ones doing it."

Ken knew what MacKenzie was thinking. The men from

SEAL Team Sixteen were playing the part of the tangos—terrorists—as the six-man SAS team from England trained, practicing the rescue of a hostage. That hostage being, of course, the one and only Gordie MacKenzie, so freaking full of himself it was a wonder he wasn't bobbing against the ceiling like a helium balloon.

MacKenzie was thinking about the fact that his SAS *boys* were dressed for a rescue mission. They had the gear and the MREs in case they got hungry. They had the firepower.

So to speak.

The automatic weapons both teams were using didn't shoot real bullets. They were part of a kickass computer program that worked like a state of the art, hightech paintball game. Except instead of covering the other players with bright colored paint, a direct hit was registered, via satellite, in the mainframe computer. A hit severe enough to "kill" disabled an individual player's ability to use any of the weapons—even one stolen from the enemy.

The weapons Ken and his SEALs had been given—only two to split between the five of them—didn't work quite as well as the seven pseudo–machine guns and sidearms that the SAS team had in their posession. Nah, unless tangos were bankrolled by a patron such as Osama Bin Laden, they often couldn't afford anything but cheap-as-shit, rusty, or obsolete weapons. And the computer program, in an attempt to make the Ts weapons seem as rusty, obsolete, and cheap as shit as possible, would occasionally and randomly cause them to jam.

That program was a neat little piece of training software. Ken knew it inside and out.

He ought to, he'd helped design it.

Its one major flaw was something that could be uncomfortable to train with in hot weather—something they didn't have to worry about on a freeze-yer-balls-off winter day like today. The program required all the players in the training op to wear specially designed, long-sleeved uniforms made of fabric laced with a sensor grid.

So, in actuality, the computer didn't register the fact that a *player* died. It registered the fact that the player's *uniform* died.

"You know, it's tempting," Ken told Gordie, "but I'm not a thief. I'm not going to steal your money by taking that bet."

"Ach, but I have no problem stealing *yours*. Humor me, lad."

"If you insist. But don't say I didn't warn you. Now, take off your *focking* clothes, Mackenzie, or we'll take 'em off for you."

Gordie stared at him. "You're serious."

"Yes, I am."

"You're going to focking cheat, aren't you, you bastard—"

Ken nodded to Gilligan, Jenk, and Silverman, who wrestled the Scotsman to the ground. He hummed happily to himself as he untied his own boots and kicked them off to get his legs free from his pants. This was going to be fun. "Hey, Lopez, you got scissors in your medical kit?"

"Absolutely, Chief."

Jenk tossed him Gordie's pants, and Ken stepped into them. Yeah, the two men definitely had the same height and build. Gordie's uniform shirt quickly followed, and he slipped that on, too. "You know how to cut hair?" he asked Lopez.

The SEAL team's hospital corpsman looked at him, looked at Gordie who was now being dressed in Ken's uniform like a giant, uncooperative Barbie doll, and smiled. "How hard could it be?"

"Let's go with something nice and short today." Ken sat down on a partially charred log someone had dragged inside, either to sit on or in an attempt to burn the place down. "I'd like the look that all the SAS *boys* are sporting these days. I think it would look *smashing* on me." He caught a glimpse of his reflection in the hut's only remaining window.

With the exception of his hair—which grew much too quickly and tended to stand straight up when he ran his hands through it—in a certain light, especially when he tipped his head a certain way, Ken looked a little bit like George Clooney, too.

"Captain," he murmured to himself in a perfect imitation of Scotty, honed from years of watching way too much *Star Trek*—a lonely, dorky, smartass loser of a kid who longed for a father more like Mr. Spock, ruled by logic instead of the kind of raw emotion that could make a man put his fist through walls. "The warp engines cannae take anymore. . . ."

It was the waiting that was the hardest part.

Ken had been born without the patience gene. His biggest challenge in becoming a SEAL had been in learning to wait, learning to lie silently in ambush, constantly alert as the seconds became minutes became hours became days.

Gilligan, Lopez, and Silverman were out there now, dug into the dirt, communing with the bugs that were still alive under the blanket of brown leaves and fallen pine needles.

Somehow it was easier to wait in an ambush position. but Ken was here, waiting for a signal, sitting on his butt in this stupid hut.

Ach, laddie, but he was nae Kenneth Karmody any longer. No, he was handsome Gordon MacKenzie now, and aye, he had the short hair and overinflated ego to prove it.

The sun was low in the sky and the shadows nice and long when Gilligan—Dan Gillman—finally gave forth with one of his freakishly authentic turkey calls. Apparently, Gillman entered turkey-calling contests at county fairs and won first prize all the time. Ken wasn't sure exactly what he won—a trophy of a turkey or a trophy of a grown man standing on a stage and acting like a turkey.

But the signal was his heads-up. The SAS boys had finally moved into position outside the hut. What the hell had taken them so long to find this place?

Ken ignored Gordie's reproachful eyes as he tested the ropes that bound the man and checked the bandana he'd stuffed in his mouth as a gag. "Won't be long now."

Gordie made a string of muted noises that might've been him trying to say, "You dumb focker, when I get free, I'm going to kick your bluddy arse."

"I'm sure you'll try, me wee laddie," Ken murmured back to him as he jammed his own favorite winter hat—the one with the ear flaps that completely covered his hair—onto Gordie's head.

He glanced at Jenk, who also appeared to be tied and

gagged, at least at first glance. In case any of the naughty SAS *boys* peeped in through the windows.

"Ready?"

Jenk nodded. With his cheeks rosy from the chill in the air, and his eyes bright with excitement, he looked more like a kid who'd just put a frog in his teacher's drawer than a deadly Navy SEAL. But that was part of his particular charm.

Ken squeezed the trigger of the pseudo-automatic. Two short bursts, aimed at the floor.

"Get down," he shouted in Gordie's accent. "Get on the focking floor! Yer dead—so dinna ye move!"

He counted out the seconds it would have taken him to bind and gag two men, and then, crawling on his stomach, pulling his weapon behind him, he pushed at the door, propping it so that it would stay open. With great drama, aware that all eyes were on him, he dragged himself down the steps and into the dirt, leaves, and fallen pine needles outside of the hut.

He was Gordie, he was Gordie, he was Gordie. Keep the accent up, keep his face down in the shadows.

"If you're out there, boys, I sure enough now could use some help," he called in a low voice. Gordie's voice. Allie, allie, ox in tree, boy-Os. "I had a bit of a fall, and my ankle's focked up good. I think it's broken for real."

Ah, shite, that last bit sounded far more like John Lennon than Gordie MacKenzie. Still, maybe Gordie sounded like John Lennon when he was in serious pain, because—jackpot!—here they came.

Four of 'em, silently slipping out of the brush and shadows like ghosts, coming to his aid. That meant two were hanging back.

And there it was again. Gilligan's wild turkey. Which meant his teammates had pinpointed the locations of the other two SAS boys who were cautious enough to stay hidden.

Once these four got close enough to see his face in the twilight, the game would move to the next phase. The chaos phase. His favorite. Ken clenched his teeth so he wouldn't smile.

"I've got two kills in the cabin," Ken reported à la Gordie.

"Which means there's only three of 'em out there, with one weapon between 'em. Because I've got their other right here."

He pulled it up into a firing position, and damn, Gordie was at least half right. His boys *were* pretty good, considering the fact they never should have left the cover of the brush in the first place.

Either they had great intuition or 20/40 vision, because he didn't get a single shot off.

They fired, he was hit, and then he *couldn't* get a shot off. The sensors in the uniform screwed with the computer in the automatic weapon, rendering it useless.

To him.

Although he was dead, his aim was still good, and he neatly tossed the weapon back through the open doorway of the hut.

Then Jenkins was there, popping out like a nightmare jack-in-the-box, weapon blazing. And just like that, the game was over for those four wee brave SAS laddies.

It was over for the two in the bush, as well.

And the sun hadn't even fully set.

Ken went into the hut to cut Gordie free. "You lose."

"You son of a whore," Gordie accused as soon as the gag was out of his mouth.

"Actually, my mother's quite nice. Kind of conservative. You'd like her. She attends church—"

"Is everything a focking joke to you?"

Kenny considered the question carefully. "No. In fact, I took this training op very seriously—enough to completely kick your ass in record time. Six SAS boys *and* the hostage dead—killed by friendly fire no less. The computer will make a special little note of that."

"They didn't kill me, they killed *you*."

"Details, details. As in your *boys* missed an important one—such as the fact that I was wearing your uniform. If they really were the elite force that they're supposed to be, they should have been paying attention. *I* would have made a point to know everything there was to know about the computer program that was running this show."

"Sure," Gordie grumbled, "and since you're some kind of focking computer genius, you would've gone in and rewritten the program so that your opposition's weapons wouldn't fire. That's called cheating, Karmody."

"Not according to my definition, it's not," Ken said, still able to sound serene in the face of Gordie's anger because he was right. "It's called *being prepared.*"

"What about throwing your weapon to Jenkins that way? I saw you, you know. When you're dead you're supposed to play dead. That was cheating for sure. I'll bet you do it because you know you wouldn't win in a fair fight."

Ken's cool slipped a notch. "Yeah, gee, sorry, MacKenzie, you're abso-fucking-lutely right. Of course we all know real terrorists *never* cheat. And we also all know that there's never been a case of a tango—even one who's been shot in the head—managing to squeeze off a few more rounds and killing his attackers after he's as good as dead."

A year ago, this was where Kenny would've followed up on Gordie's insult by challenging him to a fair fight right there and then. Bare fists and no rules—let's see who walks away and who crawls. Come on, dickhead. Hit me. Just hit me. . . .

But a year ago, he hadn't yet made chief. With the higher rank came the responsibility to not be an asshole—particularly not in front of his men.

"I'm going to see that the results of this op are challenged," Gordie blustered. "Your CO is going to hear about this from me."

"From me, too," Ken countered, managing to smile because he knew that Gordie was baiting him, and he knew that by staying cool he was completely pissing off the other man. "My team did one fine job today. I'm going to make sure Lieutenant Commander Paoletti knows all about it."

Gordie made himself large. "My boys were supposed to learn something here today."

Ken nodded. "Yeah," he said as he stepped around Mac-Kenzie. "Let's hope they did."

THE DEFIANT HERO

by Suzanne Brockmann

"The United States refuses to negotiate with terrorists." Meg Moore remembered the warning from her job as a translator in a European embassy. Those same words will spell out a death sentence for her daughter and grandmother who have been kidnapped by a lethal group called the Extremists. Meg will do anything to meet their unspeakable demands; anything—even kill—to save her child.

When Navy SEAL Lieutenant, junior grade, John Nilsson is summoned to Washington, D.C., by the FBI to help negotiate a hostage situation, the last person he expects to see holding a foreign ambassador at gunpoint is Meg. He hasn't seen her in years, but he's never forgotten how it feels to hold her in his arms. John could lose his career if he helps her escape. She will lose her life if he doesn't. . . .

Published by Ivy Books.
Available at bookstores everywhere.

THE UNSUNG HERO
by Suzanne Brockmann

After a near-fatal head injury, Navy SEAL Lieutenant Tom Paoletti catches a terrifying glimpse of an international terrorist in his New England hometown. When he calls for help, the Navy dismisses the danger as injury-induced imaginings. In a desperate last-ditch effort to prevent disaster, Tom creates his own makeshift counterterrorist team, assembling his most loyal officers, two elderly war veterans, a couple of misfit teenagers, and Dr. Kelly Ashton—the sweet "girl next door" who has grown into a remarkable woman. The town's infamous bad boy, Tom has always longed for Kelly. Now he has one final chance for happiness, one last chance to win her heart, and one desperate chance to save the day. . . .

Published by Ivy Books.
Available in bookstores everywhere.

BODYGUARD
by Suzanne Brockmann

Threatened by underworld boss Michael Trotta, Alessandra Lamont is nearly blown to pieces in a mob hit. The last thing she wants is to put what's left of her life into the hands of the sexy, loose-cannon federal agent who seems to look right through her yet won't let her out of his sight.

FBI agent Harry O'Dell's ex-wife and son were tragic casualties in his ongoing war against organized crime. He'll do whatever it takes to bring Trotta down— even if it means sticking like glue to this blonde bombshell. But the explosive attraction that threatens to consume them both puts them into the greatest danger of all . . . falling in love.

Published by Fawcett Books.
Available in bookstores everywhere.

HEART THROB
by Suzanne Brockmann

Once voted the "Sexiest Man Alive," Jericho Beaumont had dominated the box office before his fall from grace. Now poised for a comeback, he wants the role of Laramie bad enough to sign an outrageous contract with top producer Kate O'Laughlin—one that gives her authority to supervise JB's every move, twenty-four hours a day, seven days a week.

The last thing Kate wants to do is baby-sit her leading man, and Jericho Beaumont may be more than she can handle. A player in every sense of the word, he is an actor of incredible talent—and a man with a darkly haunted past. Despite her better judgment, Kate's attraction flares into explosive passion, and she is falling fast. But is she being charmed by the real Jericho or the superstar who dazzles the world?

Published by Fawcett Books.
Available in bookstores everywhere.